This book belongs to

....

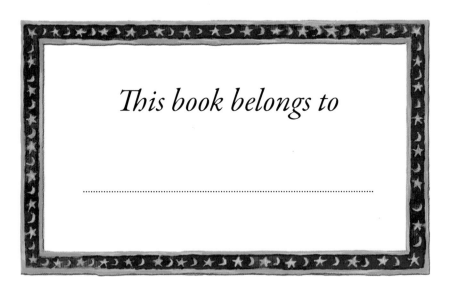

This 2009 edition published by Sandy Creek by arrangement with
Miles Kelly Publishing Ltd.

Editorial Director *Belinda Gallagher*

Art Director *Jo Brewer*

Editorial Assistant *Claire Philip*

Designer *Michelle Foster*

Americanizer *Eleanor Van Zandt*

Production Manager *Elizabeth Brunwin*

Reprographics *Stephan Davis, Ian Paulyn, Liberty Newton*

Editions Manager *Bethan Ellish*

ACKNOWLEDGMENTS

The publishers would like to thank the following artists
who have contributed to this book:

The Bright Agency: Mark Beech, Peter Cottrill, Evelyne Duverne,
Masumi Furukawa, Tom Sperling, Mike Spoor

Advocate Art: Andy Catling

Beehive Illustration: Rupert Van Wyk

Made with paper from a sustainable forest

www.mileskelly.net
info@mileskelly.net

ISBN–13 978-1-4351-1901-7

Printed and bound in China

2 4 6 8 10 9 7 5 3 1

50 Bedtime Stories

Compiled by Tig Thomas

Sandy Creek

Contents

Bold Lads and Brave Girls

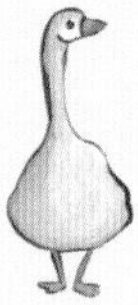

Strange and Magical Tales

READING TIME

Along the Road

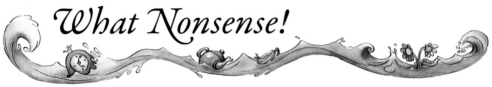

What Nonsense!

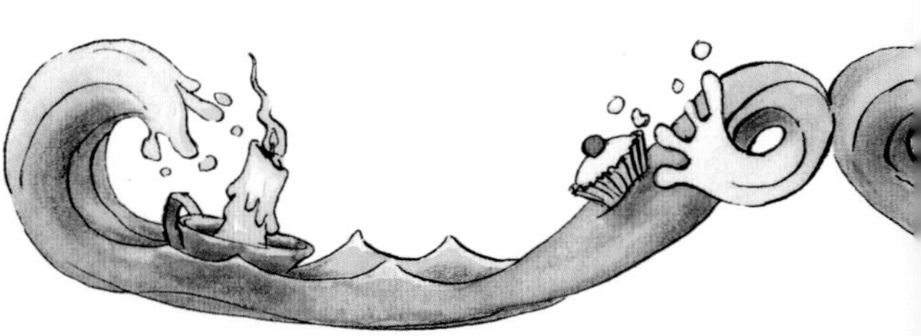

Birds, Beasts, and Dragons

Good and Bad Wishes

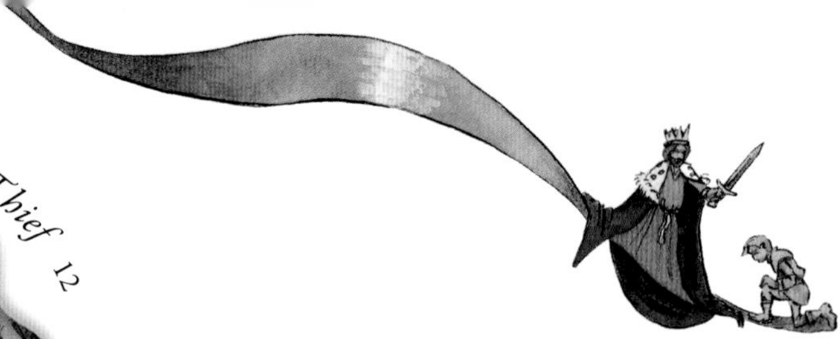

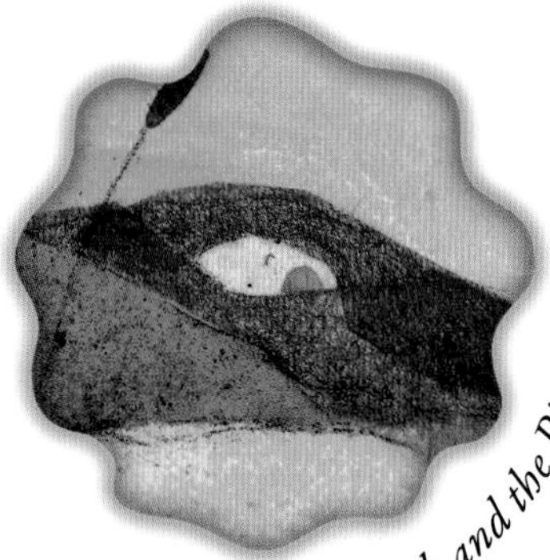

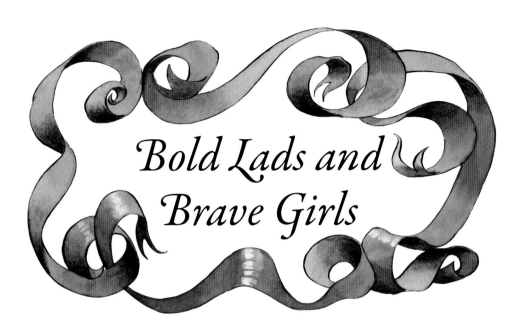

Bold Lads and Brave Girls

Jack the Cunning Thief

By Joseph Jacobs

READING TIME: 25 MINUTES

*T*here was a poor farmer who had three sons, and on the same day the three boys went to seek their fortune. The eldest two were sensible young men—but the youngest, Jack, never did much at home that was any use. He loved to be setting snares for rabbits and inventing all sorts of funny tricks to annoy people at first and then set them laughing.

The three parted at a crossroads, and Jack took the lonesomest. The day turned out rainy, and he was wet and weary, you may depend, at nightfall, when he came

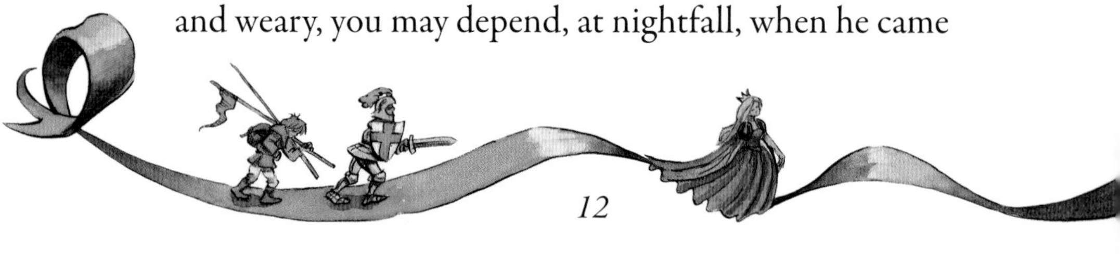

to a lonesome house a little off the road.

"What do you want?" said a bleary-eyed old woman, who was sitting at the fire.

"My supper and a bed, to be sure," said he.

"You can't get it," said she.

"What's to hinder me?" said he.

"The owners of this house," said she, "six tough men that go out until three or four o'clock in the morning each night. And if they find you when they get back they'll skin you alive at the very least."

"Well, I think," said Jack, "that their very most couldn't be much worse. Come, give me something out of the cupboard, for here I'll stay. Skinning is not much worse than catching your death of cold in a ditch or under a tree such a night as this."

Well, she grew afraid, and gave him a good supper, and when he was going to bed, he said that if she let any of the six honest men disturb him when they came home she'd be sorry for it. But when he awoke in the morning, there were six ugly-looking rascals standing around his bed. He leaned on his elbow and looked at them with great contempt. "Who are you," said the chief, "and what's your business?"

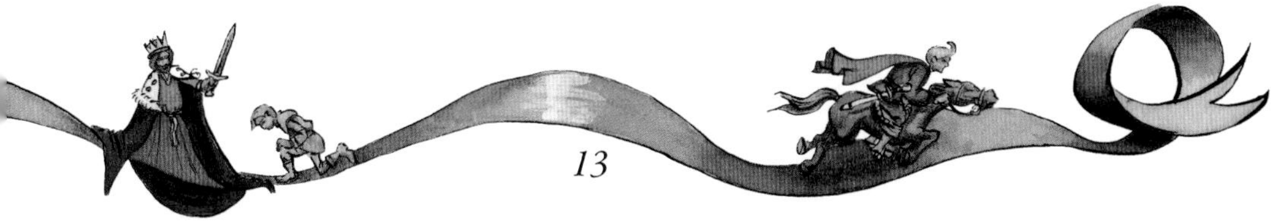

"My name," said he, "is Master Thief, and my business just now is to find apprentices and workmen. If I find you any good, maybe I'll give you a few lessons."

They were a little cowed by that; said the head man, "Well, get up, and after breakfast, we'll see who is to be the master, and who the apprentice."

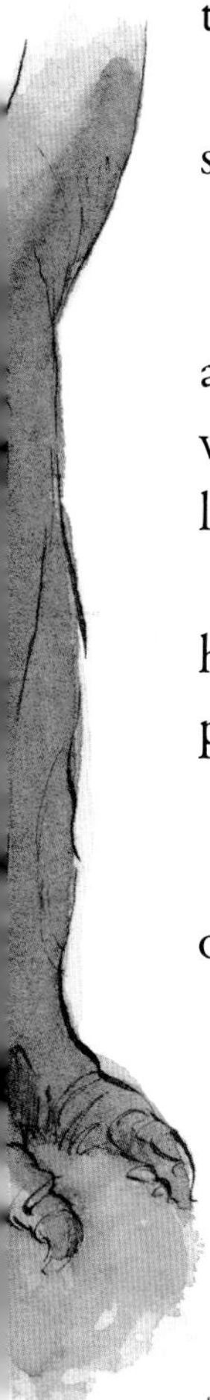

They had just finished breakfast, when what should they see but a farmer driving a fine large goat to market.

"Will any of you," said Jack, "undertake to steal that goat from the owner before he gets out of the wood, and that without the smallest violence?"

"I couldn't do it," said one, and "I couldn't do it," said another.

"I'm your master," said Jack, "and it's up to me do it."

He slipped out through the trees where there was a bend in the road and laid down his right shoe in the very middle of it. Then he ran on to another bend and laid down his left shoe and went and hid himself.

When the farmer saw the first shoe, he said to himself, "That would be worth something if it had its pair, but it is worth nothing by itself."

He went on until he came to the second shoe.

"What a fool I was," he thought, "not to pick up the other! I'll go back for it."

So he tied the goat to a sapling in the hedge, and returned for the shoe. But Jack, who was behind a tree, had it already on his foot, and when the man was beyond the bend, he picked up the other shoe, untied the goat, and led it off through the wood.

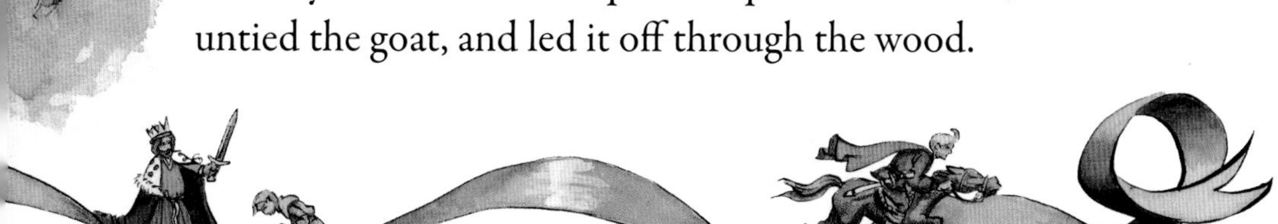

Alas! The poor man was confused—he was unable to find the first shoe, and when he came back, he couldn't find the second either, nor his goat.

"Woe's me!" said he. "What will I do after promising Johanna to buy her a shawl? I'll go and drive another beast to the market unknownst. I'd never hear the last of it if she found out what a fool I made of myself."

The thieves were in great admiration at Jack and wanted him to tell them how he had tricked the farmer, but he wouldn't tell them.

By and by, they saw the poor man driving a fine fat sheep the same way.

"Who'll steal that sheep," said Jack, "before it's out of the wood, and no roughness used?"

"I couldn't," said one, and "I couldn't," said another.

"I'll try," said Jack. "Give me a good rope."

The poor farmer was jogging along and thinking of his misfortune, when he saw a man hanging from the bough of a tree. "Lord save us!" said he. "The corpse wasn't there an hour ago." He went on about half a quarter of a mile, and there was another corpse again hanging over the road. "God between us and harm," said he. "Am I in my right senses?"

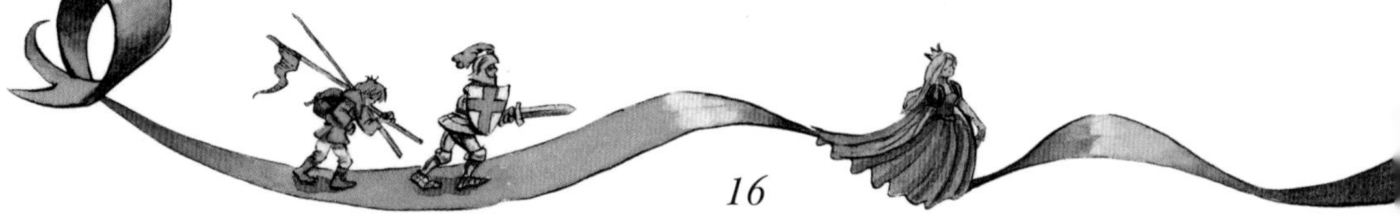

There was another turn about the same distance, and just beyond it the third corpse was hanging.

"Murder!" said he. "I'm beside myself. What would bring three hanged men so near one another? I must be mad. I'll go back and see if the others are there still."

He tied the sheep to a sapling, and back he went. But when he was past the bend, down came Jack, the corpse, who untied the sheep, and drove it home to the robbers' house. You all may think how the poor farmer felt when he could find no one dead or alive going or coming, nor his sheep, nor the rope.

"Oh, misfortunate day!" cried he. "What'll Joan say to me now? My morning gone, and the goat and sheep lost. I must sell something to make the price of the shawl. Well, the fat bullock is in the nearest field. She won't see me taking it."

Well, if the robbers were not surprised when Jack came in with the sheep! "If you do another trick like this," said the captain, "I'll hand over command to you."

They soon saw the farmer going by again, driving a fat bullock this time.

"Who'll bring that fat bullock here," said Jack, "and use no violence?"

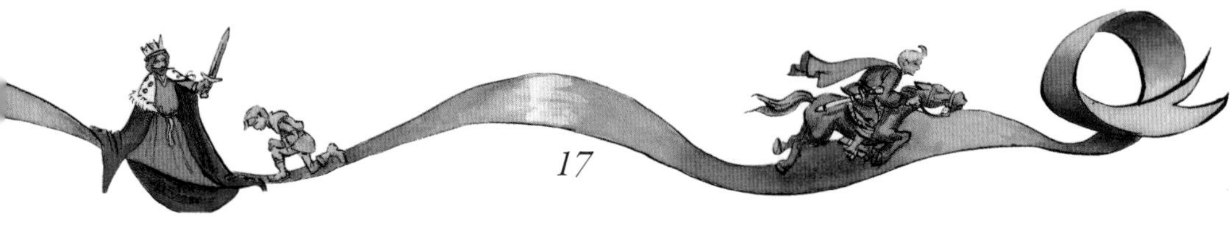

"I couldn't," said one, and "I couldn't," said another.

"I'll try," said Jack, and away he went into the wood.

The farmer was nearly at the spot where he had seen the first shoe, when he heard the bleating of a goat off at his right in the wood. He cocked his ears, and the next thing he heard was the baa-ing of a sheep.

"Blood alive!" said he. "Maybe these are my own that I lost." There was more bleating and more baa-ing.

"There they are, as sure as shooting," said he, and he tied his bullock to a sapling that grew in the hedge, and away he went into the wood. When he got near the place where the cries came from, he heard them a little before him, and on he followed them. At last, when he was about half a mile from the spot where he had tied the beast, the cries stopped altogether. After searching and searching till he was tired, he returned for his bullock—but there wasn't the ghost of a bullock there, nor anywhere else that he searched.

This time, when the thieves saw Jack and his prize coming, they couldn't help shouting out, "Jack must be our chief!" So there was nothing but feasting and drinking, hand to fist, the rest of the day. Before they went to bed, they showed Jack the cave where their

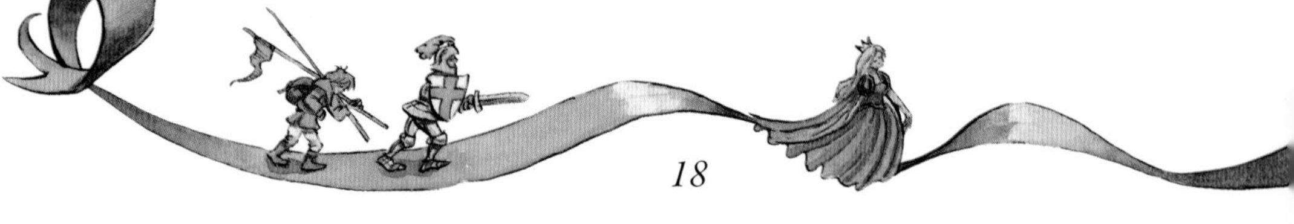

money was hid, and all their disguises in another cave, and swore obedience to him.

One morning, when they were at breakfast, about a week after, said they to Jack, "Will you mind the house for us today while we are at the fair of Mochurry? We haven't had a spree for ever so long; you must get your turn whenever you like."

"Never say't twice," said Jack, and off they went.

After they were gone, Jack said to the wicked housekeeper, "Do these fellows ever give you a present?"

"Ah, catch them at it! Indeed, and they don't."

"Well, come along with me, and I'll make you a rich woman."

He took her to the treasure cave, and while she was in raptures, gazing at the heaps of gold and silver, Jack filled his pockets as full as they could hold, put more into a little bag, and walked out, locking the door on the old hag and leaving the key in the lock.

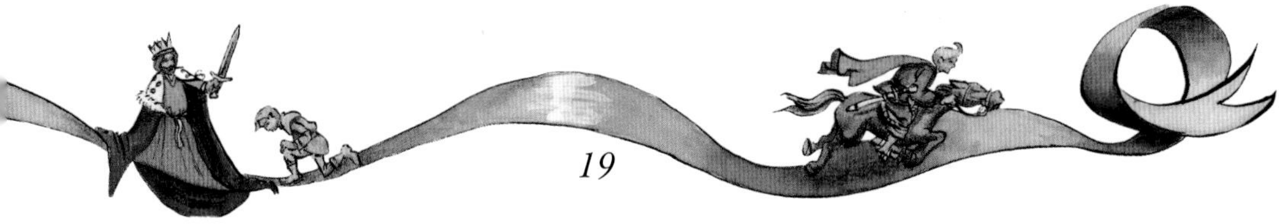

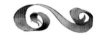

He then put on a rich suit of clothes, took the goat and the sheep and the bullock, and drove them before him to the farmer's house.

Johanna and her husband were at the door, and when they saw the animals, they clapped their hands and laughed for joy.

"Do you know who owns these beasts, neighbors?"

"Sure, they're ours!"

"I found them straying in the wood. Is that bag with ten guineas in it that's hung around the goat's neck yours?"

"Faith, it isn't."

"Well, you may as well keep it for a godsend—I don't want it."

"Heaven be in your road, good gentleman!"

Jack traveled on till he came to his father's house, in the dusk of the evening. He went in and said, "God save all here!"

"God save you kindly, sir!"

"Could I have a night's lodging here?"

"Oh, sir, our place isn't fit for the likes of a gentleman such as you."

"Oh, come now, don't you know your own son?"

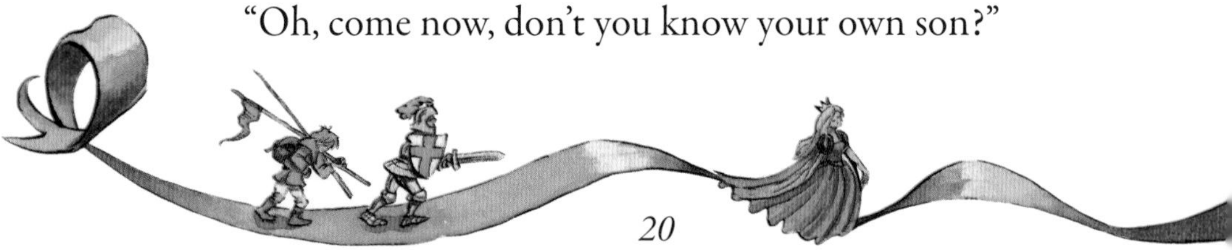

Well, they opened their eyes, and it was a struggle to see who'd have him in their arms first.

"But, Jack, where did you get the fine clothes?"

"Oh, you may as well ask me where I got all that money," said he, emptying his pockets on the table.

Well, they got in a great fright, but when he told them his adventures, they were easier in their minds, and all went to bed in great content.

"Father," said Jack, next morning, "go over to the landlord, and tell him I wish to be married to his daughter."

"Faith, I'm afraid he'd only set the dogs on me. If he asks me how you made your money, what'll I say?"

"Tell him I am a master thief, and that there is no one equal to me in the three kingdoms, that I am worth a thousand pounds, and all taken from the biggest rogues unhanged. Speak to him when the young lady is by."

"It's a strange message you're sending me on, I'm afraid it won't end well."

The old man came back in two hours.

"Well, what news?"

"Strange news, enough. The lady didn't seem a bit unwilling I suppose it's not the first time you spoke to

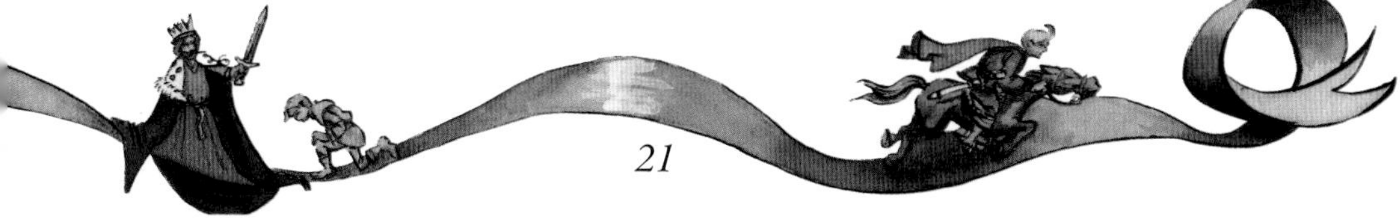

her, and the squire laughed, and said you would have to steal the goose off o' the spit in his kitchen next Sunday, and he'd see about it."

"Oh! That won't be hard, anyway."

Next Sunday, after the people came from early Mass, the squire and all his people were in the kitchen, and the goose turning before the fire. The kitchen door opened, and a miserable old beggar man, with a big bag on his back, put in his head.

"Would the mistress have anything for me when dinner is over, your honor?"

"To be sure. We have no room here for you just now; sit in the porch for a while."

"God bless your honor's family, and yourself!"

Soon someone sitting near the window cried out, "Oh, sir, there's a big hare scampering like the devil around the yard. Shall we run out and catch it?"

"Catch a hare indeed! Much chance you'd have; sit where you are."

That hare made its escape into the garden, but Jack, who was in the beggar's clothes, soon let another out of the bag.

"Oh, master, there it is still running around. It can't

make its escape—let us have a chase. The hall door is locked on the inside, and Mr. Jack can't get in."

"Stay quiet, I tell you."

In a few minutes he shouted out again that the hare was there still, but it was the third which Jack had just given its liberty. Well after that, the servants couldn't be kept in any longer. Out raced every mother's son of them, and the squire after them.

"Shall I turn the spit, your honor, while they're catching the hare?" said the beggar.

"Do, and don't let anyone in for your life."

"Faith, an' I won't, you may depend on it."

The third hare got away after the others, and when they all came back from the hunt, there was neither beggar nor goose in the kitchen.

"Credit to you, Jack," said the landlord, "you've outdone me this time."

Well, while they were thinking of making another dinner, a messenger came from Jack's father to beg that the squire and the mistress and the young lady would step across the fields and take a share of what God sent.

There was no dirty mean pride about the family, and they walked over and got a dinner with roast turkey and

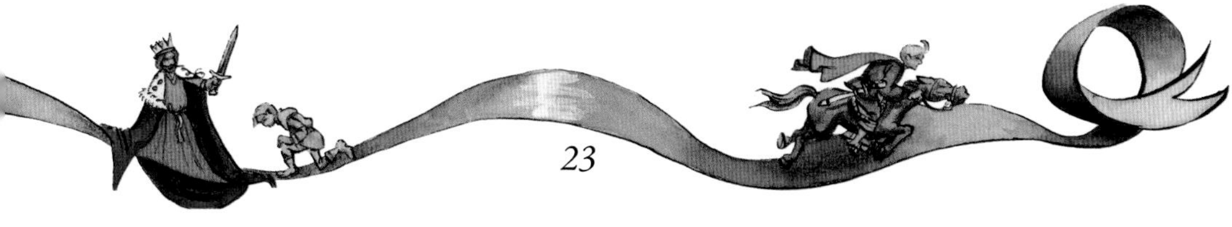

roast beef and their own roast goose, and the squire had like to burst his waistcoat with laughing at the trick, and Jack's good clothes and good manners did not take away any liking the young lady had for him already.

While they were taking their punch at the old oak table in the nice clean little parlor with the sanded floor, the squire said, "You can't be sure of my daughter, Jack, unless you steal away my six horses from under the six men that will be watching them tomorrow night in the stable."

"I'll do more than that," said Jack, "for a pleasant look from the young lady," and the young lady's cheeks turned as red as fire.

Monday night the six horses were in their stalls, and a man on every horse, and a good glass of whiskey under every man's waistcoat, and the door was left wide open for Jack. They were merry enough for a long time, and joked and sang, and were pitying the poor fellow. But the small hours crept on, and the whiskey lost its power, and they began to shiver and wish it was morning. A miserable old beggar woman, with half a dozen bags, and a beard half an inch long on her chin, came to the door.

"Ah, then, tenderhearted men," said she, "would you

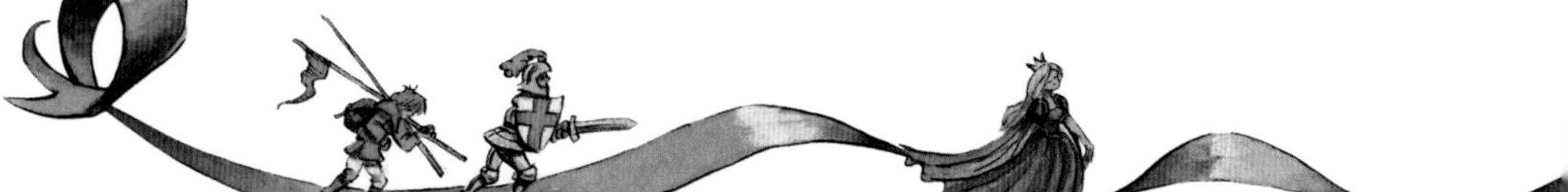

let me in and allow me a wisp of straw in the corner? The life will be froze out of me, if you don't give me shelter."

Well, they didn't see any harm in that, and she made herself as snug as she could, and they soon saw her pull out a big black bottle, and take a sup. She coughed and smacked her lips, and seemed a little more comfortable, and the men couldn't take their eyes off her.

"Good men," said she, "I'd offer you a drop of this, only you might think it too free-making."

"Oh, hang all pride," said one, "we'll take it, and thankee."

So she gave them the bottle, and they passed it around, and the last man had the manners to leave half a glass in the bottom for the old woman. They all thanked her, and said it was the best drop ever passed their tongue.

"Ah well," said she, "it's myself that's glad to show how I value your kindness in giving me shelter, I'm not without another bottle, and you may pass it around while myself finishes what the kindly man left me."

Well, what they drank out of the other bottle only gave them a relish for more, and by the time the last man got to the bottom, the first man was dead asleep in the

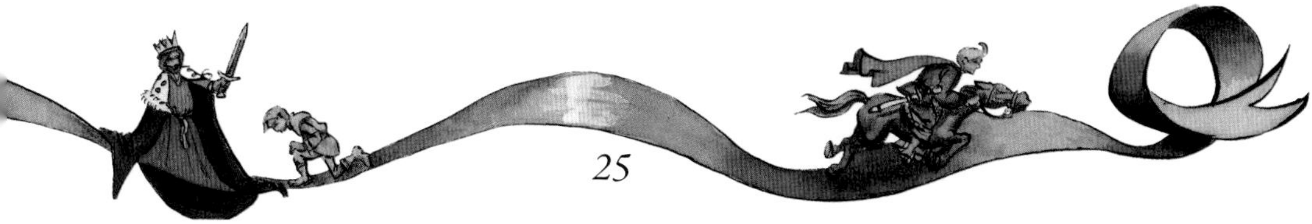

saddle, for the second bottle had a sleeping draft mixed with the whiskey. The beggar woman lifted each man down, and laid him in the manger, or under the manger, snug and comfy, drew a stocking over every horse's hoof, and led them away without any noise to one of Jack's father's outbuildings. The first thing the squire saw next

morning was Jack riding up the avenue, and five horses stepping after the one he rode.

"Confound you, Jack!" said he, "and confound the numbskulls that let you outwit them!"

He went out to the stable, and didn't the poor fellows look very ashamed o' themselves, when they could be woken up in earnest!

"After all," said the squire, when they were sitting at breakfast, "it was no great thing to outwit such ninnies. I'll be riding out on the common from one to three today, and if you can outwit me of the beast I'll be riding, I'll say you deserve to be my son-in-law."

"I'd do more than that," said Jack, "for the honor, if there was no love at all in the matter," and the young lady held up her saucer before her face.

Well, the squire kept riding about and riding about till he was tired, and no sign of Jack. He was thinking of going home at last, when what should he see but one of his servants running from the house as if he was crazy.

"Oh master, master," said he, as far as he could be heard, "fly home if you wish to see the poor mistress alive! I'm running for the surgeon. She fell down the stairs, and her neck, or her hips, or both her arms are

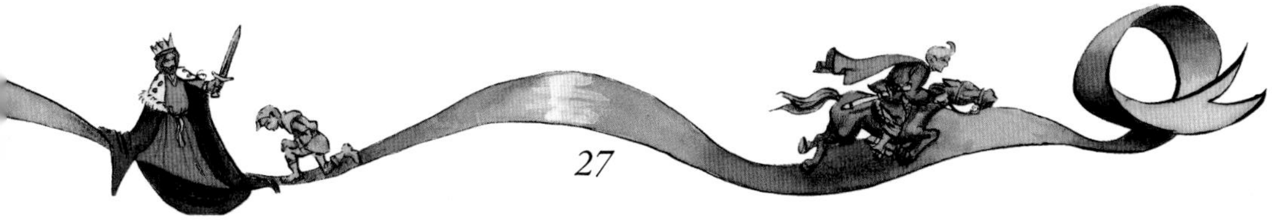

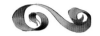

broke, and she's speechless, and it's a mercy if you find the breath in her. Fly as fast as the beast will carry you."

"But hadn't you better take the horse? It's a mile and a half to the surgeon's."

"Oh, anything you like, master. Oh, mistress, mistress, that I should ever see the day! And your pretty body disfigured as it is!"

"Here, stop your noise, and be off like wildfire! Oh, my darling, my darling, isn't this a trial?"

He tore home like a fury. He wondered to see no stir outside, and when he flew into the hall, and from that to the parlor, his wife and daughter, who were sewing at the table screeched out at the rush he made and the wild look that was on his face.

"Oh, my darling!" said he, when he could speak, "how's this? Are you hurt? Didn't you fall down the stairs? What happened at all? Tell me!"

"Why, nothing at all happened, thank God, since you rode out. Where did you leave the horse?"

Well, no one could describe the state he was in for about a quarter of an hour, between joy for his wife and anger with Jack, and shame for being tricked. The servant didn't make his appearance for a week, choosing

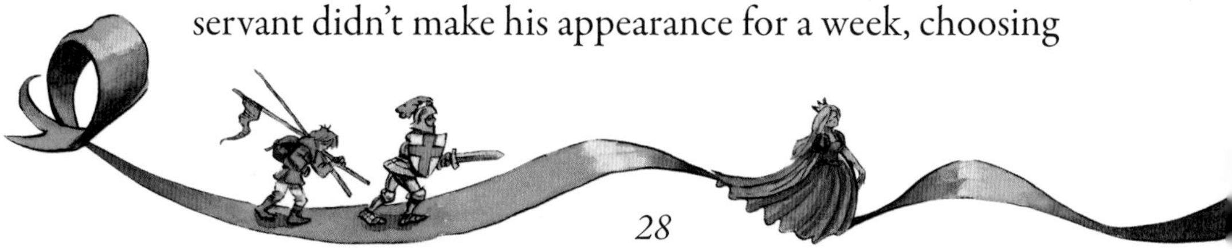

to keep a safe distance for a while—but what did the squire care with Jack's ten golden guineas in his pocket?

Jack didn't show his nose till next morning, and it was a queer reception he met.

"That was all foul play you gave," said the squire. "I'll never forgive you for the shock you gave me. But then I am so happy ever since, that I think I'll give you only one trial more. If you will take away the sheet from under my wife and myself tonight, the marriage may take place tomorrow."

"We'll try," said Jack, "but if you keep my bride from me any longer, I'll steal her away even if she was minded by fiery dragons."

When the squire and his wife were in bed, and the moon was shining in through the window, he saw a head rising over the sill to have a peep, and then bobbing down again.

"That's Jack," said the squire, pointing a gun at the lower pane, "I'll astonish him a bit."

"Oh Lord, my dear!" said the wife, "sure, you wouldn't shoot the brave fellow?"

"Indeed, an' I wouldn't for a kingdom, there's no bullet in it."

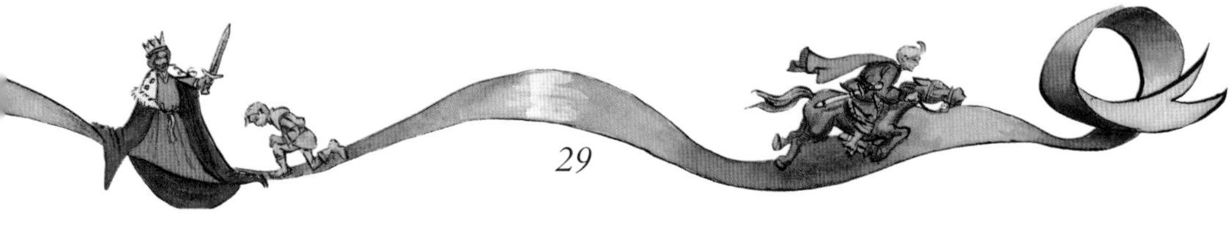

Up went the head, bang went the gun, down dropped the body, and a great crash was heard on the gravel walk.

"Oh, Lord," said the lady, "poor Jack is killed or disabled for life."

"I hope not," said the squire, and down the stairs he ran. He didn't bother to shut the door, but opened the gate and ran into the garden. His wife heard his voice at the room door, before he could be under the window and back, as she thought.

"Wife, wife!" said he from the door. "The sheet, the sheet! He is not killed, I hope, but he is bleeding like a pig. I must wipe it away as well as I can and get someone to carry him in with me." She pulled it off the bed and threw it to him. Down he ran like lightning, and he had hardly time to be in the garden, when he was back, and this time he came back in his shirt, as he went out.

"High hanging to you, Jack," said he, "for an arrant rogue!"

"Arrant rogue?" said she. "Isn't the poor fellow all cut and bruised?"

"I don't much care if he was. What do you think was bobbing up and down at the window, and fell down so

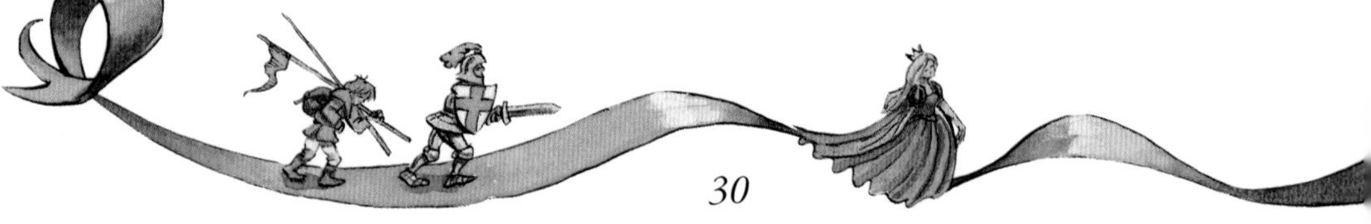

heavy on the walk? A man's clothes stuffed with straw, and a couple of stones."

"And what did you want with the sheet just now, to wipe his blood if he was only a man of straw?"

"Sheet, woman! I wanted no sheet!"

"Well, whether you wanted it or not, I threw it to you, and you standing outside o' the door."

"Oh, Jack, Jack, you terrible rascal!" said the squire. "There's no use in striving with you. We must do without the sheet for one night. We'll have the marriage tomorrow to get ourselves out of trouble."

So married they were, and Jack turned out to be a good husband. And the squire and his lady were never tired of praising their son-in-law, Jack the Cunning Thief.

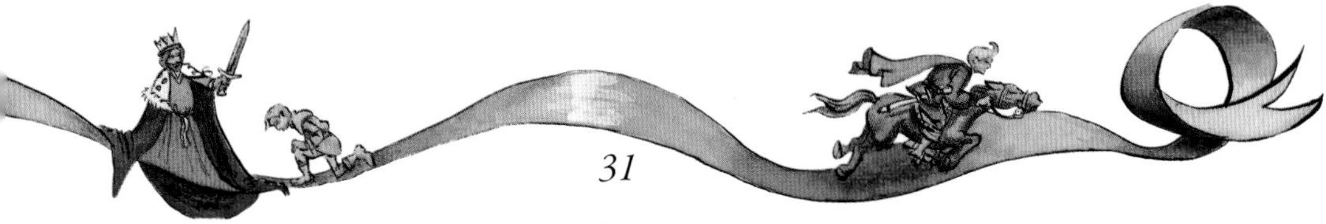

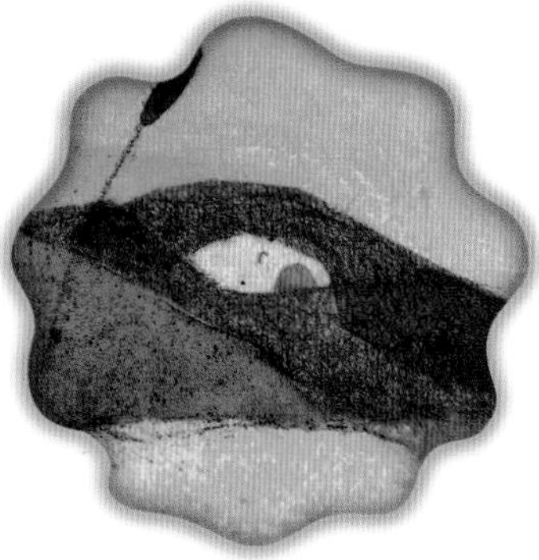

The Fish and the Ring

By Flora Annie Steel

READING TIME: 10 MINUTES

Once upon a time there lived a baron who was a great magician, and could tell by his arts and charms everything that was going to happen at any time.

Now this great lord had a little son born to him as heir to all his castles and lands. So when the little lad was about four years old, the baron, wishing to know what his fortune would be, looked in his Book of Fate to see what it foretold.

And, lo and behold! It was written that this much-loved, much-prized heir to all the great lands and castles

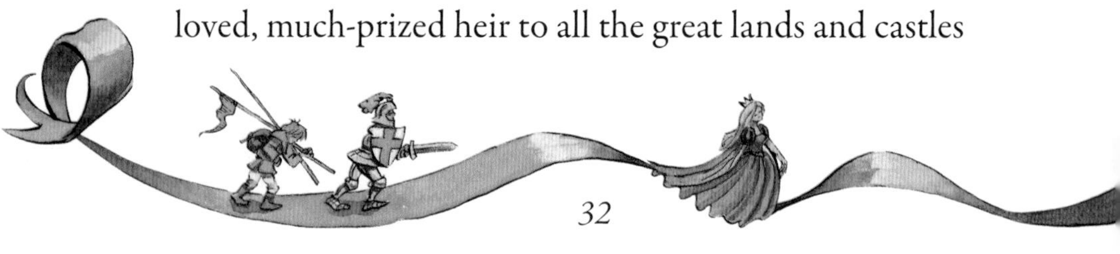

was to marry a low-born maiden. So the baron was dismayed, and set to work by more arts and charms to discover if this maiden were already born and, if so, where she lived.

And he found out that she had just been born in a very poor house, where the poor parents already had five children.

So he called for his horse and rode far away, until he came to the poor man's house, and there he found the poor man sitting at his doorstep very sad and doleful.

"What is the matter, my friend?" asked he, and the poor man replied:

"May it please your honor, a little lass has just been born to our house, and we have five children already, and where the bread is to come from to fill the sixth mouth, we know not."

"If that be all your trouble," said the baron readily, "maybe I can help you. So don't be downhearted. I am just looking for such a little lass to be a companion to my son, so, if you will, I will give you ten crowns for her."

Well! The man he nigh jumped for joy, since he was to get good money, and his daughter, so he thought, a good home. Therefore he brought out the child then and

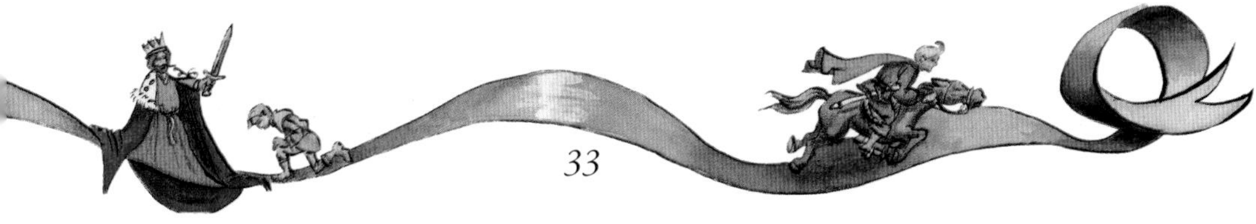

there, and the baron, wrapping the babe in his cloak, rode away. But when he got to the river he flung the little thing into the swollen stream, and said to himself as he galloped back to his castle:

"There goes Fate!"

But, you see, he was just sore mistaken. For the little lass didn't sink. The stream was very

swift, and her long clothes kept her up till she caught in a snag just opposite a fisherman, who was mending his nets.

Now the fisherman and his wife had no children, and they were just longing for a baby, so when the good man saw the little lass he was overcome with joy and took her home to his wife, who received her with open arms.

And there she grew up, the apple of their eyes, into the most beautiful maiden that ever was seen.

Now, when she was about fifteen years of age, it so happened that the baron and his friends went a-hunting along the banks of the river and stopped to get a drink of water at the fisherman's hut. And who should bring the water out but, as they thought, the fisherman's daughter.

The young men of the party noticed her beauty, and one of them said to the baron, "She should marry well; read us her fate, since you are so learned in the art."

Then the baron, scarce looking at her, said carelessly, "I could guess her fate! Some wretched yokel or other. But, to please you, I will cast her horoscope by the stars. So tell me, girl, what day you were born?"

"That I cannot tell, sir," replied the girl, "for I was picked up in the river about fifteen years ago."

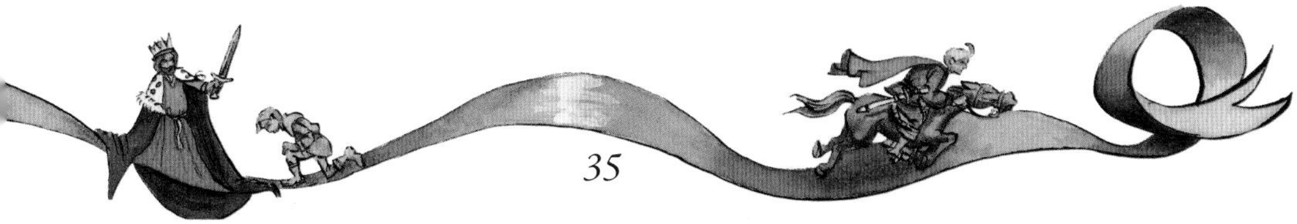

Then the baron grew pale, for he guessed at once that she was the little lass he had flung into the stream and that Fate had been stronger than he was. But he kept his own counsel and said nothing at the time. Afterward, however, he thought out a plan, so he rode back and gave the girl a letter.

"See you!" he said. "I will make your fortune. Take this letter to my brother, who needs a good girl, and you will be settled for life."

Now the fisherman and his wife were growing old and needed help, so the girl said she would go, and took the letter.

And the baron rode back to his castle saying to himself once more:

"There goes Fate!"

For what he had written in the letter was this:

Dear Brother, take the bearer and put her to death immediately.

But once again he was sore mistaken, since on the way to the town where his brother lived, the girl had to stop the night in a little inn. And it so happened that that very night a gang of thieves broke into the inn, and not content with carrying off all that the innkeeper possessed, they searched the pockets of the guests, and found the letter that the girl carried. And when they read it, they agreed that it was a mean trick and a shame. So their captain sat down and, taking pen and paper, wrote instead:

> *Dear Brother, take the bearer and marry her to my son without delay.*

Then, after putting the note into an envelope and sealing it up, they gave it to the girl and bade her go on her way. So when she arrived at the brother's castle, though he was rather surprised, he gave orders for a wedding feast to be prepared. And the baron's son, who was staying with his uncle, seeing the girl's great beauty, was not unwilling, so they were fast wedded.

Well! When the news was brought to the baron, he was beside himself, but he was determined not to be outdone by Fate. So he rode quickly to his brother's and

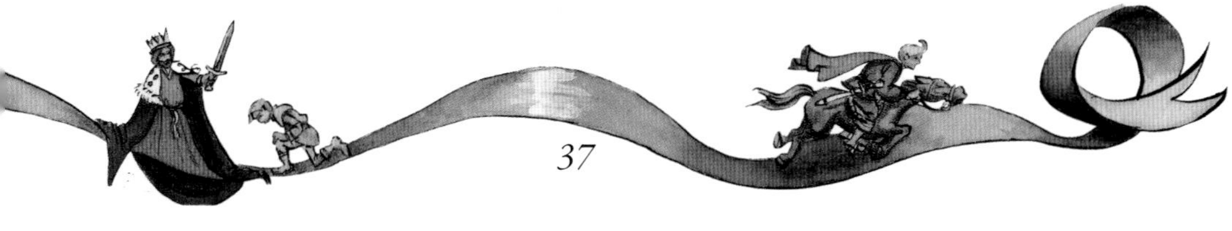

pretended to be quite pleased. And then one day, when no one was near, he asked the young bride to come for a walk with him, and when they were close to some cliffs, seized hold of her, and was for throwing her over into the sea. But she begged hard for her life.

"It is not my fault," she said. "I have done nothing. It is Fate. But if you will spare my life I promise that I will fight against Fate also. I will never see you or your son again until you desire it. That will be safer for you, since, see you, the sea might preserve me, as the river did."

Well! The baron agreed to this. So he took off his gold ring from his finger and flung it over the cliffs into the sea and said:

"Never dare to show me your face again till you can show me that ring likewise."

And with that he let her go.

Well! The girl wandered on, and she wandered on, until she came to a nobleman's castle, and there, as they needed a kitchen girl, she took work.

Now one day, as she was cleaning a big fish, she looked out of the kitchen window, and who should she see driving up to dinner but the baron and his young son, her husband. At first she thought that, to keep her

promise, she must run away, but afterward she remembered that they would not see her in the kitchen, so she went on with her cleaning of the big fish.

And, lo and behold! She saw something shine in its inside, and there, sure enough, was the baron's ring! She was glad enough to see it, I can tell you, so she slipped it onto her thumb. But she went on with her work, and dressed the fish as nicely as ever she could, and served it up as pretty as may be, with parsley sauce and butter.

Well! When it came to table the guests liked it so well that they asked the host who cooked it. And he called to his servants, "Send up the cook who cooked that fine fish, that she may get her reward."

Well! When the girl heard she was wanted she made herself ready, and with the gold ring on her thumb, went boldly into the dining hall. And all the guests when they

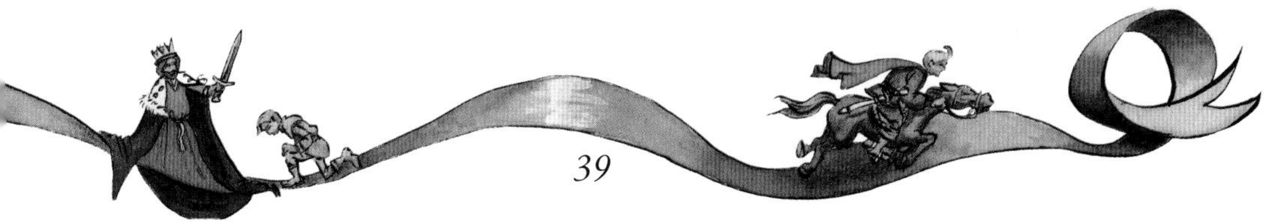

saw her were struck dumb by her wonderful beauty. And the young husband started up gladly, but the baron, recognizing her, jumped up angrily and looked as if he would kill her. So, without one word, the girl held up her hand before his face, and the gold ring shone and glittered on it, and she went straight up to the baron, and laid her hand with the ring on it before him on the table.

Then the baron understood that Fate had been too strong for him, so he took her by the hand, and, placing her beside him, turned to the guests and said:

"This is my son's wife. Let us drink a toast in her honor."

And after dinner he took her and his son home to his castle, where they all lived as happy as could be forever afterward.

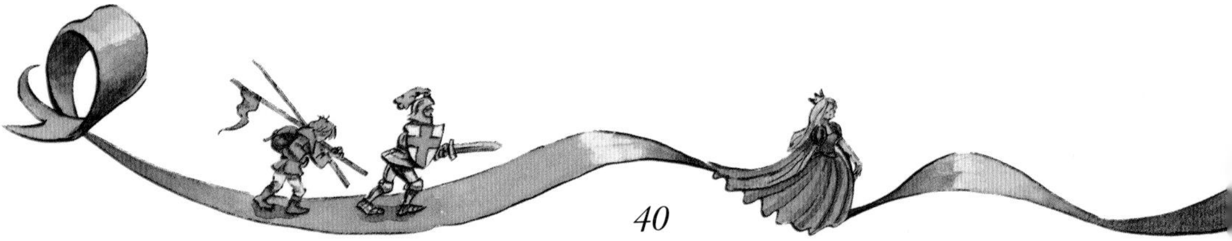

Cap o' Rushes

By Joseph Jacobs

READING TIME: 10 MINUTES

*W*ell, there was once a very rich gentleman, and he had three daughters, and he thought he'd see how fond they were of him. So he said to the first, "How much do you love me, my dear?"

"Why," said she, "as I love my life."

"That's good," said he.

So he said to the second, "How much do you love me, my dear?"

"Why," said she, "better than all the world."

"That's good," said he.

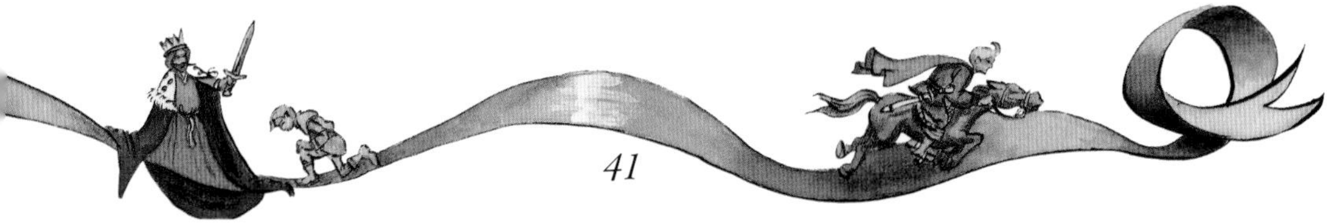

So he said to the third, "How much do you love me, my dear?"

"Why, I love you as fresh meat loves salt," said she.

Well, he was angry. "You don't love me at all," said he, "and in my house you stay no more." So he drove her out there and then, and shut the door in her face.

Well, she went away on and on till she came to a marsh, and there she gathered a lot of rushes and made them into a kind of cloak with a hood, to cover her from head to foot and to hide her fine clothes. And then she went on and on till she came to a great house.

"Do you want a maid?" said she.

"No, we don't," said they.

"I have nowhere to go," said she, "and I ask no wages, and do any sort of work," said she.

"Well," said they, "if you like to wash the pots and scrape the saucepans you may stay."

So she stayed there and washed the pots and scraped the saucepans and did all the dirty work. And because she gave no name they called her "Cap o' Rushes."

Well, one day there was to be a great dance a little way off, and the servants were allowed to go and look on at the grand people. Cap o' Rushes said she was too tired

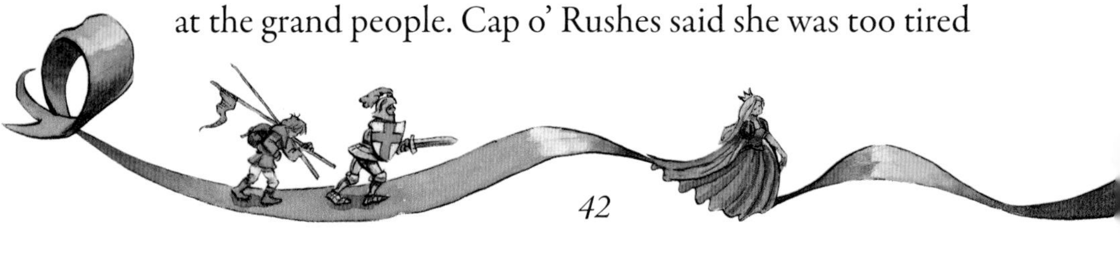

to go, so she stayed at home.

But when they were gone, she offed with her cap o' rushes and cleaned herself, and went to the dance. And no one there was so finely dressed as she.

Well, who should be there but her master's son, and what should he do but fall in love with her the minute he set eyes on her. He wouldn't dance with anyone else.

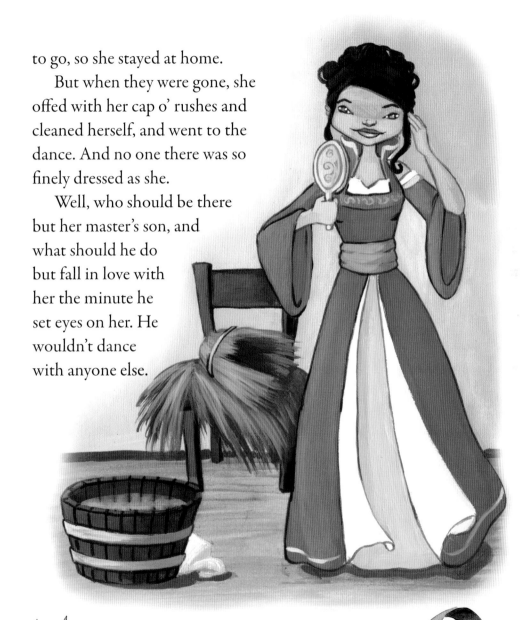

But before the dance was done, Cap o' Rushes slipped off, and away she went home. And when the other maids came back, she was pretending to be asleep with her cap o' rushes on.

Well, next morning they said to her, "You did miss a sight, Cap o' Rushes!"

"What was that?" said she.

"Why, the beautifullest lady you ever saw, dressed right gay and grand. The young master, he never took his eyes off her."

"Well, I should have liked to have seen her," said Cap o' Rushes.

"Well, there's to be another dance this evening, and perhaps she'll be there."

But, come the evening, Cap o' Rushes said she was too tired to go with them. However, when they were gone, she offed with her cap o' rushes and cleaned herself, and away she went to the dance.

The master's son had been reckoning on seeing her, and he danced with no one else, and never took his eyes off her. But before the dance was over, she slipped off, and home she went, and when the maids came back she pretended to be asleep with her cap o' rushes on.

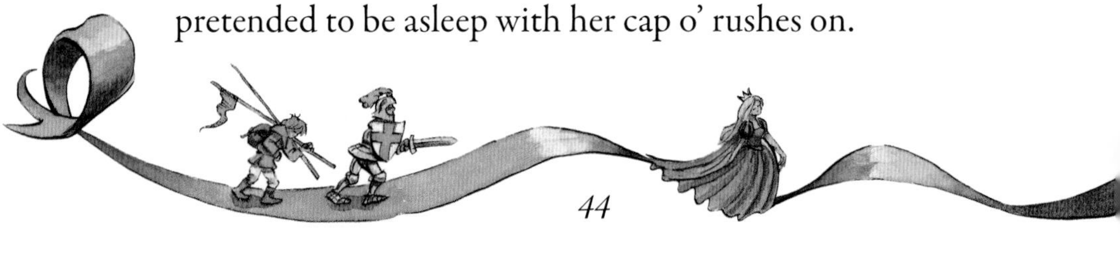

Next day they said to her again, "Well, Cap o' Rushes, you should ha' been there to see the lady. There she was again, gay and grand, and the young master he never took his eyes off her."

"Well, there," said she, "I should have liked to have seen her."

"Well," said they, "there's a dance again this evening, and you must go with us, for she's sure to be there."

Well, come that evening, Cap o' Rushes said she was too tired to go, and do what they would, she stayed at home. But when they were gone, she took off her cap o' rushes and cleaned herself, and away she went to the dance.

The master's son was very glad when he saw her. He danced with none but her and never took his eyes off her. When she wouldn't tell him her name, nor where she came from, he gave her a ring and told her if he didn't see her again he should die.

Well, before the dance was over, off she slipped, and home she went, and when the maids came home she was pretending to be asleep with her cap o' rushes on.

Well, next day they said to her, "There, Cap o' Rushes, you didn't come last night, and now you won't

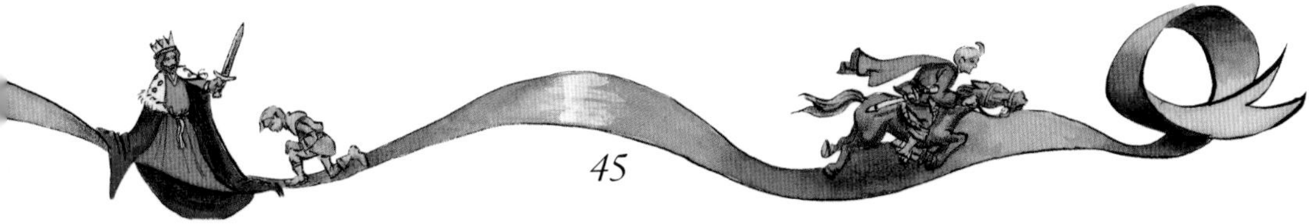

see the lady, for there's no more dances."

"Well, I should have liked to have seen her," said she.

The master's son tried every way to find out where the lady had gone, but go where he might, and ask whom he might, he never heard anything about her. And he got worse and worse for the love of her till he had to keep his bed.

"Make some gruel for the young master," they said to the cook. "He's dying for the love of the lady." The cook had set about making it when Cap o' Rushes came in.

"What are you doing?" said she.

"I'm going to make some gruel for the young master," said the cook, "for he's dying for love of the lady."

"Let me make it," said Cap o' Rushes.

Well, the cook wouldn't at first, but at last she said yes, and Cap o' Rushes made the gruel. And when she had made it, she slipped the ring into it on the sly before the cook took it upstairs.

The young man drank it, and then he saw the ring at the bottom.

"Send for the cook," said he. So up she came.

"Who made this gruel here?" said he.

"I did," said the cook, for she was frightened.

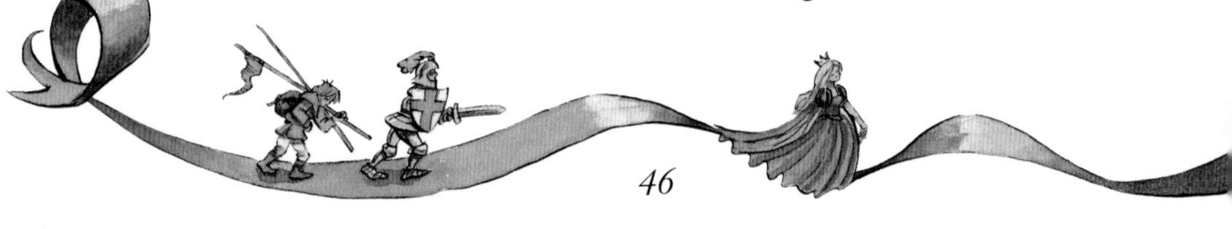

And he looked at her.

"No, you didn't," said he. "Say who did it, and you shan't be harmed."

““Well, then, 'twas Cap o' Rushes," said she.

"Send Cap o' Rushes here," said he.

So Cap o' Rushes came.

"Did you make my gruel?" said he.

"Yes, I did," said she.

"Where did you get this ring?" said he.

"From him that gave it me," said she.

"Who are you, then?" said the young man.

"I'll show you," said she. And she took off her cap o' rushes, and there she was in her beautiful clothes.

Well, the master's son soon recovered, and they were to be married in a little time. It was to be a very grand wedding, and everyone was asked far and near. And Cap o' Rushes's father was asked. But she never told anybody who she was.

But before the wedding, she went to the cook, and she said:

"I want you to dress every dish without a grain of salt."

"That'll be nasty," said the cook.

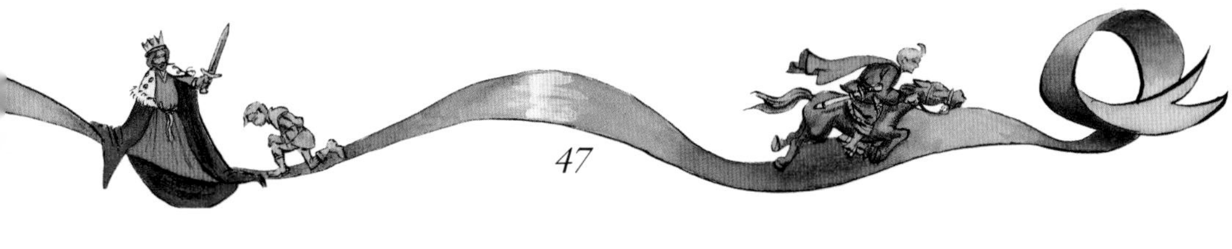

"That doesn't matter," said she.

"Very well," said the cook.

Well, the wedding day came, and they were married. And after they were married, all the company sat down to the dinner. When they began to eat the meat, it was so tasteless they couldn't eat it. But Cap o' Rushes's father tried first one dish and then another, and then he burst out crying.

"What is the matter?" said the master's son to him.

"Oh!" said he, "I had a daughter. And I asked her how much she loved me. And she said, 'As much as fresh meat loves salt.' And I turned her from my door, for I thought she didn't love me. And now I see she loved me best of all. And she may be dead for aught I know."

"No, father, here she is!" said Cap o' Rushes. And she went up to him and put her arms around him.

And so they were all happy ever after.

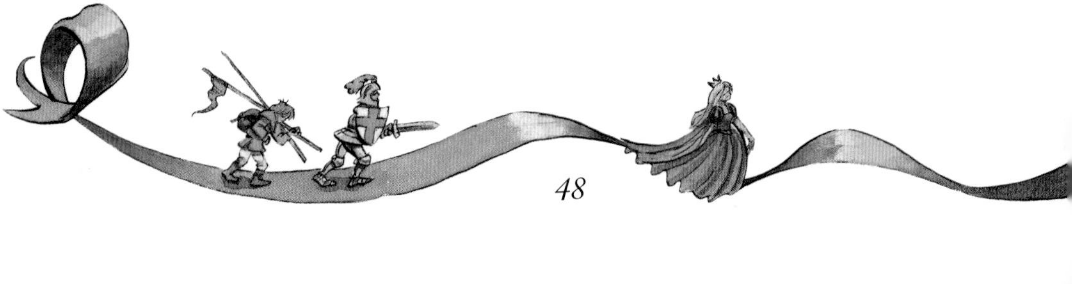

The Four Clever Brothers

By the Brothers Grimm

READING TIME: 10 MINUTES

A poor man once said to his four sons, "Dear children, I have nothing to give you. You must go out into the wide world and try your luck. Begin by learning some craft or another, and see how you can get on."

So the four brothers took their walking sticks in their hands and their little bundles on their shoulders, and after bidding their father goodbye, went out of the gate together. When they had gone some way they came to four crossways, each leading to a different country.

Then the eldest said, "Here we must part, but on this

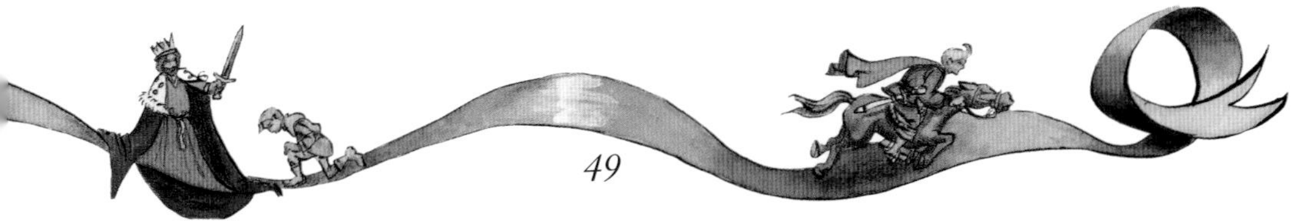

day in four years' time we will come back to this spot, and in the meantime each must try to see what he can do for himself."

So each brother went his way, and as the eldest was hastening on he met a man, who asked him where he was going and what he wanted.

"I am going to try my luck in the world, and should like to begin by learning some art or trade," answered he.

"Then," said the man, "Come with me, and I will teach you to become the most cunning thief that has ever been."

"No," said the other, "that is not an honest calling, and what can one look to earn but the gallows?"

"Oh!" said the man. "You need not fear the gallows, for I will teach you only to steal what will be fair game. I meddle with nothing but what no one else can get or care anything about."

So the young man agreed to follow his trade, and he soon showed himself so clever that nothing could escape him that he had once set his mind upon.

The second brother also met a man, who, when he found out what he was setting out upon, asked him what craft he meant to follow.

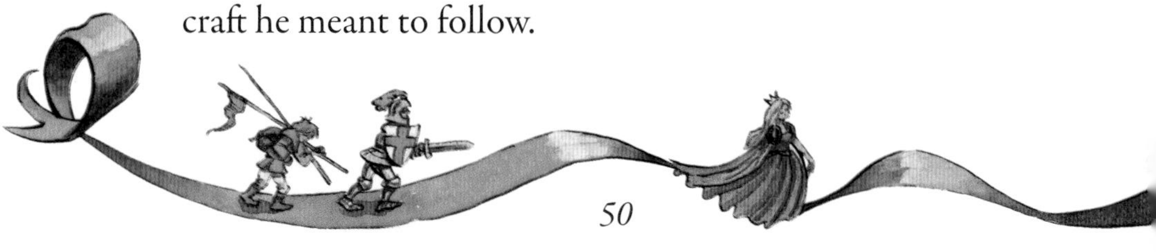

"I do not know," said he.

"Then come with me, and be a stargazer. It is a noble art, for nothing can be hidden from you when once you understand the stars." The plan pleased him much, and he soon became such a skillful stargazer that when he had served out his time and wanted to leave, his master gave him a glass and said, "With this you can see all that is passing in the sky and on earth, and nothing can be hidden from you."

The third brother met a huntsman, who took him with him, and taught him so well about hunting that he became very clever in the craft of the woods. When he left, his master gave him a bow and said, "Whatever you shoot at with this bow you will be sure to hit."

The youngest brother likewise met a man who asked him what he wished to do. "Would not you like," said he, "to be a tailor?"

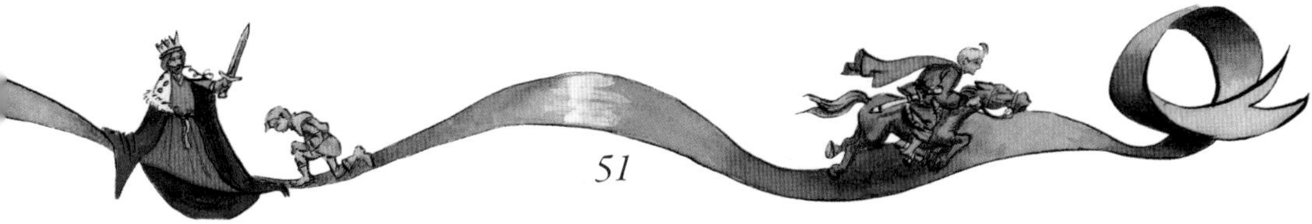

"Oh, no!" said the young man. "Sitting cross-legged from morning to night, working backward and forward with a needle would never suit me."

"Oh!" answered the man. "That is not my sort of tailoring. Come with me, and you will learn quite another kind of craft from that."

Not knowing what better to do, he came into the plan, and learned tailoring from the beginning. When he left, his master gave him a needle and said, "You can sew anything with this, be it as soft as an egg or as hard as steel, and the joint will be so fine that no seam will be seen."

After the space of four years, at the time agreed upon, the four brothers met at the four crossroads. Having welcomed each other, they set off toward their father's home, where they told him all that had happened to them and how each had learned some craft.

Then, one day, as they were sitting before the house under a very high tree, the father said, "I should like to try what each of you can do in this way." So he looked up, and said to the second son, "At the top of this tree there is a chaffinch's nest; tell me how many eggs there are in it."

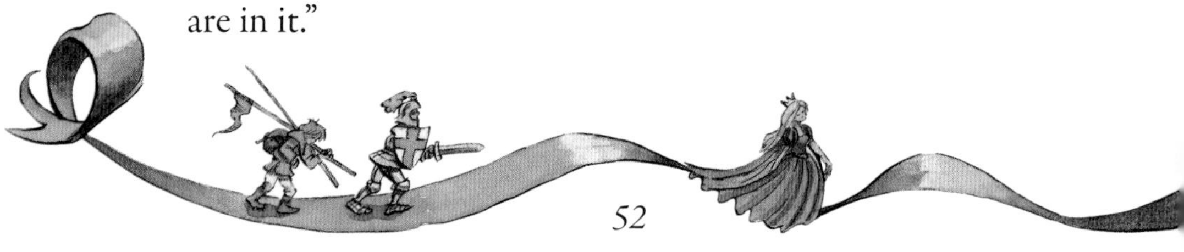

The stargazer took his glass, looked up, and said, "Five."

"Now," said the father to the eldest son, "take away the eggs without letting the bird that is sitting upon them and hatching them know anything of what you are doing."

So the cunning thief climbed up the tree and brought back to his father the five eggs from under the bird, and it never saw or felt what he was doing, but kept sitting at its ease.

Then the father took the eggs, and put one on each corner of the table, and the fifth in the middle, and said to the huntsman, "Cut all the eggs in two pieces at one shot." The huntsman took up his bow, and at one shot struck all the five eggs as his father wished.

"Now comes your turn," said he to the young tailor, "sew the eggs and the young birds in them together again, so neatly that the shot shall have done them no harm." Then the tailor took his needle, and sewed the eggs as he was told, and when he had done, the thief was sent to take them back to the nest and put them under the bird without its knowing it. Then she went on sitting, and hatched them, and in a few days they

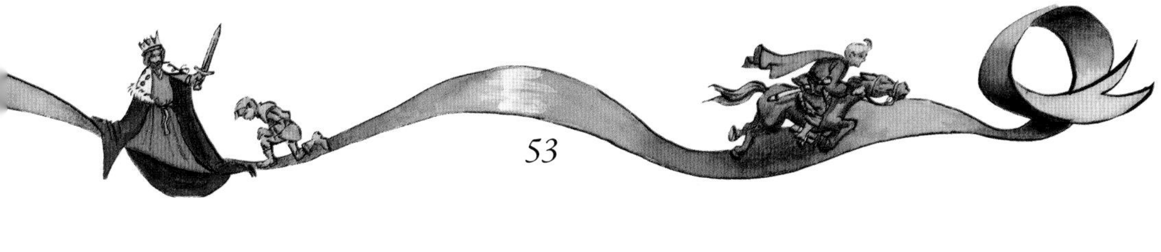

crawled out. They had only a little red streak across their necks, where the tailor had sewn them together.

"Well done, sons!" said the old man. "You have made good use of your time, and learned something worth knowing, but I am sure I do not know which ought to have the prize. I wish that a time might soon come for you to turn your skill to some account!"

Not long after this, there was a great bustle in the country, for the king's daughter had been carried off by a mighty dragon. The king mourned over his loss day and night and made it known that whoever brought her back to him should have her for a wife. Then the four brothers said to each other, "Here is a chance for us let us try what we can do."

And they agreed to see whether they could not set the princess free. "I will soon find out where she is," said the stargazer, as he looked through his glass, and he soon cried out, "I see her far off, sitting upon a rock in the sea, and I can spy the dragon close by, guarding her."

Then he went to the king, and asked for a ship for himself and his brothers, and they sailed together over the sea, till they came to the right place. There they found the princess sitting, as the stargazer had said,

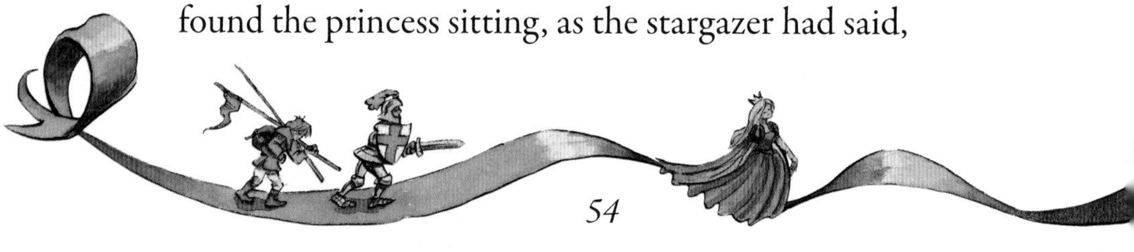

on the rock, and the dragon was lying asleep, with his head upon her lap. "I dare not shoot at him," said the huntsman, "for I should kill the princess also."

"Then I will try my skill," said the thief, and he went and stole her away from under the dragon, so quietly that the beast did not know it, but went on snoring.

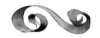

Then away they hastened with her, full of joy, in their boat toward the ship, but soon came the dragon roaring behind them through the air, for it had awakened and missed the princess. But when it got over the boat, and wanted to pounce upon them and carry off the princess, the huntsman took up his bow and shot it straight through the heart so that it fell down dead. They were still not safe, for it was such a great beast that in its fall it overset the boat, and they had to swim in the open sea upon a few planks. So the tailor took his needle, and with a few large stitches put some of the planks together, and he sat down upon these, and sailed about and gathered up all the pieces of the boat, and then tacked them together so quickly that the boat was soon ready, and they then reached the ship and got home safely.

When they had brought home the princess to her father, there was great rejoicing, and he said to the four brothers, "One of you shall marry her, but you must settle among yourselves which it is to be." Then there arose a quarrel between them, and the stargazer said, "If I had not found the princess out, all your skill would have been of no use; therefore she ought to be mine."

"Your seeing her would have been of no use," said the

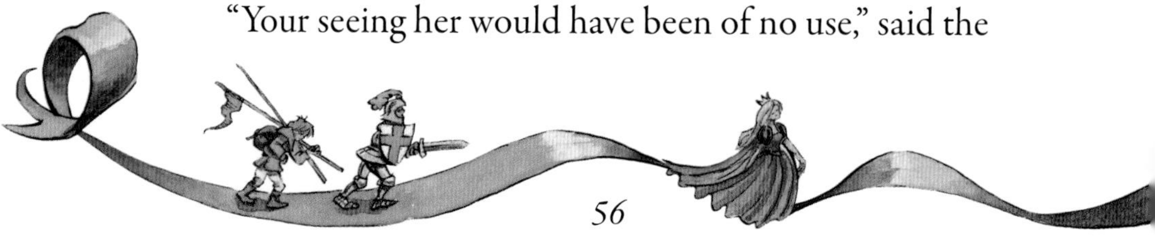

thief, "if I had not taken her away from the dragon; therefore she ought to be mine."

"No, she is mine," said the huntsman, "for if I had not killed the dragon, it would, after all, have torn you and the princess into pieces."

"And if I had not sewn the boat together again," said the tailor, "you would all have been drowned; therefore she is mine."

Then the king said, "Each of you is right, and as all cannot have the young lady, the best way is for none of you to have her. The truth is, there is somebody she likes a great deal better. But to make up for your loss, I will give each of you half a kingdom." So the brothers agreed that this plan would be much better than either quarreling or marrying a lady who had no mind to have them. And the king then gave to each half a kingdom, as he had said, and they lived very happily the rest of their days, and took good care of their father, and somebody took better care of the young lady, than to let either the dragon or one of the craftsmen have her again.

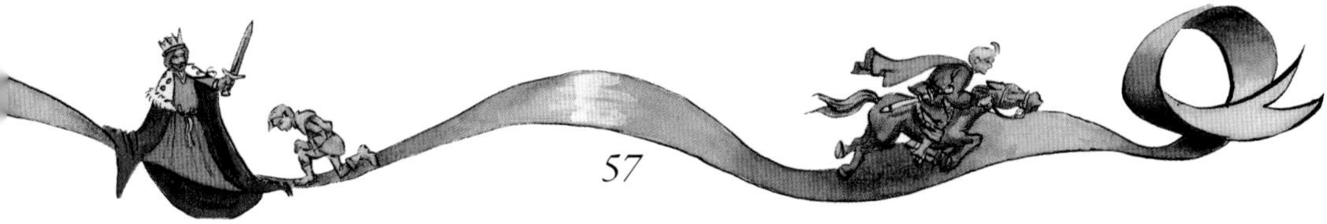

Tattercoats

By Flora Annie Steel

READING TIME: 10 MINUTES

*I*n a magnificent palace by the sea there once dwelled a very rich old lord, who had neither wife nor children living and only one little granddaughter, whose face he had never seen in all her life. He hated her bitterly, because at her birth his favorite daughter had died, and when the old nurse brought him the baby he swore that she might live or die as she liked, but he would never look on her face as long as she lived.

So he turned his back, and sat by his window looking out over the sea, and weeping great tears for his lost

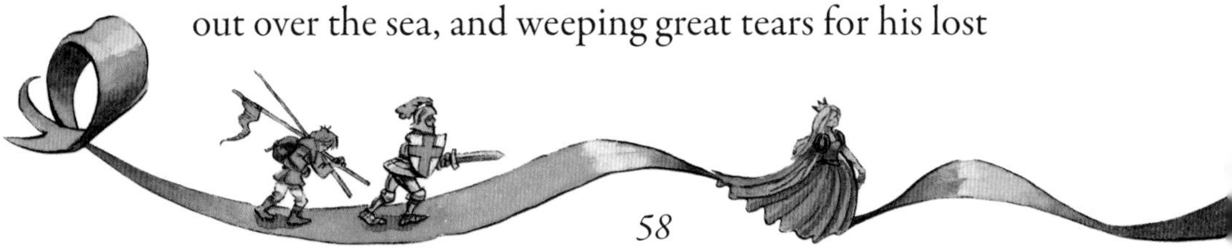

daughter, till his white hair and beard grew down over his shoulders and twined around his chair and crept into the chinks of the floor, and his tears, dropping onto the window ledge, wore a channel through the stone and ran away in a little river to the great sea. Meanwhile, his granddaughter grew up with no one to care for her, or clothe her. Only the old nurse, when no one was by, would sometimes give her a dish of scraps from the kitchen, or a torn petticoat from the rag bag, while the other servants of the palace would drive her from the house with blows and mocking words, calling her "Tattercoats" and pointing to her bare feet and shoulders, till she ran away, crying, to hide among the bushes.

So she grew up, with little to eat or to wear, spending her days out of doors, her only companion a gooseherd, who fed his flock of geese on the common. And this gooseherd was a merry little chap, and when she was hungry, or cold, or tired, he would play to her so gaily on his little pipe, that she forgot all her troubles and would fall to dancing with his flock of noisy geese for partners.

Now one day people told each other that the king was traveling through the land and was to give a great ball for all the lords and ladies of the country in a nearby

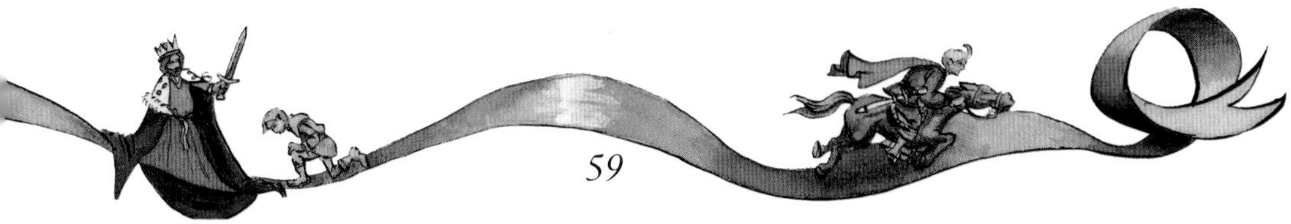

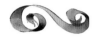

town, and that the prince, his only son, was to choose a wife from among the maidens in the company.

In due time one of the royal invitations to the ball was brought to the palace by the sea, and the servants carried it up to the old lord, who still sat by his window, wrapped in his long white hair and weeping into the little river that was fed by his tears.

But when he heard the king's command, he dried his eyes and bade them bring shears to cut him loose, for his hair had bound him a prisoner, and he could not move. And then he sent for rich clothes and jewels, which he put on, and he ordered the servants to saddle the white horse with gold and silk, that he might ride to meet the king. But he quite forgot that he had a granddaughter to take to the ball.

Meanwhile Tattercoats sat by the kitchen door weeping, because she could not go to see the grand doings. And when the old nurse heard her crying, she went to the lord of the palace and begged him to take his granddaughter with him to the king's ball.

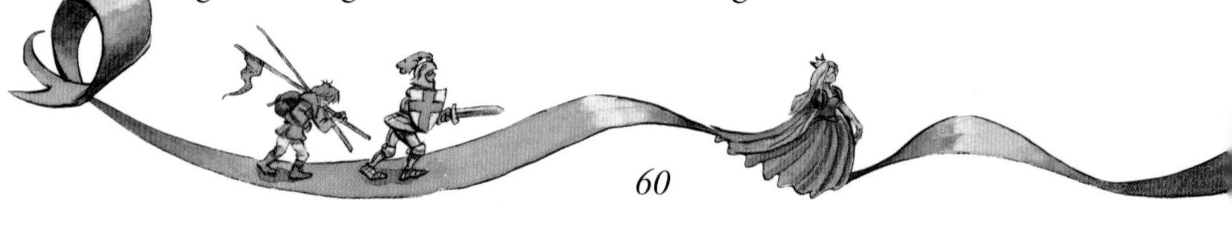

But he only frowned and told her to be silent, while the servants laughed and said, "Tattercoats is happy in her rags, playing with the gooseherd! Let her be—it is all she is fit for."

A second, and then a third time, the old nurse begged him to let the girl go with him, but she was answered only by black looks and fierce words, till she was driven from the room by the jeering servants, with blows and mocking words.

Weeping over her ill-success, the old nurse went to look for Tattercoats, but the girl had been turned from the door by the cook, and had run away to tell her friend the gooseherd how unhappy she was because she could not go to the king's ball.

Now when the gooseherd had listened to her story, he bade her cheer up, and proposed that they should go together into the town to see the king, and all the fine things. And when she looked sorrowfully down at her rags and bare feet, he played a note or two upon his pipe, so gay and merry that she forgot all about her tears and her troubles, and before she well knew, the gooseherd had taken her by the hand, and she and he, and the geese before them, were dancing down the road toward town.

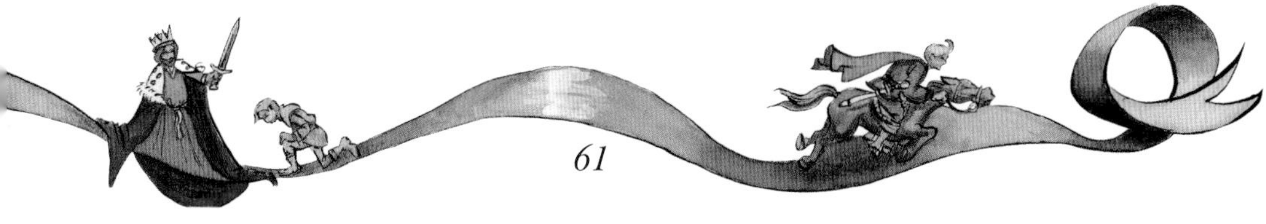

Before they had gone very far, a handsome young man, splendidly dressed, rode up and stopped to ask the way to the castle where the king was staying, and when he found that they too were going, he got off his horse and walked beside them along the road.

"You seem merry folk," he said, "and will be good company."

"Good company, indeed," said the gooseherd, and played a new tune which was not a dance.

It was a curious tune, and it made the strange young man stare and stare and stare at Tattercoats till he couldn't see her rags—till he couldn't, to tell the truth, see anything but her beautiful face.

Then he said, "You are the most beautiful maiden in the world. Will you marry me?"

Then the gooseherd smiled to himself, and played sweeter than ever.

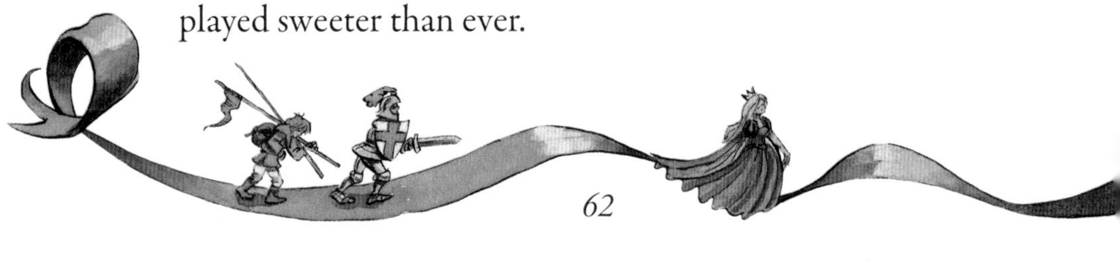

But Tattercoats laughed. "Not I," said she. "You would be finely put to shame, and so would I be, if you took a goose girl for your wife! Go and ask one of the great ladies you will see tonight at the king's ball, and do not mock poor Tattercoats."

But the more she refused him, the sweeter the pipe played, and the deeper the young man fell in love, till at last he begged her to come that night at twelve to the king's ball, just as she was, with the gooseherd and his geese, in her torn petticoat and bare feet, and see if he wouldn't dance with her before the king and the lords and ladies, and present her to them all, as his dear and honored bride.

Now at first Tattercoats said she would not, but the gooseherd said, "Take fortune when it comes, little one."

So when night came, and the hall in the castle was full of light and music, and the lords and ladies were dancing before the king, just as the clock struck twelve, Tattercoats and the gooseherd, followed by his flock of noisy geese, hissing and swaying their heads, entered at the great doors, and walked straight up the ballroom, while on either side the ladies whispered, the lords laughed, and the king, seated at the far end, stared in amazement.

But as they came in front of the throne Tattercoats's lover rose from beside the king and came to meet her. Taking her by the hand, he kissed her thrice before them all and turned to the king.

"Father!" he said, for it was the prince himself, "I have made my choice, and here is my bride, the loveliest girl in all the land, and the sweetest as well!"

Before he had finished speaking, the gooseherd had put his pipe to his lips and played a few notes that sounded like a bird singing far off in the woods, and as he played, Tattercoats's rags were changed to shining robes sewn with glittering jewels, a golden crown lay

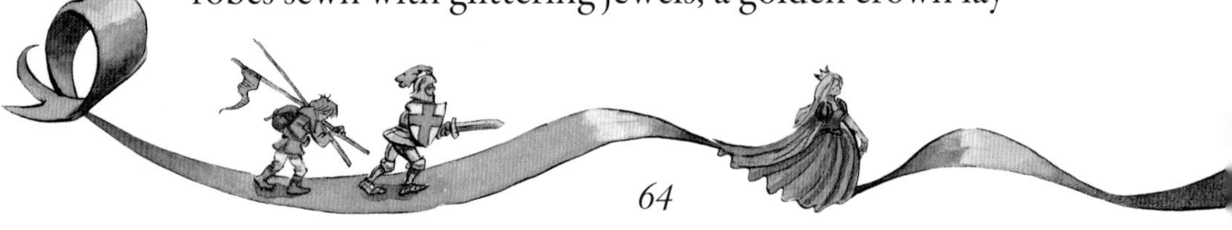

upon her hair, and the flock of geese behind her became a crowd of dainty pages, bearing her long train.

And as the king rose to greet her as his daughter, the trumpets sounded loudly in honor of the new princess, and the people outside in the street said to each other:

"Ah! Now the prince has chosen for his wife the loveliest girl in all the land!"

But the gooseherd was never seen again, and no one knew what became of him, while the old lord went home once more to his palace by the sea, for he could not stay at court, when he had sworn never to look on his granddaughter's face.

So there he still sits by his window—if you could only see him—weeping more bitterly than ever. And his white hair has bound him to the stones, and the river of his tears runs away to the great sea.

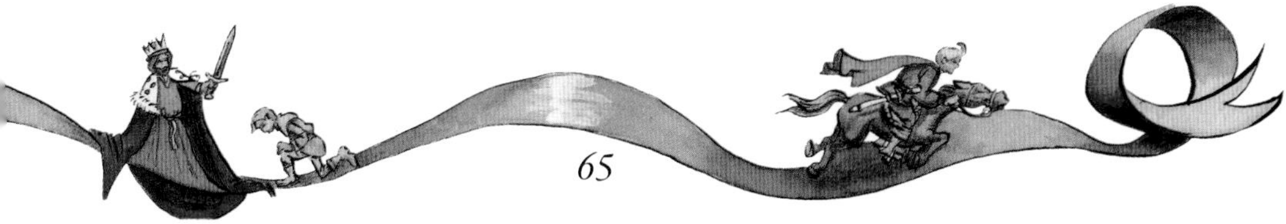

The Clever Apprentice

By Walter Gregor

READING TIME: 3 MINUTES

A shoemaker once engaged an apprentice. A short time after the apprenticeship began, the shoemaker asked the boy what he would call him when addressing him.

"Oh, I would just call you master," answered the apprentice.

"No," said the master, "you must call me master above all masters."

Continued the shoemaker, "What would you call my trousers?"

Apprentice: "Oh, I would call them trousers."

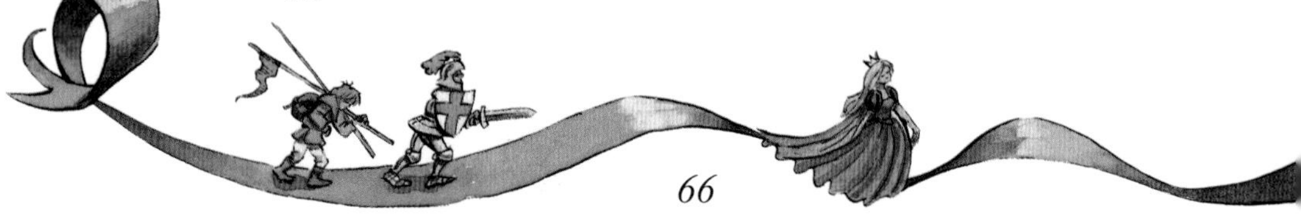

Shoemaker: "No, you must call them struntifers. And what would you call my wife?"

Apprentice: "Oh, I would call her mistress."

Shoemaker: "No, you must call her the Fair Lady Permoumadam. And what would you call my son?"

Apprentice: "Oh, I would call him Johnny."

Shoemaker: "No, you must call him John the Great. And what would you call the cat?"

Apprentice: "Oh, I would call him pussy."

Shoemaker: "No, you must call him Great Carle Gropus. And what would you call the fire?"

Apprentice: "Oh, I would call it fire."

Shoemaker: "No, you must call it Fire Evangelist. And what would you call the peat stack?"

Apprentice: "Oh, I would just call it peat stack."

Shoemaker: "No, you must call it Mount Potago. And what would you call the well?"

Apprentice: "Oh, I would call it well."

Shoemaker: "No, you must call it the Fair Fountain. And, last of all, what would you call the house?"

Apprentice: "Oh, I would call it house."

Shoemaker: "No, you must call it the Castle of Mungo."

The shoemaker, after giving this lesson to his

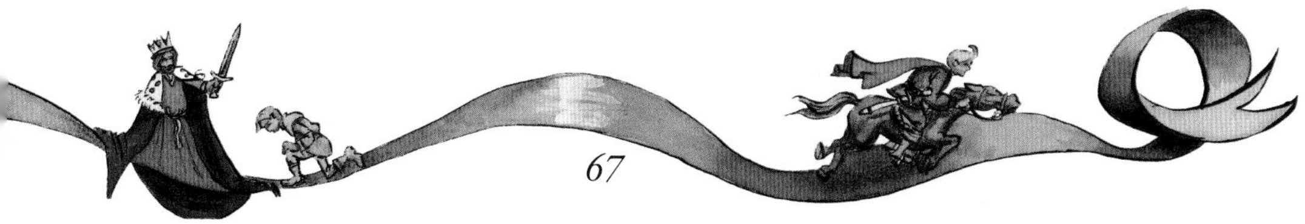

apprentice, told him that the first day he managed to use all these words at once, and was able to do so without making a mistake, the apprenticeship would be at an end.

The apprentice was not long in making an occasion for using the words. One morning he got out of bed before his master and lit the fire. He then tied some bits of paper to the tail of the cat and threw the animal into the fire. The cat ran out with the papers all in a blaze and landed in the peat stack, which caught fire.

The apprentice hurried to his master and cried out, "Master above all masters, start up and jump into your struntifers, and call upon Sir John the Great and the Fair Lady Permoumadam, for Carle Gropus has caught hold of Fire Evangelist, and he is out to Mount Potago, and if you don't get help from the Fair Fountain, the whole of Castle Mungo will be burned to the ground!"

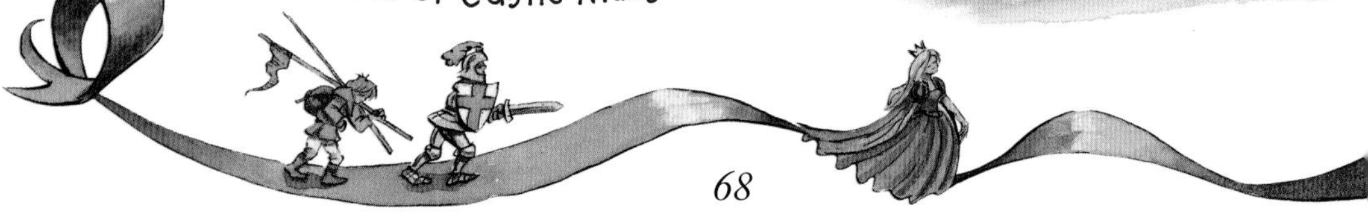

The Ogre's Bride

By Juliana Horatia Gatty Ewing

READING TIME: 10 MINUTES

This story is set in a time when it was important for a girl to be a good housewife in order to find a husband. Girls were also expected to come with a dowry—a sum of money given to their new husband on the wedding day. Poor girls whose parents couldn't afford a dowry might have trouble finding a husband. But a cunning girl can usually find a way through such troubles—as Managing Molly did.

In the days when ogres were still the terror of certain districts, there was one in particular who had long kept an entire neighborhood in the grip of fear without

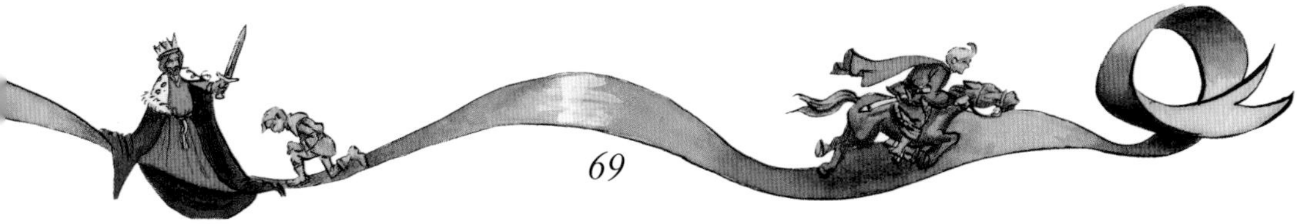

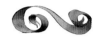

anyone daring to challenge his tyranny.

By thefts and by heavy ransoms from merchants too old and tough to be eaten, in one way and another, the ogre had become very rich, and although those who knew could tell of huge cellars full of gold and jewels, and yards and barns groaning with the weight of stolen goods, the richer he grew, the more anxious and greedy he became. Day by day, he added to his stores, for though (like most ogres) he was as stupid as he was strong, no one had ever been found, by force or fraud, to get the better of him.

What he took from the people was not their heaviest grievance. Even to be killed and eaten by him was not what they feared most. A man can die but once, and if he is a sailor, a shark may eat him, which is not so much better than being devoured by an ogre. No, that was not the worst. The worst was this—he would keep getting married. And as he liked little wives, all the short women lived in fear and dread. And as his wives always died very soon, he was constantly courting fresh ones.

Some said he ate his wives, some said he tormented them, and others said that he only worked them to death. Everybody knew it, and yet there was not a father

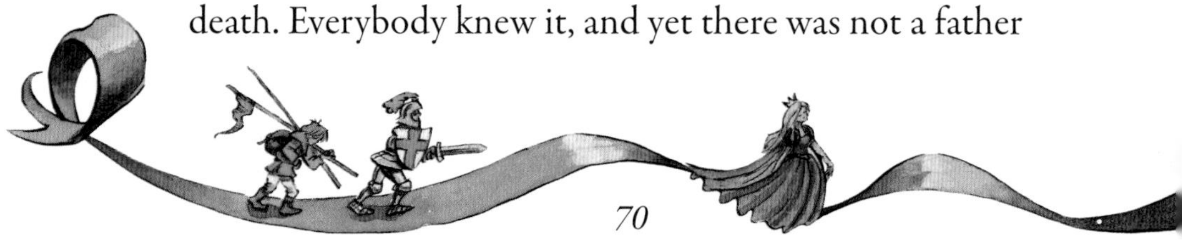

who dared refuse his daughter if she were asked for. The ogre cared for only two things in a woman: he liked her to be little and a good housewife.

Now, it was when the ogre had just lost his twenty-fourth wife (within the memory of man) that these two qualities were joined in the daughter of a certain poor farmer. He was so poor that he could not afford properly to give his daughter a dowry on her marriage, and so she had remained single. Everybody felt sure that Managing Molly must now be married to the ogre. The tall girls stretched themselves till they looked like maypoles, and said, "Poor thing!" The poor housekeepers gossiped from house to house, the heels of their shoes clacking as they went, and cried that this was what came of being too neat and careful.

And sure enough, the giant came to the farmer as he was in the field looking over his crops, and proposed to take Molly there and then. The farmer was so much put out that he did not know what he said in reply, either when he was saying it, or afterward, when his friends asked about it. But he remembered that the ogre had invited himself to supper a week from that day.

Managing Molly did not distress herself at the news.

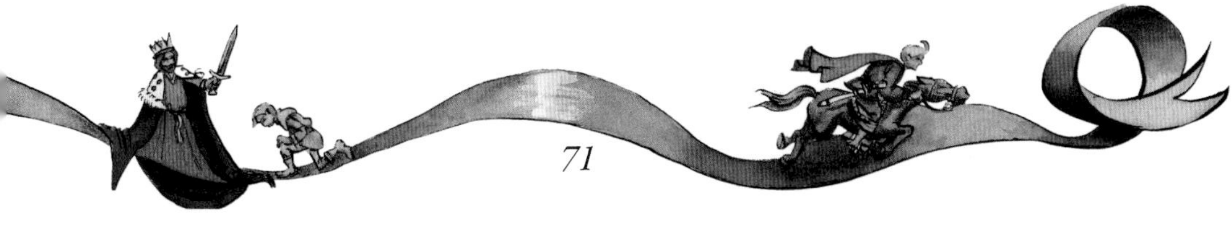

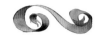

"Do what I bid you, and say as I say," said she to her father, "and if the ogre does not change his mind, you shall not come empty-handed out of the business."

By his daughter's desire, the farmer now procured a large number of hares and a barrel of white wine, which expenses completely emptied his slender moneybox. On the day of the ogre's visit, she made a delicious and savory stew with the hares in the biggest pickling tub, and the wine barrel was set on a bench near the table.

When the ogre came, Molly served up the stew, and the ogre sat down to sup, his head just touching the kitchen rafters. The stew was perfect, and there was plenty of it. For what Molly and her father ate was hardly to be counted in the tubful. The ogre was very much pleased, and said politely:

"I'm afraid, my dear, that you have been put to great trouble and expense on my account, I have a large appetite, and like to sup well."

"Don't mention it, sir," said Molly. "The fewer rats there are, the more corn. How do you cook them?"

"Not one of all the extravagant women I have had as wives ever cooked them at all," said the ogre, and he thought to himself, "Such a delicious stew out of rats!

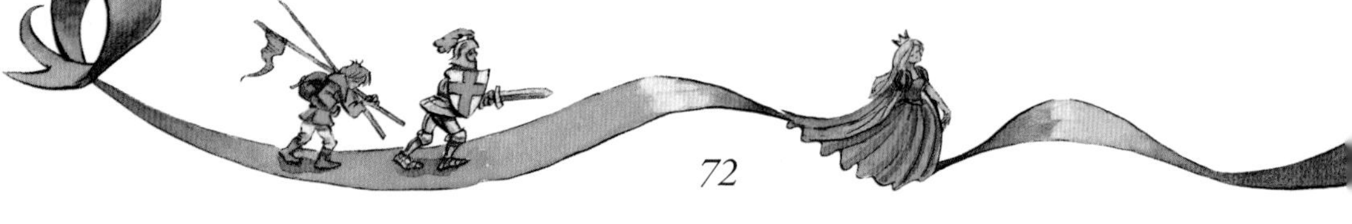

What frugality! What a housewife!"

When he opened the wine, he was no less pleased, for it was of the best.

"This must have cost you a great deal, neighbor," said he, drinking to the farmer as Molly left the room.

"I don't know that rotten apples could be better used," said the farmer, "but I leave all that to Molly. Do you brew at home?"

"We give our rotten apples to the pigs," growled the ogre. "But things will be better organized when she is my wife."

The ogre was now in great haste to arrange the match, and asked what dowry the farmer would give.

"I should never dream of giving a dowry with Molly," said the farmer, boldly. "Whoever gets her, gets dowry enough. On the contrary, I shall expect a good round sum from the man who deprives me of her. Our wealthiest farmer is just widowed, and therefore sure to be in a hurry for marriage. He would not grudge to pay well for such a wife, I'll warrant."

"I'm no churl myself," said the ogre, who was anxious to secure his thrifty bride at any price, and he named a large sum of money, thinking, "We shall live on rats henceforward, and the beef and mutton will soon cover the dowry."

"Double that, and we'll see," said the farmer, stoutly.

But the ogre became angry, and cried, "What are you thinking of, man? Who is to stop me carrying your lass

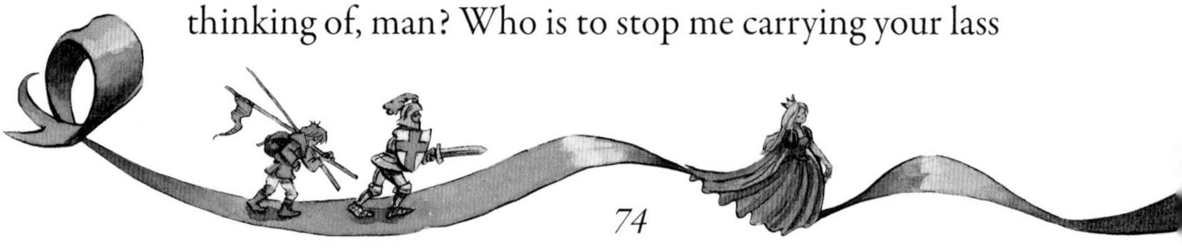

off, without 'with your leave' or 'by your leave,' dowry or none?"

"How little you know her!" said the farmer. "She is so firm that she would be cut to pieces sooner than give you any benefit of her thrift, unless you dealt fairly in the matter."

"Well, well," said the ogre, "let us meet each other." And he named a sum larger than he at first proposed, and less than the farmer had asked. This the farmer agreed to, as it was enough to make him prosperous for life.

"Bring it in a sack tomorrow morning," said he to the ogre, "and then you can speak to Molly, she's gone to bed now."

The next morning the ogre appeared, carrying the dowry in a sack, and Molly came to meet him.

"There are two things," said she, "I would ask of any lover of mine: a new farmhouse, built as I should direct, with a view to economy, and a feather bed of fresh goose feathers, filled when the old woman plucks her geese. If I don't sleep well, I cannot work well."

"That is better than asking for finery," thought the ogre, "and after all, the house will be my own." So, to save the expense of labor, he built it himself, and worked

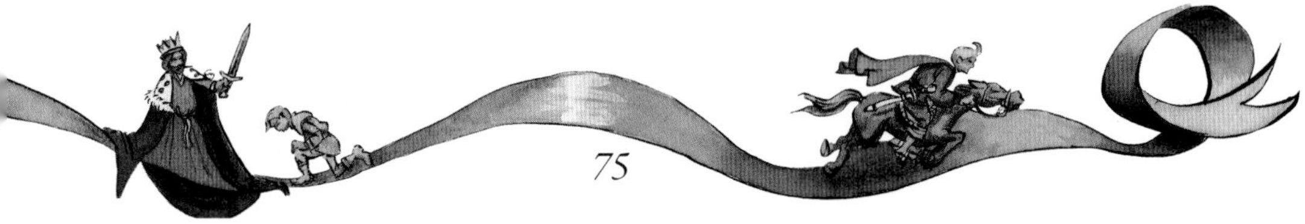

hard, day after day, under Molly's orders, till winter came. Then it was finished.

"Now for the feather bed," said Molly. "I'll sew up the ticking, and when the old woman plucks her geese, I'll let you know."

When it snows, they say that the old woman up in the sky is plucking her geese, and so at the first snowstorm Molly sent for the ogre.

"You see the feathers falling," said she. "Fill the bed."

"How am I to catch them?" cried the ogre.

"Stupid! Don't you see them lying there in a heap?" cried Molly, "get a shovel, and set to work."

The ogre carried in shovelfuls of snow to the bed, but since it melted as fast as he put it in, his labor never seemed done. Toward night, the room got so cold that the snow would not melt, and the bed was soon filled.

Molly hastily covered it with sheets and blankets and said: "Pray rest here tonight, and tell me if the bed is not comfort itself. Tomorrow we will be married."

So the tired ogre lay down on the bed he had filled, but, do what he would, he could not get warm.

"The sheets must be damp," said he, and in the morning he woke with such horrible pains that he could hardly move, and half the bed had melted away. "It's no use," he groaned, "she's a very managing woman, but to sleep on such a bed would be the death of me."

And he went off home as quickly as he could, before Molly could call upon him to be married, for she was so managing that he was afraid of her already.

When Molly found that he had gone, she sent a messenger after him.

"What does he want?" cried the ogre.

"He says the bride is waiting for you," was the reply.

"Tell him I'm too ill to be married," said the ogre.

But the messenger soon returned.

"He says she wants to know what you will give her to make up for the disappointment."

"She's got the dowry, and the farm, and the feather-bed," groaned the ogre, "What more does she want?"

"She says you've pressed the feather bed flat, and she wants some more goose feathers."

"There are geese enough in the yard," yelled the ogre, "Let the farmer drive them home."

The farmer, who overheard this order, lost no time in taking his leave, and as he passed through the yard he drove home as fine a flock of geese as you will ever see.

It is said that the ogre never recovered from the effects of sleeping on the "old woman's goose feathers," and was less powerful than before.

As for Molly, being now well dowered, she had no lack of offers of marriage, and was soon wed to her content.

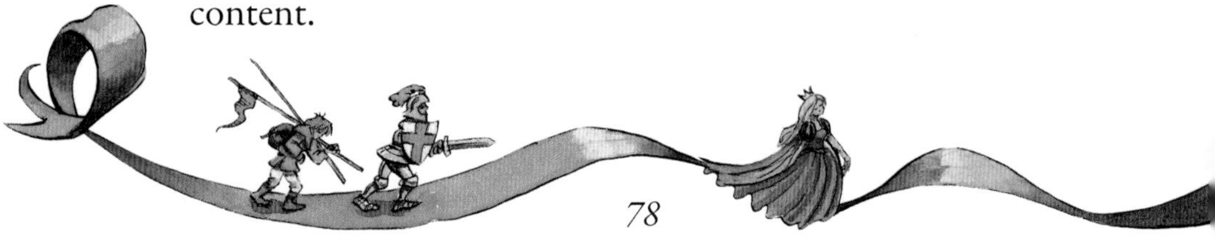

The Wise Girl

By Katharine Pyle

READING TIME: 12 MINUTES

*T*here was once a girl who was wiser than the king and all his councillors—there never was anything like it. Her father was so proud of her that he boasted about her cleverness at home and abroad. He could not keep his tongue still about it. One day he was boasting to one of his neighbors, and he said, "The girl is so clever that not even the king could ask her a question she couldn't answer, or read her a riddle she couldn't unravel."

Now it so chanced the king was sitting at a window nearby, and he overheard what the girl's father was saying.

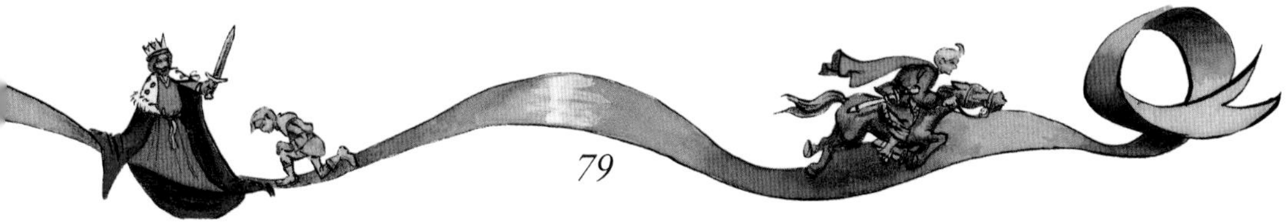

The next day he sent for the man to come before him.

"I hear you have a daughter who is so clever that no one in the kingdom can equal her, and is that so?" asked the king.

Yes, the man said, it was no more than the truth. Too much could not be said of her wit and cleverness.

That was well, and the king was glad to hear it. He had thirty eggs, they were fresh and good, but it would take a clever person to hatch chickens out of them. He then bade his chancellor get the eggs and give them to the man.

"Take these home to your daughter," said the king, "and bid her hatch them out for me. If she succeeds she shall have a bag of money for her pains, but if she fails you shall be beaten as a vain boaster."

The man was troubled when he heard this. Still, his daughter was so clever he was almost sure she could hatch out the eggs. He carried them home to her and told her exactly what the king had said. It did not take the girl long to find out that the eggs had been boiled.

When she told her father that, he made a great to-do. That was a pretty trick for the king to have played upon him. Now he would have to take a beating and all the

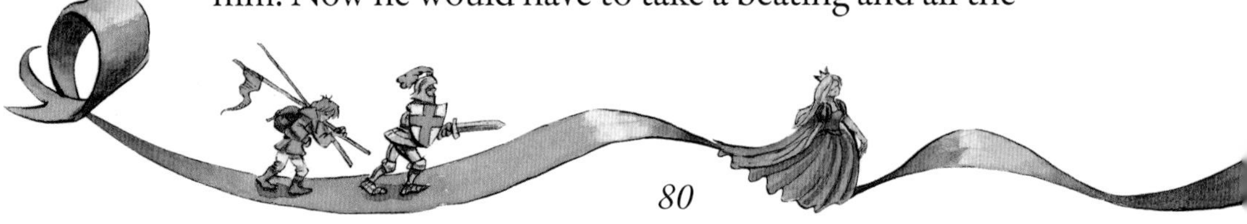

neighbors would hear about it. Would to Heaven he had never had a daughter at all if that was what came of it.

The girl, however, told him to be of good cheer. "Go to bed and sleep quietly," said she. "I will think of some way out of the trouble. No harm shall come to you, even if I have to go to the palace myself and take the beating in your place."

The next day the girl gave her father a bag of boiled beans and told him to take them out to a certain place where the king rode by every day. "Wait until you see him coming," said she, "and then begin to sow the beans." At the same time he was to call out so loudly that the king could not help but hear him.

The man took the bag of beans and went out to the field his daughter had spoken of. He waited until he saw the king coming, and then he began to sow the beans, and at the same time to cry aloud, "Come sun, come rain! Heaven grant that these boiled beans may yield me a good crop."

The king was surprised that any one should be so stupid as to think boiled beans would grow and yield a crop. He did not recognize the man, for he had seen him only once, and he stopped his horse to speak to him.

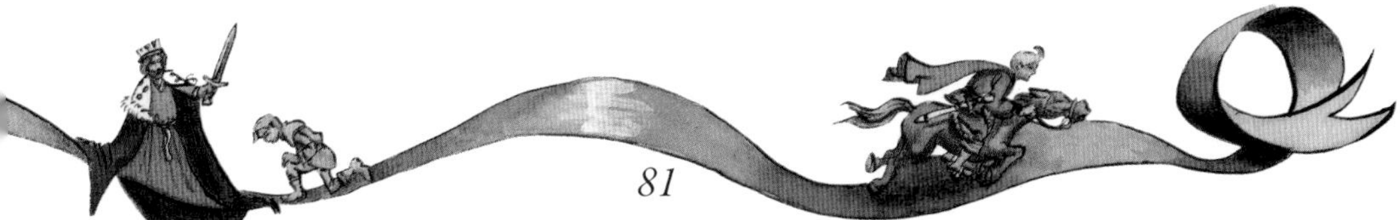

"My poor man," said he, "how can you expect boiled beans to grow? Do you not know that is impossible?"

"Whatever the king commands should be possible," answered the man. "And if chickens can hatch from boiled eggs, why should not boiled beans yield a crop?"

When the king heard this he looked at the man more closely, and then he recognized him as the father of the clever daughter.

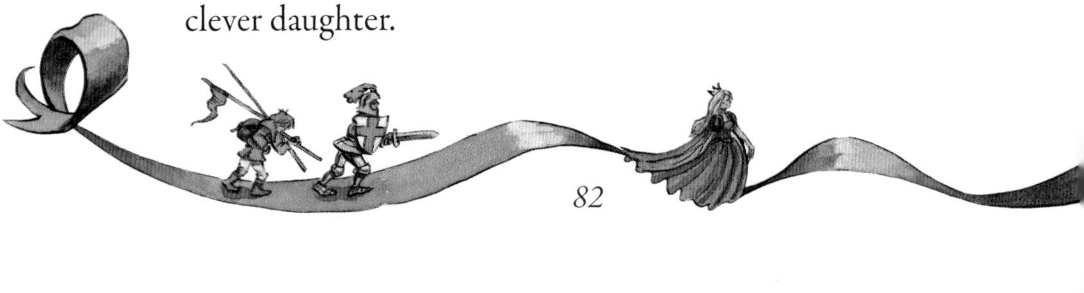

"You have indeed a clever daughter," said he. "Take your beans home and bring me back the eggs I gave you."

The man was glad when he heard that and made haste to obey. He carried the beans home, then took the eggs and brought them back to the palace of the king.

After the king had received the eggs he gave the man a handful of flax. "Take this to your clever daughter," he said, "and bid her make for me within the week a full set of sails for a large ship. If she does this she shall receive the half of my kingdom as a reward, but if she fails, you shall have a beating that you will not soon forget."

The man returned home lamenting his hard lot.

"What is the matter?" asked his daughter. "Has the king set another task that I must do?"

Yes, that he had—her father showed her the flax the king had sent her and gave her the message.

"Do not be troubled," said the girl. "No harm shall come to you. Go to bed and sleep quietly, and tomorrow I will send the king an answer that will satisfy him."

The man believed what his daughter said. He went to bed and slept quietly.

The next day the girl gave her father a small piece of wood. "Carry this to the king," said she. "Tell him I am

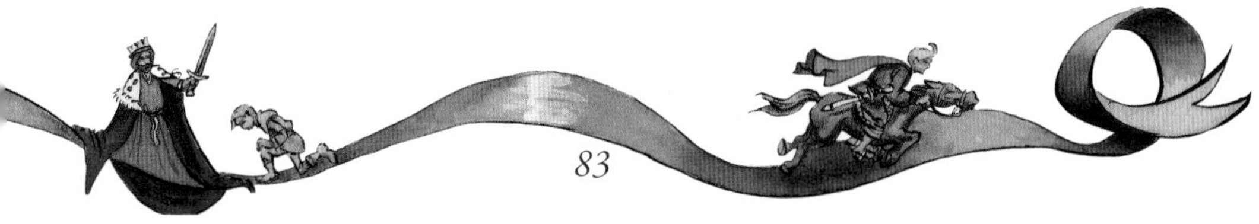

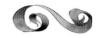

ready to make the sails, but first let him make me of this wood a large ship so that I may fit the sails to it."

The father did as the girl bade him, and the king was surprised at the cleverness of the girl in returning him such an answer.

"That is all very well," said he, "and I will excuse her from this task. But here! Here is a glass mug. Take it home to your clever daughter. Tell her it is my command that she dip out the waters from the ocean bed so that I can ride over the bottom dry shod. If she does this, I will take her for my wife, but if she fails, you shall be beaten within an inch of your life."

The man took the mug and hastened home, weeping aloud and bemoaning his fate.

"Well, and what is it?" asked his daughter. "What does the king demand of me now?"

The man gave her the glass mug and told her what the king had said.

"Do not be troubled," said the girl. "Go to bed and sleep in peace. You shall not be beaten, and soon I shall be reigning as queen over all this land."

The man had trust in her. He went to bed and dreamed he saw her sitting by the king wearing a crown.

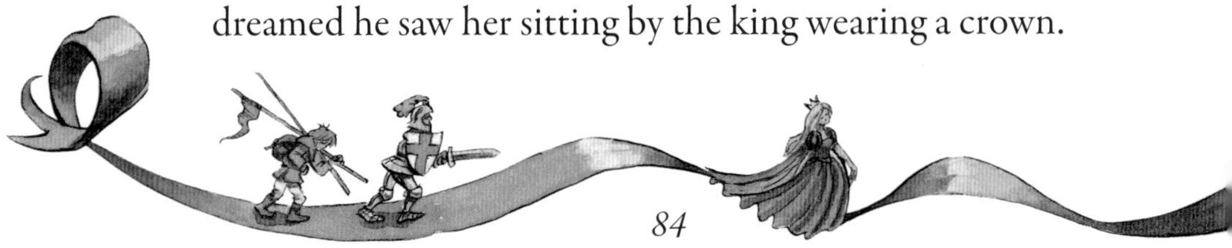

The next morning the girl gave her father a bunch of wool. "Take this to the king," she said. "Tell him that you have given me the mug, and I am willing to dip the sea dry, but first let him take this wool and stop up all the rivers that flow into the ocean."

The man did exactly as his daughter instructed him. He took the wool to the king and repeated what she had said word for word.

Then the king saw that the girl was indeed a clever one, and he sent for her to come before him.

She came just as she was, in her homespun dress and her rough shoes and with a cap on her head; but for all her mean clothing she was as pretty and fine as a flower, and the king was not slow to see it. Still, he wanted to make sure for himself that she was as clever as her messages had been.

"Tell me," said he, "what sound can be heard the farthest throughout the world?"

"The thunder that echoes through heaven and earth," answered the girl, "and your own royal commands that go from lip to lip."

This reply pleased the king greatly. "And now tell me," said he, "exactly what is my royal scepter worth?"

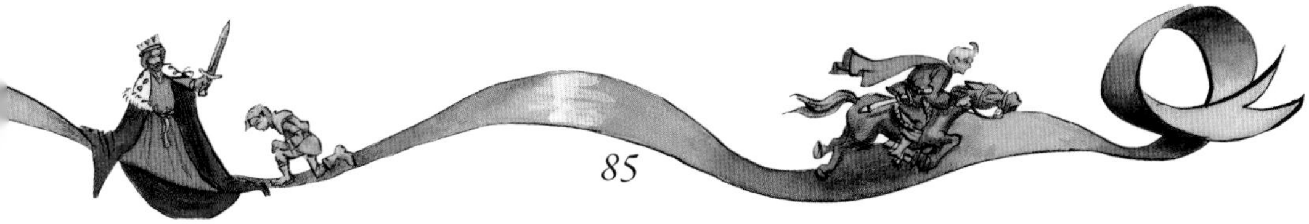

"It is worth exactly as much as the power for which it stands," the girl replied.

The king was so well satisfied with the way the girl answered that he no longer hesitated—he was determined that she should be his queen, and that they should be married at once.

The girl had something to say to this, however. "I am but a poor girl," said she, "and my ways are not your ways. It may well be that you will tire of me, or that you may be angry with me sometime, and send me back to my father's house to live. Promise that if this should happen, you will allow me to carry back with me from the castle the thing that has grown most precious to me."

The king was willing to agree to this, but the girl was not satisfied until he had written down his promise and signed it with his own royal hand. Then she and the king were married with the greatest magnificence, and she came to live in the palace and reign over the land.

Now while the girl had been only a peasant, she had been well content to dress in homespun and live as a peasant should; but after she became queen she would wear nothing but the most magnificent robes and jewels and ornaments, for that seemed to her only right and

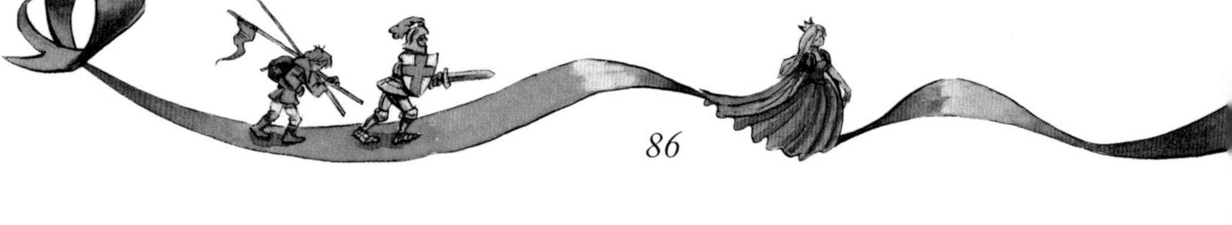

proper for a queen. But the king, who was of a very jealous nature, thought his wife did not care at all for him, but only for the fine things he could give her.

One day the king and queen were to ride abroad together, and the queen spent so much time in dressing herself that the king was kept waiting, and he became very angry. When she appeared before him, he would not even look at her. "You care nothing for me, but only for the jewels and fine clothes you wear!" he cried. "Take with you those that are the most precious to you, as I promised you, and return to your father's house. I will no longer have a wife who cares only for my possessions and not at all for me."

Very well, the girl was willing to go. "And I will be happier in my father's house than I was when I first met you," said she. Nevertheless, she begged that she might spend one more night in the palace, and that she and the king might sup together once again before she returned home. To this the king agreed, for he still loved her, even though he was so angry with her.

So he and his wife supped together that evening, and just at the last, the queen took a golden cup and filled it with wine. Then, when the king was not looking, she put

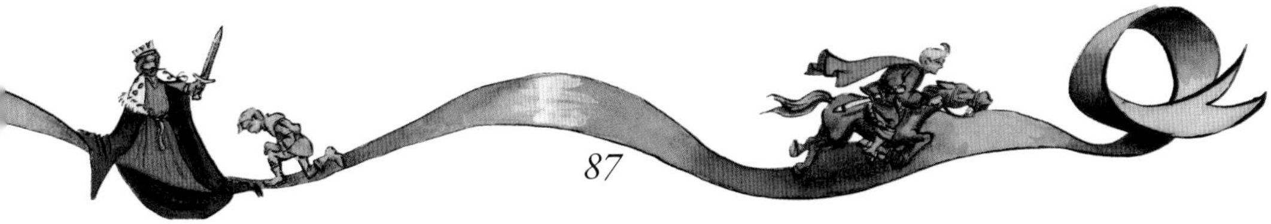

a sleeping potion in the cup and gave it to him to drink.

He took it and drank to the very last drop, suspecting nothing, but soon after, he sank down among the cushions in a deep sleep. Then the queen ordered him to be carried to her father's house and laid in the bed there.

When the king awoke the next morning, he was very

much surprised to find himself in the peasant's cottage. He raised himself upon his elbow to look about him, and at once the girl came to the bedside, and she was again dressed in the coarse and common clothes she had worn before she was married.

"What means this?" said the king. "How came I here?"

"My dear husband," said the girl, "your promise was that if you ever sent me back to my father's house I might carry with me the thing that had become most precious to me in the castle. You are that most precious thing, and I care for nothing else unless it makes me pleasing in your sight."

Then the king could no longer feel jealous or angry. He clasped her in his arms, and they kissed each other tenderly. That day they returned to the palace, and from then on the king and his peasant queen lived together in the greatest love and happiness.

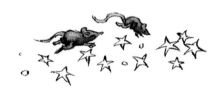

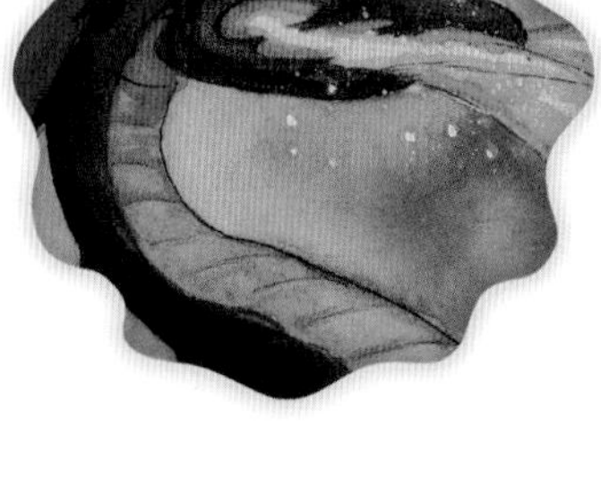

Strange and Magical Tales

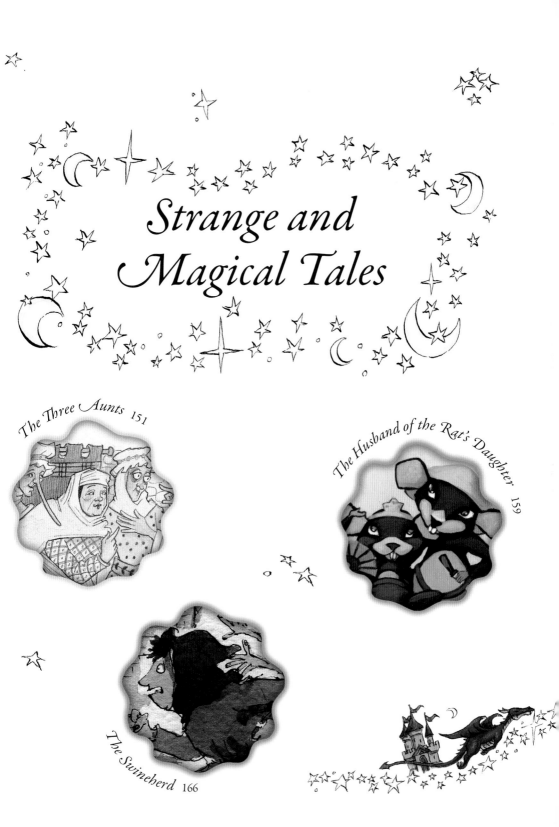

The Three Heads of the Well

By Flora Annie Steel

READING TIME: 12 MINUTES

Not all princesses sit in castles waiting to be rescued—some go out to seek their own fortunes. This princess, from the east of England, even takes a bottle of beer with her—small beer is a weak beer people drank every day when water wasn't safe to drink. You will find a wonderful old use of the word "weird" in this story, meaning to cast a spell.

Once upon a time there reigned a king in Colchester who was valiant, strong, wise, and famous throughout

the land as a good ruler. But in the midst of his glory his dear queen died, leaving him with a daughter to look after. This maiden was renowned for her beauty, kindness, and grace.

Now strange things happen—the king of Colchester heard of a lady who had immense riches, and he had a mind to marry her, although she was old, ugly, hook-nosed, and ill-tempered. Furthermore, she possessed a daughter as ugly as herself. None could give the reason why, but only a few weeks after the death of his dear queen, the king brought this loathly bride to court, and married her with great pomp and festivities. Now the very first thing she did was to poison the king's mind against his own beautiful, kind, daughter, of whom, naturally, the ugly queen and her ugly daughter were jealous.

Now when the young princess found that even her father had turned against her, she grew weary of court life and longed to get away from it. So one day, happening to meet the king alone in the garden, she went down on her knees and begged and prayed him to give her some help and let her go out into the world to seek her fortune. To this the king agreed, and he told his consort to fit the girl out for her enterprise in proper fashion. But the jealous woman gave her only a canvas bag of brown bread and hard cheese, with a bottle of small beer.

Though this was but a pitiful dowry for a king's daughter, the princess was too proud to complain, so she took it, returned her thanks, and set off on her journey through woods and forests, by rivers and lakes, over mountain and valley.

At last she came to a cave, at the mouth of which, on a stone, sat an old, old man with a white beard.

"Good day," he said, "Where are you going?"

"Reverend father," replied she, "I'm going to seek my fortune."

"And what have you for a dowry, fair damsel," said he, "in your bag and bottle?"

"Bread and cheese and small beer, father," said she, smiling. "Will it please you to partake of either?"

"With all my heart," said he, and when she pulled out her provisions he ate them nearly all. But once again she made no complaint, but bade him eat what he needed.

Now when he had finished he gave her many thanks, and said:

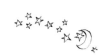

"For your beauty, and your kindness, and your grace, take this wand. There is a thick, thorny hedge before you that seems impassible. But strike it thrice with this wand, saying each time, 'Please, hedge, let me through,' and it will open a pathway for you. Then, when you come to a well, sit down on the brink of it. Do not be surprised at anything you may see, but whatever you are asked to do, please do!"

So saying, the old man went into the cave, and she went on her way. After a while she came to a high, thick, thorny hedge. When she struck it three times with the wand, saying, "Please, hedge, let me through," it opened a wide pathway for her. So she came to the well, on the brink of which she sat down, and no sooner had she done so, than a golden head without any body came up through the water, singing as it came:

"Wash me and comb me, lay me on a bank to dry
Softly and prettily to watch the passers-by."

"Certainly," she said, pulling out her silver comb. Then, placing the head on her lap, she began to comb the golden hair. When she had combed it, she lifted the golden head softly and laid it on a primrose bank to dry. No sooner had she done this than another golden head appeared, singing as it came:

"Wash me and comb me, lay me on a bank to dry
Softly and prettily to watch the passers-by."

"Certainly," said she, and after combing the golden hair, placed the golden head softly on the primrose bank, beside the first one.

Then came a third head out of the well, and it said the same thing:

"Wash me and comb me, lay me on a bank to dry
Softly and prettily to watch the passers-by."

"With all my heart," said she graciously, and after taking the head on her lap, and combing its golden hair with her silver comb, there were the three golden heads in a row on the primrose bank. She sat down to rest and looked at them, they were so quaint and pretty. As she rested, she cheerfully ate and drank the meagre portion of the brown bread, hard cheese, and small beer that the old man had left to her. Although she was a king's daughter, she was too proud to complain.

Then the first head spoke. "What shall we weird for this damsel who has been so gracious? I weird her to be so beautiful that she shall charm every one she meets."

"And I," said the second head, "weird her a voice that shall exceed the nightingale's in sweetness."

"And I," said the third head, "weird her to be so fortunate that she shall marry the greatest king alive."

"Thank you with all my heart," said she, "but don't you think I had better put you back in the well before I go on? Remember you are golden, and the passers-by might steal you."

To this they agreed, so she put them back. And when they had thanked her for her kind thought and said goodbye, she went on her journey.

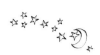

Now she had not traveled far before she came to a forest where the king of the country was hunting with his nobles. As the procession passed down the glade she stood back to avoid them, but the king caught sight of her and drew up his horse, amazed at her beauty.

"Fair maid," he said, "who are you, and where are you traveling through the forest alone?"

"I am the king of Colchester's daughter, and I go to seek my fortune," said she, and her voice was sweeter than a nightingale's.

Then the king jumped from his horse, being so struck by her that he felt it would be impossible to live without her; and falling on his knee, begged and prayed her to marry him without delay.

And he begged and prayed so well that at last she consented. So, with all courtesy, he lifted her onto his horse behind him. Commanding the hunt to follow, he returned to his palace, where the wedding festivities took place with all possible pomp and merriment. Then, ordering out the royal chariot, the happy pair departed to pay the king of Colchester a bridal visit. You may imagine the surprise and delight with which, after so short an absence, the people of Colchester saw their

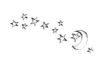

beloved, beautiful, kind, and gracious princess return in a chariot as the bride of the most powerful king in the world. The bells rang out, flags flew, drums beat, the people cheered, and all was gladness, save for the ugly queen and her ugly daughter, who were ready to burst with envy, for the despised maiden was now above them both, and went before them at every court ceremony.

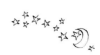

So, after the visit was ended, and the young king and his bride had gone back to their own country to live happily ever after, the ugly, ill-natured princess said to her mother, the ugly queen:

"I also will go into the world and seek my fortune. If that slovenly girl with her mincing ways got so much, what may I not get?"

So her mother agreed, and furnished her forth with silken dresses and furs, and gave her as provisions sugar, almonds, and sweetmeats of every variety, besides a large flagon of Malaga wine. Altogether a right royal dowry fit for a princess.

Armed with her plentiful package, the ugly princess set forth on her journey, following the same road as her stepsister. Thus she soon came upon the same old man with a white beard, who was seated on a stone by the mouth of a cave.

"Good day" said he. "Where are you going?"

"What's that to you, old man?" she said rudely.

"And what have you for a dowry in bag and bottle?" he asked quietly.

"Good things with which you shall not be troubled," she answered pertly.

"Will you not spare an old man something to eat?" he said.

Then she laughed. "Not a bite, not a sup, lest they should choke you, though that would be small matter to me," she replied, with a toss of her head.

"Then ill luck go with you," remarked the old man as he rose and went into the cave.

So she went on her way, and after a time came to the thick, thorny hedge. Seeing what she thought was a gap in it, she tried to pass through, but no sooner had she gotten well into the middle of the hedge than the thorns closed in around her so that she was all scratched and torn before she won her way. Thus, streaming with blood, she went on to the well, and seeing water, sat on the brink, intending to cleanse herself. But just as she dipped her hands, up came a golden head singing as it came:

"*Wash me and comb me, lay me on the bank to dry*
Softly and prettily to watch the passers-by."

"A likely story," said she. "I'm going to wash myself, thank you very much." And with that she gave the head

such a bang with her bottle that it bobbed below the water. But it came up again, and so did a second head, singing as it came:

"Wash me and comb me, lay me on the bank to dry
Softly and prettily to watch the passers-by."

"Not I," scoffed she. "I'm going to wash my hands and face and have my dinner." So she gave the second head a cruel bang with the bottle, and both heads ducked down in the water.

But when they came up again, all draggled and dripping, the third head came also, singing as it came:

"Wash me and comb me, lay me on the bank to dry
Softly and prettily to watch the passers-by."

By this time the ugly princess had cleansed herself, and, seated on the primrose bank, had her mouth full of sugar and almonds.

"Not I," said she, as well as she could. "I'm not a washerwoman nor a barber. So take that for your washing and combing."

And with that, she finished the wine, carelessly flung the empty bottle at the three heads floating in the well, and carried on greedily eating her sweets.

But this time the heads didn't duck. They looked at each other and said, "How shall we weird this rude girl for her bad manners?"

"I weird that to her ugliness shall be added blotches on her face," said the first head.

"And I weird that she shall forever be hoarse as a crow and speak as if she had her mouth full," said the second head.

"And I weird that she shall be glad to marry a cobbler," said the third head.

Then the three heads sank into the well and were no more seen, and the ugly princess went on her way. But, lo and behold! When she came to a town, the children ran from her ugly blotched face screaming with fright, and when she tried to tell them she was the king of Colchester's daughter, her voice squeaked like a corn-crake's and was hoarse as a crow's. Folk could not understand a word she said, because she spoke as if her mouth was full!

Now in the town there happened to be a cobbler, who not long before had mended the shoes of a poor old hermit, and the latter, having no money, had paid for the job by the gift of a wonderful ointment that would cure blotches on the face, and a bottle of medicine that would banish any hoarseness.

So, seeing the miserable, ugly princess in great

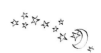

distress, he went up to her and gave her a few drops out of his bottle, and then understanding from her rich attire and clearer speech that she was indeed a king's daughter, he craftily said that if she would take him for a husband he would undertake to cure her.

"Anything! Anything!" sobbed the miserable princess.

So they were married, and the cobbler straightway set off with his bride to visit the king of Colchester. But the bells did not ring, the drums did not beat, and the people, instead of cheering, burst into loud guffaws at the cobbler in leather, and his wife in silks and satins.

As for the ugly queen, she was so enraged and disappointed that she went mad with anger and left the country. Whereupon the king, really pleased at getting rid of her so soon, gave the cobbler one hundred pounds and bade him go about his business with his ugly bride.

Which he did quite contentedly, for one hundred pounds meant much to the poor cobbler. So they went to a remote part of the kingdom and lived unhappily for many years, he cobbling shoes, and she spinning the thread for him.

The Enchanted Head

By Andrew Lang

READING TIME: 15 MINUTES

This story is set in Arabia, where many women wear veils when they go out in public. The sequins that the old woman receives are not the little sparkling disks we know, but a small gold coin minted in several countries around the Mediterranean. The modern sequin is named after the coin.

Once upon a time an old woman lived in a small cottage near the sea with her two daughters. They were very poor, and the girls seldom left the house, as they worked all day long making veils for the ladies to wear over their faces, and every morning, when the veils were

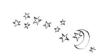

finished, the mother took them over the bridge and sold them in the city. Then she bought the food that they needed for the day, and returned home to do her share of veil making.

One morning the old woman rose even earlier than usual, and set off for the city with her wares. She was just crossing the bridge when, suddenly, she knocked against a human head, which she had never seen there before. The woman started back in horror, but what was her surprise when the head spoke, exactly as if it had a body joined onto it.

"Take me with you, good mother!" said the head imploringly. "Take me with you back to your house."

At the sound of these words the poor woman nearly went mad with terror. Have that horrible thing always at home? Never! Never! And she turned and ran back as fast as she could, not knowing that the head was jumping, dancing, and rolling after her. But when she reached her own door, it bounded in before her and stopped in front of the fire, begging and praying to be allowed to stay.

All that day there was no food in the house, for the veils had not been sold, and they had no money to buy

anything with. So they all sat silent at their work, inwardly cursing the head that was the cause of their misfortunes.

When evening came and there was no sign of supper, the head spoke, for the first time that day:

"Good mother, does no one ever eat here? During all the hours I have spent in your house not a creature has touched anything."

"No," answered the old woman, "we are not eating anything."

"And why not, good mother?"

"Because we have no money to buy any food."

"Is it your custom never to eat?"

"No, for every morning I go into the city to sell my veils, and with the few shillings I get for them I buy all we want. Today I did not cross the bridge, so of course I had nothing for food."

"Then I am the cause of your having gone hungry all day?" asked the head.

"Yes, you are," answered the old woman.

"Well, then, I will give you money and plenty of it, if you will only do as I tell you. In an hour, as the clock strikes twelve, you must be on the bridge at the place where you met me. When you get there, call out 'Ahmed!' three times, as loud as you can. Then a man will appear, and you must say to him: 'The head, your master, desires you to open the trunk and to give me the green purse that you will find in it.'"

"Very well, my lord," said the old woman, "I will set off at once for the bridge." And wrapping her veil around her, she went out.

Midnight was striking as she reached the spot where she had met the head so many hours before.

"Ahmed! Ahmed! Ahmed!" she cried, and immediately a huge man, as tall as a giant, stood on the bridge before her.

"What do you want?" he asked.

"The head, your master, desires you to open the trunk and to give me the green purse that you will find in it."

"I will be back in a moment, good mother," said he. And three minutes later he placed a purse full of sequins in the old woman's hand.

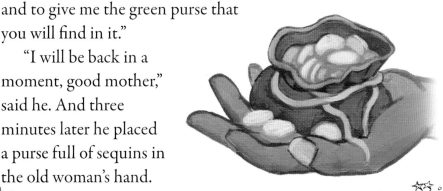

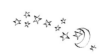

No one can imagine the joy of the whole family at the sight of all this wealth. The tiny, tumbledown cottage was rebuilt, the girls had new dresses, and their mother ceased selling veils. It was such a new thing to them to have money to spend that they were not as careful as they might have been, and by and by there was not a single coin left in the purse. When this happened their hearts sank within them, and their faces fell.

"Have you spent your fortune?" asked the head from its corner, when it saw how sad they looked. "Well, then, go at midnight, good mother, to the bridge, and call out 'Mahomet!' three times, as loud as you can. A man will appear in answer, and you must tell him to open the trunk, and to give you the red purse that he will find there."

The old woman did not need telling twice, but set off at once for the bridge.

"Mahomet! Mahomet! Mahomet!" cried she, with all her might, and in an instant a man, still larger than the last, stood before her.

"What do you want?" asked he.

"The head, your master, bids you open the trunk, and to give me the red purse that you will find in it."

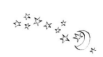

"Very well, good mother, I will do so," answered the man, and, the moment after he had vanished, he reappeared with the purse in his hand.

This time the money seemed so endless that the old woman built herself a new house and filled it with the most beautiful things that were to be found in the shops. Her daughters were always wrapped in veils that looked as if they were woven out of sunbeams, and their dresses shone with precious stones. The neighbors wondered where all this sudden wealth had sprung from, but nobody knew about the head.

"Good mother," said the head, one day, "this morning you are to go to the city and ask the sultan to give me his daughter for my bride."

"Do what?" asked the old woman in amazement. "How can I tell the sultan that a head without a body wishes to become his son-in-law? They will think that

I am mad, and I shall be laughed from the palace and stoned by the children."

"Do as I bid you," replied the head, "it is my will."

The old woman was afraid to say anything more, and, putting on her richest clothes, started for the palace. The sultan granted her an audience at once, and in a trembling voice, she made her request.

"Are you mad, old woman?" said the sultan, staring at her in amazement.

"The wooer is powerful, oh sultan, and nothing is impossible to him."

"Is that true?"

"It is, oh sultan, I swear it," she answered.

"Then let him show his power by doing three things, and I will give him my daughter."

"Command, oh gracious prince," said she.

"Do you see that hill in front of the palace?" asked the sultan.

"I see it," answered she.

"Well, in forty days the man who has sent you must make that hill vanish and plant a beautiful garden in its place. That is the first thing. Now go, and tell him what I say."

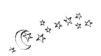

So the old woman returned and told the head the sultan's first condition.

"It is well," he replied, and said no more about it.

For thirty-nine days the head remained in his favorite corner. The old woman thought that the task set before him was beyond his powers, and that no more would be heard about the sultan's daughter. But on the thirty-ninth evening after her visit to the palace, the head suddenly spoke.

"Good mother," he said, "you must go tonight to the bridge, and when you are there cry 'Ali! Ali! Ali!' as loud as you can. A man will appear before you, and you will tell him that he is to level the hill, and to make, in its place, the most beautiful garden that ever was seen."

"I will go at once," answered she.

It did not take her long to reach the bridge that led to the city, and she took up her position on the spot where she had first seen the head and called loudly "Ali! Ali! Ali." In an instant a man appeared before her, of such a huge size that the old woman was half frightened, but his voice was mild and gentle as he said, "What is it that you want?"

"Your master bids you level the hill that stands in

front of the sultan's palace and in its place to make the most beautiful garden in the world."

"Tell my master he shall be obeyed," replied Ali, "it shall be done this moment." And the old woman went home and gave Ali's message to the head.

Meanwhile the sultan was in his palace, waiting till the fortieth day should dawn, wondering that not one spadeful of earth should have been dug out of the hill.

"If that old woman has been playing me a trick," thought he, "I will hang her! And I will put up a gallows tomorrow on the hill itself."

But when tomorrow came there was no hill—when the sultan opened his eyes he could not imagine why the room was so much lighter than usual, or why a sweet smell of flowers had filled the air.

"Can there be a fire?" he said to himself. "The sun never came in at this window before. I must get up and see." So he rose and looked out, and underneath him flowers from every part of the world were blooming, and creepers of every color hung in chains from tree to tree.

Then he remembered. "Certainly that old woman's son is a clever magician!" cried he, "I never met anyone as clever as that. What shall I give him to do next?

Let me think. Ah! I know." And he sent for the old woman, who, was waiting below.

"Your son has carried out my wishes very nicely," he said. "The garden is larger and better than that of any other king. But when I walk across it I shall need some place to rest on the other side. In forty days he must build me a palace, in which every room shall be filled with different furniture from a different country, and each more magnificent than any room ever seen." And having said this, he turned around and went away.

"Oh! He will never be able to do that," thought she. "It is much more difficult than the hill." And she walked home slowly, with her head bent.

"Well, what am I to do next?" asked the head cheerfully. And the old woman told her story.

"Dear me! Is that all? Why it is child's play," answered the head, and troubled no more about the palace for thirty-nine days. Then he told the old woman to go to the bridge and call for Hassan.

"What do you want, old woman?" asked Hassan, when he appeared, for he was not as polite as the others had been.

"Your master commands you to build the most

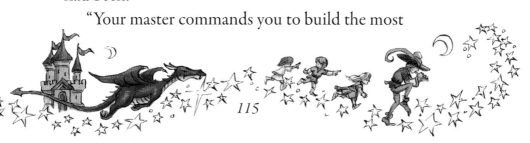

magnificent palace that ever was seen," she replied, "and you are to place it on the borders of the new garden."

"He shall be obeyed," answered Hassan. And when the sultan woke he saw, in the distance, a palace built of soft blue marble, with slender pillars of pure gold.

"That old woman's son is certainly powerful," he cried, "what shall I bid him do now?" And after thinking for some time, he sent for the old woman, who was expecting the summons.

"The garden is wonderful, and the palace the finest in the world," said he. "Let your son fill it with forty servants whose beauty shall be unequaled, all exactly like each other, and of the same height."

This time the king thought he had invented something totally impossible, and he was quite pleased with himself for his cleverness.

Thirty-nine days passed, and at midnight on the night of the last, the old woman was standing on the bridge.

"Bekir! Bekir! Bekir!" cried she. And a man appeared and inquired what she wanted.

"The head, your master, bids you find forty servants of unequaled beauty, and of the same height, and place them in the sultan's palace on the other side of the garden."

And when, on the morning of the fortieth day, the sultan went to the blue palace, and was received by the forty servants, he nearly lost his wits from surprise.

"I will assuredly give my daughter to the old woman's son," thought he. "If I were to search all the world through, I could never find a more powerful son-in-law."

And when the old woman entered his presence he

informed her that he was ready to fulfill his promise, and she was to bid her son appear at the palace without delay.

This command did not at all please the old woman, though, of course, she made no objections to the sultan.

"All has gone well so far," she grumbled, when she told her story to the head, "but what do you suppose the sultan will say when he sees his daughter's husband?"

"Never mind what he will say! Put me on a silver dish and carry me to the palace."

So it was done, though the old woman's heart beat as she laid down the dish with the head upon it.

At the sight before him, the king flew into a violent rage.

"I will never marry my daughter to such a monster," he cried. But the princess placed her head gently on his arm.

"You have given your word, my father, and you cannot break it," said she.

"But, my child, it is impossible for you to marry such a being!" exclaimed the sultan.

"Yes, I will marry him. He has a beautiful head, and I love him already."

So the marriage was celebrated, and great feasts were

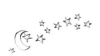

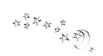

held in the palace, though the people wept tears to think of the sad fate of their beloved princess. But when the merrymaking was done, and the young couple were alone, the head suddenly disappeared—or, rather, a body was added to it, and one of the handsomest young men that ever was seen stood before the princess.

"A wicked fairy enchanted me at birth," he said, "and for the rest of the world I must always be a head only. But for you, and you only, I am a man like other men."

"And that is all I care about," said the princess.

The Broad Man, the Tall Man, and the Man with Eyes of Flame

By Alexander Chodsko

READING TIME: 16 MINUTES

There was once a king of a certain country who had a daughter who was not only exceedingly beautiful but also remarkably clever. Many kings and princes traveled from far-distant lands, each one with the hope of making her his wife. But she would have nothing to do with any one of them. Finally, it was proclaimed that she would marry the man who for three successive nights

could keep such strict watch upon her that she could not escape unnoticed. Those who failed were to have their heads cut off.

The news of this offer spread to all parts of the world. A great many kings and princes hastened to make the trial, taking their turn and keeping watch. But each one lost his life in the attempt, for they could not prevent—indeed they were not even able to see—the princess take her flight.

Now it happened that Matthias, prince of a royal city, heard of what was going on and resolved to watch through the three nights. He was young, handsome as a deer, and brave as a falcon. His father did all he could to turn him from his purpose—he used entreaties, prayers, threats. In fact, he forbade him to go, but in vain—nothing could prevent him. What could the poor father do? Worn out with contention, he was at last obliged to consent. Matthias filled his purse with gold, girded his best sword to his side, and, quite alone, started off to seek the fortune of the brave.

Walking along the next day, he met a man who seemed hardly able to drag one leg after the other.

"Where are you going?" asked Matthias.

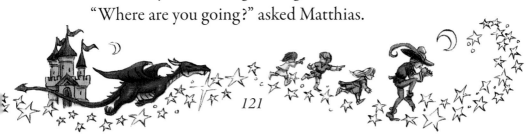

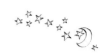

"I am traveling all over the world in search of happiness."

"What is your profession?"

"I have no profession, but I can do what no one else can. I am called Broad, because I have the power of swelling myself to such a size that there is room for a whole regiment of soldiers inside me."

So saying, he puffed himself out till he formed a barricade from one side of the road to the other.

"Bravo!" cried Matthias, delighted at this proof of his capacities. "By the way, would you mind coming with me? I, too, am traveling across the world in search of happiness."

"If there is nothing bad in it, I am quite willing," answered Broad. And they continued their journey together.

A little farther on, they met a very slender man—frightfully thin, and tall and straight as a column.

"Whither are you going, good man?" asked Matthias, filled with curiosity at his strange appearance.

"I am traveling about the world."

"To what profession do you belong?"

"To no profession, but I know something everyone

else is ignorant of. I am called Tall, and with good reason. For without leaving the earth I can stretch out and reach up to the clouds. When I walk I clear a mile at each step."

Without more ado he lengthened himself out until his head was lost in the clouds, while he really cleared a mile with each step.

"I like that, my fine fellow," said Matthias. "Come, would you not like to travel with us?"

"Why not?" replied he. "I'll come."

So they proceeded on their way together. While passing through a forest they saw a man placing tree trunks one upon another.

"What are you trying to do there?" asked Matthias, addressing him.

"I have Eyes of Flame," said he, "and I am building a pile here." So saying, he fixed his flaming eyes upon the wood, and the whole was instantly set alight.

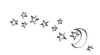

"You are a very clever and powerful man," said Matthias, "would you like to join our party?"

"All right, I am willing."

So the four traveled along together. Matthias was overjoyed to have met with such gifted companions, and he paid their expenses generously, without complaining of the enormous sum of money he had to spend on the amount of food Broad consumed.

After some days they reached the princess's palace. Matthias had told them the object of his journey and had promised each a large reward if he was successful. They gave him their word to work with a will at the task, which every one up till then had failed to accomplish. The prince bought them each a handsome suit of clothes; and when they were all presentable he sent them to tell the king, the princess's father, that he had come with his attendants to watch the princess for three nights. But he took very good care not to say who he was, nor whence he had come.

The king received them kindly, and after hearing their request said: "Reflect well before engaging yourselves in this, for if the princess escapes you will have to die."

"We very much doubt her escaping from us," they

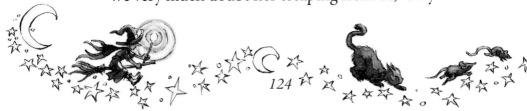

replied, "but come what will, we intend to make the attempt and to begin at once."

"My duty was to warn you," replied the monarch, smiling, "but if you still persist in your resolution, I myself will take you to the lady's apartments."

Matthias was dazzled at the loveliness of the royal maiden, while she, on her side, received the brilliant and handsome young man most graciously, not trying to hide how much she liked his good looks and gentle manner. Hardly had the king retired when Broad lay down across the threshold. Tall and the Man with Eyes of Flame placed themselves near the window, while Matthias talked with the princess and watched her every movement attentively.

Suddenly she ceased to speak, then after a few moments said, "I feel as if a shower of poppies were falling on my eyelids."

And she lay down on the couch, pretending to sleep.

Matthias did not breathe a word. Seeing her asleep, he sat down at a table near the sofa, leaned his elbows upon it, and rested his chin in the hollow of his hands. Gradually he felt drowsy and his eyes closed, as did those of his companions.

Now this was the moment the princess was waiting for. Quickly changing herself into a dove, she flew toward the window. If it had not happened that one of her wings touched Tall's hair, he would not have awakened, and he would certainly never have succeeded in catching her if it had not been for the Man with Eyes of Flame; for as soon as he knew which direction she had taken, he sent such a glance after her—that is, a flame of fire—that in the twinkling of an eye her wings were burned, and having been thus stopped, she was obliged to perch on top of a tree. From there, Tall reached her easily, and placed her in Matthias' hands, where she became a princess again. Matthias was just waking from his sleep.

Next morning and the morning after, the king was greatly astonished to find his daughter sitting by the prince's side, but he was obliged to keep silent and accept facts as they were, at the same time entertaining his guests royally. At the approach of the third night, he spoke with his daughter and begged her to practice all the magic of which she was capable and to act in such a way as to free him from the presence of intruders of whom he knew neither the rank nor the fortune.

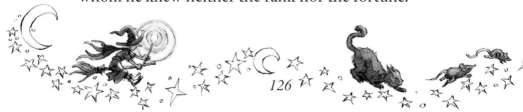

As for Matthias, he used every means in his power to bring about a happy ending to such a hitherto successful undertaking. Before entering the princess's apartments he took his comrades aside and said, "There is but one more stroke of luck, dear friends, and then we have succeeded. If we fail, do not forget that our four heads will roll on the scaffold."

"Come along," replied the three, "never fear, we shall be able to keep good watch."

When they came into the princess's room, they hastened to take up their positions, and Matthias sat down facing the lady. He would have much preferred to remain with her without being obliged to keep watch all the time for fear of losing her forever. Resolving not to sleep this time, he said to himself, "Now I will keep watch upon you, but when you are my wife I will rest."

At midnight, when sleep was beginning to overpower her watchers, the princess kept silent, and, stretching herself on the couch, shut her beautiful eyes as if she were really asleep.

Matthias, his elbows on the table, his chin in the palms of his hands, his eyes fixed upon her, admired her silently. But as sleep closes even the eyes of the eagle, so it

shut those of the prince and his companions.

The princess, who all this time had been watching them narrowly and only waiting for this moment, got up from her seat and, changing herself into a little fly, flew out of the window. Once free, she changed herself into a fish, and falling into the palace well, she plunged and hid herself in the depths of the water.

She would certainly have made her escape if, while a fly, she had not just touched the tip of the nose of the Man with Eyes of Flame. He sneezed and opened his eyes in time to notice the direction in which she had disappeared. Without losing an instant, he gave the alarm, and all four ran into the courtyard. The well was very deep, but that did not matter. Tall stretched himself to the depth, and searched in all the corners—but he was unable to find the little fish, and it seemed impossible that it could ever have been there.

"Now then, get out of that, I will take your place," said Broad.

And getting in at the top by the rim, he filled up all the inside of the well, stopping it so completely with his huge body that the water sprang out—but nothing was seen of the little fish.

"Now it is my turn," said the Man with Eyes of Flame. "I warrant I'll dislodge this clever magician."

When Broad had cleared the well of his enormous person, the water returned to its place, but it soon began to boil from the heat of the eyes of flame. It boiled and boiled, till it boiled over the rim—then, as it went on boiling and rising ever higher and higher, a little fish was seen to throw itself out on the grass, half cooked. As it touched the ground it again took the form of the princess.

Matthias went to her and kissed her tenderly.

"You have conquered, my master and husband," she said. "You have succeeded in preventing my escape. Henceforth I am yours, both by right of conquest and of my own free will."

The young man's courtesy, strength, and gentleness, as well as his beauty, were very pleasing to the princess, but her father, the king, was not so ready to approve of her choice, and he resolved not to let her go with them.

But this did not trouble Matthias, who determined to carry her off, aided by his three comrades. They soon all left the palace.

The king was furious, and he ordered his guards to follow them and bring them back under pain of death. Meanwhile Matthias, the princess, and the three comrades had already traveled a distance of some miles. When she heard the steps of the pursuers, she begged the Man with Eyes of Flame to see who they were. Having turned to look, he told her that a large army of men on horseback were advancing at a gallop.

"They are my father's guards," said she. "We shall have some difficulty in escaping them."

Then, seeing the horsemen draw nearer, she took the veil from her face and, throwing it behind her in the direction of the wind, said, "I command as many trees to spring up as there are threads in this veil."

Instantly, in the twinkling of an eye, a high, thick forest rose up between them. Before the soldiers had time to clear a pathway for themselves through this dense mass, Matthias and his companions had been able to get a great distance ahead. They even had time to take a little rest.

"Look," said the princess, "and see if they are still coming after us."

The Man with Eyes of Flame looked back, and replied that the king's guards were out of the forest and coming towards them with all speed.

"They will not be able to reach us!" cried she. And she let fall a tear from her eyes, saying as she did so, "Tear, become a river."

At the same moment a wide river flowed between them and their pursuers, and before the latter had found means of crossing it, Matthias and his party were far on in front.

"Man with Eyes of Flame," said the princess, "look behind and tell me how closely we are followed."

"They are quite near to us again," he replied. "They are almost upon our heels."

"Darkness, cover them," said she.

At these words Tall drew himself up. He stretched and stretched and stretched until he reached the clouds, and there, with his hat, he half covered the face of the sun. The side toward the soldiers was black as night,

while Matthias and his party, lit up by the shining half, went a good way without hindrance.

When they had traveled some distance, Tall uncovered the sun, and he soon joined his companions by taking a mile at each step. They were already in sight of Matthias's home, when they noticed that the royal guards were again following them closely.

"Now it is my turn," said Broad. "Go on your way in safety, and I will remain here. I shall be ready for them."

He quietly awaited their arrival, standing motionless, with his large mouth open from ear to ear. The royal army, who were determined not to turn back without having taken the princess, advanced toward the town at a gallop. They had decided among themselves that if it resisted they would lay siege to it.

Mistaking Broad's open mouth for one of the city gates, they all dashed through and disappeared.

Broad closed his mouth, and, having swallowed them, ran to rejoin his comrades in the palace of Matthias's father. He felt somewhat disturbed with a whole army inside him, and the earth groaned and trembled beneath him as he ran. He could hear the shouts of the people assembled around Matthias, as they rejoiced at his safe return.

"Ah, here you are at last, brother Broad," cried Matthias, as soon as he caught sight of him. "But what have you done with the army? Where have you left it?"

"The army is here, quite safe," answered he, patting his enormous person. "I shall be very pleased to return them as they are, for the morsel is not very easy to digest."

"Come then, let them out of their prison," said Matthias, enjoying the joke, and at the same time calling all the inhabitants to assist at the entertainment.

Broad, who looked upon it as a common occurrence, stood in the middle of the palace square, and putting his hands to his sides, began to cough. Then—it was really a sight worth seeing—at each cough horsemen and horses fell out of his mouth, one over the other, plunging, hopping, jumping, trying to see who could get out of the way the quickest. The last one had a little difficulty in getting free, for he somehow gotten into one of Broad's nostrils and was unable to move. It was only by giving a good sneeze that Broad could release him, the last of the royal cavaliers, and he lost no time in following his companions at top speed.

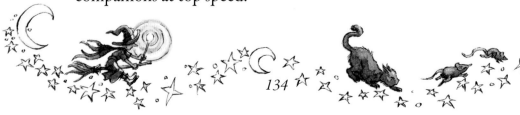

A few days later a splendid feast was given at the wedding of Prince Matthias and the princess. The king, her father, was also present. Tall had been sent to invite him. Owing to his knowledge of the road and the length of his limbs, he accomplished the journey so quickly that he was there before the royal horsemen had time to get back. It was well for them that this was so, for, had he not pleaded that their lives might be saved, their heads would certainly have been cut off for returning empty-handed.

Everything was now arranged to everybody's satisfaction. The princess's father was in the end delighted to know that his daughter was married to a gallant and noble prince, and Matthias generously rewarded his brave traveling companions, who remained with him to the end of their days.

Empty Bottles

By Howard Pyle

READING TIME: 15 MINUTES

Nicholas Flamel was a real man who lived in the fifteenth century and had a reputation as a great alchemist. It was even said that he had discovered the secret of the Philosopher's Stone, which supposedly turns base metals into gold and grants eternal life. In Harry Potter and the Philosopher's Stone, *by J.K. Rowling, Nicholas Flamel is described as having worked with Professor Dumbledore.*

*I*n the old, old days when men were wiser than they are in these times, there lived a great philosopher and magician, Nicholas Flamel. Not only did he know all the

actual sciences, but the black arts too, and magic, and whatnot. He conjured demons, so that when someone passed a house on a moonlit night, they might see imps, great and small, little and big, sitting on the chimney stacks and the ridge pole of the roof, clattering their heels on the tiles and chatting together.

He could change iron and lead into silver and gold, he discovered the elixir of life, and he might have been living even to this day had he thought it worthwhile to do so.

There was a student at the university whose name was Gebhart, who was so well acquainted with algebra and geometry that he could tell at a single glance how many drops of water there were in a bottle of wine. As for Latin and Greek—he could patter them off like his ABCs. Nevertheless, he was not satisfied with the things he knew, and wanted to learn the things that no schools could teach him. So one day he came knocking at Nicholas Flamel's door.

"Come in," said the wise man, and there Gebhart found him sitting in the midst of his books and bottles and diagrams and dust and chemicals and cobwebs, making strange figures upon the table with straws and a piece of chalk—for your true wise man can squeeze more learning out of straws and a piece of chalk than we common folk can get out of all the books in the world.

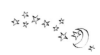

No one else was in the room but the wise man's servant, whose name was Babette.

"What is it you want?" said the wise man, looking at Gebhart over the rim of his spectacles.

"Master," said Gebhart, "I have studied day after day at the university, and from early in the morning until late at night, so that my head has hummed and my eyes were sore, yet I have not learned those things that I wish most of all to know—the arts that no one but you can teach. Will you take me as your pupil?"

The wise man shook his head.

"Many would like to be as wise as that," said he, "and few there be who can become so. Now tell me. Suppose all the riches of the world were offered to you, would you rather be wise?"

"Yes."

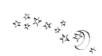

"Suppose you might have all the rank and power of a king or of an emperor, would you rather be wise?"

"Yes."

"Suppose I undertook to teach you, would you give up everything of joy and of pleasure to follow me?"

"Yes."

"Perhaps you are hungry," said the master.

"Yes," said the student, "I am."

"Then, Babette, you may bring some bread and cheese."

It seemed to Gebhart that he had learned all that Nicholas Flamel had to teach him.

It was the gray of dawn, and the master took the pupil by the hand and led him up the rickety stairs to the roof of the house, where nothing was to be seen but gray sky, high roofs, and chimney stacks, from which the smoke rose straight into the still air.

"Now," said the master, "I have taught you nearly all of the science that I know, and the time has come to show you the wonderful thing that has been waiting for us from the beginning when time was. You have given up wealth and the world and pleasure and joy and love for

the sake of wisdom. Now, then, comes the last test—whether you can remain faithful to me to the end. If you fail in it, all is lost that you have gained."

After he said that, he stripped his cloak away from his shoulders and laid bare the skin. Then he took a bottle of red liquor and began bathing his shoulder blades with it, and as Gebhart looked, he saw two little lumps bud out upon the smooth skin, and then grow and grow and grow until they became two great wings as white as snow.

"Now then," said the master, "take me by the belt and grip fast, for there is a long, long journey before us, and if you should lose your head and let go your hold, you will fall and be dashed to pieces."

Then he spread the two great wings, and away he flew as fast as the wind, with Gebhart hanging on to his belt.

Over hills, over dales, over mountains, over moors he flew, with the brown earth lying so far below that horses and cows looked like ants and men like fleas.

Then, by and by, it was over the ocean they were crossing, with the great ships that pitched and tossed below looking like wood chips in a puddle in rainy weather.

At last they came to a strange land, far, far away, and there the master landed upon a seashore where the sand was as white as silver. As soon as his feet touched the hard ground, the great wings were gone like a puff of smoke, and the wise man walked like any other body.

At the edge of the sandy beach was a great, high, naked cliff, and the only way of reaching the top was by a flight of stone steps, as slippery as glass, cut in the solid rock.

The wise man led the way, and the student followed close at his heels, every now and then slipping and stumbling, so that, had it not been for the help that the master gave him, he would have fallen more than once and have been dashed to pieces upon the rocks below.

At last they reached the top, and there found themselves in a desert, without a stick of wood or blade of grass, but only gray stones and skulls and bones bleaching in the sun.

In the middle of the plain was a castle such as the eyes of man never saw before, for it was built all of crystal from roof to cellar. Around it was a high wall of steel, and in the wall were seven gates of polished brass.

The wise man led the way straight to the middle gate

of the seven, where there hung a horn of pure silver, which he set to his lips. He blew a blast so loud and shrill that it made Gebhart's ears tingle. In an instant there sounded a great rumble and grumble like the noise of loud thunder, and the gates of brass swung slowly back.

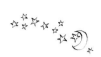

But when Gebhart saw what he saw within the gates, his heart crumbled away for fear, and his knees knocked together, for there, in the very middle of the way, stood a monstrous, hideous dragon, which blew out flames and clouds of smoke from its gaping mouth like a chimney on fire.

But the wise master was as cool as smooth water. He thrust his hand into the bosom of his jacket and drew forth a little black box, which he flung straight into the fiery mouth. Snap! The dragon swallowed the box.

The next moment it gave a great, loud, terrible cry and, clapping and rattling its wings, leaped into the air and flew away, bellowing like a bull.

If Gebhart had been wonder-struck at seeing the outside of the castle, he was ten thousand times more amazed to see the inside thereof. For as the master led the way and he followed, he passed through four-and-twenty rooms, each one more wonderful than the other. Everywhere was gold and silver and dazzling jewels that glistened so brightly that one had to shut one's eyes to their sparkle. Besides all this, there were silks and satins and velvets and laces and crystal and ebony and sandal-wood, which smelled sweeter than musk and rose leaves. All the wealth of the world brought together into one place could not make such riches as Gebhart saw with his two eyes in these four-and-twenty rooms.

His heart beat fast within him.

At last they reached a little door of solid iron, beside which hung a sword with a blade that shone like lightning. The master took the sword in one hand and laid the other upon the latch of the door. Then he turned to Gebhart and spoke for the first time since they had started upon their long journey.

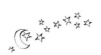

"In this room," said he, "you will see a strange thing happen, and in a little while I shall be as one dead. As soon as that comes to pass, go straightaway through to the room beyond, where you will find upon a marble table a goblet of water and a silver dagger. Touch nothing else, and look at nothing else, for if you do all will be lost to both of us. Bring the water straightaway, and sprinkle my face with it, and when that is done you and I will be the wisest and greatest men that ever lived, for I will make you equal to myself in all that I know. So now swear to do what I have just bid you, and not turn aside a hair's breadth in the going and the coming."

"I swear," said Gebhart, and crossed his heart.

Then the master opened the door and entered, with Gebhart close at his heels.

In the center of the room was a great red cockerel, with eyes that shone like sparks of fire. As soon as it saw the master it flew at him, screaming fearfully and spitting out darts of fire that blazed and sparkled like lightning.

It was a dreadful battle between the master and the cockerel. Up and down they fought, and here and there. Sometimes the student could see the wise man whirling

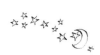

and striking with his sword, and then again he would be hidden in a sheet of flame. But after a while he made a lucky stroke, and off flew the cockerel's head. Then, lo and behold—instead of a cockerel it was a great, hairy, black demon that lay dead on the floor.

But, though the master had conquered, he looked like one sorely sick. He was just able to stagger to a couch that stood by the wall, and there he fell without breath or motion, like one dead, and as white as wax.

As soon as Gebhart had gathered his wits together he remembered what the master had said about the other room.

The door of it was also of iron. He opened it and passed within, and there saw two great tables or blocks of polished marble. Upon one was the dagger and a goblet of gold brimming with water. Upon the other lay the figure of a woman, and as Gebhart looked at her he thought her more beautiful than

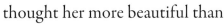

any thought or dream could picture. But her eyes were closed, and she lay like a lifeless figure of wax.

After Gebhart had gazed at her a long, long time, he took up the goblet and the dagger from the table and turned toward the door.

Then, before he left that place, he thought that he would have just one more look at the beautiful figure. So he did, and gazed and gazed until his heart melted away within him like a lump of butter, and, hardly knowing what he did, he stooped and kissed the lips.

Instantly he did so, a great humming sound filled the whole castle, so sweet and musical that it made him tremble to listen. Then suddenly the figure opened its eyes and looked straight at him.

"At last!" she said, "Have you come at last?"

"Yes," said Gebhart, "I have come."

Then the beautiful woman arose and stepped down from the table to the floor, and if Gebhart had thought her beautiful before, he thought her a thousand times more beautiful now that her eyes looked into his.

"Listen," said she. "I have been asleep for hundreds upon hundreds of years, for so it was fated to be until he should come who was to bring me back to life again.

You are he, and now you shall live with me forever. In this castle is the wealth gathered by the king of the genii, and it is greater than all the riches of the world. It and the castle likewise shall be yours. I can transport everything into any part of the world you choose, and can by my arts make you prince or king or emperor. Come."

"Stop," said Gebhart. "I must first do as my master bade me."

He led the way into the other room, the lady following him, and so they both stood together by the couch where the wise man lay. When the lady saw his face she cried out in a loud voice, "It is the great master! What are you going to do?"

"I am going to sprinkle his face with this water," said Gebhart.

"Stop!" said she. "Listen to what I have to say. In your hand you hold the water of life and the dagger of death. The master is not dead, but sleeping. If you sprinkle that water upon him he will awaken, young, handsome, and more powerful than the greatest magician that ever lived. I myself, this castle, and everything that is in it will be his, and, instead of you becoming a prince or a king or an emperor, he will be so in your place. That, I say, will happen if he wakens. Now the dagger of death is the only thing in the world that has power to kill him. You have it in your hand. You have but to give him one stroke with it while he sleeps, and he will never waken again, and then all will be yours—your very own."

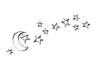

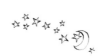

Gebhart neither spoke nor moved, but stood looking down upon his master. Then he set down the goblet very softly on the floor, and, shutting his eyes that he might not see the blow, raised the dagger to strike.

"That is all your promises amount to," said Nicholas Flamel the wise man. "After all, Babette, you need not bring the bread and cheese, for he shall be no pupil of mine."

Then Gebhart opened his eyes.

There sat the wise man in the midst of his books and bottles and diagrams and dust and chemicals and cobwebs, making strange figures upon the table with straws and a piece of chalk.

And Babette, who had just opened the cupboard door for the loaf of bread and the cheese, shut it again with a bang, and went back to her spinning.

So Gebhart had to go back again to his Greek and Latin and algebra and geometry, for after all, one cannot pour a gallon of beer into a quart pot, or the wisdom of a Nicholas Flamel into such a one as Gebhart.

As for the name of this story—why, if some promises are not bottles full of nothing but wind, there is little need to have a name for anything.

The Three Aunts

By George Webbe Dasent

READING TIME: 10 MINUTES

Once upon a time there was a poor man who lived in a hut far away in the wood and got his living by shooting. He had an only daughter, who was very pretty, and since she had lost her mother when she was a child and was now half grown up, she said she would go out into the world and earn her bread.

"Well, lassie!" said the father, "True enough you have learned nothing here but how to pluck birds and roast them, but still you may as well try to earn your bread."

So the girl went off to seek a place, and when she had

gone a little way, she came to a palace. There she stayed and got a place, and the queen liked her so well that all the other maids grew envious of her. So they made up their minds to tell the queen how the lassie said she could spin a pound of flax in four-and-twenty hours, for you must know that the queen was a great housewife, and thought much of good work.

"Have you said this? Then you shall do it," said the queen, "but you may have a little longer if you choose."

Now, the poor lassie dared not say she had never spun in all her life, but she only begged for a room to herself. That she got, and the wheel and the flax were brought up to her. There she sat sad and weeping, and knew not how to help herself. She pulled the wheel this way and that, and twisted and turned it about, but she made a poor hand of it, for she had never even seen a spinning wheel in her life.

But all at once, as she sat there, in came an old woman to her.

"What ails you, child?" she said.

"Ah!" said the lassie, with a deep sigh, "It's no good to tell you, for you'll never be able to help me."

"Who knows?" said the old wife. "Maybe I know

how to help you after all."

"Well," thought the lassie to herself, "I may as well tell her." And so she explained how fellow-servants had said she could spin a pound of flax in four-and-twenty hours.

"And here am I, wretch that I am, shut up to spin all that heap in a day and a night, when I have never ever seen a spinning wheel in all my born days."

"Well never mind, child," said the old woman, "If you'll call me 'aunt' on the happiest day of your life, I'll spin this flax for you, and so you may just go away and lie down to sleep."

Yes, the lassie was willing enough, and off she went and lay down to sleep.

Next morning when she awoke, there lay all the flax spun on the table, and that so clean and fine, no one had ever seen such even and pretty yarn.

The queen was very glad to get such nice yarn,

and she set greater store by the lassie than ever. But the rest were still more envious, and agreed to tell the queen how the lassie had said she could weave the yarn she had spun in four-and-twenty hours. So the queen said again, since she had said it she must do it. But if she couldn't quite finish it in four-and-twenty hours, the queen wouldn't be too hard upon her; she might have a little more time. This time, too, the lassie dared not say no, but begged for a room to herself, and then she would try. There she sat again, sobbing and crying, and not knowing which way to turn, when another old woman came in and asked:

"What ails you, child?"

At first the lassie wouldn't say, but at last she told her the whole story of her grief.

"Well, well!" said the old wife. "Never mind. If you'll call me 'aunt' on the happiest day of your life, I'll weave this yarn for you, and so you may just be off and lie down to sleep." Yes, the lassie was willing enough, so she went away and lay down to sleep. When she awoke, there lay the piece of linen on the table, woven so neat and close, no weave could be better. So the lassie took the piece and ran down to the queen, who was very glad to get such beautiful linen, and set greater store than ever by the lassie. But as for the others, they grew still more bitter against her, and thought of nothing but how to find out something to tell about her.

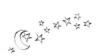

At last they told the queen that the lassie had said she could make the piece of linen into shirts in four-and-twenty hours. Well, all happened as before the lassie dared not say she couldn't sew, so she was shut up again in a room by herself, and there she sat in tears and grief. But then another old wife came, who said she would sew the shirts for her if she would call her 'aunt' on the happiest day of her life. The lassie was only too glad to do this, and then she did as the old wife told her, and went and lay down to sleep.

Next morning when she woke, she found the piece of linen made up into shirts. Such beautiful work no one had ever set eyes on, and more than that, the shirts were all marked and ready for wear. So, when the queen saw the work, she was so glad at the way in which it was sewn, that she clapped her hands, and said:

"Such sewing I never had, nor even saw, in all my born days." After that, she was as fond of the lassie as of her own children, and she said to her:

"Now, if you'd like to have the prince for your husband, you shall have him, for you will never need to hire work-women. You can sew, and spin, and weave all yourself."

So because the lassie was pretty, and the prince was glad to have her, the wedding soon came on. But just as the prince was going to sit down with the bride to the bridal feast, in came an ugly old hag with a long nose. So up got the bride and made a curtsey, and said:

"Good day, Auntie."

"That is an auntie to my bride?" asked the prince.

"Yes, she is!"

"Well, then, she'd better sit down with us to the feast," said the prince; but to tell you the truth, both he and the rest thought she was a loathsome woman to have next to you.

But just then in came another ugly old hag. She had a back so humped and broad, she had hard work to get through the door. Up jumped the bride in a trice, and greeted her with "Good day, Auntie!"

And the prince asked again if that were his bride's aunt. They both said yes, so the prince said that if that were so, she too had better sit down with them.

But they had scarce taken their seats before another ugly old hag came in, with eyes as large as saucers, and so red and bleary, it was gruesome to look at her. But up jumped the bride again, and said, "Good day, Auntie."

The prince asked her to sit down, but he wasn't very pleased, for he thought to himself, "Heaven shield me from such aunties as my bride has!" When he had sat a while, he could not keep his thoughts to himself any longer and asked:

"But how, in all the world can my bride, who is such a lovely lassie, have such loathsome, misshapen aunts?"

"I'll soon tell you how it is," said the first. "I was just as good-looking when I was her age, but the reason why I've got this long nose is, I was always kept sitting, and poking, and nodding over my spinning, and so my nose got stretched and stretched, until it got as long as you now see it."

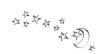

"And I," said the second, "ever since I was young, I have sat and scuttled backward and forward over my loom, and that's how my back has got so broad and humped as you now see it."

"And I," said the third, "ever since I was little, I have sat and stared and sewn, and sewn and stared, night and day, and that's why my eyes have got so ugly and red, and now there's no help for them."

"So, so!" said the prince, "'Twas lucky I came to know this, for if folk can get so ugly and loathsome by all this, then my bride shall neither spin, nor weave, nor sew all her life long."

The Husband of the Rat's Daughter

By Andrew Lang

READING TIME: 8 MINUTES

*O*nce upon a time there lived in Japan a rat and his wife who came of an old and noble race. They had one daughter, the loveliest girl in all the rat world. Her parents were very proud of her and spared no pains to teach her all she ought to know. There was not another young lady in the whole town who was as clever as she was in gnawing through the hardest wood, or who could drop from such a height onto a bed, or run away so fast

if anyone was heard coming. Great attention, too, was paid to her personal appearance, and her skin shone like satin, while her teeth were as white as pearls and beautifully pointed.

Of course, with all these advantages, her parents expected her to make a brilliant marriage, and as she grew up, they began to look around for a suitable husband.

But here a difficulty arose. The father was a rat from the tip of his nose to the end of his tail, outside as well as in, and desired that his daughter should wed among her own people. She had no lack of suitors, but her father's secret hopes rested on a fine young rat, with mustaches that almost swept the ground, whose family was still nobler and more ancient than his own. Unluckily, the mother had other views for her precious child. She was one of those people who always despised their own family and surroundings and take pleasure in thinking that they themselves are made of finer material than the rest of the world. "*My* daughter should never marry a mere rat," she declared, holding her head high. "With her beauty and talents she has a right to look for someone a little better than *that*."

So she talked to anyone that would listen to her. What the girl thought about the matter nobody knew or cared—it was not the fashion in the rat world.

Many were the quarrels that the old rat and his wife had upon the subject, and sometimes they bore on their faces certain marks that looked as if they had not kept to words only.

"Reach up to the stars is *my* motto," cried the lady one day, when she was in a greater passion than usual. "My daughter's beauty places her higher than anything upon earth!" she cried, "and I am certainly not going to accept a son-in-law who is beneath her."

"Better offer her in marriage to the sun," answered her husband impatiently. "As far as I know there is nothing greater than he."

"Well, I *was* thinking of it," replied the wife, "and as you are of the same mind, we will pay him a visit tomorrow."

So the next morning, the two rats, having spent hours in making themselves look smart, set out to see the sun, leading their daughter between them.

The journey took some time, but at length they came to the golden palace where the sun lived.

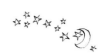

"Noble king," began the mother, "behold our daughter! She is so beautiful that she is above everything in the whole world. Naturally, we wish for a son-in-law who, on his side, is greater than all. Therefore we have come to you."

"I feel very much flattered," replied the sun, who was so busy that he had not the least wish to marry anybody. "You do me great honor by your proposal. Only, in one point you are mistaken, and it would be wrong of me to take advantage of your ignorance. There is something greater than I am, and that is the cloud. Look!" And as he spoke, a cloud spread itself over the sun's face, blotting out his rays.

"Oh, well, we will speak to the cloud," said the mother. And turning to the cloud she repeated her proposal.

"Indeed I am unworthy of anything so charming," answered the cloud, "but you make a mistake again in what you say. There is one thing that is even more powerful than I, and that is the wind. Ah, here he comes—you can see for yourself."

And she *did* see, for catching up the cloud as he passed, he threw it on the other side of the sky.

Then, tumbling father, mother, and daughter down to the earth again, he paused for a moment beside them, his foot on an old wall.

When she had recovered her breath, the mother began her little speech once more.

"The wall is the proper husband for your daughter," answered the wind, whose home consisted of a cave, which he visited only when he was not rushing around elsewhere. "You can see for yourself that he is greater than I, for he has power to stop me in my flight." And the mother, who did not trouble to conceal her wishes, turned at once to the wall.

Then something happened that was quite unexpected by everyone.

"I won't marry that ugly old wall, which is as old as my grandfather," sobbed the girl, who had not uttered one word all this time. "I would have married the sun, or the cloud, or the wind, because it was my duty, although I love the handsome young rat, and him only. But that horrid old wall—I would sooner die!"

And the wall, rather hurt in his feelings, declared that he had no claim to be the husband of so beautiful a girl.

"It is quite true," he said, "that I can stop the wind

who can part the clouds who can cover the sun, but there is someone who can do more than all these, and that is the rat. It is the rat who passes through me, and can reduce me to powder, simply with his teeth. If, therefore, you want a son-in-law who is greater than the whole world, seek him among the rats."

"Ah, what did I tell you?" cried the father. And his wife, though for the moment angry at being beaten, soon thought that a rat son-in-law was what she had always desired.

So all three returned happily home, and the wedding was celebrated three days after.

The Swineherd

By Hans Christian Andersen

READING TIME: 10 MINUTES

There was once a poor prince. He possessed a kingdom that, though small, was yet large enough for him to marry on, and married he wished to be.

Now it was certainly a little audacious of him to venture to say to the emperor's daughter, "Will you marry me?" But he did venture to say so, for his name was known far and wide. There were hundreds of princesses who would gladly have said yes, but would she say the same?

Well, we shall see.

On the grave of the prince's father grew a rose tree—a very beautiful rose tree. It bloomed only every five years, and then bore but a single rose, but oh, such a rose! Its scent was so sweet that when you smelled it you forgot all your cares and troubles. And he had also a nightingale that could sing as if all the beautiful melodies in the world were shut up in its little throat. This rose and this nightingale the princess was to have, and so they were both put into silver caskets and sent to her.

The emperor had them brought to him in the great hall, where the princess was playing "Here comes a duke a-riding" with her ladies-in-waiting. And when she caught sight of the big caskets that contained the presents, she clapped her hands for joy.

"If only it were a little pussycat!" she said. But the rose tree with the beautiful rose came out.

"But how prettily it is made!" said all the ladies-in-waiting.

"It is more than pretty," said the emperor.

But the princess felt it, and then she almost began to cry.

"Ugh! Papa," she said, "it is not artificial, it is *real*!"

"Ugh!" said all the ladies-in-waiting, "It is real!"

"Let us see first what is in the other casket before we begin to be angry," said the emperor, and there came out the nightingale. It sang so beautifully that one could scarcely utter a cross word against it.

"*Superbe*! *Charmant*!" said the ladies-in-waiting, for they all chattered French, each one worse than the other.

"How much the bird reminds me of the musical snuffbox of the late empress!" said an old courtier. "Ah, yes, it is the same tone, the same execution!"

"Yes," said the emperor, and then he wept like a little child.

"I hope that this, at least, is not real?" asked the princess.

"Yes, it is a real bird," said those who had brought it.

"Then let the bird fly away," said the princess, and she would not on any account allow the prince to come.

But he was not daunted. He painted his face brown and black, drew his cap well over his face, and knocked at the door. "Good day, Emperor," he said. "Can I get a place here as servant in the castle?"

"Yes," said the emperor, "but there are so many who ask for a place that I don't know whether there will be one for you; but still, I will think of you. Stay, it has just occurred to me that I want someone to look after the swine, for I have so very many of them."

And the prince got the job of imperial swineherd. He had a wretched little room close to the pigsties. Here he had to stay, but the whole day he sat working, and when evening came he had made a pretty little pot. All around it were little bells, and when the pot boiled they jingled most beautifully and played this tune:

"Where is Augustus dear?
Alas! He's not here, here, here!"

But the most wonderful thing was that when one held one's finger in the steam of the pot, then at once one could smell what dinner was ready in any fireplace in the town. That was indeed something quite different from the rose.

Now the princess came walking past with all her ladies-in-waiting, and when she heard the tune she stood

still and her face beamed with joy, for she also could play '*Where is Augustus dear?*'

It was the only tune she knew, but that she could play with one finger.

"Why, that is what I play!" she said. "He must be a most accomplished swineherd! Listen! Go down and ask him what the instrument costs."

And one of the ladies-in-waiting had to go down, but she put on wooden clogs because of the mud.

"What will you take for the pot?" asked the lady-in-waiting.

"I will have ten kisses from the princess," said the swineherd.

"Oh my, heaven forbid!" said the lady-in-waiting.

"Yes, I will sell it for nothing less," replied the swineherd.

"What did he say?" asked the princess urgently, when the lady-in-waiting returned.

"I really hardly like to tell you," answered the lady-in-waiting.

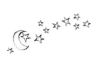

“He is disobliging!” said the princess, when she heard his price. But she had only gone a few steps when the bells rang out so prettily:

“Where is Augustus dear?
Alas! he's not here, here, here.”

“Listen!” said the princess. “‘Ask him whether he will take ten kisses from my ladies-in-waiting.”

“No, thank you,” said the swineherd. “Ten kisses from the princess, or else I keep my pot.”

“That is very tiresome!” said the princess. “But you must put yourselves in front of me, so no one can see.”

And the ladies-in-waiting placed themselves in front and then spread out their dresses, so the swineherd got his ten kisses, and she got the pot.

What happiness that was! The whole night and the whole day the pot was made to boil. There was not a fireplace in the whole town where they did not know what was being cooked, whether it was at the chancellor's or at the shoemaker's.

The ladies-in-waiting danced, clapping their hands.

“We know who is going to have soup and pancakes,

we know who is going to have porridge and sausages—isn't it interesting?'

"Yes, very interesting!" said the first lady-in-waiting.

"But don't say anything about it, for I am the emperor's daughter."

"Oh, no, of course we won't!" said everyone.

The swineherd—that is to say, the prince (though they did not know he was anything but a true swineherd)—let no day pass without making something. One day he made a rattle, which, when it was turned around, played all the waltzes and polkas that had ever been known since the world began.

"But that is *superbe*!" said the princess as she passed by. "I have never heard a more beautiful composition. Listen! Go down and ask him what this instrument costs, but I won't kiss him again."

"He wants a hundred kisses from the princess," said the lady-in-waiting who had gone down to ask him.

"He is mad!" said the princess, and then she went on, but she had only gone a few steps when she stopped.

"One ought to encourage art," she said. "I am the emperor's daughter! Tell him he shall have, as before, ten kisses, the rest he can take from my ladies-in-waiting."

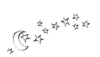

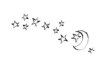

"But we don't at all like being kissed by him," said the ladies-in-waiting.

"That's nonsense," said the princess, "and if I can kiss him, you can too. Besides, remember that I give you board and lodging."

So the ladies-in-waiting had to go down to him again.

"A hundred kisses from the princess," said he, "or each keeps his own."

"Put yourselves in front of us," she said then, and so all the ladies-in-waiting put themselves in front, and he began to kiss the princess.

"What can that commotion be by the pigsties?" asked the emperor, who was standing on the balcony. He rubbed his eyes and put on his spectacles. "Why those are the ladies-in-waiting playing their games, I must go down to them."

So he took off his shoes, which were shoes, though he had trodden them down into slippers. What a hurry he was in, to be sure!

As soon as he came into the yard he walked very softly, and the ladies-in-waiting were so busy counting the kisses and seeing fair play that they never noticed the emperor. He stood on tiptoe.

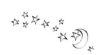

"What is that?" he said, when he saw the kissing, and then he threw one of his slippers at their heads just as the swineherd was taking his eighty-sixth kiss.

"Be off with you!" said the emperor, for he was very angry. And the princess and the swineherd were driven out of the empire.

Then the princess stood still and wept, the swineherd was scolding, and the rain was streaming down.

"Alas, what an unhappy creature I am!" sobbed the princess. "If only I had taken the beautiful prince! Alas, how unfortunate I am!"

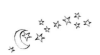

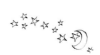

And the swineherd went behind a tree, washed the black and brown off his face, threw away his old clothes, and then stepped forward in his splendid dress, looking so beautiful that the princess was obliged to curtsy.

"I now come to this. I despise you!" he said. "You would have nothing to do with a noble prince, you did not understand the rose or the nightingale, but you would kiss the swineherd for the sake of a toy. This is what you get for it!" And he went into his kingdom and shut the door in her face, and she had to stay outside singing:

"*Where's my Augustus dear?*
Alas! he's not here, here, here!"

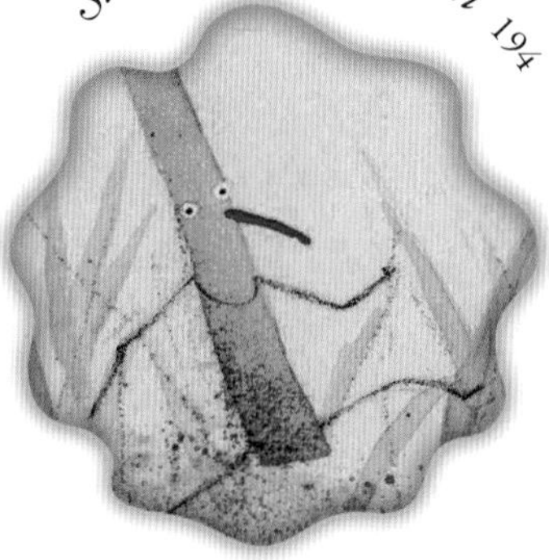

Along the Road

Hans in Luck

By Joseph Jacobs

READING TIME: 12 MINUTES

Some men are born to good luck—all they do or try to do comes right and all that falls to them isgain,all their geese are swans and all their cards are trumps. Toss them which way you will, they will always, like poor puss, alight upon their legs, and only move on so much the faster. The world may very likely not always think of them as they think of themselves, but what care they for the world? What can it know about the matter?

One of these lucky beings was neighbor Hans. Seven years he had worked hard for his master. At last he said,

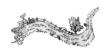

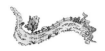

"Master, my time is up, I must go home and see my poor mother once more—so pray pay me my wages and let me go." And the master said, "You have been a faithful servant, Hans, so your pay shall be handsome." He gave him a lump of silver as big as his head.

Hans took out his handkerchief, put the piece of silver into it, threw it over his shoulder, and jogged off on his road homeward. As he went lazily on, dragging one foot after another, a man came in sight, trotting gaily along on a splendid horse. "Ah!" said Hans aloud. "What a fine thing it is to ride on horseback! There he sits as easy and happy as if he was at home, in the chair by his fireside, he trips against no stones, saves shoe leather, and gets on he hardly knows how."

Hans did not speak quietly, so the horseman heard it all, and said, "Well, friend, why do you go on foot then?"

"Ah!" said he, "I have this load to carry. To be sure it is silver, but it is so heavy that I can't hold up my head, and you must know it hurts my shoulder badly."

"What do you say of making an exchange?" said the horseman. "I will give you my horse, and you shall give me the silver, which will save you a great deal of trouble in carrying such a heavy load about with you."

“With all my heart,” said Hans, “but as you are so kind to me, I must tell you one thing—you will have a weary task to draw that silver about with you.” However, the horseman got off, took the silver, helped Hans up, gave him the bridle into one hand and the whip into the other, and said, “When you want to go very fast, smack your lips loudly together, and cry ‘Jip!’”

Hans was delighted as he sat on the horse, drew himself up, squared his elbows, turned out his toes, cracked his whip and rode merrily off, one minute whistling a merry tune, and another singing.

After a time he thought he should like to go a little faster, so he smacked his lips and cried, “Jip!” Away went the horse full gallop, and before Hans knew what he was

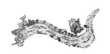

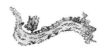

about, he was thrown off, and lay on his back by the roadside. His horse would have run off, if a shepherd who was coming by, driving a cow, had not stopped it. Hans soon came to himself, and got upon his legs again, sadly vexed, and said to the shepherd, "This riding is no joke, when a man has the luck to get upon a beast like this that stumbles and flings him off as if it would break his neck. However, I'm off now once and for all. I like your cow now a great deal better than this smart beast that played me this trick and has spoiled my best coat, you see, in this puddle, which, by the by, smells not very like a nosegay. One can walk along at one's leisure behind that cow—keep good company, and have milk, butter, and cheese every day, into the bargain. What would I give to have such a prize!"

"Well," said the shepherd, "if you are so fond of her, I will change my cow for your horse. I like to do good to my neighbors, even though I lose by it myself."

"Done!" said Hans, merrily. "What a noble heart that good man has!" thought he. Then the shepherd jumped upon the horse and wished Hans and the cow good morning, and away he rode.

Hans brushed his coat, wiped his face and hands,

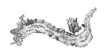

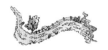

rested a while, and then drove off his cow quietly, and thought his bargain a very lucky one. "If I have only a piece of bread (and I shall always be able to get that) I can, whenever I like, eat my butter and cheese with it, and when I am thirsty I can milk my cow and drink the milk. What more can I wish for?"

When he came to an inn, he halted, ate up all his bread, and gave away his last penny for a glass of beer. When he had rested himself, he set off again, driving his cow toward his mother's village. But the heat grew greater as soon as noon came on, till at last, as he found himself on a wide heath that would take him more than an hour to cross, he began to feel so hot and parched that his tongue stuck to the roof of his mouth. "I can find a cure for this," thought he. "Now I will milk my cow and quench my thirst." So he tied her to the stump of a tree, and held his leathern cap to milk into, but not a drop was to be had. Who would have thought that this cow, which was to bring him milk and butter and cheese, was all that time utterly dry? Hans had not thought of looking to that.

While he was trying his luck in milking, and managing the matter very clumsily, the uneasy beast

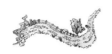

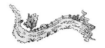

began to think him very troublesome, and at last gave him such a kick on the head as knocked him down. And there he lay a long while senseless. Luckily a butcher soon came by, driving a pig in a wheelbarrow.

"What is the matter with you, my man?" said the butcher, as he helped him up. Hans told him what had happened, how he was dry and wanted to milk his cow, but found the cow was dry too. Then the butcher gave him a flask of ale, saying, "There, drink and refresh yourself, your cow will give you no milk. Don't you see she is an old beast, good for nothing but the slaughterhouse?"

"Alas, alas!" said Hans, "Who would have thought it? What a shame to take my horse and give me only a dry cow! If I kill her, what will she be good for? I hate beef; it is not tender enough for me. If it were a pig now—like that fat gentleman you are driving along at his ease—one could do something with it; it would at any rate make sausages."

"Well," said the butcher, "I don't like to say no, when one is asked to do a neighborly thing. To please you I will change, and give you my fine fat pig for the cow."

"Heaven reward you for your kindness and self-

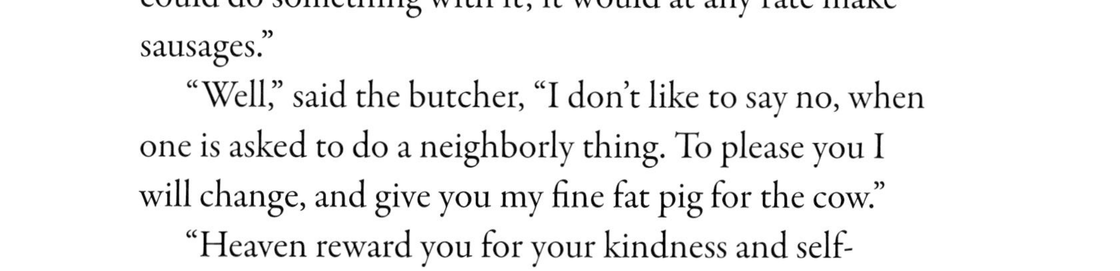

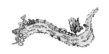

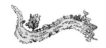

denial!" said Hans, as he gave the butcher the cow, and taking the pig off the wheelbarrow, drove it away, holding it by the string that was tied to its leg.

So on he jogged, and all seemed now to go right with him—he had met with some misfortunes, to be sure, but he was now well repaid for all. How could it be otherwise with such a traveling companion as he had at last gotten?

The next man he met was a countryman carrying a fine white goose. The countryman stopped to ask what the time was. This led to further chat, and Hans told him all his luck, how he had so many good bargains, and how all the world went gay and smiling with him. The countryman then began to tell his tale, and said he was going to take the goose to a christening. "Feel," said he, "how heavy it is, and yet it is only eight weeks old. Whoever roasts and eats it will find plenty of fat upon it, it has lived so well!"

"You're right," said Hans, as he weighed it in his hand, "but if you talk of fat, my pig is no trifle."

The countryman began to look grave, and shook his head. "Listen!" said he, "My worthy friend, you seem a good sort of fellow, so I can't help doing you a kind turn.

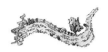

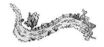

Your pig may get you into a scrape. In the village I just came from, the squire has had a pig stolen out of his sty. I was dreadfully afraid when I saw you that you had gotten the squire's pig. If you have, and they catch you, it will be bad luck for you. The least they will do will be to throw you into the horse pond. Can you swim?"

Poor Hans was greatly frightened. "Good man," cried he, "pray get me out of this. I know nothing of where the pig was either bred or born, but he may have been the squire's for all I can tell—you know this country better than I do; take my pig and give me the goose."

"I ought to have something into the bargain," said the countryman. "Give a fat goose for a pig, indeed! 'Tis not everyone would do so much for you as that. However, I will not be hard upon you, as you are in trouble." Then he took the string in his hand, and drove off the pig by a side path, while Hans went on the way homeward free from care. "After all," thought he, "that chap is pretty well taken in. I don't care whose pig it is, but wherever it came from, it has been a very good friend to me. I have much the best of the bargain. First there will be an excellent roast, then the fat will find me in goose grease for six months, and then there are all the beautiful white feathers. I will put them into my pillow, and then I am sure I shall sleep soundly. How happy my mother will be! Talk of a pig, indeed! Give me a fine fat goose."

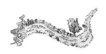

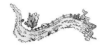

As he came to the next village, he saw a scissor grinder with his wheel, working and singing.

Hans stood looking on for a while, and at last said, "You must be well off, master grinder! You seem so happy at your work."

"Yes," said the other, "mine is a golden trade; a good grinder never puts his hand into his pocket without finding money in it—but where did you get that beautiful goose?"

"I did not buy it, I gave a pig for it."

"And where did you get the pig?"

"I gave a cow for it."

"And the cow?"

"I gave a horse for it."

"And the horse?"

"I gave a lump of silver as big as my head for it."

"And the silver?"

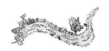

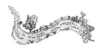

"Oh! I worked hard for that, seven long years."

"You have done well in the world," said the grinder, "now if you could find money in your pocket whenever you put your hand in it, your fortune would be made."

"Very true—but how is that to be managed?"

"How? Why, you must turn grinder like myself," said the other. "You need only a grindstone; the rest will come of itself. Here is one that is but little the worse for wear, I would not ask more than the value of your goose for it—will you buy?"

"How can you ask?" said Hans, "I should be the happiest man in the world, if I could have money whenever I put my hand in my pocket—what could I want more? There's the goose."

"Now," said the grinder, as he gave him a common rough stone that lay by his side, "this is a most excellent stone. Do but work it well enough, and you can make an old nail cut with it."

Hans took the stone, and went his way with a light heart. His eyes sparkled for joy, and he said to himself, "Surely I must have been born in a lucky hour; everything I could want or wish for comes of itself. People are so kind—they seem really to think I do them

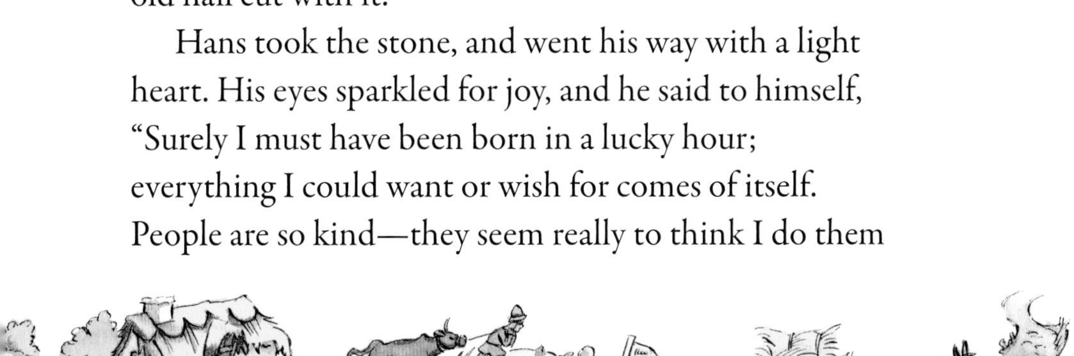

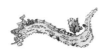

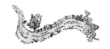

a favor in letting them make me rich, and giving me good bargains.'

In the meantime, Hans began to be tired and hungry, for he had given away his last penny in his joy at getting the cow.

At last he could go no farther, for the stone tired him sadly, and he dragged himself to the side of a river, that he might take a drink of water and rest a while. So he laid the stone carefully by his side on the bank—but, as he stooped down to drink, he forgot it and pushed it a little, and down it rolled, plump into the stream.

For a while he watched it sinking in the deep, clear water. Then he sprang up and danced for joy, and again fell upon his knees and thanked Heaven, with tears in his eyes, for its kindness in taking away his only plague, the ugly, heavy stone.

"How happy am I!" cried he. "Nobody was ever so lucky as I." Then up he got with a light heart, free from all his troubles, and walked on till he reached his mother's house, and told her how very easy the road to good luck was.

The Wind and the Sun

By James Baldwin

READING TIME: 2 MINUTES

The Wind and the Sun once had a dispute as to which was the stronger of the two.

"Do you see that traveler plodding along the road?" said the Wind. "Let us both try our strength on him. Who can first strip him of his cloak will be the winner."

"Agreed," said the Sun.

The Wind began first. He blew a blast that sent the leaves flying through air, he raised clouds of dust in the road, bent the tops of the trees to the ground, and even tore up one oak by the roots. But the traveler only

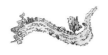

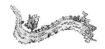

drew his cloak tightly around his shoulders and kept on his way.

Then the Sun began. He burst out from behind a cloud, and darted his beams upon the traveler's head and back. Soon the heat was so great that he stopped to wipe the sweat from his face.

"Ah!" he said, "It is so hot!"

Then he threw off his cloak, and carried it under his arm, and when he came to a tree by the roadside, he sat down under its shade to cool himself.

After that, the Wind never claimed to be stronger than the Sun.

Honorable Minu

By William H. Barker

READING TIME: 3 MINUTES

It happened one day that a poor Akim-man had to travel from his own little village to Accra—one of the big towns on the coast. This man could speak only the language of his own village—which was not understood by the men of the town. As he approached Accra he met a great herd of cows. He was surprised at the number of them and wondered to whom they could belong. Seeing a man with them, he asked him, "To whom do these cows belong?" The man did not know the language of the Akim-man, so he replied, "Minu." (I do not

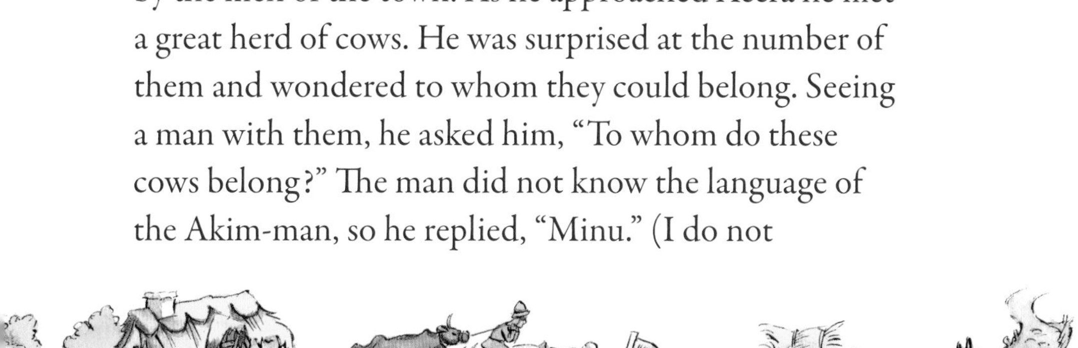

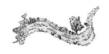

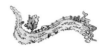

understand). The traveler, however, thought that Minu was the name of the owner of the cows and exclaimed, "Mr. Minu must be very rich."

He then entered the town. Very soon he saw a fine, large building, and he wondered to whom it might belong. The man he asked could not understand his question, so he also answered, "Minu."

"Dear me! What a rich fellow Mr. Minu must be!" cried the Akim-man.

Coming to an even finer building, with beautiful gardens around it, he again asked the owner's name. Again came the answer "Minu."

"How wealthy Mr. Minu is!" said the wondering traveler.

Next he came to the beach. There he saw a magnificent steamer being loaded in the harbor.

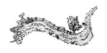

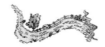

He was surprised at the great cargo that was being put on board and inquired of a bystander, "To whom does this fine vessel belong?"

"Minu," replied the man.

"To the Honorable Minu also! He is the richest man I ever heard of!" cried the Akim-man.

Having finished his business, the Akim-man set out for home. As he passed down one of the streets of the town, he met men carrying a coffin, and followed by a long procession, all dressed in black. He asked the name of the dead person, and received the usual reply, "Minu."

"Poor Mr. Minu!" cried the Akim-man. "So he has had to leave all his wealth and beautiful houses and die just as a poor person would! Well, well—in future I will be content with my tiny house and little money." And then he went home quite pleased to his own hut.

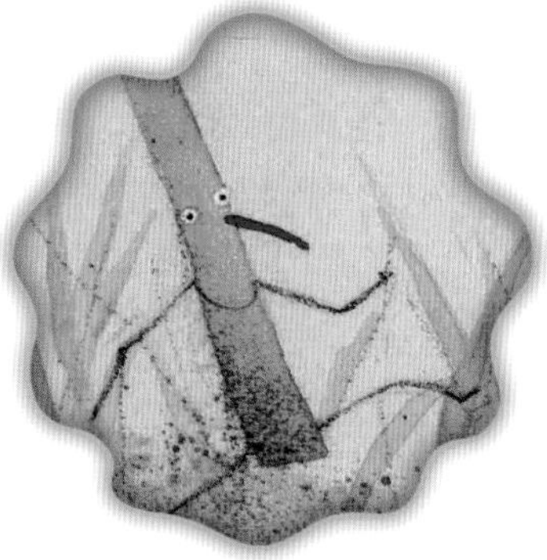

Straw, Coal, and Bean

By the Brothers Grimm

READING TIME: 3 MINUTES

An old woman lived in a village. She had gathered a serving of beans and wanted to cook them, so she prepared a fire in her fireplace. To make it burn faster she lit it with a handful of straw. While she was pouring the beans into the pot, one of them fell unnoticed to the floor, coming to rest next to a piece of straw. Soon afterward, a glowing coal jumped out of the fireplace and landed next to them.

The straw said, "Friends, where do you come from?"

The coal answered, "I jumped from the fireplace,

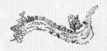

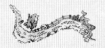

to my good fortune. If I had not forced my way out, I surely would have died. I would have burned to ash."

The bean said, "I, too, saved my skin. If the old woman had gotten me into the pot I would have been cooked to mush without mercy, just like my comrades."

"Would my fate have been any better?" said the straw. "The old woman sent all my brothers up in fire and smoke. She grabbed sixty at once and killed them. Fortunately I slipped through her fingers."

"What should we do now?" asked the coal.

"Because we have so fortunately escaped death," answered the bean, "I think that we should join together as comrades. To prevent some new misfortune from befalling us here, let us together make our way to another land."

This proposal pleased the other two, and they set forth all together.

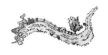

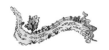

They soon came to a small brook, and because there was neither a bridge nor a walkway there, they did not know how they would get across it.

Then the straw had a good idea, and said, "I will lay myself across it and you can walk across me like on a bridge."

So the straw stretched himself from one bank to the other. The coal, who was a hot headed fellow, stepped brashly onto the newly constructed bridge, but when he got to the middle and heard the water rushing beneath him, he took fright, stopped, and did not dare to go any farther. Then the straw caught fire, broke into two pieces, and fell into the brook. The coal slid after him, hissed as he fell into the water, and gave up the ghost.

The bean, who had cautiously stayed behind on the bank, had to laugh at the event. He could not stop, and he laughed so fiercely that he burst. Now he, too, would have died, but fortunately a wandering tailor was there, resting near the brook. Having a compassionate heart, he got out a needle and thread and sewed the bean back together.

The bean thanked him most kindly. However, because he had used black thread, since that time all beans have had a black seam.

The Two Sisters

By Flora Annie Steel

READING TIME: 12 MINUTES

Once upon a time there were two sisters who were as like each other as two peas in a pod, but one was good and the other was bad-tempered. Now their father had no work, so the girls began to think of going to be servants.

"I will go first and see what I can make of it," said the younger sister, ever so cheerfully, "then you, Sis, can follow if I have good luck."

So she packed up a bundle, said goodbye, and started to look for a place, but no one in the town wanted a girl,

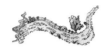

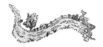

so she went farther afield into the country. And as she journeyed she came upon an oven in which a lot of loaves were baking.

Now as she passed, the loaves cried out with one voice, "Little girl! Little girl! Take us out! Please take us out! We have been baking for seven years, and no one has come to take us out. Do take us out or we shall soon be burned!"

Then, being a kind, obliging little girl, she stopped, put down her bundle, took out the bread, and went on her way, saying, "You will be more comfortable now."

After a time she came to a cow lowing beside an empty pail, and the cow said to her, "Little girl! Little girl! Milk me! Please milk me! Seven years have I been waiting, but no one has come to milk me!"

So the kind girl stopped, put down her bundle, milked the cow into the pail, and went on her way saying, "Now you will be more comfortable."

By and by she came to an apple tree so laden with fruit that its branches were nigh to break, and the apple tree called to her:

"Little girl! Little girl! Please shake my branches. The fruit is so heavy I can't stand straight!"

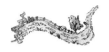

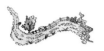

Then the kind girl stopped, put down her bundle, and shook the branches so that the apples fell off, and the tree could stand straight. Then she went on her way saying, "You will be more comfortable now."

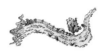

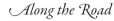

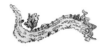

So she journeyed on till she came to a house where an old witch lived. Now this witch wanted a maid, and promised good wages. So the girl agreed to stay with her and try how she liked service. She had to sweep the floor and keep the house clean and tidy and the fire bright and cheery. But there was one thing the witch said she must never do, and that was look up the chimney.

"If you do," said the witch, "something will fall down on you, and you will come to a bad end."

Well, the girl swept and dusted and made up the fire, but never a penny of wages did she see. Now the girl wanted to go home, as she did not like witch service, for the witch used to have boiled babies for supper and bury the bones under some stones in the garden. But she did not like to go home penniless, so she stayed on, sweeping and dusting and doing her work, just as if she was pleased.

Then one day, as she was sweeping up the hearth, down tumbled some soot, and, without remembering she was forbidden to look up the chimney, she looked up to see where the soot came from. And, lo and behold—a big bag of gold fell plump into her lap.

Now the witch happened to be out on one of her

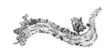

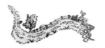

witch errands, so the girl thought it a fine opportunity to be off home.

So she tucked up her petticoats and started to run home, but she had gone only a little way when she heard the witch coming after her on her broomstick. Now the apple tree she had helped to stand straight happened to be quite close, so she ran to it and cried,

"Apple tree! Apple tree, hide me
So the old witch can't find me,
For if she does she'll pick my bones,
And bury me under the garden stones."

Then the apple tree said, "Of course I will. You helped me to stand straight, and one good turn deserves another."

So the apple tree hid her finely in its green branches; and when the witch flew past saying,

"O Tree of mine! Tree of mine!
Have you seen my naughty little maid
With a willy willy wag and a great big bag,
She's stolen my money—all I had?"

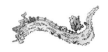

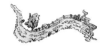

The apple tree answered,

"No, Mother dear,
Not for seven year!"

So the witch flew on the wrong way, and the girl got down, thanked the tree politely, and started again. But just as she got to where the cow was standing beside the pail, she heard the witch coming again, so she ran to the cow and cried,

"Cow! Cow, please hide me
So the witch can't find me,
If she does she'll pick my bones,
And bury me under the garden stones!"

"Certainly I will," answered the cow. "Didn't you milk me and make me comfortable? Hide yourself behind me and you'll be quite safe."

And when the witch flew by and called to the cow,

"O Cow of mine! Cow of mine!
Have you seen my naughty little maid

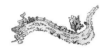

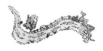

With a willy willy wag and a great big bag,
Who stole my money—all I had?"

The cow just said politely,

"*No, Mother dear,*
Not for seven year!"

Then the old witch went on in the wrong direction, and the girl started fresh on her way home, but just as she got to where the oven stood, she heard that horrid old witch coming behind her again, so she ran as fast as she could to the oven and cried,

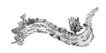

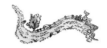

"O Oven! Oven! hide me
So as the witch can't find me,
For if she does she'll pick my bones,
And bury them under the garden stones."

Then the oven said, "I am afraid there is no room for you, as another batch of bread is baking, but there is the baker—ask him."

So she asked the baker, and he said, "Of course I will. You saved my last batch from being burned, so run into the bakehouse; you will be quite safe there, and I will settle the witch for you."

So she hid in the bakehouse, only just in time, for there was the old witch calling angrily,

"O Man of mine! Man of mine!
Have you seen my naughty little maid
With a willy willy wag and a great big bag,
Who's stole my money—all I had?"

Then the baker replied, "Look in the oven. She may be there."

And the witch alighted from her broomstick and

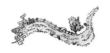

peered into the oven, but she could see no one.

"Creep in and look in the farthest corner," said the baker slyly, and the witch crept in. Bang! He shut the door on her, and there she was roasting. And when she came out with the bread, she was all crisp and brown, and had to go home as best she could and put cold cream all over her!

But the kind, obliging little girl got safe home with her bag of money.

Now the ill-tempered elder sister was very envious of this good luck and determined to get a bag of gold for herself. So she, in her turn, packed up a bundle and started to seek service by the same road. But when she came to the oven, and the loaves begged her to take them out because they had been baking seven years and were nigh to burning, she tossed her head and said, "A likely story indeed, that I should burn my fingers to save your crusts. No, thank you!"

And with that she went on till she came across the cow standing waiting to be milked beside the pail. But when the cow said, "Little girl! Little girl! Milk me! Please milk me, I've waited seven years to be milked."

She only laughed and replied, "You may wait another

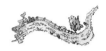

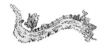

seven years for all I care. I'm not your dairymaid!"

And with that she went on till she came to the apple tree, all overburdened by its fruit. But when it begged her to shake its branches, she only giggled and, plucking one ripe apple, said, "One is enough for me, you can keep the rest yourself." And with that she went on munching the apple, till she came to the witch's house.

Now the witch, though she had gotten over being crisp and brown from the oven, was dreadfully angry with all little maids, and made up her mind this one should not trick her. So for a long time she never went out of the house; thus the ill-tempered sister never had a chance of looking up the chimney, as she had meant to do at once. And she had to dust and clean and brush and sweep ever so hard, until she was quite tired out.

But one day, when the witch went into the garden to bury her bones, she seized the moment, looked up the chimney, and, sure enough, a bag of gold fell plump into her lap!

Well! She was off with it in a moment, and ran and ran till she came to the apple tree, when she heard the witch behind her. So she cried as her sister had done,

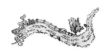

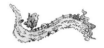

"Apple tree! Apple tree, hide me
So the old witch can't find me,
For if she does she'll break my bones,
Or bury me under the garden stones."

But the apple tree said, "No room here! I've too many apples." So she had to run on, and when the witch on her broomstick came flying by and called,

"O Tree of mine! Tree of mine!
Have you seen a naughty little maid
With a willy willy wag and a great big bag,
Who's stolen my money—all I had?"

The apple tree replied, "Yes, Mother dear, she's gone down there."

Then the witch went after her, caught her, gave her a thorough good beating, took the bag of money away from her, and sent her home without a penny payment for all her dusting, sweeping, brushing, and cleaning.

I Wonder

By Kate Douglas Wiggin

READING TIME: 12 MINUTES

*O*nce on a time there was a man who had three sons—Peter, Paul, and the least of all, whom they called Youngling. I can't say the man had anything more than these three sons, for he hadn't one penny to rub against another. He told the lads, over and over again, that they must go out into the world and try to earn their bread, for at home there was nothing to be looked for but starving to death.

Now nearby the man's cottage was the king's palace, and, you must know, just against the windows a great

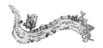

oak had sprung up, which was so stout and tall that it took away all the light. The king had said he would give untold treasure to the man who could fell the oak, but no one was man enough for that, for as soon as one chip of the oak's trunk flew off, two grew in its stead.

A well, too, the king desired, which was to hold water for the whole year, for all his neighbors had wells, but he hadn't any, and that he thought a shame. So the king said he would give both money and goods to anyone who could dig him such a well as would hold water for a whole year round, but no one could do it, for the palace lay high, high up on a hill, and they could dig only a few inches before they came upon rock.

But since the king had set his heart on having these two things done, he had it given out far and wide, in all the churches of his dominion, that he who could fell the big oak in the king's courtyard and get him a well that would hold water the whole year round, should have the princess and half the kingdom.

Well! You may easily know there was many a man who came to try his luck, but all their hacking and hewing, all their digging and delving, were of no avail. The oak grew taller and stouter at every stroke, and the rock grew no softer.

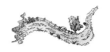

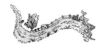

So one day the three brothers thought they'd set off and try, too, and their father hadn't a word against it; for even if they didn't get the princess and half the kingdom, it might happen that they would get a place somewhere with a good master, and that was all he wanted. So when the brothers said they thought of going to the palace, their father said "Yes" at once, and Peter, Paul and Youngling went off from their home.

They had not gone far before they came to a fir wood, and up along one side of it rose a steep hillside, and as they went they heard something hewing and hacking away up on the hill among the trees.

"I wonder now what it is that is hewing away up yonder?" said Youngling.

"You are always so clever with your wonderings," said Peter and Paul, both at once. "What wonder is it, pray, that a woodcutter should stand and hack up on a hillside?"

"Still, I'd like to see what it is, after all," said Youngling, and up he went.

"Oh, if you're such a child, it'll do you good to go and take a lesson," cried out his brothers after him.

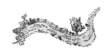

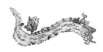

But Youngling didn't care about what they said; he climbed the steep hillside toward where the noise came, and when he reached the place, what do you think he saw?

Why, an ax that stood there hacking and hewing, all by itself, at the trunk of a fir tree.

"Good day," said Youngling. "So you stand here all alone and hew, do you?"

"Yes, here I've stood and hewed and hacked a long, long time, waiting for you, my lad," said the ax.

"Well, here I am at last," said Youngling, as he took the ax, pulled it off its haft, and stuffed both head and haft into his bag.

So when he climbed down again to his brothers, they began to jeer and laugh at him.

"And now, what funny thing was it you saw up on the hillside?" they said.

"Oh, it was only an ax we heard," said Youngling.

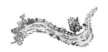

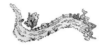

When they had gone a bit farther they heard something digging and shoveling.

"I wonder, now," said Youngling, "what it is digging and shoveling up yonder at the top of the rock?"

"Ah, you're always so clever with your wonderings," said Peter and Paul again, "as if you'd never heard a woodpecker hacking and pecking at a hollow tree."

"Well, well," said Youngling, "I think it would be a piece of fun just to see what it really is."

And so off he set to climb the rock, while the others laughed and made fun of him. But he didn't care a bit for that. Up he clambered, and when he got near the top, what do you think he saw? Why, a spade that stood there digging and delving.

"Good day," said Youngling. "So you stand here all alone, and dig and delve?"

"Yes, that's what I do," said the spade, "and that's what I've done this many a long day, waiting for you, my lad."

"Well, here I am," said Youngling again, as he took the spade and knocked off its handle, and put it into his bag, and then he climbed down again to his brothers.

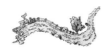

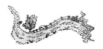

"Well, what was it, so strange and rare," said Peter and Paul, "that you saw up there at the top of the rock?"

"Oh," said Youngling, "nothing more than a spade, that was what we heard."

So they went on again a good bit, till they came to a brook. They were thirsty after their long walk, and so they sat beside the brook to have a drink.

"I have a great fancy to see where this brook comes from," said Youngling.

So up alongside the brook he went, in spite of all that his brothers shouted after him. Nothing could stop him. On he went.

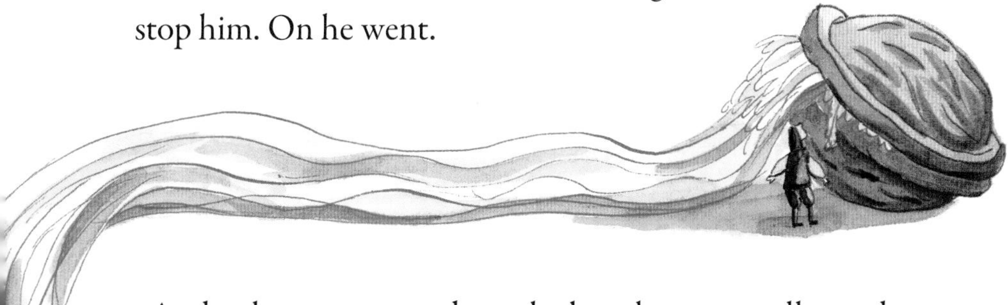

And as he went up and up, the brook grew smaller and smaller, and at last, a little way farther on, what do you think he saw? Why, a great walnut, and out of that the water trickled.

"Good day," said Youngling again. "So you lie here and trickle, and run down all alone?"

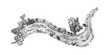

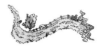

"Yes, I do," said the walnut "and here have I trickled and run this many a long day, waiting for you, my lad."

"Well, here I am," said Youngling, as he took a lump of moss and plugged up the hole, so that the water wouldn't run out. Then he put the walnut into his bag, and ran down to his brothers.

"Well," said Peter and Paul, "have you found where the water comes from? A rare sight it must have been!"

"Oh, after all, it was only a hole it ran out of," said Youngling, and the others laughed and made game of him again, but Youngling didn't mind that a bit.

So when they had gone a little farther, they came to the king's palace. But since every man in the kingdom had heard that he might win the princess and half the realm if he could only fell the big oak and dig the king's well, so many had come to try their luck that the oak was now twice as stout and big as it had been at first—for you will remember that two chips grew for every one they hewed out with their axes.

So the king had now laid it down as a punishment that if anyone tried and couldn't fell the oak, he should be put on a barren island, and both his ears were to be clipped off. But the two brothers didn't let themselves be frightened by this threat; they were quite sure they could fell the oak. Peter, as he was the eldest, was to try his hand first, but it went with him as with all the rest who had hewn at the oak—for every chip he cut, two grew in its place. So the king's men seized him and clipped off both his ears and put him out on the island.

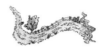

Now Paul was to try his luck, but he fared just the same. When he had hewn two or three strokes, they began to see the oak grow, and so the king's men seized him, too, and clipped his ears and put him out on the island; and they clipped his ears closer, because they said he ought to have taken a lesson from his brother.

So now Youngling was to try.

"If you want to look like a marked sheep, we're quite ready to clip your ears at once, and then you'll save yourself some trouble," said the king, for he was angry with him for his brothers' sake.

"Well, I'd just like to try first," said Youngling, and so he was given permission. Then he took his ax out of his bag and fitted it to its handle.

"Hew away!" said he to his ax, and away it hewed, making the chips fly again, so that it wasn't long before down came the oak.

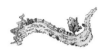

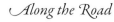

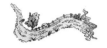

When that was done, Youngling pulled out his spade and fitted it to its handle.

"Dig away!" said he to his spade, and so the spade began to dig and delve till the earth and rock flew out in splinters, and he soon had the well deep enough, you may believe.

And when he had gotten it as big and deep as he chose, Youngling took out his walnut and laid it in one corner of the well, and pulled the plug of moss out.

"Trickle and run," said Youngling, and so the nut trickled and ran till the water gushed out of the hole in a stream, and in a short time the well was full.

So as Youngling had felled the oak that shaded the king's palace, and dug a well in the palace yard, he got the princess and half the kingdom, as the king had said. But it was lucky for Peter and Paul that they had lost their ears, else they might have grown tired of hearing how everyone said, each hour of the day, "Well, after all, Youngling wasn't so much out of his mind when he took to wondering."

Rosy's Journey

By Louisa May Alcott

READING TIME: 20 MINUTES

Rosy was a little girl who lived with her mother in a small house in the woods. They were very poor, for the father had gone away to dig for gold, and had not come back. They had to work hard to get food to eat and clothes to wear. The mother spun yarn when she was able, for she was often sick, and Rosy did all she could to help. She milked the red cow and fed the hens, dug the garden, and went to town to sell the yarn and the eggs.

She was very good and sweet, and everyone loved her, but the neighbors were all poor, and could do little to

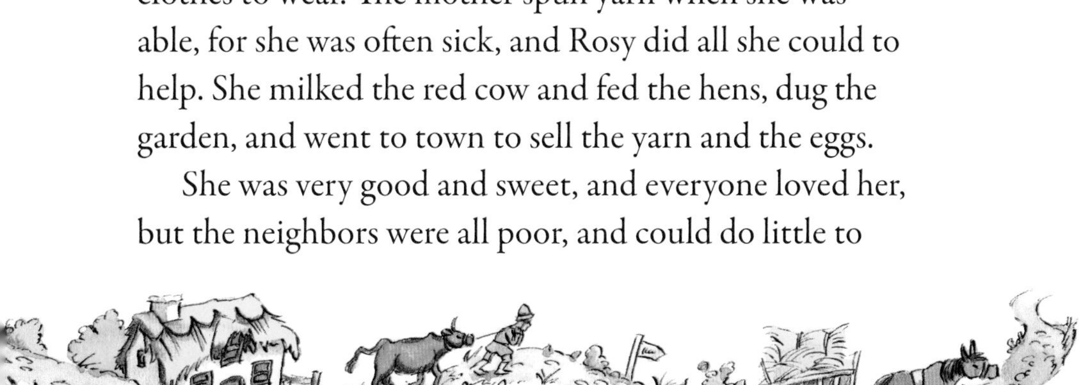

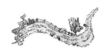

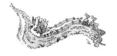

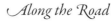

help the child. So, when at last the mother died, the cow and hens and house had to be sold to pay the doctor and the debts. Then Rosy was left all alone, with no mother, no home, and no money to buy clothes or food.

"What will you do?" said the people, who were very sorry for her.

"I will go and find my father," answered Rosy, bravely.

"But he is far away, and you don't know just where he is, up among the mountains. Stay with us and spin on your little wheel, and we will buy the yarn and take care of you."

"No, I must go, for Mother told me to, and Father will be glad to have me. I'm not afraid, for everyone is good to me," said Rosy, gratefully.

Then the people gave her a warm red cloak, and a basket with a little loaf and bottle of milk in it, and some pennies to buy more to eat when the bread was gone. They all kissed her, and wished her good luck, and she trotted away through the woods to find her father.

For some days she got on very well, for the woodcutters were kind, and let her sleep in their huts and gave her things to eat. But by and by she came to lonely places, where there were no houses, and then she

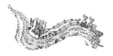

was afraid, and used to climb up in the trees to sleep and had to eat berries and leaves.

She made a fire at night so wild beasts would not come near her, and if she met other travelers, she was so young and innocent no one had the heart to hurt her. She was kind to everything she met, so all little creatures were friends to her, as we shall see.

One day, as she was resting by a river, she saw a tiny fish on the bank, nearly dead for want of water.

"Poor thing! Go and be happy again," she said, softly taking him up, and dropping him into the cool river.

"Thank you, dear child, I'll not forget, but will help you some day," said the fish, when he had taken a good drink and felt better.

"Why, how can a tiny fish help such a great girl as I am?" said Rosy, laughing.

"Wait and see," answered the fish, as he swam away with a flap of his little tail.

Rosy went on her way, and forgot all about it. But she never forgot to be kind, and soon after, as she was looking in the grass for strawberries, she found a field-mouse with a broken leg.

"Please help me! Take me to my nest, or my babies

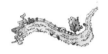

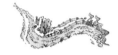

will starve," cried the poor little mouse.

"Yes, I will, and have some berries, so that you can rest till your leg is better, and still have something to eat."

Rosy took the mouse carefully in her little hand and tied up the broken leg with a leaf of spearmint and a blade of grass. Then she carried her to the nest under the roots of an old tree, where four baby mice were squeaking sadly for their mother. She made a bed of thistledown for the sick mouse, and put close within reach all the berries and seeds she could find, and brought an acorn-cup of water from the spring, so they could be comfortable.

"Good little Rosy, I shall pay you for all this kindness some day," said the mouse, when she was done.

"I'm afraid you are not big enough to do much," answered Rosy, as she ran off to continue on her journey.

"Wait and see," called the mouse, and all the little ones squeaked as if they said the same.

Some time after, as Rosy lay up in a tree, waiting for the sun to rise, she heard a great buzzing close by and saw a fly caught in a cobweb that went from one twig to another. A big spider was trying to spin him all up, and the poor fly was struggling to get away before his legs and wings were helpless.

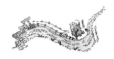

Rosy put up her finger and pulled down the web, and the spider ran away at once to hide under the leaves. But the fly sat on Rosy's hand, cleaning his wings, and buzzing so loud for joy that it sounded like a little trumpet.

"You've saved my life, and I'll save yours, if I can," said the fly, twinkling his bright eye at Rosy.

"You silly thing, you can't help me," answered Rosy, climbing down, while the fly buzzed away, saying, like the mouse and fish, "Wait and see, wait and see."

Rosy trudged on and on, till at last she came to the sea. The mountains were on the other side, but how should she get over the wide water? No ships were there, and she had no money to hire one if there had been any, so she sat on the shore, very tired and sad, and cried a few big tears as salty as the sea.

"Hello!" called a bubbly sort of voice close by, and the fish popped up his head. Rosy ran to see him.

"I've come to help you over the water," said the fish.

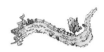

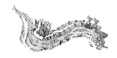

"How can you, when I need a ship, and someone to show me the way?" answered Rosy.

"I shall just call my friend the whale, and he will take you over better than a ship, because he won't get wrecked. Don't mind if he spouts and flounces about a good deal; he is only playing—so you needn't be frightened."

Down dived the little fish, and Rosy waited to see what would happen, for she didn't believe such a tiny thing could really bring a whale to help her.

Presently what looked like a small island came floating through the sea, and turning around, so that its tail touched the shore, the whale said, in a roaring voice that made her jump. "Come aboard, little girl, and hold on tight. I'll carry you wherever you like."

It was rather a slippery bridge, and Rosy was rather scared at this big, strange boat, but she got safely over, and held on fast. Then, with a roll and a plunge, off went the whale, spouting water, while his tail steered him like the rudder of a ship. Rosy liked it, and looked down into the deep sea, where all sorts of strange and lovely things were to be seen. Great fishes came and looked at her, dolphins played near to amuse her,

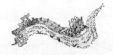

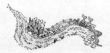

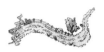

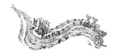

the pretty nautilus sailed by in its transparent boat, and porpoises made her laugh with their rough play. Mermaids brought her pearls and red coral to wear, and sea-apples to eat, and at night sang her to sleep with their sweet lullabies.

So she had a very pleasant voyage, and ran on shore with many thanks to the good whale, who gave a splendid spout and swam away. Then Rosy traveled along till she came to a desert. Hundreds of miles of hot sand, with no trees or brooks or houses.

"I never can go that way," she said, "I should starve, and soon be worn out walking in that hot sand. What shall I do?"

"*Quee, quee!*
Wait and see.
You were good to me,
So here I come,
From my little home,
To help you willingly,"

said a friendly voice, and there was the mouse, looking at her with its bright eyes full of gratitude.

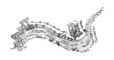

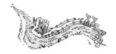

"Why, you dear little thing, I'm very glad to see you, but I'm sure you can't help me across this desert," said Rosy, stroking its soft back.

"That's easy enough," answered the mouse, rubbing its paws briskly. "I'll just call my friend the lion, he lives here, and he'll take you across with pleasure."

"Oh, I'm afraid he'd rather eat me. How dare you call that fierce beast?" cried Rosy, much surprised.

"I gnawed him out of a net once, and he promised to help me. He is a noble animal and he will keep his word."

Then the mouse sang, in its shrill little voice:

"O lion, grand,
Come over the sand,
And help me now, I pray!
Here's a little lass,
Who wants to pass,
Please carry her on her way."

In a moment a loud roar was heard, and a splendid yellow lion, with fiery eyes and a long mane, came bounding over the sand to meet them.

"What can I do for you, tiny friend?" he said, looking

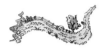

at the mouse, who was not a bit frightened, though Rosy hid behind a rock, expecting every moment to be eaten.

Mousie told him, and the good lion said pleasantly, "I'll take the child along. Come on, my dear, sit on my back and hold fast to my mane, for I'm swift, and you might fall off."

Then he crouched down like a great cat, and Rosy climbed up, for he was so kind she could not fear him, and away they went, racing over the sand till her hair whistled in the wind. As soon as she got her breath, she thought it great fun to go flying along, while other lions and tigers rolled their fierce eyes at her, but dared not touch her, for this lion was king of all, and she was quite safe. They met a train of camels with loads on their backs, and the people traveling with them wondered what strange thing was riding that fine lion. It looked like a very large monkey in a red cloak, but went so fast they never saw that it was a little girl.

"How glad I am that I was kind to the mouse, for if the good little creature had not helped me, I never could have crossed this desert," said Rosy, as the lion walked awhile to rest himself.

"And if the mouse had not gnawed me out of the net

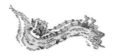

I never should have come at her call. You see, little people can conquer big ones and make them gentle and friendly by kindness," answered the lion.

Then away they went again, faster than ever, till they came to the green country. Rosy thanked the good beast, and he ran back, for if anyone saw him, they would try to catch him.

"Now I have only to climb up these mountains and find father," thought Rosy, as she saw the great hills before her, with many steep roads winding up to the top, and far, far away rose the smoke from the huts where the men lived and dug for gold. She started off bravely but took the wrong road, and after climbing a long while found that the path ended in rocks over which she could not go. She was very tired and hungry, for her food was gone, and there were no houses in this wild place. Night was coming on, and it was so cold she was afraid she would freeze before morning, but she dared not go on lest she should fall down some steep hole and be killed. Much discouraged, she lay down on the moss and cried a little, then she tried to sleep, but something kept buzzing in her ear, and looking carefully she saw a fly prancing about on the moss, as if anxious to

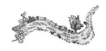

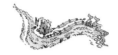

make her listen to his song:

"Rosy, my dear,
Don't cry—I'm here
To help you all I can.
I'm only a fly,
But you'll see that I
Will keep my word like a man."

Rosy couldn't help laughing to hear the brisk little fellow talk as if he could do great things, but she was very glad to see him and hear his cheerful song, so she held out her finger, and while he sat there told him all her troubles.

"Bless your heart! My friend the eagle will carry you right up the mountains and leave you at your father's door," cried the fly, and he was off with a flit of his gauzy wings, for he meant what he said.

Rosy was not at all afraid after the whale and the lion, so when a great eagle swooped down and alighted near her, she just looked at his sharp claws, big eyes, and crooked beak as coolly as if he had been a cock-robin.

He liked her courage, and said kindly in his rough

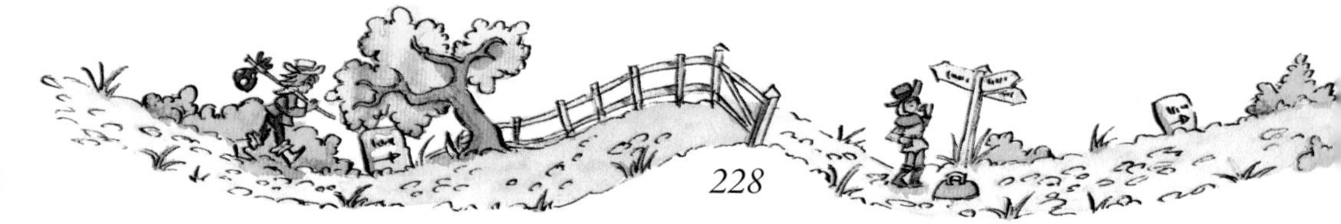

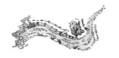

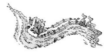

voice, "Hop up, little girl, and sit among my feathers. Hold me fast round the neck, or you may grow dizzy and fall."

Rosy nestled down among the thick brown feathers, and put both arms around his neck, and away they went, up, up, up, higher and higher, till the trees looked like grass, they were so far below. At first it was very cold, and Rosy cuddled deeper into her feather bed. Then, as they came nearer to the sun, it grew warm, and she peeped out to see the huts standing in a green spot on the top of the mountain.

"Here we are. You'll find all the men are down in the mine at this time. They won't come up till morning, so you will have to wait for your father. Goodbye, good luck, my dear." And the eagle soared away, higher still, to his nest among the clouds.

It was night now, but fires were burning in all the houses, so Rosy went from hut to hut trying to find her father's, that she might rest while she waited. At last, in one, the picture of a pretty little girl hung on the wall, and under it was written, "My Rosy." Then she knew that this was the right place, and she ate some supper, put on more wood and went to bed, for she wanted to be fresh when her father came in the morning.

While she slept a storm came on—thunder rolled and lightning flashed, the wind blew a gale, and rain poured—but Rosy never waked till dawn, when she heard men shouting:

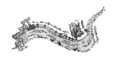

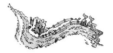

"Quick! Run, run! The river is rising!"

Rosy ran out to see what was the matter, though the wind nearly blew her away. She found that so much rain had made the river overflow till it began to wash the banks away.

"What shall I do? What shall I do?" cried Rosy, watching the men rush about like ants, getting their bags of gold ready to carry off before the water swept them away, if it became a flood.

As if in answer to her cry, Rosy heard a voice close by:

"Splash, dash!
Rumble and crash!
Here come the beavers gay,
See what they do,
Rosy, for you,
Because you helped me one day."

And there in the water was the little fish swimming about, while an army of beavers began to pile up earth and stones in a high bank to keep the river back. How they worked, digging and heaping with teeth and claws, and beating the earth hard with their strange tails like shovels! Rosy and the men watched them work, glad to be safe, while the storm cleared up, and by the time the dam was made, all danger was over. Rosy looked into the faces of the rough men, hoping her father was there, and was just going to ask one of them about him, when a great shouting rose up again, and everyone ran to the pit hole, shouting:

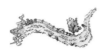

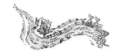

"The sand has fallen in! The poor fellows will be smothered! How can we get them out? How can we get them out?"

Rosy ran too, feeling as if her heart would break, for her father was down in the mine and would die soon if air did not come to him. The men dug as hard as they could, but it was a long job and they feared they would not be in time.

Suddenly hundreds of moles came scampering along, and began to burrow down through the earth, making many holes for air to go in, for they know how to build galleries through the ground better than men can. Everyone was so surprised they stopped to look on, for the dirt flew like rain as the busy little fellows scratched and bored as if making an underground railroad.

"What does it mean?" said the men. "They work

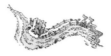

faster than we can, and better, but who sent them? Is this strange little girl a fairy?"

Before Rosy could speak, all heard a shrill, small voice singing:

"*They come at my call,*
And though they are small,
They'll dig the passage clear.
I never forget,
We'll save them yet,
For love of Rosy dear."

Then all saw a little gray mouse sitting on a stone, waving her tail about and pointing with her tiny paw to show the moles where to dig.

The men laughed, and Rosy was telling them who she was, when a cry came from the down in the pit, and they saw that the way was clear so they could pull the buried men up.

In a minute they got ropes and soon had ten poor fellows safe on the ground, pale and dirty, but all alive, and all shouting as if they were crazy:

"Tom's got it! Tom's got it! Hooray for Tom!"

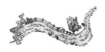

"What is it?" cried the others, and then they saw Tom come up with the biggest lump of gold ever found in the mountains.

Everyone was glad of Tom's luck, for he was a good man, and had worked a long time, and been sick, and couldn't go back to his wife and child. When he saw Rosy, he dropped the lump, and caught her up in his arms, saying:

"My little girl! She's better than a million pounds of gold."

Then Rosy was very happy and went back to the hut, and had a lovely time telling her father all about her troubles, adventures, and travels. He cried when he heard that her poor mother had died before she could have any of the good things that the gold would buy them.

"We will go away and be happy together in the pleasantest home I can find, and never part any more, my darling," said her father, kissing Rosy as she sat on his knee with her arms around his neck.

She was just going to say something very sweet to comfort him, when a fly lit on her arm and buzzed loudly:

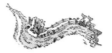

"Don't drive me away,
But hear what I say,
Bad men want the gold,
They will steal it tonight,
And you must take flight,
So be quiet and busy and bold."

"I was afraid someone would try to take my gold away. I'll pack up at once, and we will creep off while the other men are still busy at work. I'm afraid we can't travel fast enough to be safe if they miss us and come after," said Tom, while he bundled his lump of gold into a bag. He looked very sober, for some of the miners were wild fellows, and might kill him for the sake of his gold. But the fly sang again:

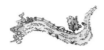

"Slip away with me,
And you will see
What a wise little thing am I,
For the road I show
No man can know,
Since it's up in the pathless sky."

Then they followed the fly to a quiet nook in the wood, and there were the eagle and his mate waiting to fly away with them so fast and so far that no one could follow. Rosy and the bag of gold were put on the mother eagle, Tom sat astride the king bird, and away they flew to a great city, where the little girl and her father lived happily together all their lives.

The Meester Stoorworm

By Katharine Pyle

READING TIME: 25 MINUTES

"Stoorworm" is a Scottish word for a mighty sea serpent, and the Meester Stoorworm is the master of all the sea serpents, so you can imagine how fearsome it would be.

There was once a lad, and what his real name was nobody remembered, unless it was the mother who bore him, but what everyone called him was Ashipattle. They called him that because he sat among the ashes of the fire to warm his toes.

He had six older brothers, and they did not think much of him. All the tasks they scorned to do

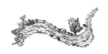

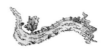

themselves they put upon Ashipattle. He gathered the sticks for the fire, he swept the floor, he cleaned the cow barn, he ran the errands, and all he got for his pains was kicks and cuffs and mocking words. Still he was a merry fellow, and as far as words went he gave his brothers as good as they sent.

Ashipattle had one sister, and she was very good and kind to him. In return for her kindness he told her long stories of trolls and giants and heroes and brave deeds, and as long as he would tell, she would sit and listen. But his brothers could not stand his stories and used to throw clods at him to make him be quiet. They were angry because Ashipattle was always the hero of his own stories, and in his tales there was nothing he dared not do.

Now while Ashipattle was still a lad, but a tall, stout one, a great misfortune fell upon the kingdom, for a stoorworm rose up out of the sea, and of all stoorworms it was the greatest and the worst. For this reason it was called the Meester Stoorworm. Its length stretched half around the world, its one eye was as red as fire, and its breath was so poisonous that whatever it breathed upon was withered.

There was great fear and lamentation throughout the

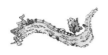

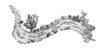

land because of the worm, for every day it drew nearer to the shore, and every day the danger from it grew greater. When it was first discovered, it was so far away that its back was no more than a low, long, black line upon the horizon, but soon it was near enough for them to see the horns upon its back, and its scales, and its one fierce eye, and its nostrils that breathed out and in.

In their fear the people cried upon the king to save them from the monster, but the king had no power to save them more than any other man. His sword, Snickersnapper, was the brightest and sharpest and most wonderful sword in all the world, but it would need a longer sword than Snickersnapper to pierce through that great body to the monster's heart. The king summoned his councillors—all the wisest men in the kingdom—and they consulted and talked together,

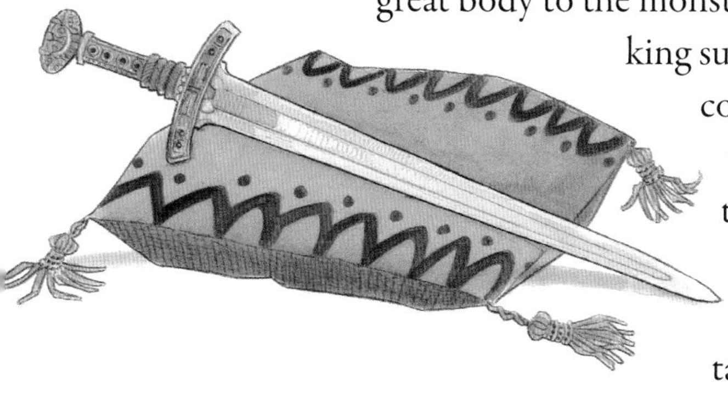

but none of them could think of any plan to beat or drive the stoorworm off, so powerful it was.

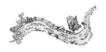

Now there was in that country a sorcerer, and the king had no love for him. Still, when all the wise men and councillors could think of no plan for destroying the stoorworm, the king said, "Let us send for this sorcerer, and have him brought before us, and hear what he has to say, for 'twould seem there is no help in any of us for this evil that has come upon us."

So the sorcerer was brought, and he stood up in the council and looked from one to another. Last of all he looked at the king, and there his eyes rested.

"There is one way, and only one," said he, "by which the land can be saved from destruction. We must let the king's only daughter, the Princess Gemlovely, be given to the stoorworm as a sacrifice, and it will be satisfied and leave us alone."

No sooner had the sorcerer said this than a great tumult arose in the council. The councillors were filled with horror, and cried aloud that the sorcerer should be torn to pieces for speaking such words.

But the king arose and bade them be silent, and he was as white as death.

"Is this the only way to save my people?" he asked.

"It is the only way I know of," answered the sorcerer.

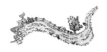

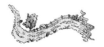

The king stood still and white for a time. "Then," said he, "if it is the only way, so let it be. But first let it be proclaimed, far and wide throughout my kingdom, that there is a heroic deed to be done. Whosoever will do battle with the stoorworm and slay it, or drive it off, shall have the Princess Gemlovely for a bride, and the half of my kingdom, and my sword Snickersnapper for his own, and after my death he shall rule as king over all the realm."

Then the king dismissed the council, and they went away in silence, with dark and heavy looks.

The proclamation was sent out as the king had commanded, and when this news went out, many a man wished he might win the three prizes for himself. For what better was there to be desired than a beauteous wife, a kingdom to reign over, and the most famous sword in all the world? But fine as were the prizes, only six-and-thirty bold hearts came to offer themselves for the task, so great was the fear of the stoorworm. Of this number, the first twelve who looked at the stoorworm fell ill at sight of him and had to be carried home. The next twelve did not stay to be carried, but ran home on their own legs and shut themselves up in strong

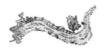

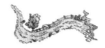

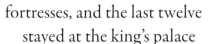

fortresses, and the last twelve stayed at the king's palace with their hearts in their stomachs and their wrists too weak with fear to strike a blow, even to win a kingdom.

So there was nothing left but for the princess to be offered up to the stoorworm, for it was better that one should be lost, even though that one were the princess, than that the whole country should be destroyed.

Then there was great grief and lamenting throughout the land, for the Princess Gemlovely was so kind and gentle that she was beloved by all, both high and low. Only Ashipattle heard it all unmoved. He said nothing, but sat by the fire and thought and thought, and what his thoughts were he told to nobody.

The day was set when the princess was to be offered up to the stoorworm, and the night before there was a great feast at the palace, but a sad feast it was. Little was eaten and less was said. The king sat with his back to the light and bit his fingers, and no one dared to speak to him.

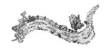

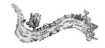

In the poorer houses there was a great stir and bustle and laying out of coats and dresses, for many were planning to go to the seashore to see the princess offered up to the stoorworm—though a gruesome sight it would be to see. Ashipattle's father and brothers were planning to go with the rest, but his mother and sister wept, and said they would not see it for anything in the world.

Now Ashipattle's father had a horse named Feetgong, and he was not much to look at. Nevertheless the farmer treasured him, and it was not often he would let anyone use him but himself. When the farmer rode Feetgong he could make him go like the wind—none faster—and that without beating him, either. Then when the farmer wished him to stop, Feetgong would stand as still as though he were frozen to the ground; no one could make him budge. But if anyone other than the farmer rode him, it was quite different. Feetgong would jog along, and not even a beating would drive him faster, and then if one wanted him to stop, that was as hard to do as it was to start him. Ashipattle was sure there was some secret about this, that his father had a way to make him go that no one knew about, but what that way was he could not find out.

The day before the beauteous Gemlovely was to be sacrificed, Ashipattle said to his mother, "Tell me something; how is it that Feetgong will not go for you or my brothers or any one, but when my father mounts him he goes like the wind—none faster?"

Then his mother answered, "Indeed, I do not know."

"It seems a strange thing that my father would not tell you that," said Ashipattle, "and you his own true wife."

To this his mother answered nothing.

"A strange thing," said Ashipattle, "and in all the years you've lived together not a thing have you kept back from him, whether he wished it or no. But even a good husband always holds back some secret from his wife."

Still his mother spoke never a word, but Ashipattle could see that she was thinking.

That night Ashipattle lay awake long after the others were asleep. He heard his father snoring and his brothers, too, but it seemed his mother could not sleep. She turned and twisted and sighed aloud, until at last she awakened her husband.

"What ails you," he asked, "that you turn and twist in bed and sigh so loud that a body scarce can sleep?"

"It's no wonder I sigh and cannot sleep," answered his wife. "I have been thinking and turning things over in my mind, and I can see very plainly that you do not love me as a good husband should love his wife."

"How can you say that?" asked her husband. "Have I not treated you well in all these years? Have I not shown my love in every way?"

"Yes, but you do not trust me," said his wife. "You do not tell me what is in your heart."

"What have I not told you?"

"You have never told me about Feetgong; you have never told me why it is that he goes like the wind whenever you mount him, and when anyone else rides him he is so slow there is no getting anywhere with him." Then she began to sob as if her heart would break. "You do not trust me," said she.

"Wait, wait!" cried the good man. "That is a secret I had never thought to tell anyone, but since you have set your heart on knowing—listen! Only you must promise not to tell a living soul what I tell you now."

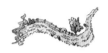

His wife promised.

"Then this is it," said her husband. "When I want Feetgong to go moderately fast, I slap him on the right shoulder; when I want him to stop, I slap him on the left shoulder, and when I want him to go like the wind, I blow upon the dried windpipe of a goose that I always carry in the right-hand pocket of my coat."

"Now indeed I know that you love me when you tell me this," said his wife. And then she went to sleep, for she was satisfied.

Ashipattle waited until near morning, and then he arose and dressed himself. He put on the coat of one brother, and the breeches of another, and the shoes of a third, and so on, for his own clothes were nothing but rags. He felt in the right-hand pocket of his father's coat, and there, sure enough, he found the dried windpipe of a goose. He took that and he took a pot of burning peat, and covered it over so it would keep hot, and he took also a big kitchen knife. Then he went out and led Feetgong from the stable. He sprang upon his back and slapped him on the right shoulder, and away they went.

The noise awoke the good man and he jumped from bed and ran to the window. There was someone riding away on his dear Feetgong. Then he called out at the top of his voice, "Hi, Hi, Ho, Feetgong, whoa!"

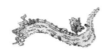

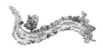

When Feetgong heard his master calling he stopped and stood stock-still. But Ashipattle whipped out the dried windpipe of the goose and blew upon it, and away went Feetgong like the wind—none could go faster. No one could overtake them.

After a while, and not so long either, they came to the seashore, and there, a little way out from the shore, lay the king's own boat with the boatman in it. He was keeping the boat there until day dawned. Then the king and his court would come, bringing the beauteous Gemlovely to offer up to the stoorworm. They would put her in the boat and set the sails to carry her toward him.

Ashipattle looked out across the water, and he could see the black back of the beast rising out of the sea like a long, low mountain.

He lighted down from Feetgong and called across the water to the boatman,

"Hello, friend! How fares it with you out there?"

"Bitterly, bitterly!" answered the boatman. "Here I sit and freeze all night, for it is cold on the water."

"I have a fire here in the pot," called Ashipattle. "Draw your boat into shore and come and warm yourself, for I can see that you are almost perished."

"That I may not do," answered the man. "The king and his court may come at any time, and they must find me ready and waiting for them as the commands were."

Then Ashipattle put his pot down on the shore and stood and thought a bit. Suddenly he dropped on his knees and began to dig in the sand as though he had gone mad. "Gold! Gold!" he shouted.

"What is the matter?" called the boatman. "What have you found?"

"Gold! Gold!" shouted Ashipattle, digging faster than ever.

The boatman thought Ashipattle must certainly have found a treasure in the sand. He made haste to bring the boat to land. He sprang out upon the shore, and pushing Ashipattle aside, he dropped on his knees and began to scoop out the sand. But Ashipattle did not wait to see whether he found anything. He caught up the pot and leaped into the boat, and before the boatman could stop him he pushed off from the shore.

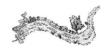

Too late, the boatman saw what he was doing. He ran down to the edge of the water and shouted and stormed and cried to Ashipattle to come back, but Ashipattle paid no heed to him. He never even turned his head. He set the sail and steered over toward where the great monster lay, with the waves washing up and breaking into foam against him.

And now the dawn was breaking. It was time for the monster to awake, and down the road from the castle came riding the king and all his court. Princess Gemlovely rode among them on a milk-white horse; she looked as white as snow.

When the king and all the others reached the shore there stood the boatman, wringing his hands and lamenting, and the boat was gone.

"What is this?" asked the king. "What have you done with my boat, and why are you standing here?"

"Look! Look!" cried the boatman, and he pointed out to sea.

The king looked, and then first he saw Ashipattle in the boat, sailing away toward the monster—for before, his eyes had been dim with sorrow, and he had seen naught but what was close before him.

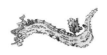

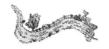

The king looked, and all the court looked with him, and a great cry arose, for they guessed that Ashipattle was sailing out to do battle with the stoorworm.

As they stood staring, the sun shone red and the monster awoke. Slowly, slowly his great jaws opened in a yawn, and as he yawned the water rushed into his mouth like a great flood and on down his throat. Ashipattle's boat was caught in the swirl and swept forward faster than any sail could carry it. Then slowly the monster closed his mouth, and all was still save for the foaming and surging of the waters.

Ashipattle steered his boat close in against the monster's jaws, and it lay there, rocking in the tide, while he waited for the stoorworm to yawn again.

Slowly, slowly, the great jaws gaped, and the flood rushed in, foaming. Ashipattle's boat was swept in with the water and it almost crushed against one of the monster's teeth, but Ashipattle fended it off, and was carried down into the stoorworm's throat.

Down, down went the boat with Ashipattle in it. The sound of surging waters filled his ears. It was light in

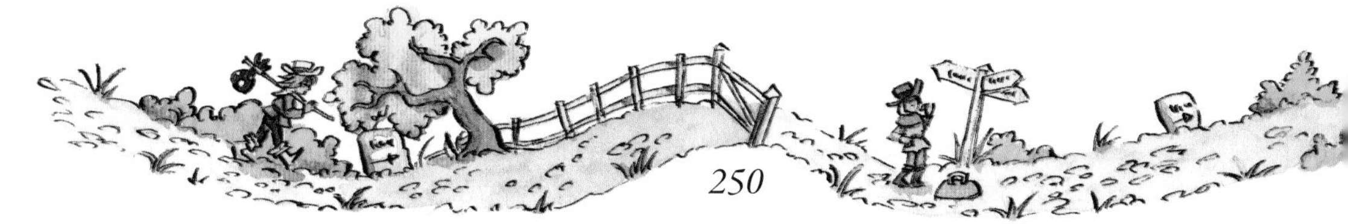

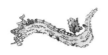

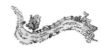

the monster's throat, for the roof and the sides of it were glowing so he could see everything.

As he swept on, the roof above him grew lower and the water grew shallower, for it drained off into passages that opened off from the throat into the rest of the body.

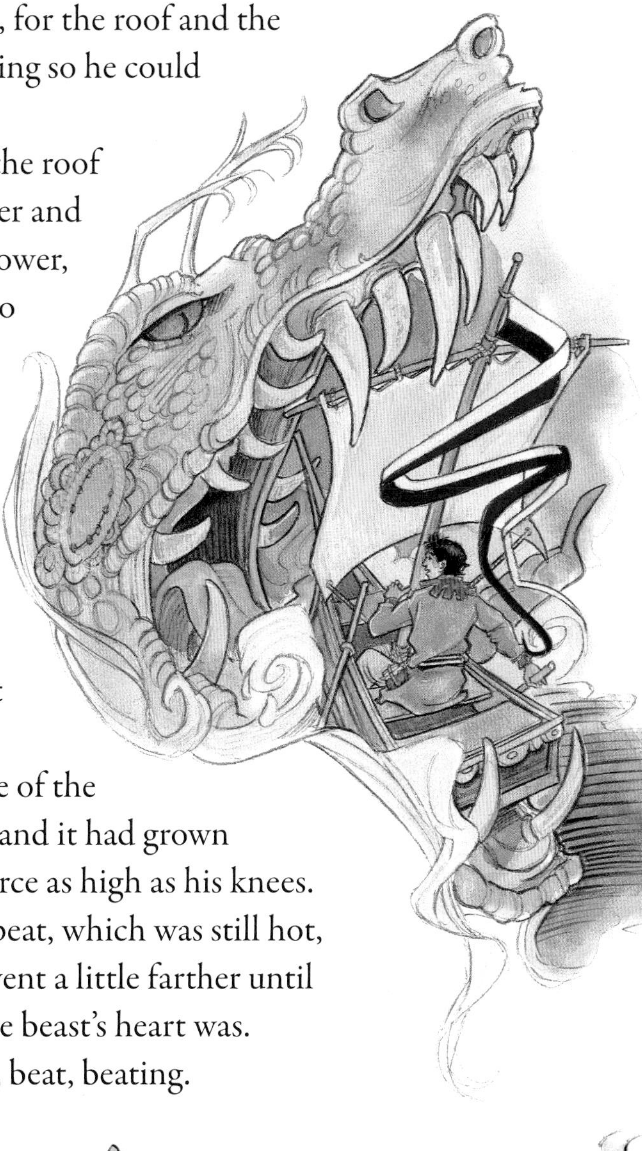

At last the roof grew so low that the mast of the boat wedged against it. Then Ashipattle stepped over the side of the boat into the water, and it had grown so shallow it was scarce as high as his knees. He took the pot of peat, which was still hot, and the knife, and went a little farther until he came to where the beast's heart was. He could see it beat, beat, beating.

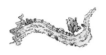

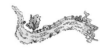

Ashipattle took his knife and dug a hole in the heart, and emptied the hot peat into it. Then he blew and blew on the peat. He blew until his cheeks almost cracked with blowing, and it seemed as though the peat would never burn. But at last it flared up, the oil of the heart trickled down upon it, and the flame burst into a blaze. Higher and higher waxed the fire. All the heart shone red with the light of it.

Then the lad ran back and jumped into the boat and pushed it clear of the roof. And none too soon, for as the fire burned deeper into the heart, the monster felt the burn of it and began to writhe and twist. Then he gave a great cough that sent the waters surging back out of his body and into the sea again in a mighty flood.

Ashipattle's boat was caught in the rush and swept like a straw up out of the stoorworm's throat and into the light of day. The monster spewed him and his boat all the way across the sea and up on the shore, almost at the king's feet.

The king himself sprang from his steed and ran to help Ashipattle to his feet. Then everyone fled back to a high hill, for the sea was rising in a mighty flood with the beating and tossing of the stoorworm.

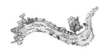

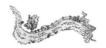

Then began such a sight as never was seen before and perchance will never be seen again. For first the monster flung his tail so high that it seemed as though it would strike the sun from the sky.

Next it fell into the sea with such a slap as sent the waves high up the rocks, and now it was his head that flung aloft, and the tongue caught on the point of the crescent moon and hung there, and for a while it looked as though the moon would be pulled from the sky, but it stood firm, and the monster's tongue tore, so that the head dropped back into the sea with such force that the teeth flew out of its mouth, and these teeth became the Orkney Islands.

Again its head reared high and fell back, and more teeth flew out, and these became the Shetland Islands. The third time his head rose and fell, and teeth flew out; they became the Faroe Islands.

So the monster beat and thrashed and struggled, while the king and the princess and Ashipattle and all the people looked on with fear at the dreadful and horrific sight.

But at last the struggle became weaker, for the heart was almost burned out. Then the stoorworm curled up and lay still, for it was dead, and its great coils became the place called Iceland. So was the monster killed, and that was the manner of its death!

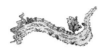

But the king turned to Ashipattle and called him "Son," and took the hand of the Princess Gemlovely and laid it in the lad's hand, for now she was to be his bride, as the king had promised.

Then they all rode back to the palace together, and the king took the sword Snickersnapper and gave it to Ashipattle for him to keep as his own.

A great feast was spread in honor of the slaying of the stoorworm. All who chose to come were welcome, and all was mirth and rejoicing.

The honest farmer, Ashipattle's father, and his mother and his sister and his brothers heard of the feast and put on their best clothes and came, but the farmer had no Feetgong to ride. When they entered the great hall and saw Ashipattle sitting there at the King's right hand in the place of honor, with the Princess Gemlovely beside him, they could hardly believe their eyes, for they had not known he was the hero everyone was talking about. But Ashipattle looked at them and nodded, and all was well.

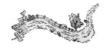

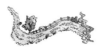

Not long after that, Ashipattle and the princess were married, and a grand wedding it was, I can tell you. And after the old king died Ashipattle became ruler of the whole realm, and he and the princess lived in mutual love and happiness together the rest of their long lives.

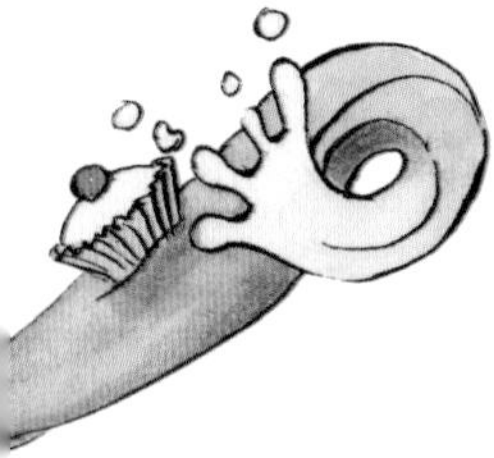

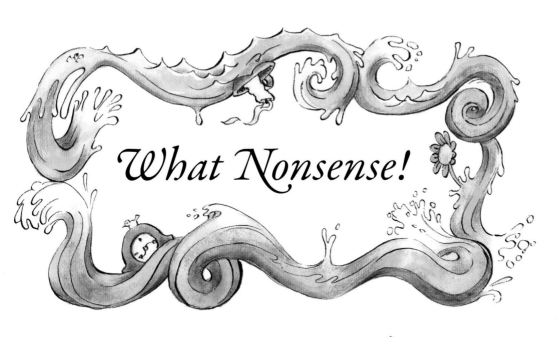

What Nonsense!

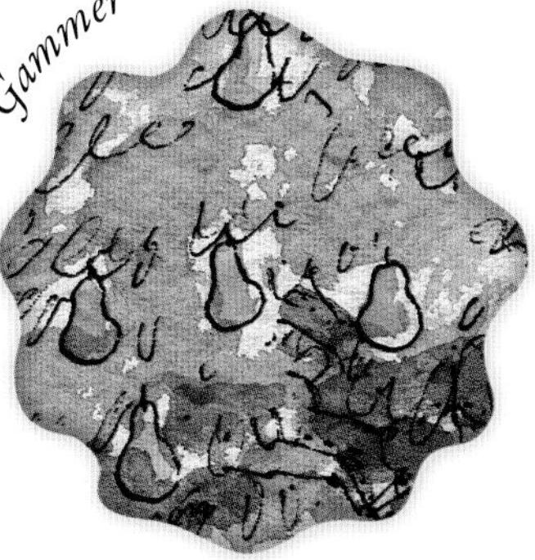

Nail Soup

By Gabriel Djurklou

READING TIME: 10 MINUTES

This story beautifully illustrates how a selfish person may be tricked into being generous so long as they think they're getting something for free.

There was once a tramp who went plodding his way through a forest. The distance between the houses was so great that he had little hope of finding a shelter before the night set in. But all of a sudden, he saw some lights between the trees. He then discovered a cottage, where there was a fire burning on the hearth. "How nice it would be to roast one's self before that fire and to get a bite of something," he thought, and so he dragged himself toward the cottage.

Just then an old woman came toward him.

"Good evening!" said the tramp.

"Good evening," said the woman. "Where do you come from?"

"South of the sun, and east of the moon," said the tramp. "And now I am on the way home again, for I have been all over the world with the exception of this parish," he said.

"You must be a great traveler, then," said the woman. "What is your business here?"

"Oh, I want a shelter for the night," he said.

"I thought as much," said the woman. "But you may as well get away from here at once, for my husband is not at home, and my place is not an inn," she said.

"My good woman," said the tramp, "you must not be so cross and hardhearted, for we are both human beings and should help one another."

"Help one another?" said the woman. "Help? Did you ever hear such a thing? Who'll help me, do you think? I haven't got a morsel in the house! No, you'll have to look for quarters elsewhere," she said.

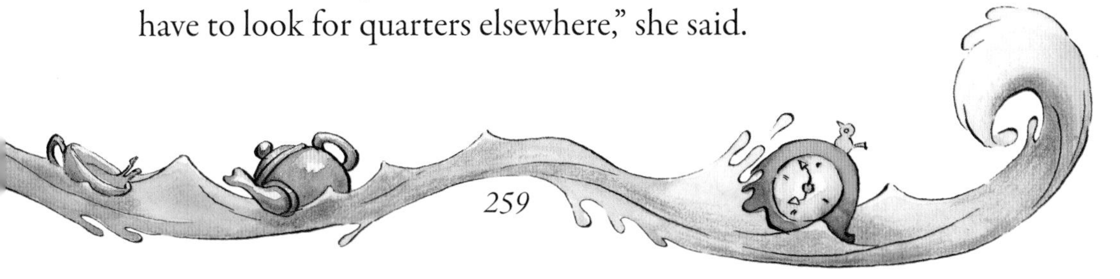

But the tramp was like the rest of his kind. He did not consider himself beaten at the first rebuff. Although the old woman grumbled and complained as much as she could, he was just as persistent as ever and went on begging and praying like a starved dog, until at last she gave in, and he got permission to lie on the floor for the night.

"That was very kind," he thought, and he thanked her for it.

"Better on the floor without sleep, than suffer cold in the forest deep," he said, for he was a merry fellow, this tramp, and was always ready with a rhyme.

When he came into the room, he could see that the woman was not so badly off as she had pretended. But she was a greedy and stingy woman of the worst sort and was always complaining and grumbling.

He now made himself very agreeable and asked her in his most insinuating manner for something to eat.

"Where am I to get it from?" said the woman. "I haven't tasted a morsel myself the whole day."

But the tramp was a cunning fellow. "Poor old granny, you must be starving," he said. "Well, I suppose I shall have to ask you to have something with me, then."

"Have something with you!" said the woman. "You don't look as if you could ask anyone to have anything! What have you got to offer one, I should like to know?"

"He who far and wide does roam sees many things not known at home, and he who many things has seen has wits about him and senses keen," said the tramp. "Better dead than lose one's head! Lend me a pot, granny!"

The old woman now became very inquisitive, as you may guess, and so she let him have a pot. He filled it with water and put it on the fire, and then he blew with all his might till the fire was burning fiercely all around it. Then he took a four-inch nail from his pocket, turned it three times in his hand, and put it into the pot.

The woman stared with all her might. "What's this going to be?" she asked.

"Nail broth," said the tramp.

The old woman had seen and heard a good deal in her time, but making broth with a nail—well, she had never heard the like before.

"That's something for poor people to know," she said, "and I should like to learn how to make it."

If she wanted to learn how to make it she had only to watch him, he said, and he went on stirring the broth. The old woman sat on the floor, her hands clasping her knees and her eyes following his hand as he stirred the broth.

"This generally makes good broth," he said, "but this time it will very likely be rather thin, for I have been making broth the whole week with the same nail. If one only had a handful of sifted oatmeal to put in, that would make it all right," he said. "But what one has to go without, it's no use thinking more about," and so he stirred the broth again.

"Well, I think I have a scrap of flour somewhere," said the old woman, and she went out to fetch some, and it was both good and fine. The tramp began putting the flour into the broth, and went on stirring, while the woman sat staring now at him and then at the pot until her eyes nearly burst their sockets.

"This broth would be good enough for company," he said, putting in one handful of flour after another. "If I had only a bit of salted beef and a few potatoes to put in, it would be fit for gentlefolks, however particular they might be," he said. "But what one has to go without, it's no use thinking more about."

When the old woman really began to think it over, she thought she had some potatoes, and perhaps a bit of beef as well, and these she gave the tramp, who went on stirring, while she sat and stared as hard as ever.

"This will be grand enough for the best in the land," he said.

"Well, I never!" said the woman, "and just fancy—all with a nail!" He was really a wonderful man, this tramp! He could do more than drink a sup and turn the tankard up, he could.

"If one had only a little barley and a drop of milk, we could ask the king himself to have some of it," he said. "For this is what he has every blessed evening—that I know, for I have been in service under the king's cook," he said.

"Dear me! Ask the king to have some! Well, I never!" exclaimed the woman, slapping her knees. She was quite awestruck at the tramp and his grand connections.

"But what one has to go without, it's no use thinking more about," said the tramp.

And then she remembered she had a little barley, and as for milk, well, she wasn't quite out of that, she said, for her best cow had just calved. And then she went to fetch both the one and the other.

The tramp went on stirring, and the woman sat staring, one moment at him and the next at the pot.

Then all at once the tramp took out the nail. "Now it's ready, and now we'll have a real good feast," he said. "But to this kind of soup the king and the queen always take a small drink or two, and one sandwich at least. And then they always have a cloth on the table when they eat," he said. "But what one has to go without, it's no use thinking more about."

But by this time the old woman herself had begun to feel quite grand and fine, I can tell you. And if that was all that was wanted to make it just as the king had it, she thought it would be nice to have it just the same way for once, and play at being king and queen with the tramp. She went straight to a cupboard and brought out the brandy bottle, glasses, butter and cheese, smoked beef and veal, until at last the table looked as if it were decked out for company.

Never in her life had the old woman had such a grand feast, and never had she tasted such broth, and just imagine, made only with a nail! She was in such a good and merry humor at having learned such an economical way of making broth that she did not know what to do.

So they ate and drank, and drank and ate, until they become both tired and sleepy.

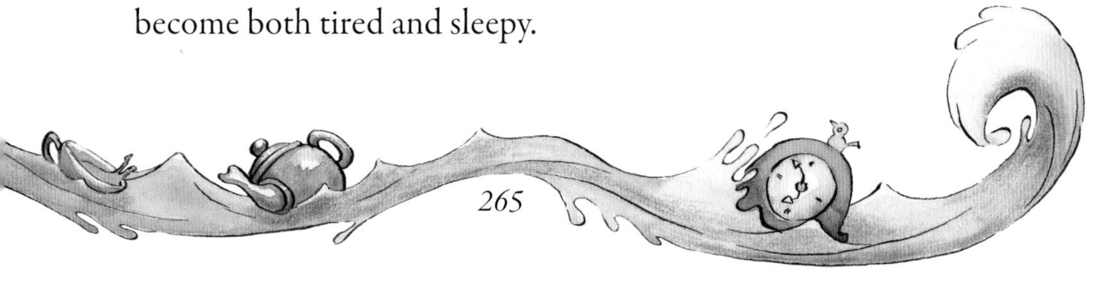

The tramp was now going to lie down on the floor. But that would never do, thought the old woman. No, that was impossible. "Such a grand person must have a bed to lie in," she said.

He did not need much pressing. "It's just like the sweet Christmastime," he said, "and a nicer woman I never came across. Ah, well! Happy are they who meet with such good people," said he, and he lay down on the bed and went to sleep.

And next morning when he woke, the first thing he got was coffee and a small brandy. When he was going, the old woman gave him a bright dollar piece. "And thanks, many thanks, for what you have taught me," she said. "Now I shall live in comfort, since I have learned how to make broth with a nail."

"Well it isn't very difficult, if one only has something good to add to it," said the tramp as he went on his way.

The woman stood at the door staring after him. "Such people don't grow on every bush," she said.

The Haughty Princess

By Patrick Kennedy

READING TIME: 8 MINUTES

There was once a very worthy king, whose daughter was the greatest beauty that could be seen far or near, but she was as proud as Lucifer, and no king or prince would she agree to marry. Her father was tired out at last, and invited every king and prince and duke and earl that he knew or didn't know to come to his court to give her one more trial. They all came, and next day after breakfast they stood in a row on the lawn, and the princess walked along in front of them to make her choice. One was fat, and said she, "I won't have you, beer

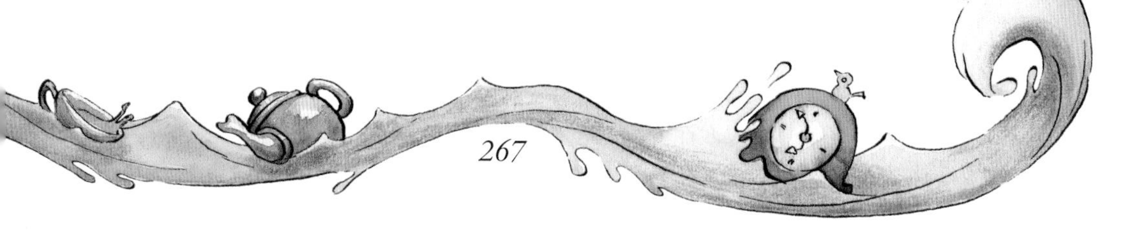

barrel!" One was tall and thin, and to him she said, "I won't have you, ramrod!" To a white-faced man she said, "I won't have you, pale death!" and to a red-cheeked man she said, "I won't have you, cockscomb!"

She stopped a little before the last of all, for he was a fine man in face and form. She wanted to find some defect in him, but he had nothing remarkable but a ring of brown curling hair under his chin. She admired him a little, and then

carried it off with, "I won't have you, whiskers!"

So all went away, and the king was so vexed he said to her, "Now to punish your impudence, I'll give you to the first beggar man or singing lazy thing that calls." And, sure enough, a fellow in rags, and hair that came to his shoulders, and a bushy red beard all over his face, came next morning and began to sing before the parlor window.

When the song was over, the hall door was opened, the singer asked in, the priest brought, and the princess married to Beardy. She roared and she bawled, but her father didn't mind her. "There," said he to the bridegroom," is five guineas for you. Take your wife out of my sight, and never let me lay eyes on you or her again."

Off he led her, and dismal enough she was. The only thing that gave her relief was the tones of her husband's voice and his genteel manners.

"Whose wood is this?" said she, as they were going through one.

"It belongs to the king you called whiskers yesterday." He gave her the same answer about meadows and cornfields, and at last a fine city.

"Ah, what a fool I was!" said she to herself. "He was a fine man, and I might have had him for a husband." At last they were coming up to a poor cabin. "Why are you bringing me here?" said the poor lady.

"This was my house," said he, "and now it's yours."

She began to cry, but she was tired and hungry, and went in with him. There was neither a table set out, nor a fire burning, and she was obliged to help her husband to light it, and boil their dinner, and clean up the place after. The next day he made her put on a woolen gown and a cotton handkerchief. When she had her house cleaned up and no business to keep her employed, he brought home willows, peeled them, and showed her how to make baskets. But the hard twigs bruised her delicate fingers, and she began to cry. Well, then he asked her to mend their clothes, but the needle drew blood from her fingers, and she cried again.

He couldn't bear to see her tears, so he bought a boxful of earthenware pots, and sent her to the market to sell them. This was the hardest trial of all, but she looked so handsome and sorrowful, and had such a nice air about her, that all her pots and jugs and plates and dishes were gone before noon.

Well, her husband was so glad, he sent her with another box the next day. But her luck was deserting her. A drunken huntsman came riding up, and his beast got in among her wares, and broke them all. She went home crying, and her husband wasn't at all pleased. "I see," said he, "you're not fit for business. Come along, I'll get you a kitchen maid's place in the palace. I know the cook."

So the poor thing was obliged to stifle her pride once more. She was kept very busy, and she went home to her husband every night, carrying her payment of scraps of leftover food, wrapped in papers in her side pockets.

A week after she got the job, there was great bustle in the kitchen. The king was going to be married, but no one knew who the bride was to be. Well, in the evening the cook filled the princess's pockets with cold meat and

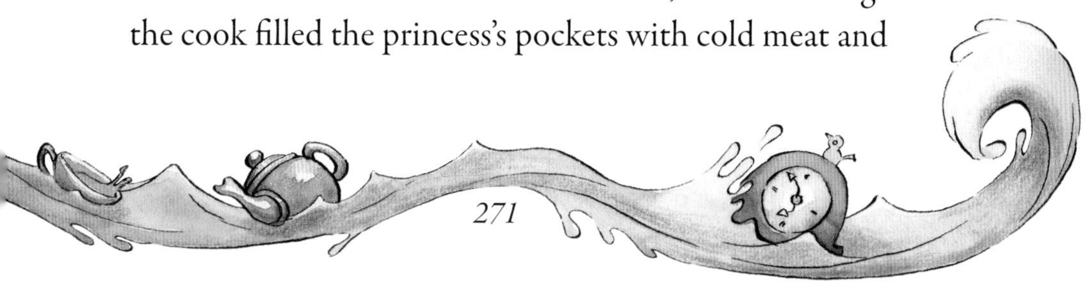

steamed puddings, and then, said she, "Before you go, let us have a look at the great doings in the big parlor." So they came near the door to get a peep, and who should come out but the king himself, as handsome as you please, and he was no other but King Whiskers himself.

"Your handsome helper must pay for her peeping," said he to the cook, when he spotted them, "and dance a jig with me."

Whether the princess would or not, he held her hand and brought her into the parlor. The fiddlers struck up, and away went him with her. But they hadn't danced two steps when the meat and the puddings flew out of her pockets. Everyone roared with laughter, and she flew to the door, crying piteously. But she was soon caught by the king, and taken into the back parlor.

"Don't you know me, my darling?" said he. "I'm King Whiskers, your husband the ballad singer, and the drunken huntsman. Your father knew me well enough when he gave you to me, and all was to drive your pride out of you."

Well, she didn't know how she was with fright and shame and joy. Love was uppermost, anyhow, for she laid her head on her husband's breast and cried like a child.

The maids of honor soon had her away and dressed her as fine as hands and pins could do it, and there were her mother and father, too, and while the company were wondering what end of the handsome girl and the king, he and his queen, whom they didn't know in her fine clothes, and the other king and queen, came in, and such rejoicings and fine doings as there were, none of us will ever see, anyway.

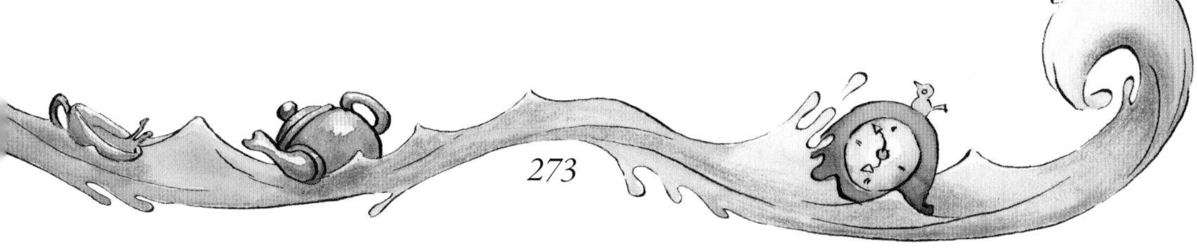

Nasreddin Hodja and the Smell of Soup

Anon

READING TIME: 3 MINUTES

Nasreddin Hodja is what you might call a wise fool. He comes up with answers other people would never have thought of! He is a popular figure in Turkish folklore, and there are many tales about him.

A beggar was walking along the road of the main market. He had begged a small piece of bread for himself, dry and old, and that was all he had to eat that day. Hoping to get something to put on it, he went to a nearby restaurant and begged for a small portion of food, but was ordered out of the inn empty handed. As he walked out, he stopped to stare at the rich people enjoying the bowls of good savory soup. He leaned over one of the cauldrons that bubbled and hissed on the charcoal fire and took a deep breath to savor its good smell, then turned sadly to go. At that moment the innkeeper came out and seized his arm.

"Not so fast! You haven't paid!" he exclaimed.

"Payment? But I have had nothing," stammered the confused beggar, "I was only enjoying the smell of your soup."

"Then you must pay for the smell," insisted the innkeeper. "Do you think I cook my soup for a beggar to steal a smell from? I saw you take it."

The poor beggar had no money to pay, of course,

so the innkeeper dragged him off to Nasreddin Hodja, the judge. Hodja listened to the case most carefully, considering both the innkeeper's angry exclamations, and the beggar's protests that he had taken nothing.

"And you say you have no money?" he asked the poor man.

"Not a penny," stammered the terrified beggar.

Then Hodja turned to the innkeeper.

"So you insist on being paid for the smell?" he inquired.

"Indeed I do," said the innkeeper.

"Then I myself will pay you," said Hodja.

He drew some coins out of his pocket and beckoned the innkeeper closer. The man went eagerly forward.

Hodja held the coins in his hands up to the innkeeper's ear and shook his hand gently so the coins rang together.

"You may go," he said.

The innkeeper said angrily, "But my payment . . ."

"This man took the smell of the soup," said Hodja, "and you have been paid with the sound of the money. Now go on your way."

The Box of Robbers

By L. Frank Baum

READING TIME: 15 MINUTES

No one intended to leave Martha alone that afternoon, but it happened that everyone was called away, for one reason or another. Mrs. McFarland was attending the weekly card party. Sister Nell's young man had called quite unexpectedly to take her for a long drive. Papa was at the office, as usual. It was Mary Ann's day out. As for Emeline, she certainly should have stayed in the house and looked after the little girl, but Emeline had a restless nature.

"Would you mind, miss, if I just crossed the alley to

speak a word to Mrs. Carleton's girl?" she asked Martha.

"'Course not," replied the child. "You'd better lock the back door, though, and take the key, for I shall be upstairs."

"Oh, I'll do that, of course, miss," said the delighted maid, and ran away to spend the afternoon with her friend, leaving Martha quite alone in the big house, and locked in, into the bargain.

The little girl read a few pages in her new book, sewed a few stitches in her embroidery, and started to "play visiting" with her four favorite dolls. Then she remembered that in the attic was a doll's playhouse that hadn't been used for months, so she decided she would dust it and put it in order.

Filled with this idea, the girl climbed the winding stairs to the big room under the roof. It was well lit by three dormer windows and was warm and pleasant. Around the walls were rows of boxes and trunks, piles of old carpeting, pieces of damaged furniture, bundles of discarded clothing, and other odds and ends of more or less value.

The doll's house had been moved, but after a search Martha found it over in a corner near the big chimney.

She drew it out and noticed that behind it was a black wooden chest, which Uncle Walter had sent over from Italy years and years ago—before Martha was born, in fact. Mamma had told her about it one day, how there was no key to it, because Uncle Walter wished it to remain unopened until he returned home, and how this wandering uncle, who was a mighty hunter, had gone into Africa to hunt elephants and had never been heard from afterward.

The little girl looked at the chest curiously, now that it had by accident attracted her attention.

It was quite big—bigger even than Mamma's traveling trunk—and was studded all over with tarnished brass-headed nails. It was heavy, too, for when Martha tried to lift one end of it, she found she could not stir it a bit. But there was a place in the side of the cover for a key. She stooped to examine the lock and saw that it would take a rather big key to open it.

Then, as you may suspect, the little girl longed to open Uncle Walter's big box and see what was in it. For we are all curious, and little girls are just as curious as the rest of us.

"I don't b'lieve Uncle Walter'll ever come back,"

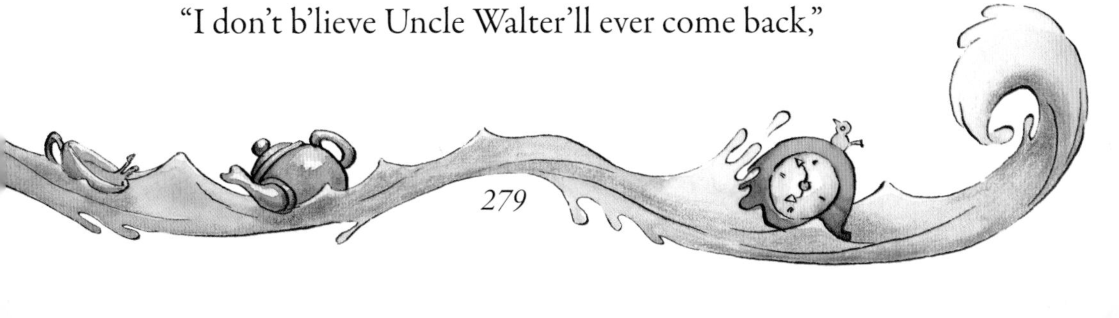

she thought. "Papa said once that some elephant must have killed him. If I only had a key." She stopped and clapped her little hands together as she remembered a big basket of keys on the shelf in the linen closet. They were of all sorts and sizes—perhaps one of them would unlock the mysterious chest!

She flew down the stairs, found the basket, and returned with it to the attic. Then she sat down before the brass-studded box and began trying one key after another in the curious old lock. Some were too large, but most were too small. One would go into the lock but would not turn, another stuck so fast that she feared for a time that she would never get it out again. But at last, when the basket was almost empty, an oddly shaped, ancient brass key slipped easily into the lock. With a cry of joy, Martha turned the key with both hands, then she heard a sharp "click," and the next moment the heavy lid flew up of its own accord!

Martha leaned over the edge of the chest. The sight that met her eyes caused her to start back in amazement.

Slowly and carefully a man unpacked himself from the chest, stepped out upon the floor, stretched his limbs, and then took off his hat and bowed politely to the astonished child.

He was tall and thin and his face seemed tanned or sunburned.

Then another man emerged from the chest, yawning and rubbing his eyes like a sleepy schoolboy. He was of middle size, and his skin seemed as badly tanned as that of the first.

While Martha stared openmouthed at the remarkable sight, a third man crawled from the chest. He had the same complexion as his fellows but was short and fat.

All three were dressed in a curious manner. They wore short jackets of red velvet braided with gold and knee breeches of sky-blue satin with silver buttons. Over their stockings were laced wide ribbons of red and yellow and blue, while their hats had broad brims with high, peaked crowns, from which fluttered yards of bright-colored ribbons.

They had big gold rings in their ears and rows of knives and pistols in their belts. Their eyes were black and glittering, and they wore long, fierce mustaches, curling at the ends like a pig's tail.

"My! You were heavy," exclaimed the fat one, when he had pulled down his velvet jacket and brushed the dust from his sky-blue breeches. "And you squeezed me all out of shape."

"It was unavoidable, Luigi," responded the thin man, lightly. "The lid of the chest pressed me down upon you."

"As for me," said the middle-sized man, "you must acknowledge I have been your nearest friend for years, so do not be disagreeable."

"Who are you?" asked Martha, who until now had been too astonished to be frightened.

"Permit us to introduce ourselves," said the thin man,

flourishing his hat gracefully. "This is Luigi," the fat man nodded, "and this is Beni," the middle-sized man bowed, "and I am Victor. We are three bandits—Italian bandits."

"Bandits!" cried Martha, with a look of horror.

"Exactly. Perhaps in all the world there are not three other bandits so terrible and fierce as ourselves," said Victor proudly.

"'Tis so," said the fat man, nodding gravely.

"But it's wicked!" exclaimed Martha.

"Yes, indeed," replied Victor. "We are extremely and tremendously wicked. Perhaps in all the world you could not find three men more wicked than those who now stand before you."

"'Tis so," said the fat man, approvingly.

"But you shouldn't be so wicked," said the girl. "It's—it's—naughty!"

Victor cast down his eyes and blushed.

"Naughty!" gasped Beni, with a horrified look.

"'Tis a hard word," said Luigi, sadly, and buried his face in his hands.

"I little thought," murmured Victor, in a voice broken by emotion, "ever to be so reviled! Yet, perhaps you spoke thoughtlessly. You must consider, miss, that our wickedness has an excuse. For how are we to be bandits, let me ask, unless we are wicked?"

Martha was puzzled and shook her head thoughtfully. Then she remembered something.

"You can't remain bandits any longer," said she, "because you are now in America."

"America!" cried the three, together.

"Certainly. You are on Prairie Avenue, in Chicago. Uncle Walter sent you here from Italy in this chest."

The bandits seemed greatly bewildered by this announcement. Luigi sat down on an old chair with a broken rocker and wiped his forehead with a yellow silk handkerchief. Beni and Victor fell back upon the chest and looked at her with pale faces and staring eyes.

When he had somewhat recovered himself, Victor spoke.

"Your Uncle Walter has greatly wronged us," he said, reproachfully. "He has taken us from our beloved Italy, where bandits are highly respected, and brought us to a strange country where we shall not know whom to rob or how much to ask for a ransom."

"'Tis so!" said the fat man, slapping his leg sharply.

"And we had such fine reputations in Italy!" said Beni, regretfully.

"Perhaps Uncle Walter wanted to reform you," suggested Martha.

"Are there, then, no bandits in Chicago?" asked Victor.

"Well," replied the girl, blushing in her turn, "we do not call them bandits."

"Then what shall we do for a living?" inquired Beni, despairingly.

"A great deal can be done in a big American city," said the child. "My father is a lawyer," (the bandits shuddered) "and my mother's cousin is a police inspector."

"Ah," said Victor, "that is a good employment.

The police need to be inspected, especially in Italy."

"Everywhere!" added Beni.

"Then you could do other things," continued Martha, encouragingly." You could be clerks in a department store. Some people even become aldermen to earn a living."

The bandits shook their heads sadly.

"We are not fitted for such work," said Victor. "Our business is to rob."

Martha tried to think.

"It is rather hard to get positions in the gas office," she said, "but you might become politicians."

"No!" cried Beni, with sudden fierceness, "Bandits we have always been, and bandits we must remain!"

"'Tis so!" agreed the fat man.

"Even in Chicago there must be people to rob," remarked Victor, with cheerfulness.

Martha was distressed.

"I think they have all been robbed," she objected.

"Then we can rob the robbers, for we have experience and talent beyond the ordinary," said Beni.

"Oh dear, oh dear!" moaned the girl, "why did Uncle Walter ever send you here in this chest?"

The bandits became interested.

"That is what we should like to know," declared Victor, eagerly.

"But no one will ever know, for Uncle Walter was lost while hunting elephants in Africa," she continued, with conviction.

"Then we must accept our fate and rob to the best of our ability," said Victor. "So long as we are faithful to our beloved profession, we need not be ashamed."

"'Tis so!" cried the fat man.

"Brothers! We will begin now. Let us rob the house we are in."

"Good!" shouted the others and sprang to their feet.

Beni turned threateningly upon the child.

"Remain here!" he commanded. "If you stir one step your blood will be on your own head!" Then he added, in a gentler voice: "Don't be afraid, that's the way all bandits talk to their captives. But of course we wouldn't hurt a young lady under any circumstances."

"Of course not," said Victor.

The fat man drew a big knife from his belt and flourished it about his head.

"S'blood!" he shouted, fiercely.

"S'bananas!" cried Beni, in a terrible voice.

"Confusion to our foes!" hissed Victor.

And then the three bent themselves nearly double and crept stealthily down the stairway with cocked pistols in their hands and glittering knives between their teeth, leaving Martha trembling with fear and too horrified even to cry for help.

How long she remained alone in the attic she never knew, but finally she heard the catlike tread of the returning bandits and saw them coming up the stairs in single file.

All bore heavy loads of plunder in their arms, and Luigi was balancing a mince pie on the top of a pile of her mother's best evening dresses. Victor came next, with an armful of bric-a-brac, a brass candelabra, and the parlor clock. Beni had the family Bible, the basket of silverware from the sideboard, a copper kettle, and Papa's fur overcoat.

"Oh, joy!" said Victor, putting down his load, "It is pleasant to rob once more."

"Oh, ecstasy!" said Beni, but he let the kettle drop on his toe and immediately began dancing around in anguish, while he muttered queer words in Italian.

"We have much wealth," continued Victor, holding the mince pie while Luigi added his spoils to the heap, "and all from one house! America must be a rich place."

With a dagger he then cut himself a piece of the pie and handed the remainder to his comrades. Whereupon all three sat upon the floor and consumed the pie while Martha looked on sadly.

The next moment they were startled by the ringing of the electric doorbell, which was heard plainly even in the remote attic.

"What's that?" demanded Victor in a hoarse voice, as the three scrambled to their feet with drawn daggers.

Martha ran to the window and saw it was only the postman, who had dropped a letter in the box and gone away again. But the incident gave her an idea of how to get rid of her troublesome bandits, so she began wringing her hands as if in great distress and cried out:

"It's the police!"

The robbers looked at one another with genuine alarm, and Luigi asked, tremblingly:

"Are there many of them?"

"A hundred and twelve!" exclaimed Martha, after pretending to count them.

"Then we are lost!" declared Beni, "for we could never fight so many and live."

"Are they armed?" inquired Victor, who was shivering as if cold.

"Oh, yes," said she. "They have guns and swords and pistols and axes and—and—"

"And what?" demanded Luigi.

"And cannons!"

The three wicked ones groaned aloud, and Beni said, in a hollow voice: "I hope they will kill us quickly and not put us to the torture."

Suddenly Martha turned from the window.

"You are my friends, are you not?" she asked.

"We are devoted!" answered Victor.

"We adore you!" cried Beni.

"We would die for you!" added Luigi, thinking he was about to die anyway.

"Then I will save you," said the girl.

"How?" asked the three, with one voice.

"Get back into the chest," she said. "I will then close the lid, so they will be unable to find you."

They looked around the room in a dazed and irresolute way, but she exclaimed: "You must be quick!

They will soon be here to arrest you."

Then Luigi sprang into the chest and lay flat upon the bottom. Beni tumbled in next and packed himself in the back side. Victor followed after pausing to kiss her hand in a graceful manner.

Then Martha ran up to press down the lid, but could not make it catch.

"You must squeeze down," she said to them.

Luigi groaned.

"I am doing my best, miss," said Victor, who was nearest the top, "but although we fitted in very nicely before, the chest now seems rather small for us."

"'Tis so!" came the muffled voice of the fat man from the bottom.

"I know what takes up the room," said Beni.

"What?" inquired Victor, anxiously.

"The pie," returned Beni.

"'Tis so!" came from the bottom, in faint accents.

Then Martha sat upon the lid and pressed it down with all her weight. To her great delight the lock caught, and, springing down, she exerted all her strength and turned the key.

This story should teach us not to interfere in matters that do not concern us. For had Martha refrained from opening Uncle Walter's mysterious chest, she would not have been obliged to carry downstairs all the plunder the robbers had brought into the attic.

The Husband who was to Mind the House

By Peter Christen Asbjørnsen

READING TIME: 5 MINUTES

Once upon a time there was a man who was so bad tempered and cross that he never thought his wife did anything right in the house. One evening, in hay-making time, he came home, scolding and shouting and showing his teeth and making a commotion.

"Dear love, don't be so angry, that's a good man," said his wife. "Tomorrow let's change jobs. I'll go out with the mowers and mow, and you can mind the house at home."

Yes, the husband thought that would do very well. He was quite willing, he said.

So early the next morning, his wife took a scythe over her neck and went out into the hay field with the mowers and began to mow, but the man was to mind the house and do the work at home.

First of all, he wanted to churn the butter, but when he had churned awhile, he got thirsty and went down to the cellar to tap a barrel of ale. He had just knocked in the stopper, and was putting in the tap, when he heard the pig come into the kitchen above. As as fast as he could, he ran up the cellar steps, with the tap in his hand, to keep the pig from upsetting the churn, but when he got there, the pig had already knocked the churn over and

was rolling and grunting in the cream that was all over the floor.

He got so angry that he quite forgot the ale barrel and ran at the pig as hard as he could. He caught it, too, just as it ran out of doors, and gave it such a powerful kick that he killed it on the spot. Then he remembered he had the tap in his hand, but when he got down to the cellar, all the ale had run out of the barrel.

Then he went into the milk shed and found enough cream left to fill the churn again, and so he began to churn, for they had to have butter at dinner. When he had churned a bit, he remembered that their milk cow was still shut up in the barn, and hadn't had a bit to eat or a drop to drink all morning, although the sun was high. It occurred to him that it was too far to take her down to the meadow, so he'd just get her up on the roof, for it was a sod roof, and a fine crop of grass was growing there. The house was close against a steep hill, and he thought if he laid a plank across to the back of the roof he'd easily get the cow up.

But he couldn't leave the churn, for his little baby was crawling about on the floor. "If I leave it," he thought, "the child will tip it over." So he took the churn on his back and went out with it, but then he thought he'd better first draw water for the cow before he put her on the roof. So he picked up a bucket to draw water out of the well, but as he stooped over the edge of the well, all the cream ran out of the churn over his shoulder and down into the well.

Now it was near dinnertime, and he hadn't even gotten the butter yet, so he thought he'd best boil the porridge, and he filled the pot with water and hung it over the fire. When he had done that, it occurred to him that the cow might fall off the roof and break her legs or her neck. So he climbed up on the house to tie her up. He tied one end of the rope to the cow's neck. He slipped the other end down the chimney and tied it around his own leg. Then he had to hurry, for the water was now boiling in the pot, and he had still to grind the oatmeal.

He began to grind away, but while he was hard at it, the cow fell off the roof, dragging the man up the chimney by the rope. There he stuck fast, and as for the cow, she hung halfway down the wall, swinging between heaven and earth, for she could neither get down nor up.

Now the wife waited seven lengths and seven

breadths for her husband to come and call her home to dinner, but he never came. At last she thought she'd waited long enough, and went home. But when she got home and saw the cow hanging there, she ran up and cut the rope with her scythe. When she did this, her husband fell down from within the chimney. When the old woman came inside, she found him upside down with his head in the porridge pot.

The Six Soldiers of Fortune

By the Brothers Grimm

READING TIME: 12 MINUTES

There was once a man who was a Jack-of-all-trades. He had served in the war and had been brave and bold, but at the end of it he was sent about his business with three farthings and his discharge.

"I am not going to stand this," said he. "Wait till I find the right man to help me, and the king shall give me all the treasures of his kingdom before he has done with me."

Then, full of wrath, he went into the forest, and he saw one standing there by six trees that he had rooted up

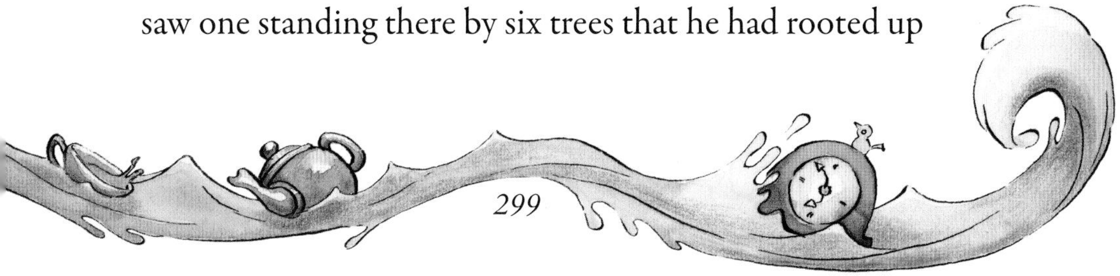

as if they had been stalks of corn. And he said to him,

"Will you be my man, and come along with me?"

"All right," answered he, "I must just take this bit of wood home to my father and mother." And taking one of the trees, he bound it around the other five, and putting the bundle of sticks on his shoulder, he carried it off. Then soon coming back, he went along with his leader, who said, "Two such as we can stand against the whole world."

And when they had gone on a little while, they came to a huntsman who was kneeling on one knee and taking careful aim with his rifle.

"Huntsman," said the leader, "what are you aiming at?"

"Two miles from here," answered he, "there sits a fly on the bough of an oak tree. I mean to put a bullet into its left eye."

"Oh, come along with me," said the leader. "Three of us together can stand against the world."

The huntsman was quite willing to go with him, and so they went on till they came to seven windmills, whose sails were going around briskly, and yet there was no wind blowing from any quarter, and not a leaf stirred.

"Well," said the leader, "I cannot think what ails the windmills, turning without wind," and he went on with his followers about two miles farther, and then they came to a man sitting up in a tree, holding one nostril and blowing with the other.

"Now then," said the leader, "what are you doing up there?"

"Two miles from here," answered he, "there are seven windmills. I am blowing, and they are going around."

"Oh, go with me," cried the leader. "Four of us together can stand against the world."

So the blower got down and went with them, and after a time they came to a man standing on one leg, and the other had been taken off and was lying near him.

"You seem to have got a handy way of resting yourself," said the leader to the man.

"I am a runner," answered he, "and in order to keep myself from going too fast I have taken off a leg, for when I run with both, I go faster than a bird can fly."

"Oh, go with me," cried the leader. "Five of us together may well stand against the world."

So he went with them all together, and it was not long before they met a man with a little hat on, and he wore it just over one ear.

"Manners! Manners!" said the leader. "With your hat like that, you look like a fool."

"I dare not put it straight," answered the other. "If I did, there would be such a terrible frost that the very birds would be frozen and fall dead from the sky to the ground."

"Oh, come with me," said the leader. "We six together may well stand against the whole world."

So the six went on until they came to a town where the king had caused it to be made known that whoever would run a race with his daughter and win it might become her husband, but that whoever lost must lose his head into the bargain. And the leader came forward and said one of his men should run for him.

"Then," said the king, "his life too must be put in pledge, and if he fails, his head and yours too must fall."

When this was quite settled and agreed upon, the leader called the runner, and strapped his second leg onto him.

"Now, look out," said he, "and take care that we win."

It had been agreed that the one who should bring water first from a far distant brook should be accounted winner. Now the king's daughter and the runner each took a pitcher, and they started both at the same time, but in one moment, when the king's daughter had gone but a very little way, the runner was out of sight, for his running was as if the wind rushed by. In a short time he reached the brook, filled his pitcher full of water, and turned back again. About halfway home, however, he was overcome with weariness, and setting down his pitcher, he lay down on the ground to sleep. But in order to awaken soon again by not lying too soft, he had taken a horse's skull that lay near and placed it under his head for a pillow. In the meanwhile the king's daughter, who really was a good runner, good enough to beat an ordinary man, had reached the brook and filled her pitcher, and was hastening with it

back again, when she saw the runner lying asleep.

"The day is mine," said she with much joy, and she emptied his pitcher and hastened on. And now all had been lost but for the huntsman, who was standing on the castle wall, and with his keen eyes saw all that happened.

"We must not be outdone by the king's daughter," said he, and he loaded his rifle and took so good an aim that he shot the horse's skull from under the runner's head without doing him any harm. And the runner awoke and jumped up, and saw his pitcher standing empty and the king's daughter far on her way home. But, not losing courage, he ran swiftly to the brook, filled it again with water, and for all that, he got home ten minutes before the king's daughter.

"Look you," said he, "this is the first time I have really stretched my legs. Before it was not worth the name of running."

The king was vexed, and his daughter yet more so, that she should be beaten by a discharged common soldier, and they took counsel together how they might rid themselves of him and of his companions at the same time.

"I have a plan," said the king. "Do not fear but that

we shall be quit of them forever." Then he went out to the men and bade them to feast and be merry and eat and drink, and he led them into a room that had a floor of iron, and the doors were iron, the windows had iron frames and bolts. In the room was a table set out with costly food.

"Now, go in there and make yourselves comfortable," said the king.

And when they had gone in, he had the door locked and bolted. Then he called the cook, and told him to make a big fire underneath the room, so that the iron floor of it should be red hot. And the cook did so, and the six men began to feel the room growing very warm, by reason, as they thought at first, of the good dinner. But as the heat grew greater and greater, and they found the doors and windows fastened, they began to think it was an evil plan of the king's to suffocate them.

"He shall not succeed, however," said the man with the little hat, "I will bring on a frost that shall make the fire feel ashamed of itself, and creep out of the way."

So he set his hat straight on his head, and immediately there came such a frost that all the heat passed away and the food froze in the dishes. After an hour or two had passed, and the king thought they must have all perished in the heat, he caused the door to be opened, and went himself to see how they fared. And when the door flew back, there they were all six quite

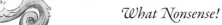

safe and sound, and they said they were, quite ready to come out, so that they might warm themselves, for the great cold of that room had caused the food to freeze in the dishes. Full of wrath, the king went to the cook and scolded him, and asked why he had not done as he was ordered.

"It is hot enough there—you may see for yourself," answered the cook. And the king looked and saw an immense fire burning underneath the room of iron, and he began to think that the six men were not to be gotten rid of in that way. And he thought of a new plan by which it might be managed, so he sent for the leader and said to him,

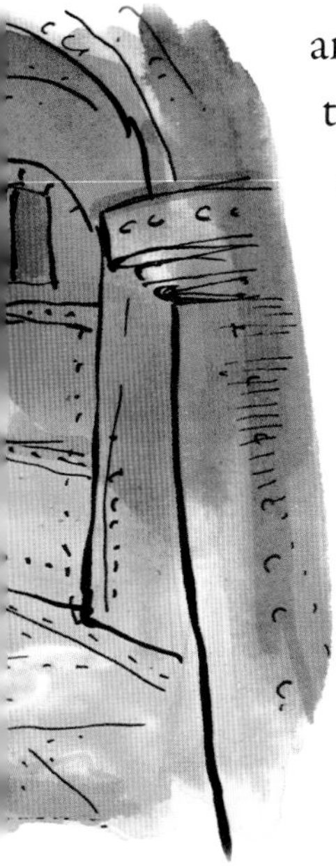

"If you will give up your right to my daughter, and take gold instead, you may have as much as you like."

"Certainly, my lord king," answered the man, "let me have as much gold as my servant can carry, and I give up all claim to your daughter."

And the king agreed that he should come again in a fortnight to fetch the gold. The man then called together all the tailors in the kingdom, and set them to work to make a sack, and it took them a fortnight. And when it was ready, the strong man who had been found rooting up trees took it on his shoulder, and went to the king.

"Who is this immense fellow carrying on his shoulder a bundle of cloth as big as a house?" cried the king, terrified to think how much gold he would carry off. And a ton of gold was dragged in by sixteen strong men, but he put it all into the sack with one hand, saying, "Why don't you bring some more? This hardly covers the bottom!" So the king bade them fetch by degrees the whole of his treasure, and even then the sack was not half full.

"Bring more!" cried the man, "These few scraps go no way at all!" Then at last seven thousand wagons laden with gold collected through the whole kingdom were driven up, and he threw them in his sack, oxen and all.

"I will not look too closely," said he, "but take what I can get, so long as the sack is full." And when all was put in, there was still plenty of room.

"I must make an end of this," he said. "If it is not full, it is so much the easier to tie up." And he hoisted it on his back and went off with his comrades.

When the king saw all the wealth of his realm carried off by a single man, he was full of wrath, and he bade his cavalry mount, and follow after the six men, and take the sack away from the strong man.

Two regiments were soon up to them, and called them to consider themselves prisoners and to deliver up the sack or be cut in pieces.

"Prisoners, say you?" said the man who could blow, "Suppose you first have a little dance together in the air." And holding one nostril and blowing through the other, he sent the regiments flying head over heels, over the hills and far away. But a sergeant who had nine wounds and was a brave fellow begged not to be put to so much shame. And the blower let him down easily, so that he came to no harm, and he bade him go to the king and tell him that whatever regiments he liked to send, more should be blown away just the same. And the king, when he got the message, said, "Let the fellows be, they have some right on their side." So the six comrades carried home their treasure, divided it among them, and lived contented till they died.

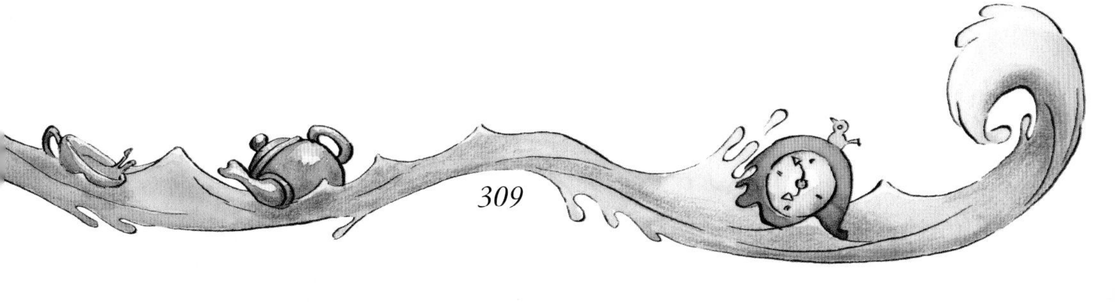

Nasreddin Hodja and the Pot

Anon

READING TIME: 2 MINUTES

Nasreddin Hodja went to his neighbor to borrow a large cooking pot for a few days. When he returned it, the neighbor was surprised to find a smaller pot inside, which he had never seen before.

"What's this, Nasreddin?" he said

"Oh, your pot gave birth while in my house," Nasreddin replied. "And naturally, as the larger pot is yours, so the smaller pot belongs to you also, so I have brought it to you."

"What a fool!" thought the man, but he smiled and accepted the pot, pleased at his good fortune.

Some days later, Nasreddin asked if might borrow the pot again. After a few weeks, the neighbor went to Nasreddin's house to ask for it back.

"Oh, I am sorry to tell you," said Nasreddin, "but your pot has died."

"Don't be so foolish" said the neighbor angrily. "Cooking pots don't die!"

"Are you sure?" said Nasreddin. "You didn't seem surprised when you heard it had given birth."

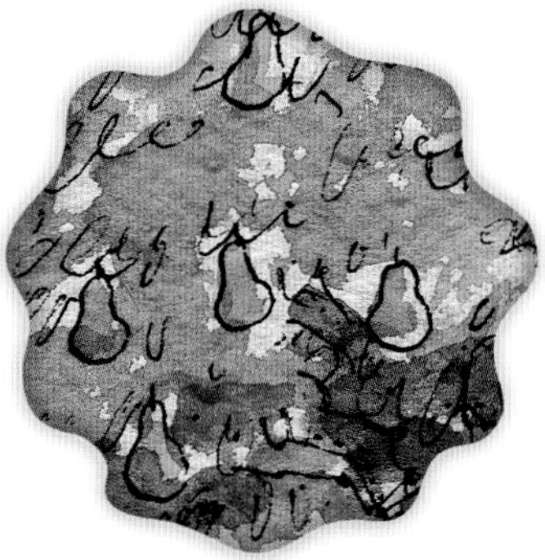

Sir Gammer Vans

By Joseph Jacobs

READING TIME: 4 MINUTES

Last Sunday morning at six o'clock in the evening, as I was sailing over the tops of the mountains in my little boat, I met two men on horseback riding on one mare. So I asked them, could they tell me whether the little old woman was dead yet who was hanged last Saturday week for drowning herself in a shower of feathers?

They said they could not positively inform me, but if I went to Sir Gammer Vans he could tell me all about it.

"But how am I to know the house?" said I.

"Ho, 'tis easy enough," said they, "for 'tis a brick

house, built entirely of flints, standing alone by itself in the middle of sixty or seventy others just like it."

"Oh, nothing in the world is easier," said I.

"Nothing can be easier," said they. So I went on my way.

Now this Sir Gammer Vans was a giant and a bottle maker. And as all giants who are bottle makers usually pop out of a little thumb-bottle from behind the door, so did Sir Gammer Vans.

"How d'ye do?" said he.

"Very well, I thank you," said I.

"Have some breakfast with me?"

"With all my heart," said I.

So he gave me a slice of beer, and a cup of cold veal. And there was a little dog under the table that picked up all the crumbs.

"Hang him," says I.

"No, don't hang him," said he, "for he killed a hare yesterday. And if you don't believe me, I'll show you the hare alive in a basket."

So he took me into his garden to show me the curiosities. In one corner there was a fox hatching eagles' eggs. In another there was an iron apple tree, entirely

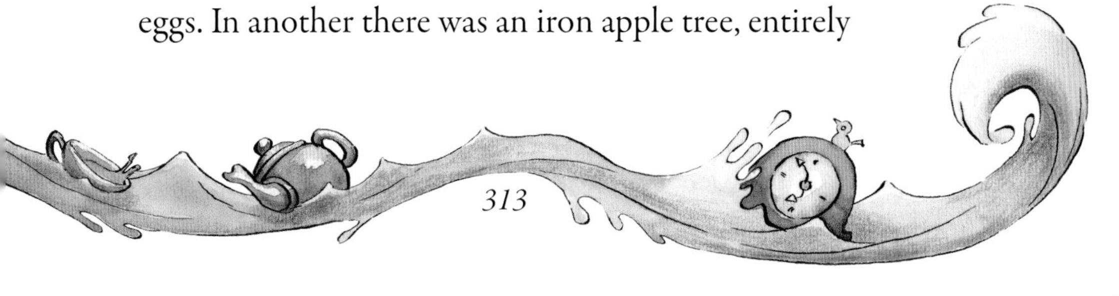

covered with pears and lead. In the third there was the hare that the dog killed yesterday, alive in the basket.

Then he took me into the park to show me his deer. And I remembered that I had a warrant in my pocket to shoot venison for his majesty's dinner. So I set fire to my bow, poised my arrow, and shot among them. I broke seventeen ribs on one side, and twenty-one and a half on the other, but my arrow passed clean through without ever touching it, and the worst was I lost my arrow. However, I found it again in the hollow of a tree. I felt it. It felt clammy. I smelled it. It smelled of honey.

"Oh, ho," said I. "Here's a bee's nest," when out sprang a flight of partridges. I shot at them. Some say I killed eighteen, but I am sure I killed thirty-six, besides a dead salmon that was flying over the bridge, out of which I made the best apple pie I ever tasted.

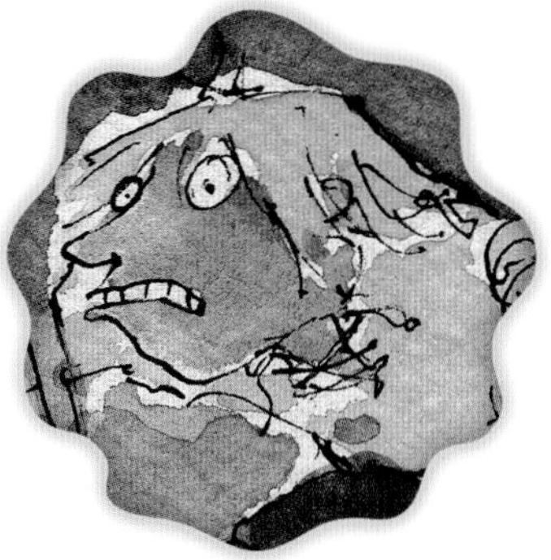

Lazy Jack

By Flora Annie Steel

READING TIME: 5 MINUTES

*O*nce upon a time there was a boy whose name was Jack, and he lived with his mother on some land. They were very poor, and the old woman got her living by spinning, but Jack was so lazy that he would do nothing but bask in the sun in the hot weather, and sit by the corner of the hearth in wintertime. So they called him Lazy Jack. His mother could not get him to do anything for her, and at last told him, one Monday, that if he did not begin to work for his porridge she would turn him out to get his living as he could.

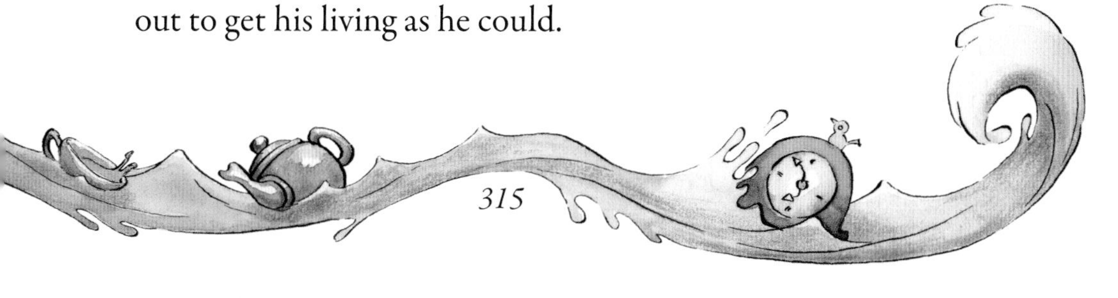

This roused Jack, and he went out and hired himself for the next day to a neighboring farmer for a penny, But as he was coming home, never having had any money before, he lost it in passing over a brook.

"You stupid boy," said his mother, "you should have put it in your pocket."

"I'll do so another time," replied Jack.

Well, the next day, Jack went out again and hired himself to a cow keeper, who gave him a jar of milk for his day's work. Jack took the jar and put it into the large pocket of his jacket, spilling it all long before he got home.

"Dear me!" said the old woman, "you should have carried it on your head."

"I'll do so another time," said Jack.

So the following day, Jack hired himself again to a farmer, who agreed to give him a cream cheese for his services. In the evening Jack took the cheese and went home with it on his head. By the time he got home the cheese was all spoiled, part of it being lost and part matted with his hair.

"You stupid lout," said his mother, "you should have carried it very carefully in your hands."

"I'll do so another time," replied Jack.

Now the next day, Lazy Jack again went out, and hired himself to a baker, who would give him nothing for his work but a large tomcat. Jack took the cat, and began carrying it very carefully in his hands, but in a short time pussy scratched him so much that he was compelled to let it go.

When he got home, his mother said to him, "You silly fellow, you should have tied it with a string and dragged it along after you."

"I'll do so another time," said Jack.

So on the following day, Jack hired himself to a butcher, who rewarded him by the handsome present of a shoulder of mutton. Jack took the mutton, tied it with a string, and trailed it along after him in the dirt, so that by the time he had got home the meat was completely spoiled. His mother was this time quite out of patience with him, for the next day was Sunday, and she was obliged to make do with cabbage for her dinner.

"You ninney-hammer," said she to her son, "you should have carried it on your shoulder."

"I'll do so another time," replied Jack.

Well, on the Monday, Lazy Jack went once more and

hired himself to a cattle keeper, who gave him a donkey for his trouble. Now though Jack was strong, he found it hard to hoist the donkey onto his shoulders, but at last he did it, and began walking home slowly with his prize. Now it so happened that in the course of his journey he

passed a house where a rich man lived with his only daughter, a beautiful girl who was deaf and dumb. And she had never laughed in her life, and the doctors said she would never speak till somebody made her laugh. So the father had given out that any man who made her laugh would receive her hand in marriage. Now this young lady happened to be looking out of the window when Jack was passing by with the donkey on his shoulders, and the poor beast with its legs sticking up in the air was kicking violently and heehawing with all its might. Well, the sight was so comical that she burst out into a great fit of laughter, and immediately recovered her speech and hearing. Her father was overjoyed, and fulfilled his promise by marrying her to Lazy Jack, who was thus made a rich gentleman. They lived in a large house, and Jack's mother lived with them in great happiness until she died.

The Three Sillies

By Joseph Jacobs

READING TIME: 10 MINUTES

*O*nce upon a time there was a farmer and his wife who had one daughter, and she was courted by a gentleman. Every evening he used to come and see her, and stop to supper at the farmhouse, and the daughter used to be sent down into the cellar to draw the beer for supper. So one evening she had gone down to draw the beer, and she happened to look up at the ceiling while she was drawing, and she saw a mallet stuck in one of the beams. It must have been there a long, long time, but somehow or other she had never noticed it before, and she began thinking. She thought it was very dangerous to have that mallet there, and said to herself: "Suppose him and me was to be married, and we was to have a son, and he was to grow up to be a man, and come down into the cellar to draw the beer, like as I'm doing now, and the mallet was to fall on his head and kill him, what a dreadful thing it would be!" And she put down the candle and the jug, and sat herself down and began crying.

Well, they began to wonder upstairs how it was that she was so long drawing the beer, and her mother went down to see after her, and she found her sitting on the settle crying, and the beer running over the floor. "Why, whatever is the matter?" said her mother.

"Oh, mother!" said she, "look at that horrid mallet! Suppose we was to be married, and was to have a son, and he was to grow up, and was to come down to the cellar to draw the beer, and the mallet was to fall on his head and kill him, what a dreadful thing it would be!"

"Dear, dear! What a dreadful thing it would be!" said the mother, and she sat her down aside of the daughter and started crying too. Then after a bit the father began to wonder that they didn't come back, and he went down into the cellar to look after them himself, and there they two sat crying, and the beer running all over the floor. "Whatever is the matter?" said he.

"Why," said the mother, "look at that horrid mallet. Just suppose, if our daughter and her sweetheart was to be married, and was to have a son, and he was to grow up, and was to come down into the cellar to draw the beer, and the mallet was to fall on his head and kill him, what a dreadful thing it would be!"

"Dear, dear! So it would!" said the father, and he sat himself down aside of the other two, and started crying.

Now the gentleman got tired of staying up in the kitchen by himself, and at last he went down into the cellar too, to see what they were after, and there they three sat crying side by side, and the beer running all over the floor. And he ran straight and turned the tap. Then he said: "Whatever are you three doing, sitting there crying, and letting the beer run all over the floor?"

"Oh!" said the father, "look at that horrid mallet! Suppose you and our daughter was to be married, and was to have a son, and he was to grow up, and was to come down into the cellar to draw the beer, and the mallet was to fall on his head and kill him!"

And then they all started crying worse than before.

But the gentleman burst out laughing and reached up and pulled out the mallet, and then he said: "I've traveled many miles, and I never met three such big sillies as you three before, and now I shall start out on my travels again, and when I can find three bigger sillies than you three, then I'll come back and marry your daughter." So he wished them goodbye and started off on his travels, and left them all crying because the girl had lost her sweetheart.

Well, he set out, and he traveled a long way, and at last he came to a woman's cottage that had some grass growing on the roof. And the woman was trying to get her cow to go up a ladder to the grass, and the poor thing would not go. So the gentleman asked the woman what she was doing. "Why," she said, "look at all that beautiful grass. I'm going to get the cow onto the roof to eat it. She'll be safe, for I shall tie a string around her neck, and pass it down the chimney, and tie it to my wrist as I go about the house, so she can't fall off without my knowing."

"Oh, you poor silly!" said the gentleman, "you should cut the grass and throw it down to the cow!" But the woman thought it was easier to get the cow up the ladder than to get the grass down, so she pushed and coaxed her up, and tied a string around her neck, and passed it down the chimney, and fastened it to her wrist.

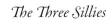

The gentleman went on his way, but he hadn't gone far when the cow tumbled off the roof and hung by the string tied around her neck, and it strangled her. The weight of the cow tied to her wrist pulled the woman up the chimney, and she stuck fast halfway and was covered in soot. Well, that was one big silly.

And the gentleman went on and on, and he went to an inn to stay the night, and they were so full at the inn that they had to put him in a room with two beds, and another traveler was to sleep in the other bed. The other man was a very pleasant fellow, and they got very friendly together, but in the morning, when they were both getting up, the gentleman was surprised to see the other hang his trousers on the knobs of the chest of drawers and run across the room and try to jump into them, and he tried over and over again, and couldn't manage it, and the gentleman wondered whatever he was doing it for. At last he stopped and wiped his face with his handkerchief. "Oh dear," he said, "I do think trousers are the most awkward kind of clothes that ever were. I can't think who could have invented such things. It takes me the best part of an hour to get into mine every morning, and I get so hot! How do you manage yours?" So the gentleman burst out laughing, and showed him how to put them on, and he was very much obliged to him, and said he never should have thought of doing it that way. So that was another big silly.

Then the gentleman went on his travels again, and he came to a village, and outside the village there was a pond, and around the pond was a crowd of people. And they had rakes and brooms and pitchforks reaching into the

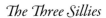

pond. The gentleman asked what was the matter.

"Why," they said, "the moon's tumbled into the pond, and we can't rake her out anyhow!" So the gentleman burst out laughing, and told them to look up into the sky, and that it was only the shadow in the water. But they wouldn't listen to him, and abused him shamefully, and he got away as quick as he could.

So there was a whole lot of sillies bigger than those three sillies at home. So the gentleman turned back home again and married the farmer's daughter, and if they didn't live happy forever after, that's nothing to do with you or me.

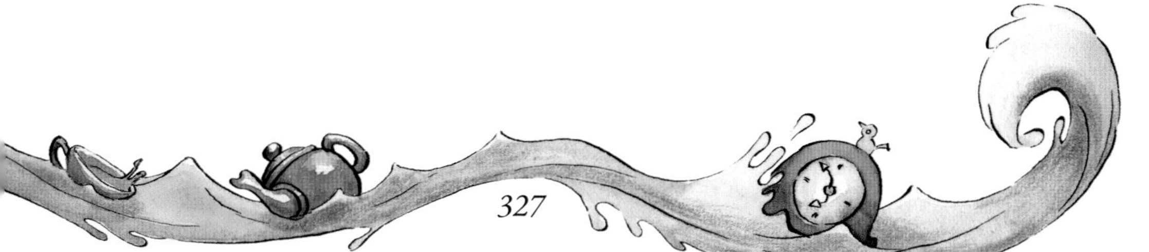

Tikki Tikki Tembo

Anon

READING TIME: 5 MINUTES

Once upon a time in faraway China there lived two brothers, one named Sam and one named Tikki Tikki Tembo No Sarimbo Hari Kari Bushkie Perry Pem Do Hai Kai Pom Pom Nikki No Meeno Dom Barako.

Now one day the two brothers were playing near the well in their garden when Sam fell into the well, and Tikki Tikki Tembo No Sarimbo Hari Kari Bushkie Perry Pem Do Hai Kai Pom Pom Nikki No Meeno Dom Barako ran to his mother, shouting, “Quick, Sam has fallen into the well. What shall we do?”

"What?" cried the mother, "Sam has fallen into the well? Run and tell father!"

Together they ran to the father and cried, "Quick, Sam has fallen into the well. What shall we do?"

"Sam has fallen into the well?" cried the father. "Run and tell the gardener!"

Then they all ran to the gardener and shouted, "Quick, Sam has fallen into the well. What shall we do?"

"Sam has fallen into the well?" cried the gardener, and then he quickly fetched a ladder and pulled the poor boy from the well, who was wet and cold and frightened, and ever so happy to still be alive.

Some time afterward, the two brothers were again playing near the well.

This time Tikki Tikki Tembo No Sarimbo Hari Kari Bushkie Perry Pem Do Hai Kai Pom Pom Nikki No Meeno Dom Barako fell into the well, and Sam ran to his mother, shouting, "Quick, Tikki Tikki Tembo No Sarimbo Hari Kari Bushkie Perry Pem Do Hai Kai Pom Pom Nikki No Meeno Dom Barako has fallen into the well. What shall we do?"

"What?" cried the mother, "Tikki Tikki Tembo No Sarimbo Hari Kari Bushkie Perry Pem Do Hai Kai Pom Pom Nikki No Meeno Dom Barako has fallen into the well? Run and tell father!"

Together they ran to the father and cried, "Quick, Tikki Tikki Tembo No Sarimbo Hari Kari Bushkie Perry Pem Do Hai Kai Pom Pom Nikki No Meeno Dom Barako has fallen into the well. What shall we do?"

"Tikki Tikki Tembo No Sarimbo Hari Kari Bushkie Perry Pem Do Hai Kai Pom Pom Nikki No Meeno Dom Barako has fallen into the well?" cried the father. "Run and tell the gardener!"

So they all ran to the gardener and shouted, "Quick, Tikki Tikki Tembo No Sarimbo Hari Kari Bushkie Perry Pem Do Hai Kai Pom Pom Nikki No Meeno Dom Barako has fallen into the well. What shall we do?"

"Tikki Tikki Tembo No Sarimbo Hari Kari Bushkie Perry Pem Do Hai Kai Pom Pom Nikki No Meeno Dom Barako has fallen into the well?" cried the gardener, and then he quickly fetched a ladder and pulled Tikki Tikki Tembo No Sarimbo Hari Kari Bushkie Perry Pem Do Hai Kai Pom Pom Nikki No Meeno Dom Barako from the well, but the poor boy had been in the water so long that he had drowned.

And from that time forth, the Chinese have given their children short names.

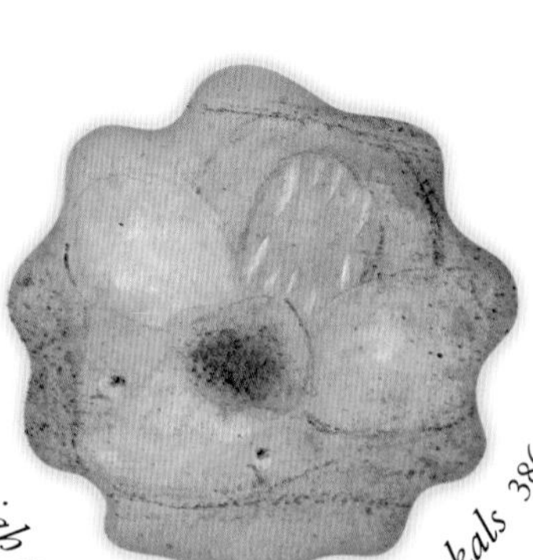

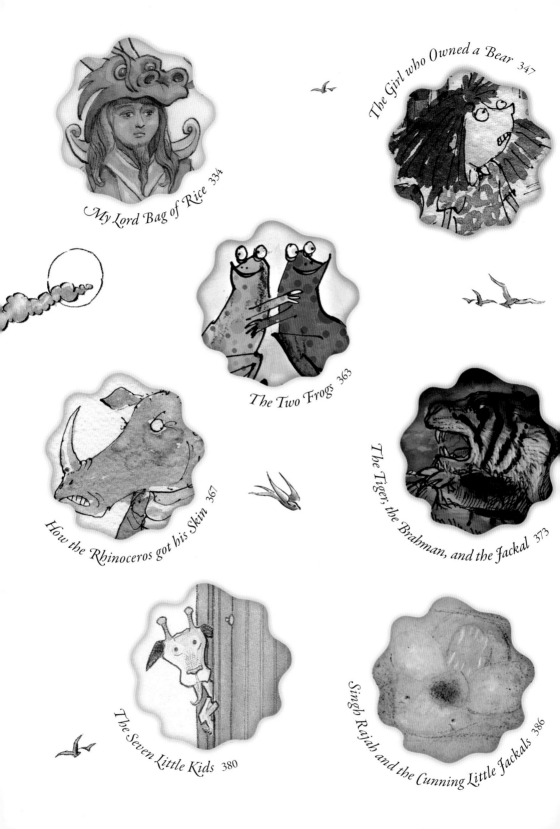

Birds, Beasts, and Dragons

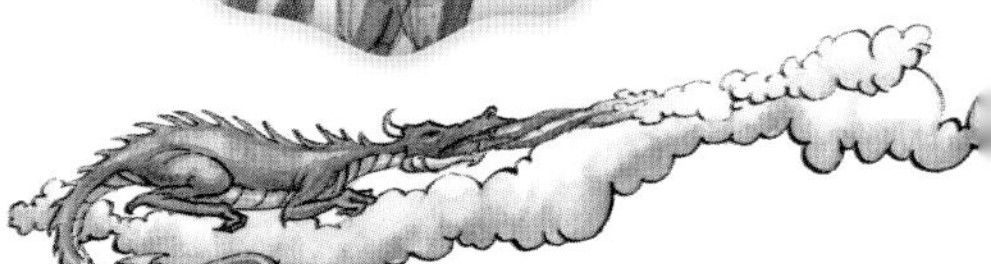

My Lord Bag of Rice

By Yei Theodora Ozaka

READING TIME: 14 MINUTES

Long, long ago there lived in Japan a brave warrior known to all as Tawara Toda, or "My Lord Bag of Rice." His true name was Fujiwara Hidesato, and there is a very interesting story of how he came to change his name.

One day he went out in search of adventures, for he had the nature of a warrior and could not bear to be idle. So he buckled on his two swords, took his huge bow in his hand, and, slinging his quiver on his back, started out. He had not gone far when he came to the bridge of Seta-no-Karashi spanning one end of the beautiful Lake Biwa.

No sooner had he set foot on the bridge than he saw lying right across his path a huge serpent-dragon. Its body was so big that it looked like the trunk of a large pine tree, and it took up the whole width of the bridge. One of its huge claws rested on the parapet of one side of the bridge, while its tail lay right against the other. The monster seemed to be asleep, and as it breathed, fire and smoke came out of its nostrils.

At first Hidesato could not help feeling alarmed at the sight of this horrible reptile lying in his path, for he must either turn back or walk right over its body. He was a brave man, however, and putting aside all fear went forward dauntlessly. Crunch, crunch! He stepped now on the dragon's body, now between its coils, and without even one glance backward, he went on his way.

He had gone only a few steps when he heard someone calling him from behind. On turning back he was much surprised to see that the monster dragon had entirely disappeared, and in its place was a strange-looking man, who was bowing most ceremoniously to the ground. His red hair streamed over his shoulders and was surmounted by a crown in the shape of a dragon's head, and his sea-green dress was patterned with shells.

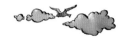

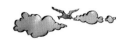

Hidesato knew at once that this was no ordinary mortal, and he wondered much at the strange occurrence. Where had the dragon gone in such a short space of time? Or had it transformed itself into this man, and what did the whole thing mean? While these thoughts passed through his mind, he had come up to the man on the bridge and now addressed him:

"Was it you that called me just now?"

"Yes, it was I," said the man, "I have an earnest request to make to you. Do you think you can grant it to me?"

"If it is in my power to do so I will," answered Hidesato, "but first tell me who you are?"

"I am the dragon king of the lake, and

my home is in these waters just under this bridge."

"What is it you have to ask of me?" said Hidesato.

"I want you to kill my mortal enemy the centipede, who lives on the mountain beyond." And the dragon king pointed to a high peak on the opposite shore of the lake.

"I have lived for many years in this lake, and I have a large family of children and grandchildren. For some time past we have lived in terror, for a monster centipede has discovered our home, and night after night it comes and carries off one of my family. I am powerless to save them. If it goes on much longer like this, not only shall I lose all my children, but I myself must fall a victim to the monster. I am, therefore, very unhappy, and in my extremity I determined to ask the help of a human being. For many days, with this intention, I have waited on the bridge in the shape of the horrible serpent-dragon that you saw, in the hope that some strong, brave man would come along. But all who came this way, as soon as they saw me were terrified and ran away as fast as they could. You are the first man I have found able to look at me, without fear, so I knew at once that you were a man of great courage. I beg you to have pity upon me. Will you not help me and kill my enemy the centipede?"

Hidesato felt very sorry for the dragon king on hearing his story, and readily promised to do what he could to help him. The warrior asked where the centipede lived, so that he might attack the creature at once. The dragon king replied that its home was on the mountain Mikami, but since it came every night at a certain hour to the palace of the lake, it would be better to wait till then.

So Hidesato was conducted to the palace of the dragon king, under the bridge. Strangely, as he followed his host downward the waters parted to let them pass, and his clothes did not even feel damp as he passed through the flood. Never had Hidesato seen anything so beautiful as this palace built of white marble beneath the lake. He had often heard of the sea king's palace at the bottom of the sea, where all the servants were saltwater fish, but here was a magnificent building in the heart of Lake Biwa. The dainty goldfish, red carp, and silvery trout waited upon the dragon king and his guest.

Hidesato was astonished at the feast that was spread for him. The dishes were crystallized lotus leaves and flowers, and the chopsticks were of the rarest ebony. As soon as they sat down, the sliding doors opened and ten lovely goldfish dancers came out, and behind them followed ten red carp musicians. Thus the hours flew by till midnight, and the beautiful music and dancing had banished all thoughts of the centipede. The dragon king was about to pass the warrior a fresh cup of wine when the palace was suddenly shaken by a tramp, tramp, tramp! It was as if a mighty army had begun to march not far away.

Hidesato and his host both rose to their feet and rushed to the balcony, and the warrior saw on the opposite mountain two great balls of glowing fire coming nearer and nearer. The dragon king stood by the warrior's side, trembling with fear.

"The centipede! The centipede! Those two balls of fire are its eyes. It is coming for its prey! Now is the time to kill it."

Hidesato looked where his host pointed, and in the dim light of the starlit evening, behind the two balls of fire, he saw the long body of an enormous centipede winding around the mountains, and the light in its terrifying eyes glowed like many distant lanterns moving slowly toward the shore. Hidesato showed no fear. He tried to calm the dragon king.

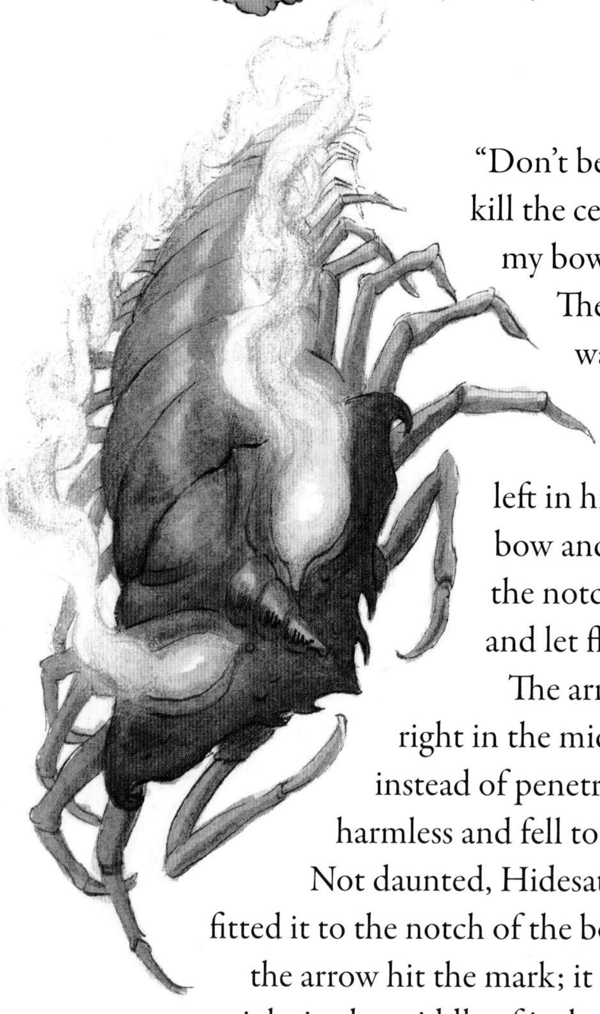

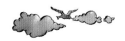

"Don't be afraid. I shall surely kill the centipede. Just bring me my bow and arrows."

The dragon king did as he was bid, and the warrior noticed that he had only three arrows left in his quiver. He took the bow and, fitting an arrow to the notch, took careful aim and let fly.

The arrow hit the centipede right in the middle of its head, but instead of penetrating, it glanced off harmless and fell to the ground.

Not daunted, Hidesato took another arrow, fitted it to the notch of the bow, and let fly. Again the arrow hit the mark; it struck the centipede right in the middle of its head, only to glance off and fall to the ground. The centipede was invulnerable to weapons! When the dragon king saw that even this brave warrior's arrows were powerless to kill the centipede, he lost heart and began to tremble with fear.

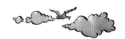

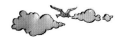

The warrior saw that he had now only one arrow left in his quiver, and if this one failed he could not kill the centipede. He looked across the waters. The huge reptile had wound its horrid body seven times around the mountain and would soon come down to the lake. Nearer and nearer gleamed the fiery eyes, and the light of its hundred feet began to throw reflections in the still waters of the lake.

Then suddenly the warrior remembered that human saliva was deadly to centipedes. But this was no ordinary centipede. This was so monstrous that even to think of such a creature made him creep with horror. Hidesato determined to try one more time. So taking his last arrow and first putting the end of it in his mouth, he fitted the notch to his bow, took careful aim once more and let fly.

The arrow again hit the centipede right in the middle of its head, but instead of glancing off harmlessly as before, it struck home to the creature's brain. Then, with a convulsive shudder, the serpentine body stopped moving, and the fiery light of its great eyes and hundred feet darkened to a dull glare like the sunset of a stormy day, and then went out in blackness. A great darkness now overspread the heavens, thunder rolled and lightning flashed, and the wind roared in fury, and it seemed as if the world were coming to an end. The dragon king and his children and retainers all crouched in different parts of the palace, frightened to death, for the building was shaken to its foundations. At last the dreadful night was over. Day dawned beautiful and clear. The centipede was gone from the mountain.

Then Hidesato called to the dragon king to come out with him on the balcony, for the centipede was dead and he had nothing more to fear.

All the inhabitants of the palace came out shouting with joy, and Hidesato pointed to the lake. There lay the body of the dead centipede floating on the water, which was dyed red with its blood.

The gratitude of the dragon king knew no bounds.

The whole family came and bowed down before the warrior, calling him their preserver and the bravest warrior in all Japan.

Another feast was prepared, more sumptuous than the first. All kinds of fish, prepared in every imaginable way—raw, stewed, boiled and roasted, served on coral trays and crystal dishes—were put before him, and the wine was the best that Hidesato had ever tasted in his life. The sun shone brightly and the lake glittered like a liquid diamond. The palace was a thousand times more beautiful by day than by night.

His host tried to persuade the warrior to stay a few days, but Hidesato insisted on going home, saying that he had now finished what he had come to do, and must return. The dragon king and his family were all very sorry to have him leave so soon, but since he would go, they begged him to accept a few small presents (so they said) in token of their gratitude to him for delivering them forever from their terrible enemy the centipede.

As the warrior stood in the porch taking leave, a train of fish was suddenly transformed into a retinue of men, all wearing ceremonial robes and dragons' crowns on their heads to show that they were servants of the great dragon king. The presents that they carried were as follows:

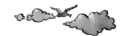

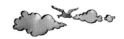

First, a large bronze bell.
Second, a bag of rice.
Third, a roll of silk.
Fourth, a cooking pot.
Fifth, another bell.

Hidesato did not want to accept all these presents, but as the dragon king insisted, he could not well refuse.

The dragon king himself accompanied the warrior as far as the bridge, and then took leave of him with many bows and good wishes, leaving the procession of servants to accompany Hidesato to his house with the presents.

The warrior's household and servants had been very much concerned when they found that he did not return the night before, but they finally concluded that he had been kept by the violent storm and had taken shelter somewhere. When the servants on the watch for his return caught sight of him, they called to everyone that he was approaching, and the whole household turned out to meet him, wondering what the retinue of men, bearing presents and banners, that followed him, could mean.

As soon as the dragon king's retainers had put down the presents they vanished, and Hidesato told all that had happened to him.

The presents that he had received from the grateful dragon king were found to be of magic power. Only the bell was ordinary, and since Hidesato had no use for it, he presented it to the temple nearby, where it was hung up, to boom out the hour of day over the neighborhood.

However much was taken from from the single bag of rice for the meals of the warrior and his whole family, the supply in the bag never grew less.

The roll of silk, too, never grew shorter, though time after time long pieces were cut off to make the warrior a new suit of clothes to go to court in at the New Year.

The cooking pot was magical, too. No matter what was put into it, it cooked deliciously whatever was wanted without any heating—truly a very economical saucepan.

The fame of Hidesato's fortune spread far and wide, and as there was no need for him to spend money on rice, silk, or heating, he became very rich and prosperous, and was henceforth known as "My Lord Bag of Rice."

The Girl who Owned a Bear

By L. Frank Baum

READING TIME: 14 MINUTES

Mamma had gone downtown to shop. She had asked Nora to look after Jane Gladys, and Nora promised she would. But it was her afternoon for polishing the silver, so she stayed in the pantry and left Jane Gladys to amuse herself alone in the big living room upstairs. The little girl did not mind being alone, for she was working on her first piece of embroidery—a sofa pillow for Papa's birthday present. So she crept into the big bay window and curled herself up on the broad windowsill while she bent her brown head over her work.

Soon the door opened and closed again, quietly. Jane Gladys thought it was Nora, so she didn't look up until she had taken a couple more stitches on a forget-me-not. Then she raised her eyes and was astonished to find a strange man in the middle of the room, who regarded her earnestly.

He was short and fat and seemed to be breathing heavily from his climb up the stairs. He held a hat in one hand, and underneath his other elbow was tucked a good-sized book. He was dressed in a black suit that looked old and rather shabby, and his head was bald upon the top.

"Excuse me," he said, while the child gazed at him in surprise. "Are you Jane Gladys Brown?"

"Yes, sir," she answered.

"Very good, very good, indeed!" he remarked, with a queer sort of smile. "I've had quite a hunt to find you, but I've succeeded at last."

"How did you get in?" inquired Jane Gladys, with a growing distrust of her visitor.

"That is a secret," he said, mysteriously.

This was enough to put the girl on her guard. She looked at the man and the man looked at her, and both looks were grave and somewhat anxious.

"What do you want?" she asked, straightening herself up with a dignified air.

"Ah! Now we are coming to business," said the man, briskly. "I'm going to be quite frank with you. Your father has abused me in a most ungentlemanly manner."

Jane Gladys got off the windowsill and pointed her small finger at the door.

"Leave this room 'meejitly!" she cried, her voice trembling with indignation. "My papa is the best man in the world. He never abused anybody!"

"Allow me to explain, please," said the visitor, without paying any attention to her request to go away. "Your father may be very kind to you, for you are his little girl, you know. But when he's downtown in his office he's inclined to be rather severe, especially on book agents. Now, I called on him the other day and asked him to buy the "Complete Works of Peter Smith," and what do you suppose he did?"

She said nothing.

"Why," continued the man, with growing excitement,

"he ordered me from his office, and had me put out of the building by the janitor! What do you think of such treatment as that from the "best man in the world," eh?"

"I think he was quite right," said Jane Gladys.

"Oh, you do? Well," said the man, "I resolved to be revenged. So, as your father is big, strong and dangerous, I have decided to be revenged upon his little girl."

Jane Gladys shivered.

"What are you going to do?" she asked.

"I'm going to present you with this book," he answered, taking it from under his arm. Then he sat down on the edge of a chair, placed his hat on the rug, and drew a fountain pen from his vest pocket.

"I'll write your name in it," said he. "How do you spell Gladys?"

"G-l-a-d-y-s," she replied.

"Thank you. Now this," he continued, rising and handing her the book with a bow, "is my revenge for your father's treatment of me. Perhaps he'll be sorry he didn't buy the "Complete Works of Peter Smith." Goodbye, my dear."

He walked to the door, gave her another bow, and left the room, and Jane Gladys could see that he was

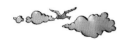

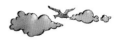

laughing to himself as if very much amused.

When the door had closed behind the strange little man, the child sat down in the window again and glanced at the book. It had a red and yellow cover, and the word "Thingamajigs" was written across the front cover in big letters.

Then she opened it, curiously, and saw her name written in black letters upon the first white page.

"He was a funny little man," she said to herself thoughtfully.

She turned the next page, and saw a big picture of a clown, dressed in green and red and yellow. He had a very white face with three-cornered spots of red on each cheek and over the eyes. While she looked at this the book trembled in her hands, the page crackled and creaked, and suddenly the clown jumped out of it and stood upon the floor beside her, becoming instantly as big as any ordinary clown.

After stretching his arms and legs and yawning in a rather impolite manner, he gave a silly chuckle and said,

"This is better! You don't know how cramped one gets, standing so long upon a page of flat paper."

Perhaps you can imagine how startled Jane Gladys was, and how she stared at the clown who had just leaped out of the book.

"You didn't expect anything of this sort, did you?" he asked, leering at her in clown fashion. Then he turned around to take a look at the room, and Jane Gladys laughed in spite of her astonishment.

"What amuses you?" demanded the clown.

"Why, the back of you is all white!" cried the girl. "You're only a clown in front of you."

"Quite likely," he returned, in an annoyed tone. "The artist made a front view of me. He wasn't expected to make the back of me, for that was against the page of the book."

"But it makes you look so funny!" said Jane Gladys, laughing until her eyes were moist with tears.

The clown looked sulky and sat down upon a chair so she couldn't see his back.

"I'm not the only thing in the book," he remarked crossly.

This reminded her to turn another page, and she had scarcely noted that it contained the picture of a monkey when the animal sprang from the book with a great crumpling of paper and landed upon the window seat beside her.

"He he he he he!" chattered the creature, springing to the girl's shoulder and then to the center table. "This is great fun! Now I can be a real monkey instead of a picture of one."

"Real monkeys can't talk," said Jane Gladys.

"How do you know? Have you ever been one yourself?" inquired the animal, and then he laughed loudly, and the clown laughed, too, as if he enjoyed the remark.

The girl was quite bewildered by this time. She thoughtlessly turned another page, and before she had time to look twice, a gray donkey leaped from the book and stumbled from the window seat to the floor with a great clatter.

"You're clumsy enough, I'm sure!" said the child, indignantly, for the beast had nearly upset her.

"Clumsy! And why not?" demanded the donkey, in an angry voice. "If the silly artist had drawn you out of perspective, as he did me, I guess you'd be clumsy yourself."

"What's wrong with you?" asked Jane Gladys.

"My front and rear legs on the left side are nearly six inches too short, that's what's the matter! If that artist didn't know how to draw properly, why did he try to make a donkey at all?"

"I don't know," replied the child, seeing an answer was expected.

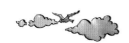

"I can hardly stand up," grumbled the donkey, "and the least little thing will topple me over."

"Don't mind that," said the monkey, making a spring at the chandelier and swinging from it by his tail until Jane Gladys feared it would fall from the ceiling, "the artist has made my ears as big as that clown's, and everyone knows a monkey hasn't any ears to speak of—much less to draw."

"He should be prosecuted," remarked the clown, gloomily. "I haven't any back."

Jane Gladys looked from one to the other with a puzzled expression upon her sweet face, and turned another page of the book.

Swift as a flash there sprang over her shoulder a tawny, spotted leopard, which landed upon the back of a big leather armchair and turned upon the others with a fierce movement.

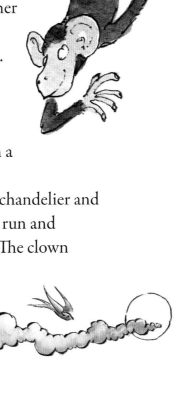

The monkey climbed to the top of the chandelier and chattered with fright. The donkey tried to run and straightway tipped over onto his left side. The clown grew paler than ever, but he sat still in his chair and gave a low whistle of surprise.

The leopard crouched upon the back of the chair, lashed his tail from side to side, and glared at all of them by turns, including Jane Gladys.

"Which of us are you going to attack first?" asked the donkey, trying hard to get upon his feet again.

"I can't attack any of you," snarled the leopard. "The artist made my mouth shut, so I haven't any teeth, and he forgot to make my claws. But I'm a frightful-looking creature, nevertheless, am I not?"

"Oh, yes," said the clown, indifferently. "I suppose you're frightful-looking enough. But if you have no teeth nor claws we don't mind your looks at all."

This annoyed the leopard so much that he growled horribly, and the monkey laughed at him.

Just then the book slipped from the girl's lap, and as she made a movement to catch it, one of the pages near the back opened wide. She caught a glimpse of a fierce grizzly bear looking at her from the page, and quickly threw the book to the ground. It fell with a crash in the middle of the room, but beside it stood the great grizzly, who had wrenched himself from the page before the

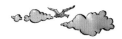

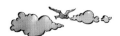

book had closed.

"Now," cried the leopard from his perch, "you'd better look out for yourselves! You can't laugh at him as you did at me. The bear has both claws and teeth."

"Indeed I have," said the bear, in a low, deep, growling voice. "And I know how to use them, too. If you read in that book you'll find I'm described as a remorseless grizzly, whose only business in life is to eat up little girls—shoes, dresses, ribbons, and all! And then, the author says, I smack my lips and glory in my wickedness."

"That's awful!" said the donkey, sitting upon his haunches and shaking his head sadly. "What do you suppose possessed the author to make you so hungry for girls? Do you eat animals, too?"

"The author does not mention my eating anything but little girls," replied the bear.

"Very good," remarked the clown, drawing a long breath of relief. "You may begin eating Jane Gladys as soon as you wish. She laughed because I had no back."

"And she laughed because my legs are out of perspective," brayed the donkey.

"But you also deserve to be eaten," screamed the leopard from the back of the leather chair, "for you laughed and poked fun at me because I had no claws nor teeth! Don't you suppose, Mr. Grizzly, you could manage to eat a clown, a donkey, and a monkey after you finish the girl?"

"Perhaps so, and a leopard into the bargain," growled the bear. "It will depend on how hungry I am. But I must begin on the little girl first, because the author says I prefer girls to anything."

Jane Gladys was much frightened on hearing this conversation, and she began to realize what the man meant when he said he gave her the book to be revenged. Surely Papa would be sorry he hadn't bought the "Complete Works of Peter Smith" when he came home and found his little girl eaten up by a grizzly bear—shoes, dress, ribbons, and all!

The bear stood up and balanced himself on his rear legs.

"This is the way I look in the book," he said. "Now watch me eat the little girl."

He advanced slowly toward Jane Gladys, and the monkey, the leopard, the donkey, and the clown all stood around in a circle and watched the bear with much interest.

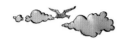

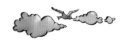

But before the grizzly reached her, the child had a sudden thought, and cried out, "Stop! You mustn't eat me. It would be wrong."

"Why?" asked the bear, in surprise.

"Because I own you. You're my private property," she answered.

"I don't see how you make that out," said the bear, in a disappointed tone.

"Why, the book was given to me, my name's on the front page. And you belong, by rights, in the book. So you mustn't dare to eat your owner!"

The grizzly hesitated.

"Can any of you read?" he asked.

"I can," said the clown.

"Then see if she speaks the truth. Is her name really in the book?"

The clown picked it up and looked at the name.

"It is," said he. "Jane Gladys Brown, and written quite plainly in big letters."

The bear sighed.

"Then, of course, I can't eat her," he decided.

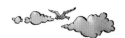

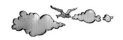

"That author is as disappointing—as most authors are."

"But he's not as bad as the artist," exclaimed the donkey, who was still trying to stand up straight.

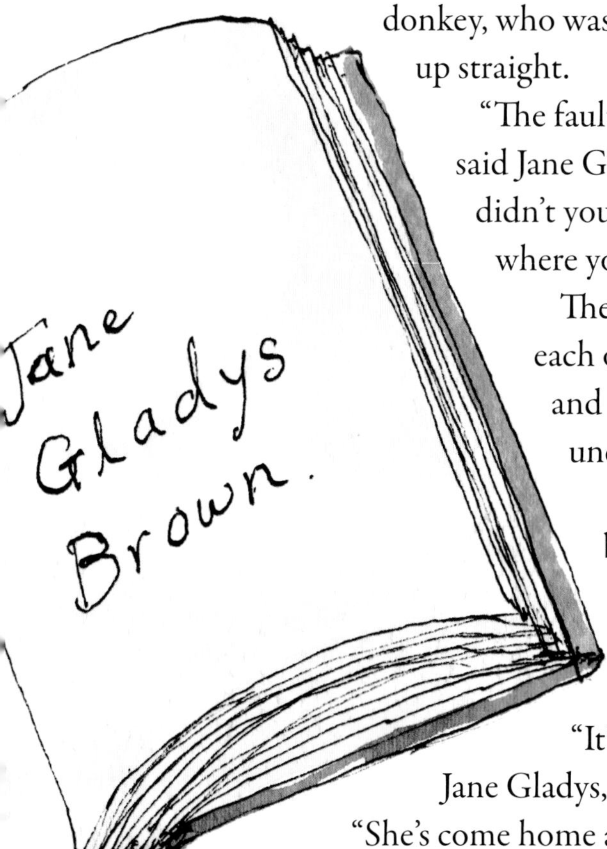

"The fault lies with yourselves," said Jane Gladys, severely. "Why didn't you stay in the book, where you were put?"

The animals looked at each other in a foolish way, and the clown blushed under his white paint.

"Really," began the bear, and then he stopped short.

The door bell rang loudly.

"It's Mamma!" cried Jane Gladys, springing to her feet. "She's come home at last. Now, you stupid creatures—"

But she was interrupted by them all making a rush for the book. There was a swish and a whirr and a rustling of leaves, and an instant later the book lay upon the floor looking just like any other book, while Jane Gladys's strange companions had all disappeared.

This story should teach us to think quickly and clearly upon all occasions, for had Jane Gladys not remembered that she owned the bear, he probably would have eaten her before the bell rang.

The Two Frogs

By Andrew Lang

READING TIME: 5 MINUTES

Once upon a time in the country of Japan there lived two frogs, one of whom made his home in a ditch near the town of Osaka, on the sea coast, while the other dwelled in a clear little stream that ran through the city of Kyoto. At such a great distance apart, they had never even heard of each other, but, funnily enough, the idea came into both their heads at once that they should like to see a little of the world, and the frog who lived at Kyoto wanted to visit Osaka, and the frog who lived at Osaka wished to go to Kyoto, where the great mikado had his palace.

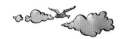

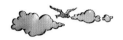

So one fine morning in the spring they both set out along the road that led from Kyoto to Osaka, one from one end and the other from the other. The journey was more tiring than they expected, for they did not know much about traveling, and halfway between the two towns there arose a mountain that had to be climbed. It took them a long time and a great many hops to reach the top, but there they were at last, and what was the surprise of each to see another frog before him!

They looked at each other for a moment without speaking and then fell into conversation, explaining the cause of their meeting so far from their homes. It was delightful to find that they both felt the same wish—to learn a little more of their native country—and since there was no sort of hurry, they stretched themselves out in a cool, damp place and agreed that they would have a good rest before they parted to go their ways.

"What a pity we are not bigger," said the Osaka frog. "Then we could see both towns from here, and tell if it is worth our while going on."

"Oh, that is easily managed," returned the Kyoto frog. "We have only got to stand up on our hind legs, and hold on to each other, and then we can each look at the town he is traveling to."

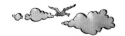

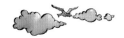

This idea pleased the Osaka frog so much that he at once jumped up and put his front paws on the shoulder of his friend, who had risen also. There they both stood, stretching themselves as high as they could and holding each other tightly, so that they might not fall down.

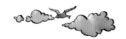

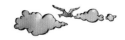

The Kyoto frog turned his nose toward Osaka, and the Osaka frog turned his nose toward Kyoto, but the foolish things forgot that when they stood up their great eyes lay in the backs of their heads, and that though their noses might point to the places to which they wanted to go, their eyes beheld the places from which they had come.

"Dear me!" cried the Osaka frog, "Kyoto is exactly like Osaka. It is certainly not worth such a long journey. I shall go home!"

"If I had had any idea that Osaka was only a copy of Kyoto I should never have traveled all this way," exclaimed the frog from Kyoto. As he spoke, he took his hands from his friend's shoulders and they both fell down on the grass. Then they took a polite farewell of each other and set off for home again, and to the end of their lives they believed that Osaka and Kyoto, which are as different to look at as two towns can be, were as alike as two peas in a pod.

How the Rhinoceros got his Skin

By Rudyard Kipling

READING TIME: 6 MINUTES

A Parsee is a member of a religious sect found mainly in India, although the religion started in Persia (modern day Iran). Nowadays, it is usually spelled "Parsi."

Once upon a time, on an uninhabited island on the shores of the Red Sea, there lived a Parsee from whose hat the rays of the sun were reflected in oriental splendor. And the Parsee lived by the Red Sea with nothing but his hat and his knife and a cooking stove of the kind that you must

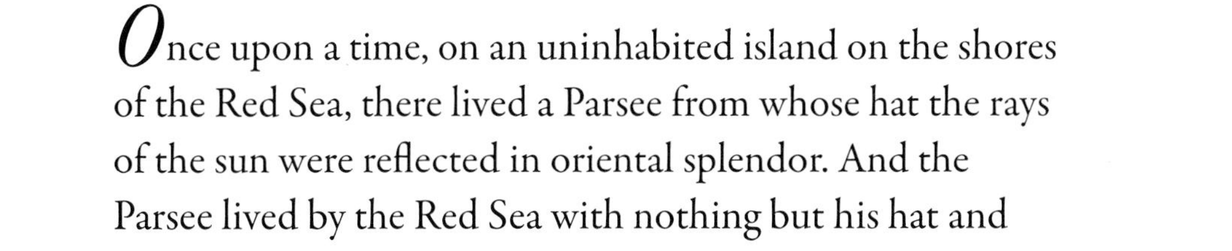

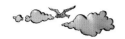

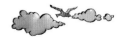

particularly never touch. And one day he took flour and water and currants and plums and sugar and things, and made himself one cake that was two feet across and three feet thick. It was indeed a superior dish, and he put it on the stove because he was allowed to cook on that stove, and he baked it and he baked it till it was all done brown and smelled most delicious. But just as he was going to eat it, there came down to the beach from the Altogether Uninhabited Interior one rhinoceros with a horn on his nose, two piggy eyes, and few manners. In those days the rhinoceros's skin fitted him quite tight. There were no wrinkles in it anywhere. He looked exactly like a Noah's Ark rhinoceros, but of course much bigger. All the same, he had no manners then, and he has no manners now, and he never will have any manners. He said, "How!" and the Parsee left that cake and climbed to the top of a palm tree with nothing on but his hat, from which the rays of the sun were always reflected in oriental splendor. And the rhinoceros upset the oil stove with his nose, and the cake rolled on the sand, and he spiked that cake on the horn of his nose and he ate it, and he went away waving his tail, to the desolate and Exclusively Uninhabited Interior that is next to the islands of Mazanderan,

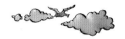

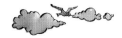

Socotra, and Promontories of the Larger Equinox. Then the Parsee came down from his palm tree and put the stove on its legs and recited the following poem, which, as you have not heard, I will now proceed to relate:

> "*Them that takes cakes*
> *Which the Parsee man bakes*
> *Makes dreadful mistakes.*"

And there was a great deal more in that than you would think. Because, five weeks later, there was a heat wave in the Red Sea, and everybody took off all the clothes they had. The Parsee took off his hat, but the rhinoceros took off his skin and carried it over his shoulder as he came down to the beach to bathe. In those days it buttoned underneath with three buttons and looked like a raincoat. He said nothing whatever about the Parsee's cake, because he had eaten it all, and he never had any manners, then, since, or henceforward. He waddled straight into the water and blew bubbles through his nose, leaving his skin on the beach.

Presently the Parsee came by and found the skin, and he smiled one smile that ran all around his face two times. Then he danced three times around the skin and rubbed his hands. Then he went to his camp and filled his hat with cake crumbs, for the Parsee never ate anything but cake, and never swept out his camp. He took that skin, and he shook that skin, and he scrubbed that skin, and he rubbed that skin just as full of old, dry, stale, tickly cake crumbs and some burned currants as ever it could possibly hold. Then he climbed to the top of his palm tree and waited for the rhinoceros to come out of the water and put it on.

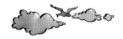

And the rhinoceros did. He buttoned it up with the three buttons, and it tickled like cake crumbs in bed. Then he wanted to scratch, but that made it worse, and then he lay down on the sands and rolled and rolled and rolled, and every time he rolled, the cake crumbs tickled him worse and worse and worse. Then he ran to the palm tree and rubbed and rubbed and rubbed himself against it. He rubbed so much and so hard that he rubbed his skin into a great fold over his shoulders and another fold underneath, where the buttons used to be (but he rubbed the buttons off), and he rubbed some more folds over his legs. And it spoiled his temper, but it didn't make the least difference to the cake crumbs.

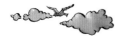

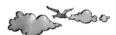

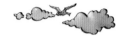

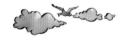

They were inside his skin and they tickled. So he went home, very angry indeed and horribly scratchy, and from that day to this, every rhinoceros has great folds in his skin and a very bad temper, all on account of the cake crumbs inside.

But the Parsee came down from his palm tree, wearing his hat, from which the rays of the sun were reflected in oriental splendor, packed up his cooking stove, and went away in the direction of Orotavo, Amygdala, the Upland Meadows of Anantarivo and the Marshes of Sonaput.

The Tiger, the Brahman, and the Jackal

By Joseph Jacobs

READING TIME: 6 MINUTES

A Brahman (now often spelled "Brahmin") is a member of the priest class in India.

Once upon a time, a tiger was caught in a trap. He tried in vain to get out through the bars, and rolled and bit with rage and grief when he failed. By chance, a poor Brahman came walking by.

"Let me out of this cage, oh holy one!" cried the tiger.

"Nay, my friend," replied the Brahman mildly.

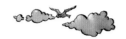

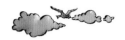

"You would probably eat me if I did."

"Not at all!" swore the tiger with many oaths. "On the contrary, I should be forever grateful, and serve you as a slave!"

Now when the tiger sobbed and sighed and wept and swore, the holy Brahman's heart softened, and at last he consented to open the door of the cage. Out popped the tiger, and seizing the poor man, cried, "What a fool you are! What is to prevent me eating you now, for after being cooped up so long I am just terribly hungry!"

In vain the Brahman pleaded for his life; the most he could gain was a promise to abide by the decision of the first three things he chose to question as to the justice of the tiger's action.

So the Brahman first asked a papal tree, a kind of fig tree, what it thought of the matter, but the papal tree replied coldly, "What have you to complain about? Don't I give shade and shelter to everyone who passes by, and don't they in return tear down my branches to feed their cattle? Don't whimper—be a man!"

Then the Brahman, sad at heart, went farther afield till he saw a buffalo turning a well-wheel, but he fared no better from it, for it answered, "You are a fool to expect gratitude! Look at me! While I gave milk they fed me on cotton-seed and oil-cake, but now I am dry they yoke me here and give me refuse as fodder!"

The Brahman, still more sad, asked the road to give him its opinion.

"My dear sir," said the road, "how foolish you are to expect anything else! Here am I, useful to everybody, yet all, rich and poor, great and small, trample on me as they go past, giving me nothing but the ashes of their pipes and the husks of their grain!"

On this, the Brahman turned back sorrowfully, and on the way he met a jackal, who called out, "Why, what's the matter, Mr. Brahman? You look as miserable as a fish out of water!"

The Brahman told him all that had occurred. "How very confusing!" said the jackal, when the recital was ended. "Would you mind telling me over again, for everything has gotten so mixed up?"

The Brahman told it all over again, but the jackal shook his head in a distracted sort of way, and still could not understand.

"It's very odd," said he, sadly. "It all seems to go in one ear and out the other! I will go to the place where it all happened, then perhaps I'll be able to give a judgment."

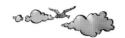

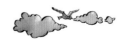

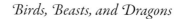

So they returned to the cage, by which the tiger was waiting for the Brahman, sharpening his teeth and claws.

"You've been away a long time!" growled the savage beast, "but now let us begin our dinner."

"Our dinner!" thought the wretched Brahman, as his knees knocked together with fright, "what a remarkably delicate way of putting it!"

"Give me five minutes, my lord!" he pleaded, "in order that I may explain matters to the jackal here, who is somewhat slow in his wits."

The tiger consented, and the Brahman began the whole story over again, not missing a single detail, and spinning as long a yarn as possible.

"Oh, my poor brain! Oh, my poor brain!" cried the jackal, wringing its paws. "Let me see! How did it all begin? You were in the cage, and the tiger came walking by—"

"Pooh!" interrupted the tiger. "What a fool you are! I was in the cage."

"Of course!" cried the jackal, pretending to tremble with fright. "Yes! I was in the cage—no I wasn't. Dear! Dear! Where are my wits? Let me see—the tiger was in the Brahman, and the cage came walking by—no, that's not it, either! Well, don't mind me, but begin your dinner, for I shall never understand!"

"Yes, you shall!" returned the tiger, in a rage at the jackal's stupidity, "I'll make you understand! Look here

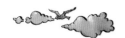

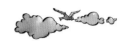

—I am the tiger—"

"Yes, I understand, my lord!"

"And that is the Brahman—"

"Yes, my lord!"

"And that is the cage—"

"Yes, my lord!"

"And I was in the cage—do you understand?"

"Yes—no—please, my lord—"

"Well?" cried the tiger impatiently.

"Please, my lord! How did you get in?"

"How! Why in the usual way, of course!"

"Oh, dear me! My head is beginning to whirl again! Please don't be angry, my lord—what is the usual way?"

At this the tiger lost patience, and, jumping into the cage, cried, "This way! Now do you understand how it was?"

"Perfectly!" said the jackal, grinning, as he swiftly shut the door, "and if you will permit me to say so, I think matters will remain as they were!"

The Seven Little Kids

By the Brothers Grimm

READING TIME: 8 MINUTES

There was once a mother goat who had seven little kids, and she was as fond of them as every mother was of her children. One day she had to go into the wood to fetch food for them, so she called them all around her.

"Dear children," said she, "I am going out into the wood and while I am gone, be on your guard against the wolf, for if he were once to get inside he would eat you up, skin, bones, and all. The wretch often disguises himself, but he may always be known by his hoarse voice and black paws."

"Mother," answered the kids, "you need not be afraid;

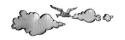

we will take care of ourselves." And the mother bleated goodbye and went on her way with an easy mind.

It was not long before someone came knocking at the door and crying out, "Open the door, my dear children, your mother has come back and brought each of you something."

But the kids knew it was the wolf by the hoarse voice.

"We will not open the door," they cried. "You are not our mother. She has a delicate and sweet voice, and your voice is hoarse—you must be the wolf!"

Then off went the wolf to a shop and bought a big lump of chalk, and ate it up to make his voice soft. Then he came back, knocked at the door and cried, "Open the door, my dear children, your mother is here and has brought each of you something."

But the wolf had put his black paws up against the window, and the kids, seeing this, cried out, "We will not open the door. Our mother has no black paws like you—you must be the wolf!"

The wolf then ran to a baker.

"Baker," said he, "I have hurt my feet; pray spread some dough over them."

And when the baker had plastered his feet with

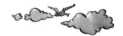

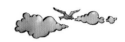

dough, the wolf ran to the miller.

"Miller," said he, "cover my paws with some white flour." But the miller refused, thinking the wolf must be meaning harm to someone.

"If you don't do it," cried the wolf, "I'll eat you up!"

And the miller was afraid and did as he was told. And that just shows what humans are.

Now the wolf arrived at the door for a third time and knocked. "Open, children!" cried he. "Your dear mother has come home and brought you each something from the wood."

"First show us your paws," said the kids, "so that we may know if you are really our mother or not."

The wolf put his paws against the window, and when the kids saw that they were white, all seemed right, so they opened the door to let their mother in.

When they opened the door and he came inside, they saw it was the wolf, and they were terrified and tried to hide themselves.

One ran under the table, the second got into the bed, the third into the oven, the fourth in the kitchen, the fifth in the cupboard, the sixth under the sink, and the seventh in the clock case. But the wolf searched and found them all. One after the other, he swallowed them down. All but the youngest, who was hidden in the clock case.

So the wolf, having gotten what he wanted, strolled forth into the green meadow, and laying himself down under a tree, fell asleep.

Not long after, the mother goat came back from the wood, and, oh! What a horrible sight met her eyes! The door was standing wide open, table, chairs, and stools all thrown about, dishes broken, quilt and pillows torn off the bed. She sought her children, but they were nowhere to be found. She called to each of them by name, but nobody answered, until she came to the name of the youngest.

"Here I am, Mother," a little voice cried, "here, in the clock case."

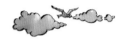

And so she helped him out and heard how the wolf had come, and eaten all the rest. And you may think how she cried for the loss of her dear children. At last, in her grief, she wandered out of doors, the youngest kid with her, and when they got to the meadow, there they saw the wolf lying under a tree and snoring so that the branches shook. The mother goat looked at him carefully on all sides, and she noticed how something inside his body was moving and struggling.

"Dear me!" thought she, "can it be that my poor children that he devoured for his evening meal are still alive?" And she sent the little kid back to the house for a pair of shears and needle and thread. Then she cut the wolf's body open. No sooner had she made one snip than out came the head of one of the kids, and then another snip, and then one after the other, the six little kids all jumped out alive and well, for in his greediness the rogue had swallowed them down whole. How delightful this was! So they comforted their dear mother and

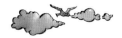

hopped about like tailors at a wedding.

"Now fetch some good hard stones," said the mother, "and we will fill his body with them as he lies asleep."

And so they fetched some in all haste and put them inside him, and the mother sewed him up so quickly again that he was none the wiser.

When the wolf at last awoke and got up, the stones inside him made him feel very thirsty, and as he was going to the brook to drink, they struck and rattled one against another. And so he cried out:

"What is this I feel inside me
Knocking hard against my bones?
How should such a thing betide me!
They were kids, and now they're stones."

So he came to the brook and stooped to drink, but the heavy stones weighed him down, so he fell over into the water and was drowned. And when the seven little kids saw it they came running up.

"The wolf is dead, the wolf is dead!" they cried, and they danced with their mother all about the place.

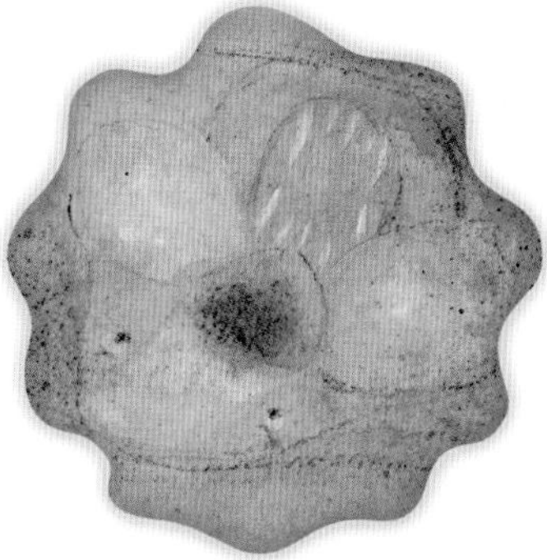

Singh Rajah and the Cunning Little Jackals

By Mary Frere

READING TIME: 5 MINUTES

This story is set in India, where Singh Rajah means "Lion King," and Rajah Jackal and Ranee Jackal mean "King and Queen Jackal."

Once upon a time, in a great jungle, there lived a great lion. He was rajah of all the country around, and every day he used to leave his den, in the deepest shadow of the rocks, and roar with a loud, angry voice and when he roared, the other animals in the jungle, who were all his subjects,

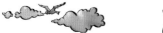

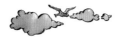

got very much frightened, and ran here and there. Singh Rajah would pounce upon them, and kill them, and gobble them up for his dinner.

This went on for a long time, until at last there were no living creatures left in the jungle but two little jackals—a Rajah Jackal and a Ranee Jackal—husband and wife.

A very hard time of it the poor little jackals had, running this way and that to escape the terrible Singh Rajah, and every day the little Ranee Jackal would say to her husband, "I am afraid he will catch us today—do you hear how he is roaring? Oh dear, oh dear!" And he would answer her, "Never fear, I will take care of you. Let us run on a mile or two. Come, come—quick, quick, quick!" And they would both run away as fast as they could.

After some time spent in this way, they found, however, one fine day, that the lion was so close upon them that they could not escape. Then the little Ranee Jackal said, "Husband, husband! I feel very frightened. The Singh Rajah is so angry he will certainly kill us at once. What can we do?" But he answered, "Cheer up, we can save ourselves yet. Come, and I'll show you how we may manage it."

So what did these cunning little jackals do, but they went to the great lion's den, and when he saw them coming, he began to roar and shake his mane, and he said, "You little wretches, come and be eaten at once. I have had no dinner for three whole days, and all that time I have been running over hill and dale to find you. ROAR! ROAR! Come and be eaten, I say!" and he lashed his tail and gnashed his teeth, and looked very terrible indeed.

Then the Rajah Jackal, creeping close up to him, said, "Great Singh Rajah, we all know you are our master, and we would have come at your bidding long ago, but indeed, sir, there is a much bigger rajah even than you in this jungle, and he tried to catch hold of us and eat us up, and frightened us so much that we were obliged to run away."

"What do you mean?" growled Singh Rajah. "There is no king in this jungle but me!"

"Ah, sire," answered the jackal, "in truth one would think so, for you are very dreadful. Your very voice is death. But it is as we say, for we, with our own eyes, have seen one with whom you could not compete, whose equal you can no more be than we are yours, whose face is as flaming fire, his step as thunder, and his power supreme."

"It is impossible!" interrupted the old lion. "But show me this rajah of whom you speak so much, that I may destroy him instantly!"

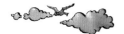

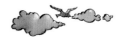

Then the little jackals ran on before him until they reached a great well, and pointing down to his own reflection in the water, they said, "See, sire, there lives the terrible king of whom we spoke."

When Singh Rajah looked down the well he became very angry, for he thought he saw another lion there. He roared and shook his great mane, and the shadow lion shook his, and looked terribly defiant. At last, beside himself with rage at the insolence of his opponent, Singh Rajah sprang down to kill him at once, but no other

lion was there—only the treacherous reflection, and the sides of the well were so steep that he could not get out again, to punish the two jackals, who peeped over the top. After struggling for some time in the deep water, he sank, to rise no more. And the little jackals threw stones down upon him from above, and danced around and around the well, singing, "Ao! Ao! Ao! Ao! The king of the forest is dead, is dead. We have killed the great lion who would have killed us! Ao! Ao! Ao! Ao! Ring-a-ting—ding-a-ting! Ring-a-ting—ding-a-ting! Ao! Ao! Ao!"

The Sagacious Monkey and the Boar

By Yei Theodora Ozaki

READING TIME: 6 MINUTES

Long, long ago, there lived in the province of Shinshin, in Japan, a traveling monkey man, who earned his living by taking around a monkey and showing off the animal's tricks. One evening the man came home in a very bad temper and told his wife to send for the butcher the next morning.

His wife was very bewildered and asked her husband, "Why do you wish me to send for the butcher?"

"It's no use taking that monkey around any longer, he's too old and forgets his tricks. I beat him with my stick all I know how, but he won't dance properly. I must now sell him to the butcher and make what money out of him I can. There is nothing else to be done."

The woman felt very sorry for the poor little animal, and pleaded for her husband to spare the monkey, but her pleading was all in vain: the man was determined to sell him to the butcher.

Now the monkey was in the next room and overheard every word of the conversation. He soon understood that he was to be killed, and he said to himself, "Barbarous, indeed, is my master! Here I have served him faithfully for years, and instead of allowing me to end my days comfortably and in peace, he is going to let me be cut up by the butcher, and my poor body is to be roasted and stewed and eaten! Woe is me! What am I to do. Ah! A bright thought has struck me! There is a wild boar living in the forest nearby. I have often heard tell of his wisdom. Perhaps if I go to him and tell him the straits I am in, he will give me his counsel. I will go and try."

There was no time to lose. The monkey slipped out of

the house and ran as quickly as he could to the forest to find the boar. The boar was at home, and the monkey began his tale of woe at once. "Good Mr. Boar, I have heard of your excellent wisdom. I am in great trouble. You alone can help me. I have grown old in the service of my master, and because I cannot dance properly now, he intends to sell me to the butcher. What do you advise me to do? I know how clever you are!"

The boar was pleased at the flattery and determined to help the monkey. He thought for a little while and then said, "Hasn't your master a baby?"

"Oh, yes," said the monkey, "he has one infant son."

"Doesn't it lie by the door in the morning when your mistress begins the work of the day? Well, I will come around early and when I see my opportunity I will seize the child and run off with it."

"What then?" said the monkey.

"Why the mother will be in a tremendous state, and before your master and mistress know what to do, you must run after me and rescue the child and take it home safely to its parents, and you will see that when the butcher comes, they won't have the heart to sell you."

The monkey thanked the boar many times and then

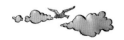

went home. He did not sleep much that night, as you may imagine, for thinking of the next day. His life depended on whether the boar's plan succeeded or not. He was the first up, waiting anxiously for what was to happen. It seemed to him a very long time before his master's wife began to move about and open the shutters to let in the light of day.

Luckily, everything happened as the boar had planned. The mother placed her child near the porch while she tidied up the house and got her breakfast ready.

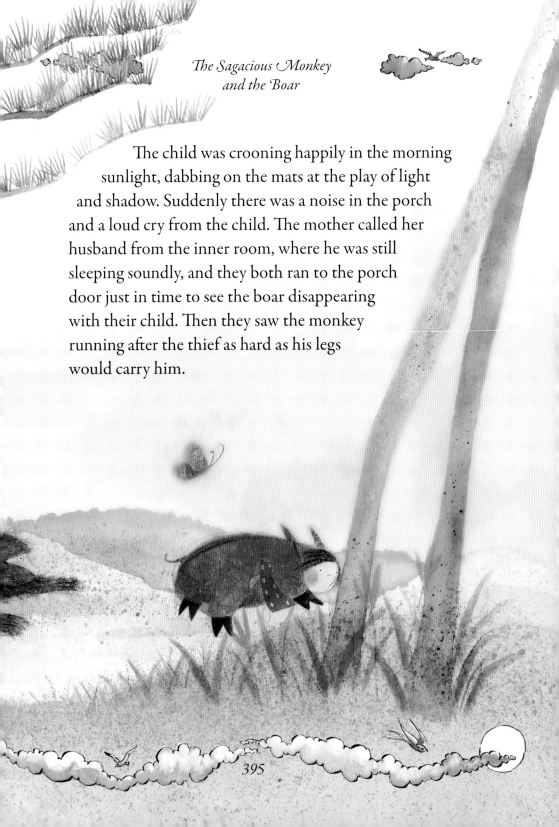

The child was crooning happily in the morning sunlight, dabbing on the mats at the play of light and shadow. Suddenly there was a noise in the porch and a loud cry from the child. The mother called her husband from the inner room, where he was still sleeping soundly, and they both ran to the porch door just in time to see the boar disappearing with their child. Then they saw the monkey running after the thief as hard as his legs would carry him.

Both the man and wife were moved to admiration at the plucky conduct of the sagacious monkey, and their gratitude knew no bounds when the faithful monkey brought the child safely back to their arms.

"There!" said the wife. "This is the animal you want to kill—if the monkey hadn't been here we should have lost our child forever."

"You are right, Wife," said the man as he carried the child into the house. "You may send the butcher back when he comes, and now give us all a good breakfast and the monkey, too."

When the butcher arrived he was sent away with an order for some boar's meat for the evening dinner, and the monkey was petted. He lived the rest of his days in peace; nor did his master ever strike him again.

How the Camel got his Hump

By Rudyard Kipling

READING TIME: 6 MINUTES

*I*n the beginning of years, when the world was so new-and-all, and the animals were just beginning to work for man, there was a camel, and he lived in the middle of a howling desert because he did not want to work, and besides, he was a howler himself. So he ate sticks and thorns and tamarisks and milkweed and prickles. He was most frustratingly idle, and when anybody spoke to him he said "Humph!" Just "Humph!" and no more.

Presently the horse came to him on Monday morning, with a saddle on his back and a bit in his mouth, and said,

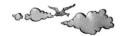

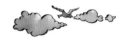

"Camel, come out and trot like the rest of us."

"Humph!" said the camel, and the horse went away and told the man.

Presently the dog came to him with a stick in his mouth, and said, "Camel, come and fetch and carry like the rest of us."

"Humph!" said the camel, and the dog went away to tell the man.

Presently the ox came to him, with the yoke on his neck, and said, "Camel, come and plow like the rest of us."

"Humph!" said the camel, and the ox went away and told the man.

At the end of the day the man called the horse and the dog and the ox together, and said, "Three, I'm very sorry for you (with the world so new-and-all), but that humph-thing in the desert can't work, or he would have been here by now, so I am going to leave him alone. You must work double-time to make up for it."

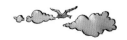

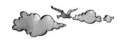

That made the Three very angry (with the world so new-and-all), and they held a palaver, and an indaba, and a punchayet, and a powwow on the edge of the desert, and the camel came chewing milkweed and laughed at them. Then he said "Humph!" and went away again.

Presently there came along the djinn in charge of All Deserts, rolling in a cloud of dust (djinns always travel that way because it is magic), and he stopped to palaver and powpow with the Three.

"Djinn of All Deserts," said the horse, "is it right for any one to be idle, with the world so new-and-all?"

"Certainly not," said the djinn.

"Well," said the horse, "there's a thing in the middle of your Howling Desert (and he's a howler himself) with a long neck and long legs, and he hasn't done a stroke of work since Monday morning. He won't trot."

"Whew!" said the djinn, whistling, "that's my camel, for all the gold in Arabia! What does he say about it?"

"He says, 'Humph!'" said the dog, "and he won't fetch and carry."

"Does he say anything else?"

"Only 'Humph!' And he won't plow," said the ox.

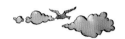

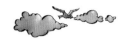

"Very good," said the djinn. "I'll humph him if you will kindly wait a minute."

The djinn rolled himself up in his dust-cloak, and took a bearing across the desert, and found the camel looking at his own reflection in a pool of water.

"My long and bubbling friend," said the djinn, "what's this I hear of you doing no work, with the world so new-and-all?"

"Humph!" said the camel.

The djinn sat down, with his chin in his hand and began to think a great magic, while the camel looked at his own reflection in the pool of water.

"You've given the Three extra work ever since Monday morning, all on account of your idleness," said the djinn, and he went on thinking magics, with his chin in his hand.

"Humph!" said the camel.

"I shouldn't say that again if I were you," said the djinn, you might say it once too often. Bubbles, I want you to work."

And the camel said "Humph!" again, but no sooner had he said it than he saw his back, that he was so proud of, puffing up and up into a great big lolloping humph.

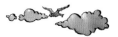

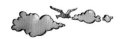

"Do you see that?" said the djinn. "That's your very own humph that you've brought upon your very own self by not working. Today is Thursday, and you've done no work since Monday, when the work began. Now you are going to work."

"How can I," said the camel, "with this humph on my back?"

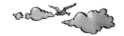

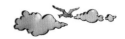

"That's made on purpose," said the djinn, "all because you missed those three days. You will be able to work now for three days without eating, because you can live on your humph, and don't you ever say I never did anything for you. Come out of the desert and go to the Three, and behave. Humph yourself!"

And the camel humphed himself, humph and all, and went away to join the Three. And from that day to this the camel always wears a humph (we call it "hump" now, not to hurt his feelings), but he has never yet caught up with the three days that he missed at the beginning of the world, and he has never yet learned how to behave.

Why the Swallow's Tail is Forked

By Florence Holbrook

READING TIME: 5 MINUTES

This is the story of how the swallow's tail came to be forked. One day the Great Spirit asked all the animals that he had made to come to his lodge. Those that could fly came first—the robin, the bluebird, the owl, the butterfly, the wasp, and the firefly. Behind them came the chicken, fluttering its wings and trying hard to keep up. Then came the deer, the squirrel, the serpent, the cat, and the rabbit. Last of all came the bear, the beaver, and the porcupine. Every one traveled as swiftly as he could, for each wished to hear the words of the Great Spirit.

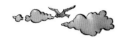

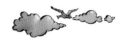

"I have called you together," said the Great Spirit, "because I often hear you scold and fret. What do you wish me to do for you? How can I help you?"

"I do not like to hunt so long for my food," said the bear.

"I do not like to build nests," said the bluebird.

"I do not like to live in the water," said the beaver.

"And I do not like to live in a tree," said the squirrel.

At last man stood before the Great Spirit and said, "O Great Father, the serpent feasts upon my blood. Will you not give him some other food?"

"And why?" asked the Great Spirit.

"Because I am the first of all the creatures you have made," answered man proudly.

Then every animal in the lodge was angry to hear the words of man. The squirrel chattered, the wasp buzzed, the owl hooted, and the serpent hissed.

"Hush, be still," said the Great Spirit. "You are, man, the first of my creatures, but I am the father of all. Each one has his rights, and the serpent must have his food. Mosquito, you are a great traveler. Now fly away and find what creature's blood is best for the serpent. You must all come back in a year and a day."

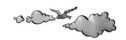

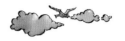

The animals straightway went to their homes. Some went to the river, some to the forest and some to the prairie, to wait for the day when they must meet at the lodge of the Great Spirit.

The mosquito traveled over the earth and stung every creature that he met to find whose blood was the best for the serpent. On his way back to the lodge of the Great Spirit, he looked up into the sky, and there was the swallow.

"Good day, swallow," called the mosquito.

"I am glad to see you, my friend," sang the swallow. "Are you going to the lodge of the Great Spirit? Have you found out whose blood is best for the serpent?"

"The blood of man," answered the mosquito.

The mosquito did not like man, but the swallow had always been his friend. "What can I do to help man?" he thought. "Oh, I know what I can do." Then he asked the mosquito, "Whose blood did you say?"

"Man's blood," said the mosquito, "that is best."

"This is best," said the swallow, and he tore out the mosquito's tongue.

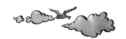

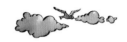

The mosquito buzzed angrily and went quickly to the Great Spirit.

"All the animals are here," said the Great Spirit. "They are waiting to hear whose blood is best for the serpent."

The mosquito tried to answer, "The blood of man," but he could not say a word. He could make no sound but "Kss-ksss-ksssss!"

"What do you say?"

"Kss-ksss-ksssss!" buzzed the mosquito angrily.

All the creatures wondered. Then said the swallow, "Great Father, the mosquito is timid and cannot answer you. I met him before we came, and he told me whose blood it was."

"Then let us know at once," said the Great Spirit.

"It is the blood of the frog," answered the swallow quickly. "Is it not so, friend mosquito?"

"Kss-ksss-ksssss!" hissed the angry mosquito.

"The serpent shall have the frog's blood," said the Great Spirit. "Man shall be his food no longer."

Now the serpent was angry with the swallow, for he did not like frog's blood. As the swallow flew near him, he seized him by the tail and tore away a little of it.

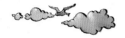

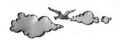

This is why the swallow's tail is forked, and it is why man always looks upon the swallow as his friend.

The White Cat

By E. Nesbit

READING TIME: 14 MINUTES

The white cat lived at the back of a shelf at the darkest end of the inside attic, which was nearly dark all over. It had lived there for years, because one of its white china ears was chipped, so that it was no longer a possible ornament for the spare bedroom.

Tavy found it at the end of a wicked and glorious afternoon. He had been left alone. The servants were the only other people in the house. He had promised to be good. He had meant to be good. And he had not been. He had done everything you can think of. He had walked

into the duck pond, and all of his clothes had been soaked through. He had climbed on a hay stack and fallen off it, and had not broken his neck, which, as Cook told him, he richly deserved to do. He had found a mouse in the trap and put it in the kitchen teapot, so that when Cook went to make tea it jumped out at her, and made her scream and cry. Tavy was sorry for this, of course, and said so like a man. He had only, he explained, meant to give her a little start. In the confusion that followed the mouse, he had eaten all the blackcurrant jam that was put out for afternoon tea, and for this too, he apologized handsomely, as soon as it was pointed out to him. He had broken a pane of the greenhouse with a stone and—but why pursue the painful theme? The last thing he had done was to explore the attic, where he was never allowed to go, and to knock down the white cat from its shelf.

The sound of its fall brought the servants. The cat was not broken—only its other ear was chipped. Tavy was put to bed. But he got out as soon as the servants had gone downstairs, crept up to the attic, secured the cat, and washed it in the bathtub. So that when Mother came back from London, Tavy, dancing impatiently at the head of the stairs, in a very wet nightshirt, flung himself upon her and cried, "I've been awfully naughty, and I'm frightfully sorry, and please may I have the white cat for my very own?"

He was much sorrier than he had expected to be when he saw that Mother was too tired even to want to know, as she generally did, exactly how naughty he had been. She only kissed him and said, "I am sorry you've been naughty, my darling. Go back to bed now."

Tavy was ashamed to say anything more about the china cat, so he went back to bed. But he took the cat with him, and talked to it and kissed it, and went to sleep with its smooth shiny shoulder against his cheek.

In the days that followed, he was extravagantly good. Being good seemed as easy as being bad usually was. This may have been because Mother seemed so tired and ill, and gentlemen in black coats and high hats came to see Mother, and after they had gone she used to cry. These things going on in a house sometimes make people good; sometimes they act just the other way. Or it may have been because he had the china cat to talk to. Anyhow, whichever way it was, at the end of the week Mother said, "Tavy, you've been a dear good boy, and a great comfort to me. You must have tried very hard to be good."

It was difficult to say, "No, I haven't, at least not since the first day," but Tavy got it said, and was hugged for his pains.

"You wanted," said Mother, "the china cat. Well, you may have it."

"For my very own?"

"For your very own. But you must be very careful not to break it. And you mustn't give it away. It goes with the house. Your Aunt Jane made me promise to keep it in the family. It's very, very old. Don't take it out of doors for fear of accidents."

"I love the white cat, Mother," said Tavy. "I love it better than all my toys."

Then Mother told Tavy several things, and that night when he went to bed Tavy repeated them all faithfully to the china cat, who was about six inches high and looked very intelligent.

"So you see," he ended, "the wicked lawyer's taken nearly all Mother's money, and we've got to leave our own lovely big white house, and go and live in a horrid little house. And Mother does hate it so."

"I don't wonder," said the china cat very distinctly.

"What!" said Tavy, halfway into his nightshirt.

"I said, I don't wonder, Octavius," said the china cat, and rose from her sitting position, stretched her china legs, and waved her white china tail.

"You can speak?" said Tavy.

"Can't you see I can? Hear, I mean?" said the cat. "I belong to you now, so I can speak to you. I couldn't before. It wouldn't have been good manners."

Tavy, his nightshirt around his neck, sat down on the edge of the bed with his mouth open.

"Come, don't look so silly," said the cat, taking a walk along the high wooden mantelpiece, "anyone would think you didn't like me to talk to you."

"I love you to," said Tavy recovering himself a little.

"Well then," said the cat.

"May I touch you?" Tavy asked timidly.

"Of course! I belong to you. Look out!" The china cat gathered herself together and jumped. Tavy caught her.

It was quite a shock to find when one stroked her that the china cat, though alive, was still china—hard, cold, and smooth to the touch, and yet perfectly brisk

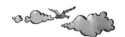

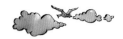

and absolutely bendable as any flesh-and-blood cat.

"Dear, dear white pussy," said Tavy, "I do love you."

"And I love you," purred the cat. "Otherwise I should never have lowered myself to begin a conversation."

"I wish you were a real cat," said Tavy.

"I am," said the cat. "Now how shall we amuse ourselves? I suppose you don't care for sport—mousing, I mean?"

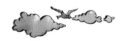

"I never tried," said Tavy, "but I think I wouldn't."

"Very well then, Octavius," said the cat. "I'll take you to the white cat's castle. Get into bed. Bed makes a good traveling carriage, especially when you haven't any other. Shut your eyes."

Tavy did as he was told. He shut his eyes, but could not keep them shut. He opened them a tiny, tiny chink, and sprang up. He was not in bed. He was on a couch of soft cloth, and the couch stood in a splendid hall, whose walls were of gold and ivory. By him stood the white cat, no longer china, but a real-life cat with fur.

"Here we are," she said. "The journey didn't take long, did it? Now we'll have that splendid supper, out of the fairytale, with the invisible hands waiting on us."

She clapped her paws—paws now as soft as white velvet—and a tablecloth floated into the room, then knives and forks and spoons and glasses. The table was set, the dishes drifted in, and they began to eat. There happened to be every single thing Tavy liked best to eat. After supper there was music and singing, and Tavy, having kissed a white, soft, furry forehead, went to bed in a gold four-poster with a counterpane of butterflies' wings. He awoke at home. On the mantelpiece sat the white cat, looking as though butter would not melt in her mouth. And all her furriness had gone with her voice. She was silent and china.

Tavy spoke to her. But she would not answer. Nor did she speak all day. Only at night, when he was getting into bed, she suddenly mewed, stretched, and said, "Make haste, there's a play acted tonight at my castle."

Tavy made haste, and was rewarded by another glorious evening in the castle of the white cat.

And so the weeks went on. Days full of an ordinary little boy's joys and sorrows, goodnesses and badnesses. Nights spent by a little prince in the magic castle of the white cat.

Then came the day when Tavy's mother spoke to him, and he, very scared and serious, told the china cat what she had said.

"I knew this would happen," said the cat. "It always does. So you're to leave your house next week. Well, there's only one way out of the difficulty. Draw your sword, Tavy, and cut off my head and tail."

"And then will you turn into a princess, and shall I have to marry you?" Tavy asked with horror.

"No, dear—no," said the cat reassuringly. "I shan't

turn into anything. But you and Mother will turn into happy people. I shall just not be any more—for you."

"Then I won't do it," said Tavy.

"But you must. Come, draw your sword, like a brave fairy prince, and cut off my head."

The sword hung above his bed, with the helmet and breastplate Uncle James had given him last Christmas.

"I'm not a fairy prince," said the child. "I'm Tavy—and I love you."

"You love your mother better," said the cat. "Come cut my head off. The story always ends like that. You love Mother best. It's for her sake."

"Yes." Tavy was trying to think it out. "Yes, I love Mother best. But I love you. And I won't cut off your head—no, not even for Mother."

"Then," said the cat, "I must do what I can!"

She stood up, waving her white china tail, and before Tavy could stop her she had leaped, not, as before, into his arms, but onto the wide hearthstone.

It was all over—the china cat lay broken inside the high brass fender. The sound of the smash brought Mother running.

"What is it?" she cried. "Oh, Tavy—the china cat!"

"She did it," sobbed Tavy. "She wanted me to cut off her head and I wouldn't."

"Don't talk nonsense, dear," said Mother sadly. "That only makes it worse. Pick up the pieces."

"There's only two pieces," said Tavy. "Couldn't you stick her together again?"

"Why," said Mother, holding the pieces close to the candle. "She's been broken before. And mended."

"I knew that," said Tavy, still sobbing. "Oh, my dear white cat, oh, oh, oh!" The last "oh" was a howl of anguish.

"Come, crying won't mend her," said Mother. "Look, there's another piece of her, close to the shovel."

Tavy stooped.

"That's not a piece of cat," he said, and picked it up.

It was a pale parchment label, tied to a key. Mother held it to the candle and read, "Key of the lock behind the knot in the mantelpiece panel in the white parlor."

"Tavy! I wonder! But where did it come from?"

"Out of my white cat, I suppose," said Tavy, his tears stopping. "Are you going to see what's in the mantelpiece panel, Mother? Are you? Oh, do let me come and see, too!"

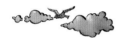

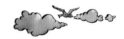

"You don't deserve," mother began, and ended, "Well, put your bathrobe on, then."

They went down the gallery, past the pictures and the stuffed birds and tables with china on them and downstairs, on to the white parlor. But they could not see any knot in the mantelpiece panel, because it was all painted white. But Mother's fingers felt softly all over it, and found a round, raised spot. It was a knot, sure enough. Then she scraped around it with her scissors, till she loosened the knot, and poked it out with the scissors point.

"I don't suppose there's any keyhole there, really," she said. But there was. And what is more, the key fitted. The panel swung open, and inside was a little cupboard with two shelves. What was on the shelves? There were old laces and old embroideries, old jewelry and old silver, there was money, and there were dusty old papers that Tavy thought most uninteresting. But Mother did not think them uninteresting. She laughed, and cried, or nearly cried, and said:

"Oh, Tavy, this was why the china cat was to be taken such care of!"

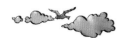

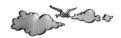

Then she told him how, one hundred and fifty years before, the head of the house had gone out to fight for the Pretender, and had told his daughter to take the greatest care of the china cat. "I will send you word of the reason by a sure hand," he said, for they parted on the open square, where any spy might have overheard anything. And he had been killed by an ambush, not ten miles from home—and his daughter had never known.

But she had kept the cat.

"And now it has saved us," said Mother. "We can stay in the dear old house, and there are two other houses that will belong to us too, I think. And, oh, Tavy, would you like some pound cake and ginger wine, dear?"

Tavy did like. And had it.

The china cat was mended, but it was put in the glass-fronted corner cupboard in the drawing room, because it had saved the house.

Now I dare say you'll think this is all nonsense, and a made-up story. Not at all. If it were, how would you account for Tavy's finding, the very next night, fast asleep on his pillow, his own white cat—the furry friend that the china cat used to turn into every evening—the dear hostess who had amused him so well in the white cat's fairy palace?

It was she, beyond a doubt, and that was why Tavy didn't mind a bit about the china cat being taken from him and kept under glass. You may think that it was just any old stray white cat that had come in by accident. Tavy knows better. It has the very same tender tone in its purr that the magic white cat had. It will not talk to Tavy, it is true, but Tavy can and does talk to it. But the thing that makes it perfectly certain that it is the white cat is that the tips of its two ears are missing just as the china cat's ears were. If you say that it might have lost its ear-tips in battle, you are the kind of person who always makes difficulties, and you may be quite sure that the kind of splendid magics that happened to Tavy will never happen to you.

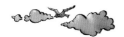

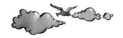

Good and Bad Wishes

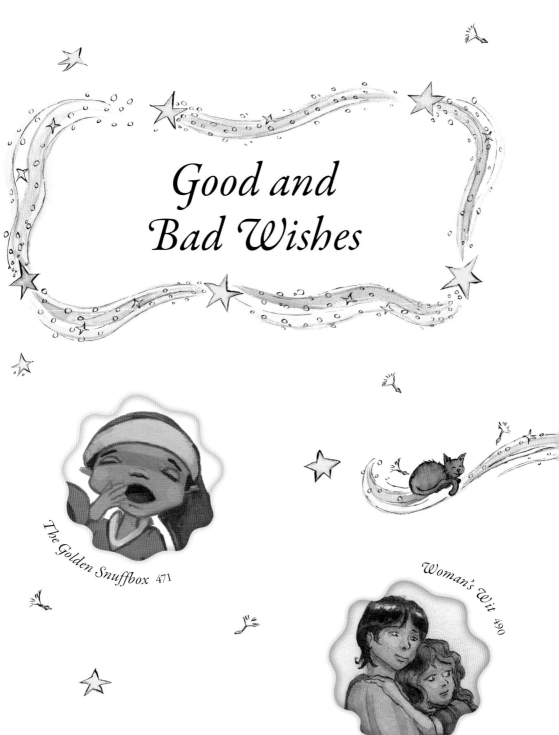

Carrie's Three Wishes

By Lucretia P. Hale

READING TIME: 20 MINUTES

People have to take great care with wishes—it is so easy to get them wrong. In this story, Carrie is an American girl living in the 19th century. She is certain she has thought of good wishes, but they still cause her a lot of trouble. The chariot she thinks of wishing for is not like a Roman chariot—it is a light carriage pulled by four horses.

Carrie Fraser was a great trouble to her mother, because she was always wishing for something she did not have.

"The other girls always have things that I don't," she complained to her mother. Her mother tried to explain

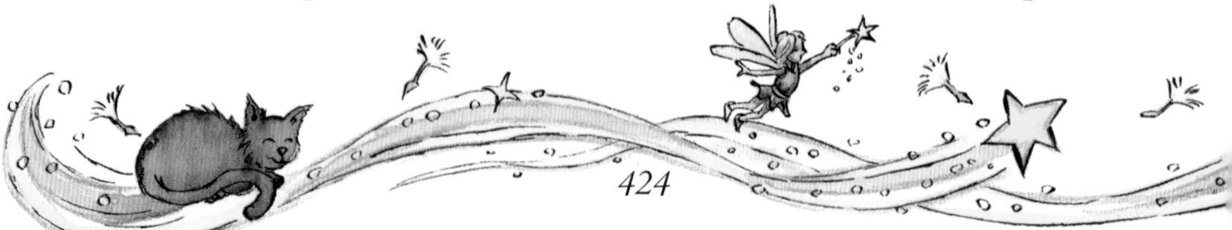

to Carrie that she had a great many things the other girls didn't have.

"But they are not always wishing for my things, just as I wish for theirs."

"That is because they are not such 'teasers' as you are," her mother would reply.

One day, as usual, she had been complaining and wishing she could have everything she wanted. Her mother said to her, "Do you remember the old story of the old couple who had their three wishes granted, and how they never got any good from it?"

"But that was because they acted like such geese," exclaimed Carrie. "I could never have been so elephantinely idiotic! First of all, they wasted one wish. They asked for a common, everyday sausage to come down the chimney, then they got into a stupid fight, and wished the sausage would settle on one of their noses, and then they had to waste their very last wish, by wishing it off again! It is too bad to have such luck come to such out-and-out idiots."

Mrs. Fraser was just setting out for the village street, to order dinner. The governor was expected to pass through and was to be met at the town hall. Jimmy, the only son in the family, had gone to see the show.

"Now, if he were a real, genuine governor," said Carrie, "like a prince in a fairytale, you would go and beseech him to grant your wishes. You would fall on your knees, or something, and he would beg you to rise, and your lovely daughter should have all that she wished."

"I am afraid you are very foolish," sighed Mrs. Fraser, "but I will see the governor. Perhaps he can advise what is best."

It seemed to Carrie as if her mother were gone a great while. "She might have gotten six dinners!" she exclaimed to herself. "How tiresome! I wish I had gone down myself, anyway. All the girls and boys have gone, and I might have seen the governor."

But she passed the time in rocking backwards and forwards in a rocking chair for when the other girls had gone downtown, and had urged her to go with them, she had been quite too lazy to go for her hat.

"Oh dear me! If I had only a chariot and four horses to go down with, and somebody to dress me and find my boots and my hat and my gloves, then it would have been worthwhile to go. I mean to make out a list of wishes, in case somebody should grant me the power to have them."

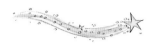

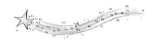

She took out a little book from her pocket and began to write down:

1. A chariot and four horses, man to drive, etc.
2. Maid to find and put on hat, boots, etc.
3. Plenty of hats, boots, and gloves for the maid to put on, and so that they could be found when wanted.

"If I had gloves in every drawer and on every shelf, I should not have to be looking for them. I might have a hat on every peg in the house except what Jimmy uses. I might have a sack over the back of every chair, and gloves in the pockets of each. The boots could be in each corner of the room and on all the top shelves. Let's see. That makes three wishes. They generally have three. If I strike out the maid, I can think of something else. Suppose I say something to eat, then. Chocolate creams! I never had enough yet."

At this moment Mrs. Fraser returned, looking quite heated and breathless. She had to fling herself into a chair by the window to recover strength enough to speak, and then her words came out in gasps.

Carrie did leave her rocking chair and tried fanning her mother, for she saw she had something to say.

"What is it? What have you seen? Have you got something for me? Is the governor coming here? Couldn't you find any dinner?"

"Yes, I saw him, I managed to see him," she gasped out. "The guns were firing, the cannon were booming, the bells were ringing."

"Oh! I dare say! I dare say!" cried Carrie, eager to hear more. "I could hear them up here. That was not worth going to town for. What did the governor say?"

"My dear! My dear!" panted Mrs. Fraser. "He said you could have your three wishes."

"What! The chariot and four horses, the maid, and, no, the maid was scratched out, not the chocolates?" asked Carrie, in wonder.

"No, no! I don't know what you mean!" said Mrs. Fraser, "but you can have three wishes, and I have hurried home, for they are to be told as the clock strikes twelve—one today, one tomorrow, one the next day—the moment the clock strikes, and I am only just in time. You are to wish, and you will have just what you wish."

Both Carrie and her mother looked at the clock. The hand was just approaching twelve. Carrie could hear a little "click" that always came from inside the clock before it struck.

"I have written out my wishes," she hurried to say, "but I don't want the chariot yet, because everybody is coming back from town. And I don't want any more hats and boots just now. But, oh! I do want some chocolate creams, and I wish this room was chock full of them."

As she spoke, the clock struck, and when it stopped she could speak no more, for the room was as full of chocolate creams as it could hold. They came rattling down upon her head, filling in all the crannies of the room. They crowded into her half-open mouth, they filled her clutching hands. Luckily, Mrs. Fraser was sitting near the open window, and the chocolate creams pushed her forward upon the sill. There were two windows. One was made of glass doors which were shut, the other, fortunately, was quite low, and Mrs. Fraser seated herself on the edge, and succeeded in passing her feet over to the other side, a torrent of chocolate creams following her as she came. She then turned to see if she could help Carrie. Carrie was trying to eat her way toward the window, and stretched out her arms to her mother, who seized her, and with all her strength pulled her through the window.

"They are fab!" exclaimed Carrie, as soon as she was free. "They are the freshest I ever ate. Golumptious!"

"Oh, Carrie," said her mother, mournfully, "how can you use such expressions now, when you have wasted your opportunity in such an extravagant wish?"

"What! A whole roomful of chocolate creams do you consider a waste?" exclaimed Carrie. "Why, we shall be envied by all our neighbors, and, Mamma, you have been sighing over our expenses. Do you not see that we can

make our fortune with chocolate creams? First, let us eat all we want before telling anybody, then let us give some to choice friends, and we will sell the rest."

All the time she was talking Carrie was putting in her hand for chocolate creams and cramming in one after another. Mrs. Fraser, too, did not refuse to taste them. How could they ever get into the parlor again, unless they were eaten up?

"I am sure we can make quite a fortune," Carrie went on. "As soon as Jimmy comes home we can calculate how much it will be. The last time I was in Boston I gave fifteen cents for a quarter of a pound, and there were just thirteen chocolate creams. Now, see. In my two hands I can hold fourteen. Now, how many times that do you suppose there are in the room?"

Mrs. Fraser could not think. Carrie was triumphant.

"Jimmy will know how to calculate, for he knows how many feet and inches there are in the room. If not, he can measure, and we can line the chocolate creams up, and see how many go to a foot, and then we can easily find out. Of course, we shall sell them cheaper than they do in Boston, and so there will be a rush for them. It will be great!"

"I am glad we happened to take this rocking chair out on the veranda this morning," said Mrs. Fraser, languidly seating herself. "I don't see how we shall ever get into the parlor again."

"Jimmy and I will eat our way in fast enough," said Carrie, laughing, and Jimmy at that moment appeared with two friends, whom he had brought home to dinner.

They were all delighted when they understood the situation, and had soon eaten a little place by the window, inside the room.

"I quite forgot to buy any dinner," exclaimed Mrs. Fraser, starting up. "I meant to have ordered a leg of mutton as I went down, and now it is too late, and eggs for a pudding. Jimmy will have to go down."

"Oh, the chocolate creams will do!" exclaimed Carrie. "Don't you see, there's our first saving, and my wish does not turn out so extravagant, after all. The boys will be glad to have chocolate creams for dinner, I'm sure."

The boys all said they would, as far as they could, when their mouths were so full.

"We must put out an advertisement," said Carrie, at last, as soon as she could stop to speak. "'Chocolate creams sold cheap!' We may as well make all we can. Suppose we look up some boxes and baskets, Jimmy, to sell them in, and you boys can go to the gate and tell people there are chocolate creams for sale."

But all the boxes and baskets were soon filled, and only a little space made in the room. Jimmy pulled out the other rocking chair which Carrie had been sitting in, and she rested herself for a while.

"I declare, I never thought before I could eat enough chocolate creams, but they are a trifle sickening."

"My dear," said Mrs. Fraser, "if you had not said 'chock full'; if you had said 'a great many' or 'a trunkful' or something of that sort."

"But I meant 'chock full,'" insisted Carrie. "I did not mean quite up to the ceiling. I didn't suppose that was what 'chock' meant. Now we know."

A great shouting was heard. All the boys of the town were gathering, and quite a crowd of people seemed coming near.

Mrs. Fraser was a widow, and there was no man in the house. Jimmy was the nearest approach to a man that she could depend upon, and here he was, leading a band of boys! She sent one of the boys she knew the best for

Mr. Stetson, the neighboring policeman, who came quickly, having already seen the crowd of boys flocking to the house.

Carrie was trying to sell off her boxes for fifteen, ten, even five cents, but the crowd could not be easily appeased, for the boys could see across the windows the chocolate creams closely packed. "The room is chock full!" they exclaimed.

Mr. Stetson examined the premises. "You'll find it hard work to get them chocolates out in a week, even if you set all the boys on them. I'd advise letting them in one by one to fill their pockets, each to pay a cent."

Even Carrie assented to this, and a line was formed, and boys let in through the window. They ate a way to the door that led into the entry, so that it could be opened and the room could be entered that way. The boys now went in at the window and came out at the door, eating as they went and filling their pockets. Carrie could not but sigh at thought of the Boston chocolates, more than a cent apiece! But the boys ate, and then the girls came and ate, but with night, all had to leave at last. It was possible to shut the window and lock it and shut the door for the night, after they had gone.

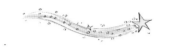

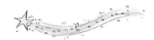

"I don't see why the chocolates should not stay on there weeks and weeks," said Carrie to her mother.

"Of course, they won't be so fresh, day after day, but they will be fresher than some in the shops.

I'm awfully tired of eating them now, and feel as if I never want to see a chocolate cream again, but I suppose I shall feel different after a night's sleep, and I think Mr. Stetson is wrong in advising us to sell them so low."

Mrs. Fraser suggested she should like to go in the parlor to sit.

"But tomorrow is the day of the picnic," said Carrie, "and we shall be outdoors anyhow. I will take chocolate creams for my share. But, dear me! My dress is on the sofa—my best dress."

"I told you, my dear, one of the last things, to take it upstairs," said Mrs. Fraser.

"And there it is, in the farthest corner of the room," exclaimed Carrie, "with all those chocolates piled on it. I'll tell you. I'll get Ben Sykes in early. He eats faster than any of the other boys, and he shall eat up toward my dress. He made a great hole in the chocolates this afternoon. I will have him come in early, and we don't go to the picnic till after twelve o'clock."

"And at twelve o'clock you have your second wish," said Mrs. Fraser.

"Yes, Mamma," said Carrie, "and I have already decided what it shall be—a chariot and four horses.

It will come just in time to take me to the picnic."

"Oh, my dear Carrie," said her mother, "do think what you are planning! Where would you keep your chariot and the four horses?"

"Oh! there will be a man to take care of them," said Carrie, "but I will think about it all night carefully."

At that very moment she went to sleep.

The next morning early, Carrie was downstairs. She found she could eat a few more chocolate creams, and Jimmy was in the same condition. She proposed to him her plan of keeping the chocolates still for sale, but eating a way to the sofa in the corner, to her best dress.

Ben Sykes came early, and a few of the other boys. The rest were kept at home, because it turned out they had eaten too many and their parents would not let them come.

A good many of the older people came with baskets and boxes, and bought some to carry away, they were so delicious and fresh.

Meanwhile Ben Sykes was eating his way toward the corner. It was very hard making any passage, for as fast as he ate out a place others, came tumbling in from the top. Carrie and Jimmy invented "a kind of a tunnel" of chairs and ironing boards, to keep open the passage, and other boys helped eat, as they were not expected to pay.

But the morning passed quickly on. Mrs. Fraser tried her best to persuade Carrie to wear another dress, but she had set her mind on this one. She had a broad blue sash to wear with it, and the sash would not go with any other dress.

She watched the clock, she watched Ben, she went in under the ironing boards to help him eat, although she had begun to loathe the taste of the chocolate creams.

Ben was splendid. He seemed to enjoy more the more he ate. Carrie watched him, as he licked them and ate with glowing eyes.

"Oh, Ben," Carrie suddenly exclaimed, "you can't seem to eat them fast enough. I wish your throat were as long as from one end of this room to the other."

At this moment the clock was striking.

Carrie was ready to scream out her second wish, but she felt herself pushed in a strange way. Ben was on all fours in front of her, and now he pushed her back, back. His neck was so long that while his head was still among the chocolates, at the far corner of the room, his feet were now out of the door.

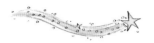

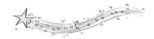

Carrie stood speechless. She had lost her wish by her foolish exclamation. The faithful Ben, meanwhile, was flinging something through the opening. It was her dress, and she hurried away to put it on.

When she came down, everybody was looking at Ben. At first he enjoyed his long neck very much. He could stand on the doorstep and put his head far out up in the cherry trees and nip off cherries, which pleased both the boys and himself.

Instead of a chariot and four horses, Carrie went off in an open wagon, with the rest of the girls. It made her feel so guilty to see Ben, with his long neck, that she got her mother's permission to spend the night with the friend in whose grounds the picnic was to be held.

She carried baskets of chocolate creams, and she found numbers of the girls, who had not eaten any, who were delighted with them, and promised to come the next day, to buy and carry away any amount of them. She began to grow more cheerful, though she felt no appetite, and instead of eating everything, as she always did at picnics, she could not even touch Mattie Somers's cream pie nor Julia Dale's doughnuts. She stayed as late as she could at her friend Mattie's, but she felt she must get home in time for her third wish, at twelve o'clock.

Would it be necessary for her to wish that Ben Sykes', neck should be made shorter? She hoped she might find that it had grown shorter in the night, then she could do as she pleased about her third wish.

She still clung to the desire for the chariot and four horses. If she had it, she and her mother and Jimmy could get into it and drive far away from everybody—from Ben Sykes and his long neck, if he still had it—and never see any of them anymore. Still, she would like to show the chariot and four horses to her friends, and perhaps Ben Sykes would not mind his long neck, and would be glad to keep it and earn money by showing himself at a circus.

So she reached home in the middle of the morning, and found the whole Sykes family there, and Ben, still with his long neck. It seems it had given him great trouble in the night. He had to sleep with his head in the opposite house, because there was not room enough on one floor at home. Mrs. Sykes had not slept a wink, and her husband had been up watching, to see that nobody stepped on Ben's neck. Ben himself appeared in good spirits, but was glad to sit in a high room, where he could support his head.

They were all in the parlor, where the chocolate creams were partially cleared away. They were in a row on two sides of the room, meeting near the center, with the underground passage, through which Ben had worked his way to Carrie's dress. Mrs. Fraser had organized a group to fill pasteboard boxes, which she had obtained from the village, and she and her friends were filling them, to send away to be sold. All the inhabitants of the town were fed up with chocolate creams.

At this moment Carrie heard a click in the clock. She looked at her mother, and as the clock struck she said steadily, "I wish that Ben's neck was all right again."

Nobody heard her, for at that moment Ben Sykes started up, saying, "I'm all right, and I have had enough.

Come along home!" And he dragged his family away with him.

Carrie fell into her mother's arms. "I'll never say 'chock full' again!" she cried, "and I'll always be satisfied with what I have got, for I can never forget what I suffered in seeing Ben's long neck!"

Good Luck is Better than Gold

By Juliana Horatia Gatty Ewing

READING TIME: 12 MINUTES

There was once upon a time a child who had Good Luck for his godfather.

"I am not Fortune," said Good Luck to the parents. "I have no gifts to bestow, but whenever he needs help I will be at hand."

"Nothing could be better," said the old couple. They were delighted. But what pleases the father often fails to satisfy the son. Moreover, every man thinks that he deserves just a little more than he has got, and does not reckon it to the purpose if his father had less.

Many a one would be thankful to have as good reasons for contentment as he who had Good Luck for his godfather.

If he fell, Good Luck popped something soft in the way to break his fall. If he fought, Good Luck directed his blows, or tripped up his adversary. If he got into a scrape, Good Luck helped him out of it, and if ever Misfortune met him, Good Luck contrived to hustle her on the pathway till his godson got safely by.

In games of chance, the godfather played over his shoulder. In matters of choice, he chose for him. And when the lad began to work on his father's farm, the farmer began to get rich. For no bird or field mouse touched a seed that his son had sown, and every plant he planted thrived when Good Luck smiled on it.

The boy was not fond of work, but when he did go into the fields, Good Luck followed him.

"Your christening day was a blessed day for us all," said the old farmer.

"He has never given me so much as a lucky sixpence," muttered Good Luck's godson.

"I am not Fortune—I make no presents," said the godfather.

By and by the old farmer died, and his son grew up and had the largest farm in the country. The other boys grew up also, and as they looked over the farmer's boundary wall, they would say, "Good morning, neighbor. That is certainly a fine farm of yours. Your cattle thrive without loss. Your crops grow in the rain and are reaped with the sunshine. Mischance never comes your road. What you have worked for, you enjoy. Such success would turn the heads of poor folk like us. At the same time one would think a man need hardly work for his living at all who has Good Luck for his godfather."

"That is very true," thought the farmer. "Many a man is prosperous, and reaps what he sows, who had no more than the clerk and the sexton for godparents at his christening."

"What is the matter, Godson?" asked Good Luck, who was with him in the field.

"I want to be rich," said the farmer.

"You will not have to wait long," replied the godfather. "In every field you sow, in every flock you rear there is increase. Your wealth is already tenfold greater than your father's."

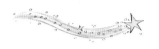

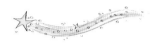

"Aye, aye," replied the farmer. "Good wages for good work. But many a young man has gold at his command who need never turn a sod, and none of the good people came to his christening. Fortunatus's Purse (a legendary self-refilling purse) now, or even a sack or two of gold."

"Peace!" cried the godfather, "I have said that I give no gifts."

Though he had not Fortunatus's Purse, the farmer now had money and to spare, and when the harvest was gathered in, he bought a fine suit of clothes and took his best horse and went to the royal city to see the sights.

The pomp and splendor, the festivities and fine clothes dazzled him.

"This is a gay life that these young courtiers lead," said he. "A man has nothing to do but to enjoy himself."

"If he has plenty of gold in his pocket," said a bystander.

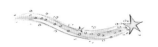

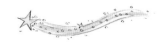

By and by the princess passed in her carriage. She was the king's only daughter. She had hair made of sunshine, and her eyes shone like stars.

"What an exquisite creature!" cried the farmer. "What would one not give to marry her?"

"She has as many suitors as hairs on her head," replied the bystander. "She wants to marry the Prince of Moonshine, but he only dresses in silver, and the king thinks he might find a richer son-in-law. The princess will go to the highest bidder."

"And I have Good Luck for my godfather, and am not even at court!" cried the farmer, and he put spurs to his horse and rode home.

Good Luck was taking care of the farm.

"Listen, godfather!" cried the young man. "I am in love with the king's daughter and want her as my wife."

"It is not an easy matter," replied Good Luck, "but I will do what I can for you. Say that by good luck you saved the princess's life, or perhaps better the king's—for they say he is selfish.

"Tush!" cried the farmer. "The king is greedy and wants a rich son-in-law."

"A wise man may bring wealth to a kingdom with his head, if not with his hands," said Good Luck, "and I can show you a district where the earth only wants mining to be flooded with wealth. Besides, there are a thousand opportunities that can be turned to account and influence. By wits and work, and with Good Luck to help him, many a poorer man than you has risen to greatness."

"Wits and work!" cried the indignant godson. "A fairy would have made a better godfather. Give me as much gold as will fill three meal-bins, and you may keep the rest of your help for those who want it."

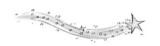

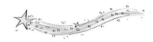

Now at this moment by Good Luck stood Dame Fortune. She liked handsome young men, and there was some little jealousy between her and the godfather, so she smiled at the quarrel.

"You would rather have had me for your godparent?" said she.

"If you would give me three wishes, I would," replied the farmer boldly, "and I would trouble you no more."

"Will you pass him over to me?" said Dame Fortune to the godfather.

"If he wishes it," replied Good Luck. "But if he accepts your gifts he has no further claim on me."

"Nor on me either," said the Dame. "Listen, young man, you mortals are apt to make a mess of your three wishes, and you may end with a sausage at your nose, like your betters."

"I have thought of it too often," replied the farmer, "and I know what I want. For my first wish I desire imperishable beauty."

"It is yours," said Dame Fortune, smiling as she looked at him.

"The face of a prince and the manners of a clown are

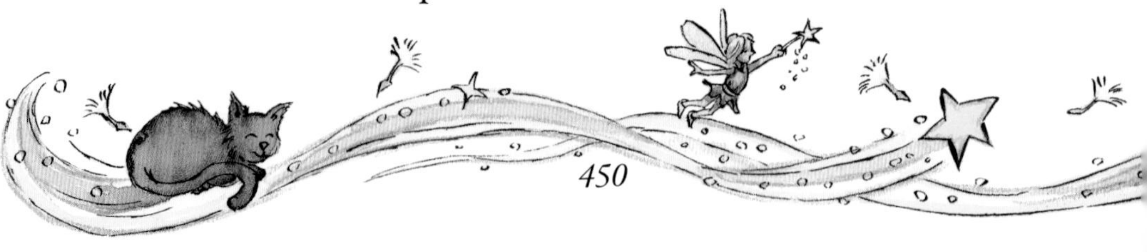

poor partners," said the farmer. "My second wish is for suitable learning and courtly manners, which cannot be gained at the plow-tail."

"You have them in perfection," said the Dame, as the young man thanked her by a graceful bow.

"Thirdly," said he, "I demand a store of gold that I can never exhaust."

"I will lead you to it," said Dame Fortune, and the young man was so eager to follow her that he did not even look back to bid farewell to his godfather.

He was soon at court. He lived in the utmost pomp. He had a suit of armor made for himself out of beaten gold. No metal less precious might come near his person, except for the blade of his sword. This had to be made of steel, for gold is not always strong enough to defend one's life or his honor. But the princess still loved the Prince of Moonshine.

"Stuff and nonsense!" said the king. "I shall give you to the Prince of Gold."

"I wish I had the good luck to please her," muttered the young prince. But he had not, for all his beauty and his wealth. However, she was to marry him, and that was the important thing.

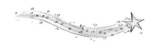

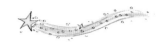

The preparations for the wedding were magnificent.

"It is a great expense," sighed the king, "but then I get the Prince of Gold for a son-in-law."

The prince and his bride drove around the city in a triumphal procession. Her hair fell over her like sunshine, but the starlight of her eyes was cold. In the train rode the Prince of Moonshine, dressed in silver, and with no color in his face. As the bridal chariot approached one of the city gates, two black ravens hovered over it and then flew away and settled on a tree. Good Luck was sitting under the tree to see his godson's triumph, and he heard the birds talking above him.

"Has the Prince of Gold no friend who can tell him that there is a loose stone above the archway that is tottering to fall?" they said.

And Good Luck covered his face with his mantle as the prince drove through.

Just as they were passing out of the gateway the stone fell on the prince's head. He wore a helmet of pure gold, but his neck was broken.

"We can't have all this expense for nothing," said the king, so he married his daughter to the Prince of Moonshine. If one can't get gold one must be content with silver.

"Will you come to the funeral?" asked Dame Fortune of the godfather.

"Not I," replied Good Luck. "I had no hand in this matter."

The rain came down in torrents. The black feathers on the ravens' backs looked as if they had been oiled.

"Caw! Caw!" said they. "It was an unlucky end."

However, the funeral was a very magnificent one, for there was no lack of gold.

The Fisherman and his Wife

By the Brothers Grimm

READING TIME: 20 MINUTES

There was once a fisherman and his wife who lived together in a hovel by the seashore. The fisherman went out every day with his hook and line to catch fish, and he angled and angled.

One day he was sitting with his rod and looking into the clear water, and he sat and sat.

At last, down went the line to the bottom of the water, and when he drew it up he found a great flounder on the hook. And the flounder said to him, "Fisherman, listen to me—let me go, I am not a real fish but an enchanted

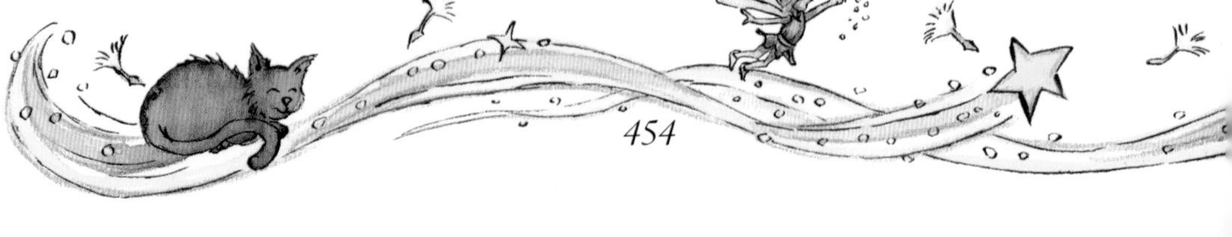

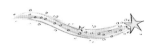

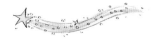

prince. What good shall I be to you if you land me? I shall not taste good, so put me back into the water again, and let me swim away."

"Well," said the fisherman, "no need of so many words about the matter. As you can speak, I had much rather let you swim away."

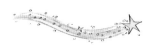

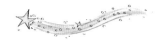

Then he put him back into the clear water, and the flounder sank to the bottom, leaving a long streak of blood behind him. Then the fisherman got up and went home to his wife in their hovel.

"Well, Husband," said the wife, "have you caught nothing today?"

"No," said the man. "That is, I did catch a flounder, but as he said he was an enchanted prince, I let him go again."

"Then, did you wish for nothing?" said the wife.

"No," said the man, "what should I wish for?"

"Oh dear!" said the wife, "and it is so dreadful always to live in this evil-smelling hovel. You might as well have wished for a little cottage. Go again and call him, tell him we want a little cottage. I daresay he will give it to us; go, and be quick."

And when he went back, the sea was green and yellow, and not nearly so clear. So he stood and said,

"O man, O man! If man you be,
Or flounder, flounder, in the sea,
Such a tiresome wife I've got,
For she wants what I do not."

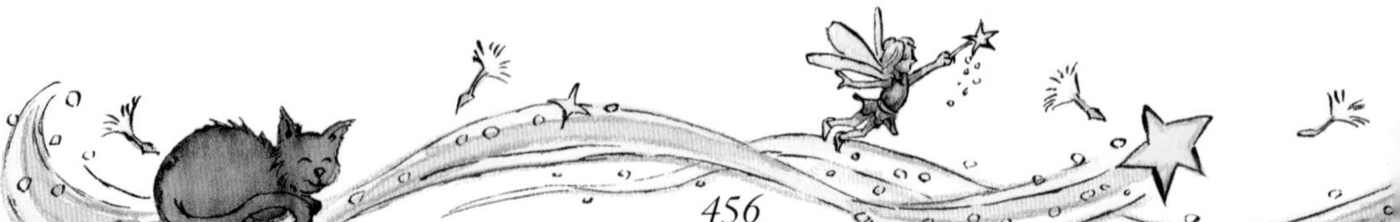

Then the flounder came swimming up and said, "Now then, what does she want?"

"Oh," said the man, "you know when I caught you my wife says I ought to have wished for something. She does not want to live any longer in the hovel and would rather have a cottage.

"Go home," said the flounder, "she has it already."

So the man went home and found, instead of the hovel, a little cottage with his wife sitting on a bench before the door. And she took him by the hand, and said to him, "Come in and see if this is not a great improvement."

So they went in, and there was a beautiful little bedroom, a kitchen and pantry, with all sorts of furniture, and iron and brass ware of the very best. And at the back was a little yard with fowls and ducks, and a little garden full of green vegetables and fruit.

"Look," said the wife, "is that not nice?"

"Yes," said the man, "if this can only last we shall be very well contented."

"We will see about that," said the wife. And after a meal they went to bed.

So all went well for a week or fortnight, when the

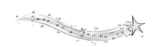

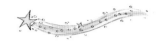

wife said, "Look here, husband, the cottage is really too confined, and the yard and garden are so small, I think the flounder had better get us a larger house, I should like very much to live in a large stone castle, so go to your fish and he will send us a castle."

"O my dear wife," said the man, "the cottage is good enough; what do we want a castle for?"

"We want one," said the wife. "Go along with you, the flounder can give us one."

"Now, Wife," said the man, "the flounder gave us the cottage, I do not like to go to him again; he may be angry."

"Go along," said the wife. "He might just as well give us it as not. Do as I say!"

The man felt very reluctant and unwilling, and he said to himself, "It is not the right thing to do."

Nevertheless he went.

So when he came to the seaside, the water was purple and dark blue and gray and thick, and not green and yellow as before. And he stood and said,

"O man, O man! If man you be,
Or flounder, flounder, in the sea,
Such a tiresome wife I've got,
For she wants what I do not."

"Now then, what does she want?" said the flounder.

"Oh," said the man, half frightened, "she wants to live in a large stone castle."

"Go home, she is already standing before the door," said the flounder.

Then the man went home, as he supposed, but when he got there, there stood, in the place of the cottage, a great castle of stone, and his wife was standing on the steps, about to go in, so she took him by the hand, and said, "Let us enter."

With that he went in with her, and in the castle was a

great hall with a marble pavement, and there were a great many servants, who led them through large doors, and the passages were decked with tapestry, and the rooms with golden chairs and tables, and crystal chandeliers hanging from the ceiling, and all the rooms had carpets. And the tables were covered with food and the best wine for anyone who wanted them. And at the back of the house was a great stable-yard for horses and cattle, and carriages of the finest besides, there was a splendid large garden, with the most beautiful flowers and fine fruit trees, and a pleasance full half a mile long, with deer and oxen and sheep and everything that they could wish for.

"There!" said the wife. "Is not this beautiful?"

"Oh yes," said the man. "If it will only last, we can live in this fine castle and be very well contented."

"We will see about that," said the wife. "In the meanwhile we will sleep upon it." With that they went to bed.

The next morning the wife was awake first, at the break of day, and she looked out and saw from her bed the beautiful country lying all around. The man took no notice of it, so she poked him in the side, and said,

"Husband, get up and just look out of the window.

Just think if we could be king over all this country. Just go to your fish and tell him we should like to be king."

"Now, Wife," said the man, "what should we be kings for? I don't want to be king."

"Well," said the wife. "If you don't want to be king, I will be king."

"Now, Wife," said the man, "what do you want to be king for? I could not ask him such a thing."

"Why not?" said the wife. "You must go directly, all the same. I must be king."

So the man went, very much put out that his wife should want to be king.

"It is not the right thing to do—not at all the right thing," thought the man. He did not at all want to go, and yet he went all the same.

And when he came to the sea, the water was quite dark gray, and rushed far inland, and had an ill smell. And he stood and said,

"O man, O man! If man you be,
Or flounder, flounder, in the sea,
Such a tiresome wife I've got,
For she wants what I do not."

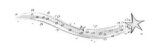

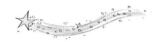

"Now then, what does she want?" said the fish.

"Oh dear!" said the man. "She wants to be king."

"Go home with you, she is so already," said the fish.

So the man went back, and as he came to the palace, he saw it was very much larger, and had great towers and splendid gateways. The herald stood before the door, and a number of soldiers with kettle drums and trumpets. And when he came inside, everything was of marble and gold, and there were many curtains with great golden tassels. Then he went through the doors of the salon to where the great throne room was, and there was his wife sitting upon a throne of gold and diamonds, and she had a great golden crown on, and the scepter in her hand was of pure gold and jewels, and on each side stood six pages in a row, each one a head shorter than the other.

So the man went up to her and said, "Well, Wife, so now you are king!"

"Yes," said the wife, "now I am king."

So then he stood and looked at her, and when he had gazed at her for some time he said,

"Well, Wife, this is fine for you to be king! Now there is nothing more to wish for."

"O Husband!" said the wife, seeming quite restless. "I am tired of this already. Go to your fish and tell him that now I am king I must be emperor."

"Now, Wife," said the man, "what do you want to be emperor for?"

"Husband," said she, "go and tell the fish I want to be emperor."

"Oh dear!" said the man, "he could not do it—I cannot ask him such a thing. There is but one emperor at a time; the fish can't possibly make any one emperor—indeed he can't."

"Now, look here," said the wife, "I am king, and you are only my husband, so will you go at once? Go along! If he was able to make me king, he is able to make me emperor, and I will and must be emperor, so go along!"

So he was obliged to go, and as he went he felt very

uncomfortable about it, and he thought to himself, "It is not at all the right thing to do; to want to be emperor is really going too far. The flounder will soon be beginning to get tired of this."

With that he came to the sea, and the water was quite black and thick, and the foam flew, and the wind blew, and the man was terrified. But he stood and said,

"*O man, O man! If man you be,*
Or flounder, flounder, in the sea,
Such a tiresome wife I've got,
For she wants what I do not."

"What is it now?" said the fish.

"Oh dear!" said the man. "My wife wants to be emperor."

"Go home," said the fish, "she is emperor already."

So the man went home, and found the castle adorned with polished marble and alabaster figures and golden gates. The troops were being marshaled before the door, and they were blowing trumpets and beating drums and cymbals, and when he entered he saw barons and earls and dukes waiting about like servants, and the doors were of bright gold. And he saw his wife sitting upon a throne made of one entire piece of gold, and it was about two miles high, and she had a great golden crown on, which was about three yards high, set with brilliants and carbuncles, and in one hand she held the scepter, and in the other the globe, and on both sides of her stood pages in two rows, all arranged according to their size, from the most enormous giant of two miles high to the tiniest dwarf of the size of my little finger, and before her stood earls and dukes in crowds. So the man went up to her and said, "Well, Wife, so now you are emperor."

"Yes," said she, "now I am emperor."

Then he went and sat down and had a good look at her, and then he said, "Well now, Wife, there is nothing left to be, now you are emperor."

"What are you talking about, Husband?" said she, "I am emperor, and next I will be pope! So go and tell the fish so."

"Oh dear!" said the man, "what is it that you don't want? You can never become pope—there is but one pope in Christendom, and the fish can't possibly do it."

"Husband," said she, "no more words about it, I must and will be pope, so go along to the fish."

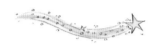

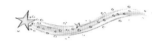

"Now, Wife," said the man, "how can I ask him such a thing? It is too bad—it is asking a little too much, and besides, he could not do it."

"What rubbish you talk!" said the wife scornfully. "If he could make me emperor then he can make me pope. Now go along and ask him, I am emperor, and you are only my husband, so go you must."

So he went, feeling very frightened, and he shivered and shook, and his knees trembled, and there arose a great wind, and the clouds flew by, and it grew very dark, and the sea rose mountains high, and the ships were tossed about, and the sky was partly blue in the middle, but at the sides very dark and red, as in a great tempest. And he felt very desponding, and stood trembling and said,

"O man, O man! If man you be,
Or flounder, flounder, in the sea,
Such a tiresome wife I've got,
For she wants what I do not."

"Well, what now?" said the fish.

"Oh dear!" said the man, "she wants to be pope."

"Go home, she is pope already," said the fish.

So he went home, and he found himself before a great church, with palaces all around. He had to make his way through a great crowd of people, and when he got inside he found the place lighted up with thousands and thousands of lights, and his wife was clothed in a golden garment, and sat upon a very high throne, and had three golden crowns on, all in the greatest priestly pomp, and on both sides of her there stood two rows of lights of all sizes—from the size of the longest tower to the smallest rushlight, and all the emperors and kings were kneeling before her and kissing her foot.

"Well, wife," said the man, and sat and stared at her, "so you are pope."

"Yes," said she, "now I am pope!"

And he went on gazing at her till he felt dazzled, as if

he were sitting in the sun. And after a little time he said,

"Well, now, wife, what is there left to be, now you are pope?"

And she sat up very stiff and straight, and said nothing.

And he said again, "Well, wife, I hope you are contented at last with being pope, you can be nothing more."

"We will see about that," said the wife.

With that they both went to bed, but she was as far as ever from being contented, and she could not get to sleep for thinking and planning what she should like to be next.

The husband, however, slept as fast as a top after his busy day, but the wife tossed and turned from side to side the whole night through, thinking all the while what she could be next, but nothing would occur to her, and when she saw the red dawn, she slipped off the bed and sat before the window to see the sun rise, and as it came up, she said, "Ah, I have it! What if I could make the sun and moon rise—Husband!" she cried, and stuck her elbow in his ribs. "Wake up, and go to your fish, and tell him I want power over the sun and moon."

The man was in such as deep sleep that when he started up he fell out of bed. Then he shook himself together and opened his eyes and said, "Oh, wife, what did you say?"

"Husband," said she, "if I cannot get the power of making the sun and moon rise when I want them, I shall never have another quiet hour. Go to the fish and tell him so."

"O Wife!" said the man, and fell on his knees to her. "The fish can really not do that for you. I grant you he could make you emperor and pope; do be contented with that, I beg of you."

And she became wild with impatience, and screamed out, "I can wait no longer, go at once!"

And so off he went, as well as he could for fright. Then a storm arose, so bad that he could hardly keep his feet, and the houses and trees were blown down, and the mountains trembled and rocks fell in the sea. The sky was quite black and thunder and lightning roared and crackled as the waves, crowned with foam, ran mountains high. When the man reached the right spot, he cried out, without being able to hear his own words,

"O man, O man! If man you be,
Or flounder, flounder, in the sea,
Such a tiresome wife I've got,
For she wants what I do not."

"Well, what now?" said the flounder.

"Oh dear!" said the man. "She wants to order about the sun and moon."

"Go home!" said the flounder. "You will find her in the old hovel."

And there they are sitting to this very day.

The Golden Snuffbox

By Flora Annie Steel

READING TIME: 20 MINUTES

A snuffbox is a little metal box, often beautifully decorated, once used for carrying around snuff, powdered tobacco that some people used to sniff (or "snuff") up their nose instead of smoking.

Once upon a time, and a very good time too, though it was not in my time, nor your time, nor for the matter of that in any one's time, there lived a man and a woman who had one son named Jack, and he was terribly fond of reading books. He read, and he read, and then, because his parents lived in a lonely house in a lonely forest and he never saw any other folk but his father and his mother,

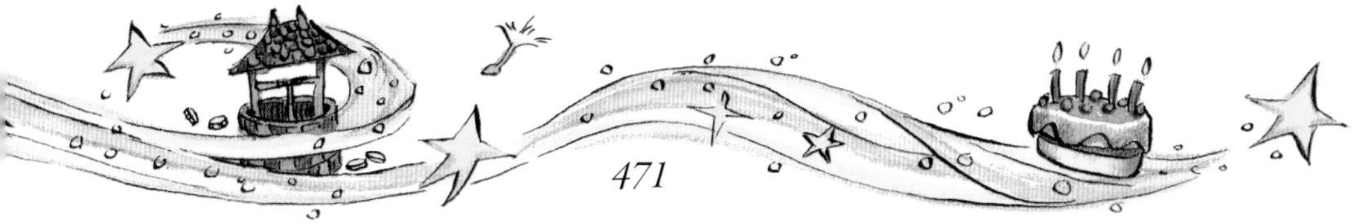

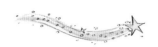

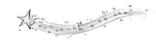

he became quite crazy to go out into the world and see charming princesses and the like.

So one day he told his mother he must be off, and she called him an air-brained addle-pate, but added that, as he was no use at home, he had better go seek his fortune.

Well, Jack hadn't gone far till he came to a field where his father was plowing. Now although the good man was dreadfully put out when he found his son was going away, he drew out of his pocket a little golden snuffbox and gave it to the lad, saying:

"If ever you are in danger of sudden death you may open the box, but not till then. It has been in our family for years and years, but, as we have lived, father and son, quietly in the forest, none of us have ever been in need of help—perhaps you may be."

So Jack pocketed the golden snuffbox and went on his way. After a time, he grew very tired and very hungry, and night closed in on him so that he could scarce see his way.

But at last he came to a large house and begged board and lodging at the back door. Now Jack was a good-looking young fellow, so the maidservant at once called him in to the fireside and gave him plenty of good meat and bread and beer. And it so happened that while he was eating his supper the master's young daughter came into the kitchen and saw him. So she went to her father and said that there was the prettiest young fellow she had ever seen in the back kitchen, and that if her father loved her he would give the young man some employment. Now the gentleman of the house was exceedingly fond of his young daughter and did not want to vex her, so he went into the back kitchen and questioned Jack as to what he could do.

"Anything," said Jack gaily, meaning, of course, that he could do any bit of work about the house.

But the gentleman saw a way of pleasing his young daughter and getting rid of the trouble of employing Jack, so he laughed and said, "If you can do anything, my good lad," said he, "you had better do this. By eight o'clock tomorrow morning you must have dug a lake four miles around in front of my mansion, and on it there must be floating a whole fleet of vessels. And they must range up in front of my mansion and fire a salute of guns. And the very last shot must break the leg of the four-post bed on which my daughter sleeps, for she is always late of a morning!"

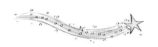

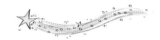

Well! Jack was terribly flabbergasted, but he managed to say, "And if I don't do it?"

"Then," said the master of the house quite calmly, "you shall die."

So he bade the servants take Jack to a turret room and lock the door on him.

Well! Jack sat on the side of his bed and tried to think things out, but he found it so difficult. Soon he decided to think no more, and after saying his prayers he lay down and went to sleep. And he did sleep! When he woke it was close on eight o'clock, and he had only time to fly to the window and look out, when the great clock on the tower began to whirr before it struck the hour. And there was the lawn in front of the house all set with beds of roses and stocks and marigolds! Well! All of a sudden he remembered the little golden snuffbox.

"I'm near enough to death," said he to himself, as he drew it out and opened it.

And no sooner had he opened it than out hopped

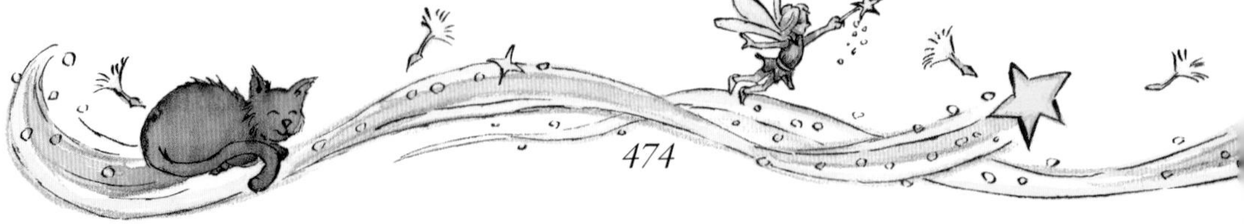

three funny little red men in red nightcaps, rubbing their eyes and yawning, for, you see, they had been locked up in the box for years and years and years.

"What do you want, Master?" they said between their yawns. But Jack heard the clock whirring and knew that he hadn't a moment to lose, so he just gabbled off his orders. Then the clock began to strike, and the little men flew out of the window, and suddenly—Bang! Bang! Bang! Bang! Bang! Bang!—Went the guns, and the last one must have broken the leg of the four-poster bed, for there at the window was the pretty young daughter in her nightcap, gazing with astonishment at the lake that was four miles around, with the fleet of vessels floating on it!

And so did Jack! He had never seen such a sight in his entire life, and he was quite sorry when the three little red men disturbed him by flying in at the window and scrambling into the golden snuffbox.

"Give us a little more time when you want us next, Master," they said sulkily. Then they shut down the lid, and Jack could hear them yawning inside as they settled down to sleep.

As you may imagine, the master of the house was fair

astonished, while as for the gay young daughter, she declared at once that she would never marry anyone else but the young man who could do such wonderful things, the truth being that she and Jack had fallen in love with each other at first sight.

But her father was cautious. "It is true, my dear," said he, "that the young fellow seems a fine boy, but for all we know it may be chance, not skill, and he may have a broken feather in his wing. So we must try him again."

Then he said to Jack, "My daughter must have a fine house to live in. Therefore by tomorrow morning at eight o'clock there must be a magnificent castle standing on twelve golden pillars in the middle of the lake, and there must be a church beside it. And all things must be ready for the bride, and at eight o'clock precisely a peal of bells from the church must ring out for the wedding. If not, you will have to forfeit your life."

This time Jack intended to give the three little red men more time for their task, but what with having enjoyed himself so much all day, and having eaten so much good food, he overslept himself, so that the big clock on the tower was whirring before it struck eight when he woke, leaped out of bed and rushed to the golden snuffbox. But he had forgotten where he had put it, and so the clock had really begun to strike before he found it under his pillow, opened it, and gabbled out his orders. And then you never saw how the three little red men tumbled over each other and yawned and stretched and made haste all at one time, so that Jack thought his life would surely be forfeit. But just as the clock struck

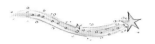

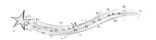

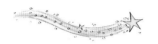

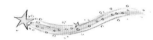

its last chime, out rang a peal of merry bells, and there was the castle standing on twelve golden pillars and a church beside it in the middle of the lake. And the castle was all decorated for the wedding, and there were crowds and crowds of servants and retainers, all dressed in their Sunday best.

Never had Jack seen such a sight before. Neither had the gay young daughter, who, of course, was looking out of the next window in her nightcap. And she looked so pretty and so gay that Jack felt quite cross when he had to step back to let the three little red men fly to their golden snuffbox. But they were far crosser than he was, and mumbled and grumbled at the hustle, so that Jack was quite glad when they shut the box down and began to snore.

Well, of course, Jack and the gay young daughter were married, and were as happy as the day is long, and Jack had fine clothes to wear, fine food to eat, fine servants to wait on him, and as many fine friends as he liked.

But it happened that one day when he was going hunting with all the ladies and gentlemen, Jack forgot to change the golden snuffbox from his waistcoat pocket to that of his scarlet hunting coat, so he left it behind him.

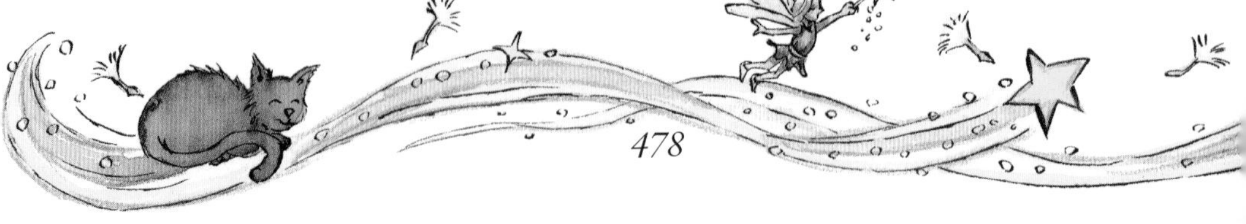

And what should happen but that the servant let it fall on the ground when he was folding up the clothes, and the snuffbox flew open and out popped the three little red men yawning and stretching.

Well! When they found out that they hadn't really been summoned, and that there was no fear of death, they were in a towering temper and said they had a great mind to fly away with the castle, golden pillars and all.

On hearing this, the servant pricked up his ears.

"Could you do that?" he asked.

"Could we?" they said, and they laughed loud. "Why, we can do anything."

Then the servant said, ever so sharp, "Then move this castle and all it contains right away over the sea where the master can't disturb us."

Now the little red men need not really have obeyed the order, but they were so cross with Jack that hardly had the servant said the words before the task was done, so when the hunting party came back, lo and behold! The castle, and the church, and the golden pillars had all disappeared!

At first all the rest set upon Jack for being a knave and a cheat. In particular, his wife's father threatened to kill him for deceiving the merry young daughter, but at last he agreed to let Jack have twelve months and a day to find the castle and bring it back.

So off Jack started on a good horse with some money in his pocket.

And he traveled far and he traveled fast, and he traveled east and west, north and south, over hills and dales and valleys and mountains and woods, but never a sign of the missing castle did he see. Now at last he came to the palace of the king of all the mice in the wide world. And there was a little mousie in a fine shirt of mail armor and a steel cap doing sentry at the front gate, and he was not for letting Jack in until he had told his errand. And when Jack had told it, he passed him on to the next mouse sentry at the inner gate, so by degrees he reached the king's chamber, where he sat surrounded by mice courtiers.

Now the king of the mice received Jack very graciously and said that he himself knew nothing of the missing castle, but, as he was king of all the mice in the whole world, it was possible that some of his subjects might know more than he. But the next morning, though there were brown mice, black mice, gray mice, white mice and piebald mice, from all parts of the world, and they all answered with one breath, "If you please, Your Majesty, we have not seen the missing castle."

Then the king said, "You must go and ask my elder brother the king of all the frogs. He may be able to tell you."

So Jack set off on the king's horse, and as he passed the outer gate he saw the little mouse sentry coming away, for its guard time was up. Now Jack was a kind-hearted lad, and he had saved some crumbs from his dinner in order to reward the little sentry for his kindness. So he put his hand in his pocket and pulled out the crumbs.

"Here you are, mousekin," he said. "That's for your trouble!"

Then the mouse thanked him kindly and asked if he would take him along to the king of the frogs.

"Not I," says Jack. "I should get into trouble with your king."

But the mousekin insisted. "I may be of some use to you," it said. So it ran up the horse's hind leg and up by its tail and hid in Jack's pocket. And the horse set off at a hard gallop, for it didn't like the mouse running over it.

So at last Jack came to the palace of the king of all the frogs, and there at the front gate was a frog doing sentry in a fine coat of mail and a brass helmet. And the frog sentry was for not letting Jack in, but the mouse called out that they came from the king of all the mice and must be let in without delay. So they were taken to the king's chamber, where he sat surrounded by frog courtiers in fine clothes. But alas! He had heard nothing of the castle on golden pillars, and though he summoned all the frogs of all the world to a grand assembly next morning, they all answered his question with, "Kro kro, Kro kro," which everyone knows stands for "no" in frog language.

So the king said to Jack, "There remains but one thing. You must go and ask my eldest brother, the king of all the birds. His subjects are always on the wing, so perhaps they have seen something."

So Jack set off, and being a kindhearted lad he gave the frog sentry, whom he met coming away from his guard, some crumbs he had saved from his dinner. And the frog asked leave to go with him, and when Jack refused to take him, he just gave one hop onto the stirrup, and a second hop onto the crupper, and the next hop he was in Jack's other pocket.

Then the horse galloped away like lightning, for it didn't like the slimy frog coming down "plop" on its back.

Well, after a time, Jack came to the palace of the king of all the birds, and there at the front gate were a sparrow and a crow marching up and down with guns on their shoulders. Now at this Jack laughed fit to split, and the mouse and the frog from his pockets called out,

"We come from the king! Let us pass."

The sentries were amazed, and let them pass in without any delay.

But when they came to the king's chamber, where he sat surrounded by all manner of birds, tomtits, wrens, cormorants, turtledoves and the like, the king said he was sorry, but he had no news of the missing castle. And though he summoned all the birds of all the world to a grand assembly next morning, not one of them had seen or heard tell of it.

So Jack was quite disconsolate till the king said, "But where is the eagle? I don't see my eagle."

So two larks flew up into the sky till they couldn't be seen and sang ever so loud, till at last the eagle appeared, all in a perspiration from having flown so fast.

Then the king said, "Have you seen a missing castle that stands upon twelve pillars of gold?"

And the eagle blinked its eyes and said, "May it please Your Majesty that is where I've been."

Then everybody rejoiced exceedingly, and when the eagle had eaten a whole calf, so as to be strong enough for the journey, he spread his wide wings, on which Jack stood, with the mouse in one pocket and the frog in the other, and started to obey the king's order to take the owner back to his missing castle as quickly as possible.

And they flew over land and they flew over sea, until at last in the far distance they saw the castle standing on its twelve golden pillars. But all the doors and windows were fast shut and barred, for, see you, the servant-master who had run away with it had gone out for the day hunting, and he always bolted doors and windows while he was absent lest someone else should run away with it.

Then Jack was puzzled to think how he should get hold of the golden snuffbox, until the little mouse said:

"Let me fetch it. There is always a mouse hole in every castle, so I am sure I shall be able to get in."

So it went off, and Jack waited on the eagle's wings till at last mousekin appeared.

"Have you got it?" shouted Jack, and the little mousie cried, "Yes!"

So every one rejoiced exceedingly, and they set off back to the palace of the king of all the birds, where Jack had left his horse, for now that he had the golden snuffbox safe, he knew he could get the castle back whenever he chose to send the three little red men to fetch it. But on the way over the sea, while Jack, who was dead tired with standing so long, lay down between the eagle's wings and fell asleep, the mouse and the eagle fell to quarreling as to which of them had helped Jack more, and they quarreled so much that at last they laid the case before the frog. Then the frog, who made a very wise judge, said he must see the whole affair from the very beginning, so the mouse brought out the golden snuffbox from Jack's pocket and began to relate where it had been found and all about it. Now, at that very moment Jack awoke, kicked out his leg, and plump went the golden snuffbox down to the very bottom of the sea!

"I thought my turn would come," said the frog, and went plump in after it.

Well, they waited, and waited, and waited for three whole days and three whole nights, but froggie never came up again, and they had just given him up in despair when his nose showed above the water.

"Have you got it?" they shouted.

"No!" says he, with a great gasp.

"Then what do you want?" they cried in a rage.

"My breath," says froggie, and he sank down again.

Well, they waited two days and two nights more, and at last up comes the little frog with the golden snuffbox in its mouth.

Then they all rejoiced exceedingly, and the eagle flew ever so fast to the palace of the king of the birds, and Jack was allowed to ride home.

But the year and a day that he had been allowed was almost gone, and even his gay young wife, after almost weeping her eyes out after her handsome young husband, had given up Jack for lost, so everyone was astounded to see him, and not over-pleased either to see him come without his castle. Indeed his father-in-law swore with many oaths that if it were not in its proper place by eight o'clock next morning, Jack's life should be forfeit.

Now this, of course, was exactly what Jack had wanted and intended from the beginning, because when death was nigh he could open the golden snuffbox and order about the little red men. But he had opened it so often of late and they had become so cross, that he was in a stew what to do, whether to give them time to show their temper, or to hustle them out of it. At last he decided to do half and half. So just as the hands of the clock were at five minutes to eight he opened the box, and stopped his ears!

Well! You never heard such a yawning, and scolding, and threatening, and blustering. What did he mean by it? Why should he take four bites at one cherry? If he was always in fear of death, why didn't he die and have done with it?

In the midst of all this the tower clock began to whirr.

"Gentlemen!" said Jack—he was really quaking with fear, "Do as you are told."

"For the last time," they shrieked. "We won't stay and serve a master who thinks he is going to die every day."

And with that they flew out of the window—and they never came back.

The golden snuffbox remained empty for evermore.

But when Jack looked out of window there was the castle in the middle of the lake on its twelve golden pillars, and there was his young wife, ever so pretty and gay in her nightcap, looking out of the window too.

So they lived happily ever after.

Woman's Wit

By Howard Pyle

READING TIME: 25 MINUTES

When man's strength fails, woman's wit prevails.

In the days when the great and wise King Solomon lived and ruled, evil spirits and demons were as plentiful in the world as wasps in summer. So King Solomon, who was so wise and knew so many potent spells that he had power over evil such as no man has had before or since, set himself to work to put those enemies of mankind out of the way. Some he conjured into bottles and sank into the depths of the sea, some he buried in the earth, some he destroyed altogether, as one burns hair in a flame.

Now, one pleasant day when King Solomon was walking in his garden with his thoughts busy as bees with this or that, he came face to face with a demon, who was a prince of his kind. "Ho, little man!" cried the evil spirit, in a loud voice. "Are you not the wise King Solomon who conjures my brethren into brass chests and glass bottles? Come, try wrestling with me, and whoever conquers shall be master over the other for all time. What do you say to such an offer as that?"

"I say yes!" said King Solomon, and, without another word, he stripped off his royal robes and stood bare breasted, man to man with the other.

The world never saw the like of that wrestling match between the king and the demon, for they struggled and strove together from the seventh hour in the morning to the sunset in the evening, and during that time the sky was clouded over as black as night, and the lightning forked and shot, and the thunder roared and bellowed, and the earth shook and quaked.

But at last the king gave the enemy an under twist and flung him down on the earth so hard that the apples fell from the trees, and then, panting and straining, he held the evil one down, knee on neck. Thereupon the sky presently cleared again, and all was as pleasant as a spring day.

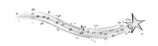

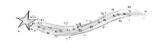

King Solomon bound the demon with spells, and made him serve him for seven years. First, he had him build a splendid palace, the like of which was not to be seen within the bounds of the seven rivers, then he made him set around the palace a garden, such as I for one wish I may see some time or other. Then, when the demon had done all that the king had asked for, the king conjured him into a bottle, corked it tightly, and set the royal seal on the stopper. Then he took the bottle a thousand miles away into the wilderness and, when no man was looking, he buried it within seven boxes set in the ground,

and this is the way the story begins.

Well, the years came and the years went, and the world grew older and older, and kept changing , so that by and by the wilderness where King Solomon had hid the bottle became a great town, with many people coming and going, and all of them as busy as bees about their own business and other folks' affairs.

Among these townspeople was a little tailor, who made clothes for many a man to wear, and who lived all alone in a little house, for he was a bachelor.

The little tailor was a thrifty soul, and by hook and by crook had managed to put by enough money to fill a small pot, and then he had to think of some safe place in which to hide it. So one night he took a spade and a lamp and went out in the garden to bury his money. He drove his spade into the ground—and clang! He struck something hard that rang under his foot with a sound as of iron. "Hello!" said the tailor to himself. "I wonder what we have we here?" And if he had known as much as you and I do, he would surely have filled in the earth, and tramped it down as quickly as he possibly could.

As it was, he scraped away the soil, and there he found a box of metal, with a ring on the lid to lift it by.

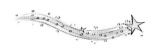

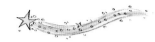

The tailor clutched the ring and bent his back, and up came the box with the damp earth sticking to it. He cleaned the mold away, and there he saw, written in red letters, these words:

OPEN NOT

You may be sure that after he had read these words he was not long in breaking open the lid of the box with his spade.

Inside the first box he found a second, and upon it the same words:

OPEN NOT

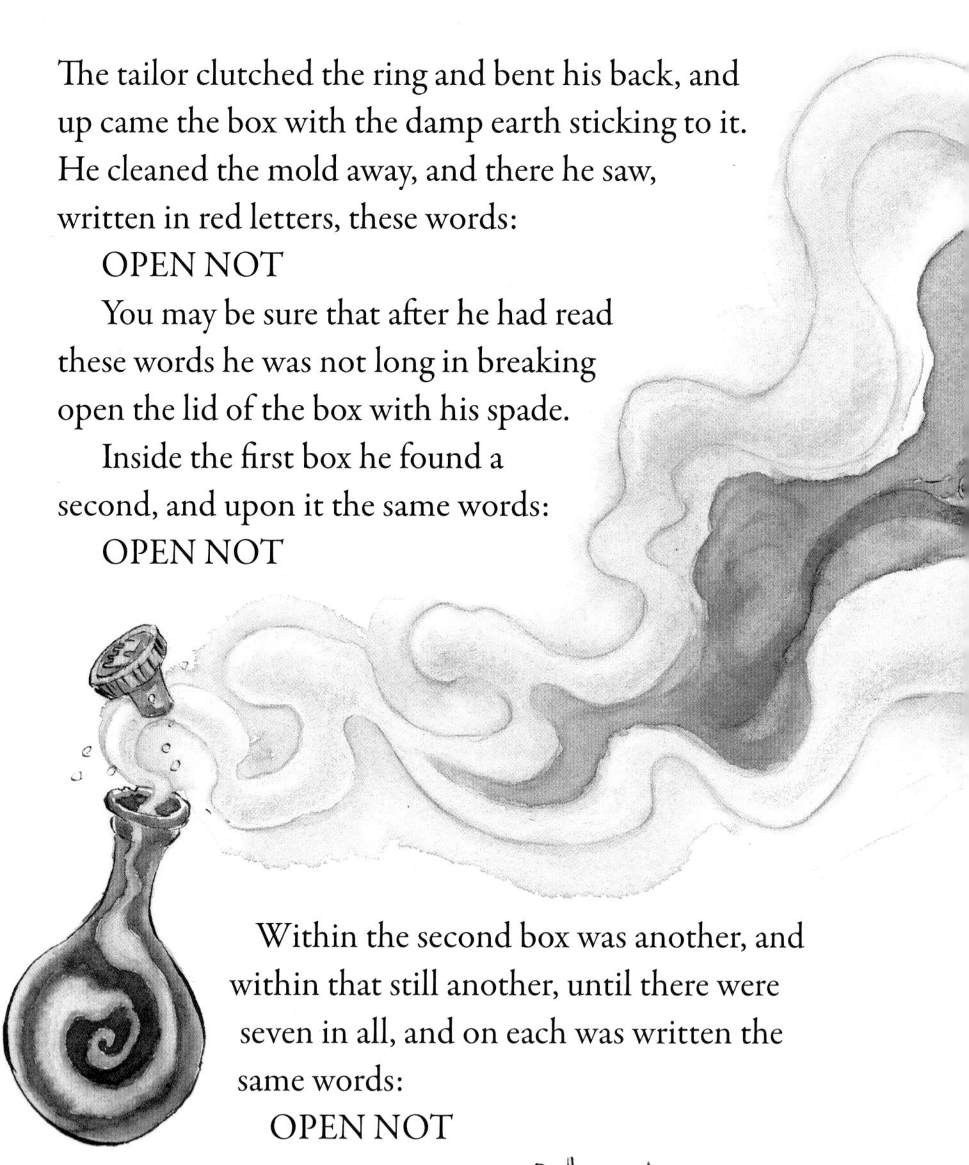

Within the second box was another, and within that still another, until there were seven in all, and on each was written the same words:

OPEN NOT

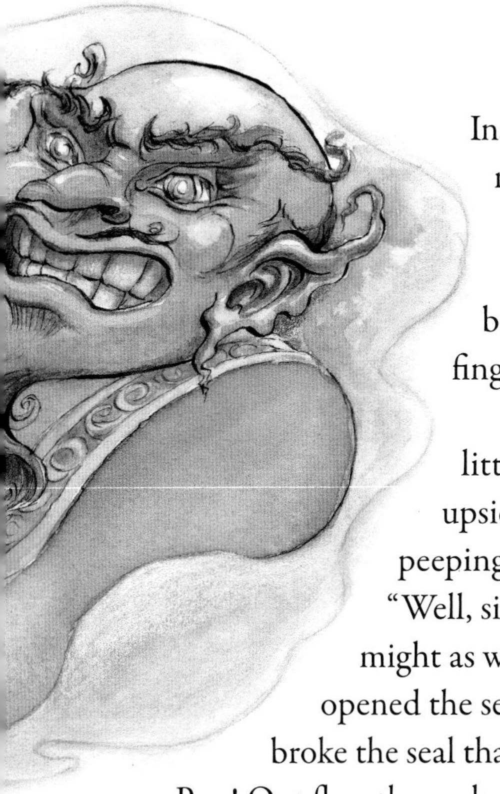

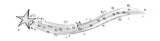

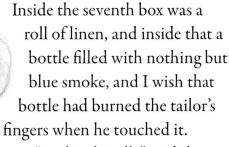

Inside the seventh box was a roll of linen, and inside that a bottle filled with nothing but blue smoke, and I wish that bottle had burned the tailor's fingers when he touched it.

"And is this all?" said the little tailor, turning the bottle upside down and shaking it, and peeping at it by the light of the lamp. "Well, since I have gone so far, I might as well open it, as I have already opened the seven boxes." Thereupon he broke the seal that stoppered it.

Pop! Out flew the cork, and puff! Out came the smoke, not all at once, but in a long thread that rose up as high as the stars, and then spread slowly until it hid their light.

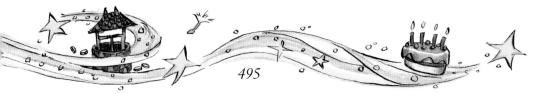

The tailor stared and goggled and gaped to see so much smoke come out of such a little bottle, and, as he goggled and stared, the smoke began to gather together again, thicker and thicker, and darker and darker, until it was as black as ink. Then out from it there stepped one with eyes that shone like sparks of fire and who had a countenance so terrible that the tailor's skin quivered and shriveled, and his tongue clove to the roof of his mouth at the sight of it.

"Who are you?" said the terrible being, in a voice that made the very marrow of the poor tailor's bones turn soft from terror.

If you please, sir," said he, "I am only a little tailor."

The evil being lifted up both hands and eyes. "How wonderful," he cried, "that one little tailor can undo in a moment that which took the wise Solomon a whole day to accomplish, and in the doing of which he well nigh broke the sinews of his heart!"

Then the demon turned to the tailor, who stood trembling like a rabbit. "Listen!" said he. "For two thousand years I lay there in that bottle, and no one came to help. You have liberated me, and so you shall not go unrewarded. Every morning at the seventh hour I will come to you and I will perform for you whatever task you may command of me—no matter how difficult.

"But there is one condition attached to the agreement, and you'll be sorry if that condition is broken. If any morning I should come to you and you have no task for me to do, I shall wring your neck as one might wring the neck of a sparrow." Thereupon he was gone in an instant, leaving the little tailor half dead with terror.

Now it happened that the prime minister of that country had left an order with the tailor for a suit of clothes, so the next morning, when the demon came, the little man set him to work on the bench, with his legs tucked up like a journeyman tailor. "I want," said he, "such and such a suit of clothes."

"You shall have them," said the demon, and thereupon he began snipping in the air, and cutting most wonderful patterns of silks and satins out of nothing at all, and the little tailor sat and gaped and stared. Then the demon began to drive the needle like a spark of fire—the like was never seen in all the seven kingdoms, for the clothes seemed to make themselves.

At last, at the end of a little while, the demon stood up and brushed his hands. "They are done," said he, and thereupon he instantly vanished. But the tailor cared little for that, for upon the bench there lay such a suit of clothes of silk and satin stuff, sewed with threads of gold and silver and set with jewels, as the eyes of man never saw before, and the tailor packed them up and marched off with them himself to the prime minister.

The prime minister wore the clothes to court that very day, and before evening they were the talk of the town. All the world ran to the tailor and ordered clothes of him, and his fortune was made. Every day the demon created new suits of clothes out of nothing at all, so that the tailor grew rich, and held his head up in the world.

As time went along, he laid heavier and heavier tasks upon the demon's back and demanded more and more of him , but all the while the demon kept his own counsel, and said never a word.

One morning, as the tailor sat in his shop window taking it easy—for he had little or nothing to do now—he heard a great hubbub in the street below, and when he looked down he saw that it was the king's daughter passing by. It was the first time that the tailor had seen her, and when he saw her his heart stood still within him and then began fluttering like a little bird, for one so beautiful was not to be met with in the four corners of the world. Then she was gone.

All that day the little tailor could do nothing but sit and think of the princess, and the next morning when the demon came he was thinking of her still.

"What have you for me to do today?" said the demon, as he always said of a morning.

The little tailor was waiting for the question.

"I would like you," said he, "to send to the king's palace, and to ask him to let me have his daughter for my wife."

"You shall have your desire," said the demon. Thereupon he smote his hands together like a clap of thunder, and instantly the walls of the room split into pieces, and there came out four-and-twenty handsome youths, clad in cloth of gold and silver. After these four-and-twenty there came another one who was the chief of them all, and before whom, splendid as they were, the four-and-twenty paled like stars in daylight. "Go to the king's palace," said the demon to that one, "and deliver this message: the tailor of tailors, the master of masters, and one greater than a king asks for his daughter to marry."

"To hear is to obey," said the other and bowed his forehead to the earth.

Never was there such a hubbub in the town as when those five-and-twenty, in their clothes of silver and gold, rode through the streets to the king's palace. As they came near, the gates of the palace flew open before them, and the king came out to meet them. The leader of the five-and-twenty leaped from his horse, and, kissing the ground before the king, delivered his message: "The tailor of tailors, the master of masters, and one greater than a king asks for your daughter to marry."

When the king heard what the messenger said, he thought and pondered a long time. At last he said, "If he who sent you is the master of masters, and greater than a king, let him send me an asking gift such as no king could send."

"It shall be as you desire," said the messenger, and thereupon the five-and-twenty rode away as they had come, followed by crowds of people.

The next morning when the demon came, the tailor was ready and waiting for him. "What have you for me to do today?" said the evil one.

"I want," said the tailor, "a gift to send to the king such as no other king could send him."

"You shall have your desire," said the demon. Thereupon he smote his hands together and summoned, not five-and-twenty young men, but fifty youths, all clad in clothes more splendid than the others.

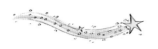

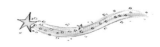

All of the fifty sat upon coal-black horses, with saddles of silver and housings of silk and velvet embroidered with gold. In the midst of all the five-and-seventy there rode a youth in cloth of silver embroidered in pearls. In his hand he bore something wrapped in a white napkin, and that was the present for the king such as no other king could give. So said the demon, "Take it to the royal palace, and tell his majesty that it is from the tailor of tailors, the master of masters, and one greater than a king."

"To hear is to obey," said the young man, and then they all rode away.

When they came to the palace the gates flew open before them, and the king came out to meet them. The young man who bore the present dismounted and lay down in the dust, and when the king bade him arise, he unwrapped the napkin, and gave to the king a goblet made of ruby, filled to the brim with pieces of gold. Moreover, the cup was of such a kind that whenever it was emptied of its money it instantly became full again. "The tailor of tailors, the master of masters, and one greater than a king sends Your Majesty this goblet and bids me, his ambassador, to ask for your daughter," said the young man.

When the king saw what had been sent him he was filled with amazement. "Surely," said he to himself, "there can be no end to the power of one who can give such a gift as this." Then to the messenger, "Tell your master that he shall have my daughter for his wife if he will build over yonder a palace such as no man ever saw or no king ever lived in before."

"It shall be done," said the young man, and then they all went away, as the others had done the day before.

The next morning when the demon appeared, the tailor was ready for him. "Build me," said he, "such and such a palace in such and such a place."

And the demon said, "It shall be done." He smote his hands together, and instantly there came a cloud of mist that covered and hid the spot where the palace was to be built. Out from the cloud there came such a banging and hammering and clapping and clattering as the people of that town never heard before. Then when evening had come, the cloud arose, and there, where the king had pointed out, stood a splendid palace as white as snow, with roofs and domes of gold and silver. As the king stood looking and wondering at this sight, there came five hundred young men riding, and one in the midst of all who wore a golden crown on his head, and upon his body a long robe stiff with diamonds and pearls. "We come," said he, "from the tailor of tailors, and master of masters, and one greater than a king, to ask you to let him have your daughter for his wife."

"Tell him to come!" cried the king, in admiration, "for the princess is his."

The next morning when the demon came, he found the tailor dancing and shouting for joy. "The princess is mine!" he cried, "So make me ready for her."

"It shall be done," said the demon, and thereupon he began to make the tailor ready for his wedding. He brought him to a marble bath of water, in which he washed away all that was coarse and ugly, and from which the little man came forth as beautiful as the sun. Then the demon clad him in the finest linen and covered him with clothes such as even the emperor of India never wore. Then he smote his hands together, and the wall of the tailor shop opened as it had done twice before, and there came forth forty servants clad in crimson and bearing bowls full of money in their hands. After them came two leading a horse as white as snow, with a saddle of gold studded with diamonds and rubies and emeralds and sapphires. After came a bodyguard of twenty warriors clad in gold armor. Then the tailor mounted his horse and rode away to the king's palace, and as he rode the slaves scattered the money among the crowd, who scrambled for it and cheered the tailor on.

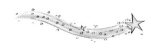

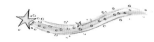

That night the princess and the tailor were married, and all the town was lit with bonfires and fireworks. The two rode away in the midst of a great crowd of nobles and courtiers to the palace that the demon had built for the tailor, and as the princess gazed upon him, she thought that she had never beheld so noble and handsome a man as her husband. So she and the tailor were the happiest couple in the whole wide world.

But the next morning the demon appeared as he had

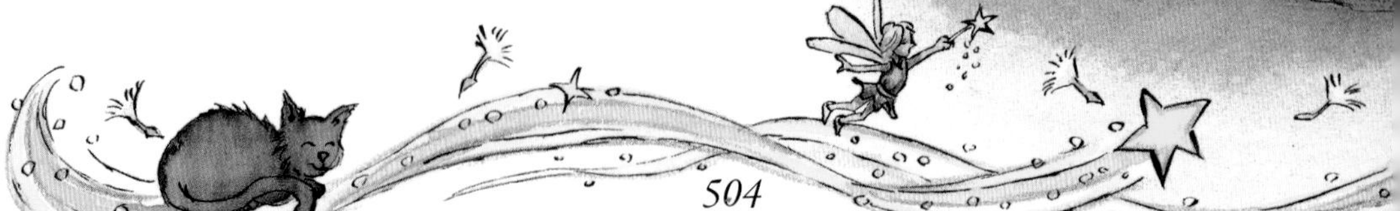

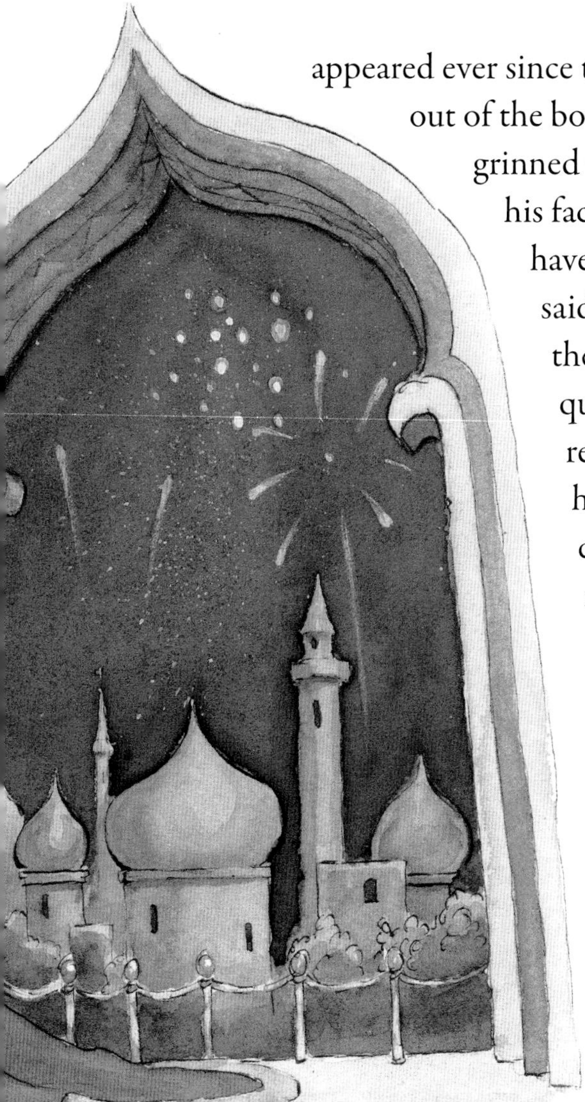

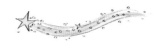

appeared ever since the tailor had let him out of the bottle, only now he grinned till his teeth shone and his face turned black. "What have you for me to do?" said he, and at the words the tailor's heart began to quake, for he remembered what was to happen to him when he could find the demon no more work to do—that his neck was to be wrung—and now he began to see that he had all that he could ask for in the world. Yes, what was there to ask for now?

"I have nothing more for you to do," said the tailor "you have done all that anyone could ask—you may go now."

"Go!" cried the demon, "I shall not go until I have done all that I have to do. Give me work, or I shall wring your neck." And his fingers began to twitch.

Then the tailor began to see into what a net he had fallen. He began to tremble. He turned his eyes up and down, for he did not know where to look for aid. Suddenly, as he looked out of the window, a thought struck him. "Maybe," thought he, "I can give the demon such a task that even he cannot do it."

"Yes, yes!" he cried, "I have thought of something for you to do. Make me out yonder in front of my palace a lake of water a mile long and a mile wide, and let it be lined throughout with white marble, and filled with water as clear as crystal."

"It shall be done," said the demon. As he spoke, he spat in the air, and instantly a thick fog arose from the earth and hid everything from sight. Then presently from the midst of the fog there came a great noise of chipping and hammering, of digging and delving, of rushing and gurgling. All day the noise and the fog continued, and then at sunset the one ceased and the other cleared away. The poor tailor looked out the window, and when he saw what he saw his teeth chattered in his head, for there was a lake a mile long and a mile broad, lined within with white marble, and filled with water as clear as crystal, and he knew that the demon would come the next morning for another task to do.

That night he slept little or none, and when the seventh hour of the morning came the castle began to rock and tremble, and there stood the demon, and his hair bristled and his eyes shone like sparks of fire.

"What have you for me to do?" said he, and the poor tailor could do nothing but look at him with a face as white as dough.

"What have you for me to do?" said the demon again, and then at last the tailor found his wits and his tongue from sheer terror. "Look!" said he, "at the great mountain over yonder. Remove it and make in its place a level plain with fields and orchards and gardens." And he thought to himself when he had spoken, "Surely, even the demon cannot do that."

"It shall be done," said the demon, and, so saying, he stamped his heel upon the ground. Instantly the earth began to tremble and quake, and there came a great rumbling like the sound of thunder. A cloud of darkness gathered in the sky, until at last all was as black as the blackest midnight. Then came a roaring and a cracking and a crashing, such as man never heard before. All day it continued, until the time of the setting of the sun, when suddenly the uproar ceased, and the darkness cleared away, and when the tailor looked out of the window the mountain was gone, and in its place were fields and orchards and gardens.

It was very beautiful to see, but when the tailor beheld it his knees began to smite together, and the sweat ran down his face in streams. All that night he walked up and down and up and down, but he could not think of one other task for the demon to do.

When the next morning came the demon appeared like a whirlwind. His face was as black as ink and smoke, and sparks of fire flew from his nostrils.

"What have you for me to do?" cried he.

"I have nothing for you to do!" piped the poor tailor.

"Nothing?" cried the demon.

"Nothing."

"Then prepare to die."

"Stop!" cried the tailor, falling on his knees, "let me

first see my wife."

"So be it," said the demon but if he had been wiser he would have said no.

When the tailor came to the princess, he flung himself on his face, and began to weep and wail. The princess asked him what was the matter, and at last, by dint of question, got the story from him, piece by piece. When she had it all she began laughing. "Why did you not come to me before?" said she, "instead of making all this trouble and uproar for nothing at all? I will give the monster a task to do." She plucked a single curling hair from her head. "Here," said she, "let him take this hair and make it straight."

The tailor was full of doubt. Nevertheless, as there was nothing better to do, he took it to the demon.

"Have you found me a task to do?" cried the demon.

"Yes," said the tailor. "It is only a little thing. Here is a hair from my wife's head; take it and make it straight."

When the demon heard what was the task that the tailor had set him to do he laughed aloud, but that was because he did not know. He took the hair and stroked it between his thumb and finger, and, when he had done, it curled more than ever. Then he looked serious, and slapped it between his palms, and that did not better matters, for it curled as much as ever. Then he frowned and began beating the hair with his palm upon his knees, and that only made it worse. All that day he labored and strove at his task trying to make that one little hair straight; and when the sun set, there was the hair just as crooked as ever. Then, as the great round sun sank red behind the trees, the demon knew that he was beaten.

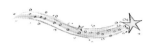

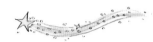

"I am conquered! I am conquered!" he howled, and he flew away, bellowing so

dreadfully that all the world shook.

So ends the story, with only this to say—where man's strength fails, woman's wit prevails.

For, to my mind, the princess—not to speak of her husband the tailor—did more with a single hair and her clever wit than King Solomon with all his wisdom.

About the Artists

Mark Beech Art has always been a large part of Mark's life. At a very early age he was inspired by the illustrations of Edward Lear and Lewis Caroll, and loved illustrating their stories himself. In 2001 Mark decided to develop a career as an illustrator and has now worked in most areas of illustration, but loves children's publishing most of all.

Carrie's Three Wishes • *The Haughty Princess*
The Ogre's Bride • *The Three Sillies* • *The Two Frogs*

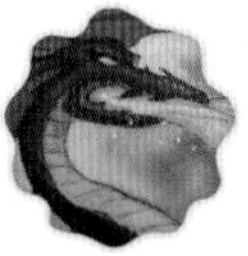

Andy Catling A graduate of the Norwich School of Art and Design, UK, Andy is a Hampshire-based illustrator. He likes to work with watercolor, gouache, and ink and is the proud owner of a very messy work table, an excessive number of brushes, and one very old mechanical pencil. Please send cookies.

Empty Bottles • *Jack the Cunning Thief* • *My Lord Bag of Rice* • *Rosy's Journey* • *Woman's Wit* • All page decoration

Peter Cottrill As well as illustrating books, Peter does some teaching and practices Shiatsu. He enjoys creating stories and scenarios. Humor and a sense of the absurd inspire Peter. Throw in some costumes and wild animals and he's even happier. For Peter, a brief is a chance to be creative and see what he can come up with, whatever the subject.

How the Camel got his Hump • *I Wonder* • *Nasreddin Hodja and the Pot* • *Nasreddin Hodja and the Smell of Soup* • *The Clever Apprentice* • *The Wind and the Sun*
The Wise Girl

Evelyne Duverne After completing a BSc in Economics, Evelyne studied painting, sculpture, animation, computer graphics, and illustration at Emile Cohl, a graphic art school in Lyon, France. She then specialized in children's illustration, becoming a freelance painter-illustrator, and now works with acrylics on paper, canvas, and cardboard. Evelyne especially likes to draw characters, getting her inspiration from the legends and tales she read as a child.

Cap o' Rushes • *Tattercoats* • *The Enchanted Head*
The Golden Head • *The Golden Snuffbox* • *The Husband of the Rat's Daughter* • *The Two Sisters* • *Tikki Tikki Tembo*

Masumi Furukawa Living in Tokyo, Japan, Masumi illustrates and writes children's books. She has worked on many books with different publishers all over the world and was recently selected to participate in the annual Bologna Book Fair illustration competition (2009).

Hans in Luck • *Singh Rajah and the Cunning Jackals*
Straw, Coal, and Bean • *The Fish and the Ring*
The Sagacious Monkey and the Boar • *Why the Swallow's Tail is Forked*

Tom Sperling After working at The Museum of Modern Art, New York, Tom pursued his interest in illustration by studying at The Art Student's League. He has twice been awarded the Paul Revere Award for Graphic Excellence and won the Small Press Book Award for Best Illustrated Young Adult Book.

Good Luck is Better than Gold • *The Broad Man, the Tall Man, and the Man with Eyes of Flame* • *The Meester Stoorworm* • *The Seven Little Kids* • *The Three Aunts*
The White Cat

Mike Spoor A professional illustrator for fifteen years, Mike also used to teach and lecture in ceramics. His illustrations are energetic and spontaneous, ranging in style from humorous animals and people, to serious, dramatic depictions of adventure and history.

Honorable Minu • *Nail Soup* • *The Box of Robbers*
The Fisherman and his Wife • *The Six Soldiers of Fortune*
The Three Heads of the Well • *The Tiger, the Brahman, and the Jackal*

Rupert Van Wyk From a very young age Rupert has been drawing and he has no intention of stopping. His work has been published in the UK, Italy, United States and South Korea. Having traveled all over the world, he now lives and works between Ravenna, Italy and London, UK.

How the Rhinoceros got his Skin • *Lazy Jack* • *Sir Gammer Vans* • *The Four Clever Brothers* • *The Girl who Owned a Bear* • *The Husband who was to Mind the House*
The Swineherd